THE HIDDEN WAR

JINN FILE

RA

The Hidden War
Copyright © 2025 by RA.

MILTON & HUGO L.L.C.
4407 Park Ave., Suite 5
Union City, NJ 07087, USA

Website: *www. miltonandhugo.com*
Hotline: *1- 888-778-0033*
Email: *info@miltonandhugo.com*

Ordering Information:
Quantity sales. Special discounts are granted to corporations, associations, and other organizations. For more information on these discounts, please reach out to the publisher using the contact information provided above.

Library of Congress Control Number:		2025906654
ISBN-13:	979-8-89285-500-6	[Paperback Edition]
	979-8-89285-501-3	[Hardback Edition]
	979-8-89285-499-3	[Digital Edition]

Rev. date: 03/10/2025

Chapter

1

The Djinn Springs into Action

Unanswered questions were attacking him like the Mongol Horde. With its damp air gripping his throat and the muddy ground pulling at his feet, it felt as if he was in a filthy tunnel. Mystery surrounded him on all sides. When he looked ahead, there was a frightening darkness; when he turned back wildly, there was a cold wind cutting his face and mossy walls of a dead-end... Resentment, pain, anger, and the humiliation of not being able to revolt...

Ali Fuat rested his head against the window, ignoring the clattering of the car. He decided to list everything from the beginning. Who was Halit Nurullah? Which group did he belong to? Did he have any actions threatening the Republic and its revolutions? How could the order to "have a coffee" be given without a detailed investigation? What was Pasha[1] Vefik's intention?

The journey had become excruciatingly long. He took out a cigarette. Just as he was about to light it, a racing motorcycle passed by. He was startled, and the lighter fell into his lap. "Damn idiot," he muttered to himself. Kenan Ferit, who was sitting in the back seat, lit his lighter. The minibus lit up briefly.

"Commander, you are distracted! If the motorcycle hadn't passed..."

"My mind is confused, Kenan!"

---

[1]   An honorary title used during the Ottoman Empire for high-ranking military officers and state officials, such as generals, governors, and viziers.

"The usual issue, Commander?"

"Both that and Pasha Vefik's headstrong behavior!" He drew on his cigarette without pleasure. The tip of the cigarette glowed like a firefly. He glanced outside. The journey did not seem to be ending.

"How much longer?" Kenan Ferit, known within the organization for his proficiency in using firearms and his handsomeness, looked at his watch. "About twenty minutes left, Commander." Ali Fuat nodded slightly.

"It has been a long time, hasn't it, Commander?"

"Yes. The last time was about three years ago, I think?"

"It was three years ago, Commander. I believe it was around this time..." Kenan Ferit called out to the front of the minibus:

"Zekeriya, which month was it?"

Zekeriya turned around, glanced briefly, and said, "Three years ago, on Thursday, March 6," without saying another word. He rarely spoke unless necessary and even then, very little. Kenan Ferit smiled, "You remember well!" Zekeriya mumbled, "Yes." and turned back. When he received no response, Kenan Ferit smiled again. He was used to Zekeriya by now. Looking at Ali Fuat, "I don't understand why it is necessary after all this time, Commander. Although, it's not so bad; we can get some exercise." Ali Fuat did not respond. His tension persisted.

"We don't know this man at all. Why was the order to 'have a coffee' given, Commander?"

"That part troubles me too!"

"No research was done, right?"

"We only know that he is a carpet merchant and that he opens Quran courses and gives scholarships to poor students. That's it!"

"So, Pasha is making us do a half-baked job!"

Ali Fuat responded with all his frustration, "Yes." The minibus fell silent again. Who was this man? Or was the Pasha having them do his personal errands? "No way," he said to himself. In the past, he had had the organization do a few small tasks for his son. But those were very minor things.

He remembered the moment the order was given. Pasha was rummaging through a blue folder, trying to find a document. With his broad face, thick eyebrows, and pale thick lips, Pasha Vefik had a stern demeanor. Although he was 62 years old, he looked much older. His eyes seemed to disappear within the wrinkles of his face. There was a knock on the door. The intelligence officer of the unit, Colonel Zeki, entered. He stood at attention and saluted Pasha.

Pasha said: "We were expecting you!"

Colonel Zeki sat down across from Ali.

"I have reviewed the file, but you should still give an overview."

"Yes, sir. The individual in question does not have an active presence. There is no detectable link to any community. If he does have a link, it is to a part of the community that we have not yet uncovered. He is involved in carpet trade. His financial situation is not bad. In the neighborhood where he lives, he has opened Quran courses. He has given scholarships to university students. He is known as Hadji Halit because he has performed the Hajj. He leads a quiet life. I don't believe he has a problematic nature."

Pasha Vefik listened with a displeased expression and suddenly tensed up. "So, you have started adding your own comments to the end of the reports, huh?"

There was a brief silence.

"You haven't obtained any information about the man, and you also state that he doesn't have a problematic nature!" he raised his voice. "You have unlimited legal and illegal resources at your disposal. But the intelligence you have brought is less than what two rookie journalists could gather!"

Colonel Zeki's jaw trembled, his lips quivered for a moment. The venom on the tip of his tongue made him want to curse Pasha with all his might. The hatred that came to the tip of his tongue poured back inside and tore at his heart. He couldn't respond.

"Alright, we will investigate the remaining part ourselves. You may leave." Colonel Zeki said, "Yes, sir," and left the room. Ali Fuat's hands were trembling. They shook violently when he was tense. Doctor had advised him to squeeze a small rubber ball. He thought about taking the ball out of his pocket for a moment. He decided against it; it wasn't the right time.

Pasha Vefik angrily closed the file and said, "Ali Fuat."

Ali Fuat straightened up and looked directly into Pasha's eyes, "Yes, sir," he replied. Pasha Vefik's order was short and clear.

"You need to have a coffee with Halit Nurullah."

He was shocked. He couldn't say, "How can you give such an order without knowing who he is?"

Pasha opened the second drawer of his desk and took out a white envelope stamped with "Top Secret." "The details are written here," he said, placing the envelope in Ali Fuat's trembling hands. Pasha Vefik, tired of Ali Fuat's dumbfounded expression, said sternly, "Understood?"

Ali Fuat, with a pale and surprised look, said, "Yes, sir."

"Report to me every six hours."

"Yes, sir."

From that moment on, he was lost in intense thoughts. He had been involved in these matters for years. The order to "have a coffee" was an order given after thorough investigation. Pasha's order was flawed, or there was something he didn't know. He was helpless. Reluctantly, he had to follow the order. "It would have been great if Commander Tuncay was with me now," he thought. Kenan Ferit's voice brought him back to reality.

"We are approaching, Commander."

The black minibus, with its very special passenger inside, entered a dirt road and stopped after advancing for another minute or two. Ali Fuat's tension had reached its peak. The cigarette he hastily placed between his lips was far from being helpful. Although he didn't want to carry out the order without a clear reason, disobedience was not an option.

His men were looking at him with questioning eyes, waiting for an order. Taking the cigarette in his left hand, he took out his phone. He entered the contact list, pressed the letter T, and hovered over "Commander Tuncay." He was indecisive for a few seconds. He pressed the call button but immediately canceled. He was extremely frustrated. He thought about calling Pasha. He wanted to talk, to ask "Why?" but he knew it would remain just a desire, he wouldn't dare. It wasn't just cowardice that held him back. A subordinate calling his commander to question the reason for an order was unheard of in the Armed Forces. It would be inappropriate. Knowing it would be useless, he took a few more puffs and realized it was time to leave this temporary refuge. He threw the cigarette out the window.

"Let's go, boys!"

The men in the car got up. Zekeriya lifted the specially designed rear quad seat. As he lifted the seats, he reached under the seats and pulled out Halit Nurullah. He was an old man in his sixties with a beard and a thin frame. His hands were handcuffed. His head was wrapped in a black cloth.

Given their purpose, it was hard to understand Zekeriya's politeness as he carefully carried the unconscious old man out of the minibus. The small man looked like a little child in Zekeriya's huge arms. They began walking towards a grove by the roadside. From behind, Zekeriya looked like a massive door of a historic mosque with his thick neck, broad shoulders, and towering height. They stopped after walking a bit and getting away from the road. Ali Fuat considered turning on his flashlight. But the moonlight was sufficient.

The conditions were quite suitable for carrying out Pasha's order to "have a coffee." He remembered a small detail. Pasha had insisted that it be done while he was unconscious. What difference does it make whether he is unconscious or awake, he whispered to himself. His men, who couldn't hear him clearly, were watching him attentively. Of course, with the heavy discipline and strict respect of the military system, they couldn't say, "We couldn't hear you, Commander, could you please repeat?" With the relative closeness brought by their similar ranks and having been together in many operations, Kenan Ferit said, "Commander!" This single word contained several questions at once. Ali Fuat glanced briefly at Kenan Ferit but didn't respond.

Remembering that detail had thoroughly confused him.

What did it mean? Unconscious or awake... Could it be that the old man had something to say? He pulled out his pocket flask. He took a couple of sips himself and then let Halit smell it. The open air and the smell of the alcohol slightly revived the old man.

It was like waking up from a dream. He scanned his surroundings with bewildered eyes. He let him smell the flask again. Halit was slowly coming to his senses. Ali Fuat wanted to ask a few questions. What did he have to do with Pasha Vefik?

Halit was slowly writhing on the grass. Ali Fuat thought about removing the handcuffs.

After all, he was an old man. There couldn't be any danger or escape attempt.

Hadji Halit directed his meaningless gazes, which he had been wandering around the environment, to those around him. He looked at each of them one by one. Kenan Ferit tightly gripped the handle of his gun.

"He is waking up, Commander."

Ali Fuat looked at Kenan and then back at Halit. The old man seemed to be moving his lips behind his beard. He listened carefully to see if he would say something. He took another sip from his flask and said, "Old man, are you awake?" Halit Nurullah didn't answer, only moving his lips. Ali Fuat couldn't make sense of it. He told Zekeriya, who was standing over him, "Shake him, let him wake up. And take off his handcuffs."

Just as Zekeriya leaned over to the old man he had carefully placed on the grass after taking him out of the car, the cool forest air turned into the heat of hell. The sound of the metal breaking rang in their ears. Hadji Halit broke his handcuffs. As soon as he got up, he grabbed Zekeriya, who was standing next to him, and lifted him into the air. In the astonished looks, he threw the 300-lbs man against a tree. He turned back and looked at Ali Fuat with a terrifying darkness in his eyes. Just as he was about to attack, a loud gunshot echoed through the forest. The elite sniper of the Black Shrouds, Kenan Ferit, had pulled the trigger just in time. Using the "safety shot" method, he sent one bullet to the head and another to the heart. Halit fell to the ground on his back. The surrounding heat suddenly disappeared. A breeze began where Halit had fallen. The wind coming from his body bent all the grass, swaying the trees and leaves, blowing through the forest.

Chapter

2

Master of the Djinn Yasin Omen

After finishing his prayer beads, Yasin Omen stood up. When he started praying at Uludag University's mosque, there were a few young people. They too left after completing their obligatory prayers. The mosque's imam and a child reading a book near the door were the only ones left.

He often saw this child. Thinking, "My devout brother must have another exam," he smiled. "Ah! My Lord, if I studied in one of these departments, would I study only from exam to exam like this? With God's permission, I would study day and night and be the top student in every class!" he thought to himself.

Since elementary school, Yasin had been the top student in his class due to his sharp intelligence. The teachers affiliated with the community were very pleased with Yasin. They expected him to rank in the top ten in the university entrance exam. Everything started when Imam Sait said, "Drink this blessed water, my child, it will open your mind." That relentless fever and severe diarrhea prevented him from taking the exam. And then... Yasin wanted to utter a hefty curse but felt ashamed in the sacred place he was in. He couldn't have cursed anyway, it would just cross his mind momentarily, but something would choke him. The words wouldn't come out.

The child reading the book was disturbed by Yasin's foolish staring after finishing his prayer and standing up. He thought of saying, "What's up, brother?" but decided against it. Pretending to read the book while assessing the situation, he concluded that Yasin was not dangerous. Although not entirely sure, he fearfully looked at him.

When Yasin noticed the boy's gaze, he averted his eyes. He shivered.

"Yasin, my son, may God accept your prayers," said the mosque's imam. After finishing his prayers, he had collected the scattered prayer beads and, thinking that Yasin was waiting for him, had approached him.

"May God be pleased with you, hodja," Yasin replied. The familiar voice was so reassuring. Yasin had relaxed. This "May God be pleased with you" was both for the good wishes after the prayer and for being there when he was under the boy's gaze.

"How are you, son? How is your father?"

"Thank God, hodja. I hope you are well too?"

"May God grant you goodness, my son. I thank God when I see young people like you who do not neglect their prayers. May God grant wisdom to other young people as well."

"Yes, hodja," said Yasin. The imam was about to give him a long sermon again. No choice but to listen. The imam continued his speech with enthusiasm:

"Look at the state of this university! Our grandfathers sacrificed thousands of lives to bring Islam here, spilling their blessed blood on every inch of this land. But now, on the land our great ancestors bestowed upon us, young people are fornicating in broad daylight. As if that weren't enough, they also interfere with our call to prayer. They say there should be no call to prayer on university grounds. Every kind of infidelity is permitted, but not the call to prayer or our veiled girls. Ah, my son! The heart of a Muslim, of any decent person, cannot bear this oppression!"

Yasin immediately joined in.

"You are right, hodja. Do you say anything to my father?"

"No, my son, what can I say? Just give him my regards."

"Peace be upon you. Will do."

Respectfully turning back, he walked towards the exit. To avoid meeting the boy's gaze again, he looked at the ground. The boy, sensing that Yasin was harmless, stared at him until he left.

Putting on his coat and shoes, Yasin exited the mosque. Although it was sunny, it was cold. He thought he had done well to bring his coat.

Bursa[2]'s weather could not be trusted; it could present you with all four seasons in one day. Especially in March...

The mosque was built about a meter below street level. He climbed the stairs. Standing on the sidewalk, he checked the road. In front of him was a huge lawn the size of several football fields. This was the central area of Uludag University, where concerts were held during annual festivals, and on sunny days, students sprawled out, lovers subtly made out. Many buildings were lined up around it: the social services building, the library, the faculties of economics and administrative sciences, engineering faculties, the educational sciences building...

He crossed the road and entered the lawn. He first decided to go to Medico-Social. From there, he thought he would go home.

The Medico-Social building, which housed Uludag University's social services, various student clubs, a cafeteria, and a hospital, was bustling with activity. He walked around and looked at the surroundings. Students who were members of clubs and involved in various activities were running back and forth. Hundreds of students were coming out of the cafeteria, and as many were going in to catch the lunch hour between 12 and 2. The Poetry and Love Club had set up a stand selling the Campus magazine. Yasin sat on the half-meter-high wall surrounding the concrete floor.

He felt sad again. He thought, "I could have been one of them." He would have joined the clubs too. He might have even become a president. And then, he could have had a girlfriend. A beautiful, brunette girlfriend!

Seated in the corner chair of honor, the president of the Poetry and Love Club, Yasin, opened the meeting. The room soon filled with group leaders and vice presidents from the club's divisions: cinema, magazine, theater, panel, organization... All the sub-groups were there. Yasin addressed the first issue, coordination, and task distribution for the festival preparations. He addressed problems one by one, giving his

---

[2]   A city in Turkey's Marmara region, known as the first capital of the Ottoman Empire and famed for its rich historical heritage. It is renowned for its green landscapes, thermal baths, mosques, and the UNESCO World Heritage village of Cumalikizik. Additionally, it is a major tourist destination due to the Uludag ski resort.

recommendations and overseeing the task assignments. His style was fluent and impressive. The girls looked at him with admiration.

He was startled by the voice of a student asking for a light for his cigarette. The boy must have found the situation strange, as he repeated, "Do you have a light?" Yasin, embarrassed, looked down and said in a low voice, "No." He stood up and walked towards the exit of the concrete area. He wanted to curse badly. He could have been one of those students. He could have attended not just Uludag but even Bogazici[3] or METU[4]. There was no university or department he couldn't get into. But... Sheikh Imam Sait didn't want it. Damn him and his... He immediately repented, walking away angrily.

He came to the front of the library building, walking on the cobbled path. He slowed his pace and looked at the parking lot to his right. There were hundreds of cars. Jeeps, BMWs, Mercedes...

He started walking through the large parking lot. The sun was directly overhead. As he approached his car, he pressed the key fob. The mechanical sound of the door locks opening sounded like pleasant music to his ears. Just as he was about to get in, he saw a long-haired, tanned, sexy girl running towards him with her breasts bouncing. Her strapless top was so low- cut that her breasts were half exposed and then covered again. This provocative movement repeated two or three times per second. The girl had probably just come out of the library. Instead of walking around the parking lot, she was cutting through it to get to the bus stops on the other side. She had seen the bus arriving at the stop and was hurrying to catch it.

Just as the girl passed by and was a few meters ahead, Yasin said, "Excuse me." The girl turned around and gave him a look as if to say, "What is it?"

---

[3]   Established in 1863 as Robert College in Istanbul, it became Bogazici University in 1971, transitioning into a public university. It is one of Turkey's most prestigious universities, known for its strong academic staff, high-quality education, and stunning campus overlooking the Bosphorus.

[4]   Middle East Technical University. Established in 1956 in Ankara, it is one of Turkey's most prestigious universities.

"You dropped this notebook," he said, holding out a notebook. The girl glanced at the bus stop and then back at Yasin , saying, "But I don't have a notebook like that!"

She spoke in a sweet, babyish tone. Yasin smiled. "How can you not? Are you saying I'm lying?" he said, imitating her bouncing movements. "You're running with your hair flying... Then you say it didn't drop from you." Yasin had said it comically, using body language. The girl smiled. Yasin felt he was on the right track.

"Look, you even wrote your name here. This is your notebook."

"Hmm. What did I write, let's see?"

Yasin, with all his foolishness, said: "Um, how about Buse?" The girl responded with a 'tsk' sound and laughed. She liked Yasin 's mannerisms.

"Betul, Aysel, Elif, Buket, Derya."

"No, you didn't get it," she said, prolonging her words. She had a very sweet way of speaking.

Yasin, caught like a thief, said, "Alright, I confess. I am a lousy liar." The girl was laughing. Yasin continued with all his theatrical skills: "Oh God, forgive this deceitful servant of yours. You created her so beautifully that I told lies just to meet her." The girl started laughing more. Yasin had his hands raised as if in prayer, smiling and watching the girl's joyful laughter. Meanwhile, seeing the bus leaving the stop, he continued his prayer. "Oh God, I made her miss her bus to get to know her. Forgive me, oh God."

Hearing this part, the girl quickly turned around. Seeing the bus leaving, she said, "Oh no…"

Yasin had been waiting for this moment. In a tempting voice, he said, "Come on, let's go together." His voice was far from the previous playful tone and was very masculine. The girl looked at the silver-colored convertible sports Mercedes. It was sparkling like a jewel under the sun. Yasin was confident and proud.

The people around were looking at him as if to say, "What is he doing?" The short blond young man standing in front of the Mercedes, scrutinizing the car, had caught everyone's attention. The preppy student who owned the car came up to Yasin, laughing loudly. Yasin continued to look at the car in the same way. He was also smiling. The preppy kid turned back and, in a mock-American accent, said, "Dude, this guy is out of it!" His friends laughed.

"Bro, if you like it so much, I'll let you take a spin," he said, laughing loudly. Yasin turned his eyes in fear. Who were these people? Why were they laughing? He immediately moved away from there. He could hear the sounds of mock laughter behind him.

If he wanted, he could get one of those cars too. The best of them! But he just couldn't bring himself to do it. He felt restrained. He couldn't break away from his sheikh's words. He walked away feeling down.

Before going home, he thought about sitting in a cafe and having some tea. After a brief moment of indecision, he went inside.

While drinking his tea, he looked at the students sitting at other tables. Mixed groups of girls and boys were chatting happily, playing backgammon, or discussing things fervently.

Yasin had gotten used to the cosmopolitan nature of the students. Long-haired boys, bald-headed ones, those wearing earrings, those with rings in their noses... What was done in the name of being marginal had become so widespread that the ordinary ones seemed more marginal. Yasin felt a sense of this.

He wondered if it was obvious that he wasn't a university student.

A girl with her hair cut short caught his attention. He looked at the sexiness given by the short hair and the girl's shapely body. She had a small, cute nose. She was laughing, talking to her female friend. Just as Yasin was engrossed in watching her, he noticed one of the men at the table glaring at him angrily. He immediately averted his gaze. His heart felt like it was being squeezed. He looked around quickly, took a couple of quick sips of his tea. He wondered, "Is he still looking?" but didn't dare check. He got up from the table and hurried out.

Chapter

3

Grand Funeral

In the central market of Konya, the shutters were opened with a prayer. Shop owners and workers greeted each other, wishing for good and profitable days. Since it wasn't fully daylight yet, some shops turned on their lights. The older shopkeepers, out of long habit, were sweeping the front of their shops. Meanwhile, the sniffling apprentices of the tea houses were rushing around, balancing trays to deliver tea for the shopkeepers' breakfast, which consisted of meat and cheese pastries.

What disrupted this routine was the reading of the "Konya Hâkimiyet" newspaper by a few shopkeepers.

"...two days ago, Halit Nurullah, a carpet dealer from Konya[5], who had been abducted by unidentified persons, was found dead in a grove near Sakarya. Halit Nurullah, who had opened Quran courses and provided scholarships for hundreds of students, was greatly loved and respected by the people. It is not yet clear why he was kidnapped or why he was killed..."

Those who read the newspaper were saddened. Soon, the entire market had received the bad news.

None of the members of the Nurullah family went to the shop that morning. The young employees told the shopkeepers that the funeral

---

[5] A city in Turkey's Central Anatolia region, known for its rich history and cultural heritage. It served as the capital of the Seljuk Empire and is home to the mausoleum of Mevlana Jalaluddin Rumi, making it a significant center of Islamic culture and Sufism.

would be held at the Kapu Mosque on Sarraflar Street after the noon prayer.

The house and courtyard were packed. Bearded men in turbans, women in black chadors, boys in white caps— hundreds of people gathered. There was a great atmosphere of mourning.

The news of Halit's death was met with sorrow in another place too. Imam Sait had received the news at midnight.

"Hello! Peace be upon you, Hodja."

"And upon you, peace."

"Hodja, it's Salih from the police."

"I recognized your voice, my son. How are you?"

"Thank God, hodja, I kiss your hands. Sorry to disturb you at this hour, but about Hodja Halit..."

"What about him? Has he been found?"

The voice on the phone gulped.

"Hodja, my condolences. He was found two hours ago near Sakarya..."

Imam Sait was very saddened. He couldn't sleep for a long time. After performing the morning prayer, he dozed off for an hour or two. He got up and started preparing for the funeral prayer.

The Kapu Mosque, the largest Ottoman mosque in Konya, was packed. The sorrowful crowd didn't know where to direct their anger, so they were tense. Frequently, shouts of "Allahu Akbar" and slogans about Sharia and the headscarf made the crowd even more agitated. National newspapers and television stations were also there.

After the funeral prayer and the burial, Imam Sait hurried to his car. One of his students opened the back door of the old Renault 19. He saw that the friends he had agreed to meet at the lodge were getting into their cars and made eye contact with some of them.

Imam Sait arrived at the lodge in the Husrev Aga neighborhood. Most of the houses were built side by side, and the entire neighborhood was affiliated with the tariqa[6] (religious order, sect).

When he went down to the lower floor of the lodge, he saw that some of his friends had arrived before him.

"Salamun alaykum" (Peace be upon you.)

Everyone in the room responded, "Wa alaykum salam" (And upon you, peace.)

The room was a spacious place with small windows, slightly below ground level. It was carpeted with beautiful rugs, and there were many cushions on the floor. He sat on the large cushion in the place of honor. There were many rooms and a large hall in the basement of the lodge. They prayed together, held conversations, and did zikr (remembrance of Allah) here. The number of meetings Imam Sait and his friends held here was increasing day by day.

The expected people arrived. Imam Sait thought it was time to start the meeting and began speaking.

"In the name of Allah, the Most Gracious, the Most Merciful. Brothers, my condolences to all of us."

The crowd was listening attentively.

"While the Islamic world is burning under the sun of infidelity, deprived of the shade of the caliphate[7], while our women are being forced to uncover their heads, our call to prayer is being made in Turkish, and

---

[6]   In Islamic mysticism, a Sufi order or spiritual path where followers (dervishes) gather to seek closeness to God and attain spiritual enlightenment through specific rules and rituals. Today, modern meaning, it typically refers to religious communities or groups within Islam that gather around a specific leader, following their own teachings, rituals, and rules. In contemporary usage, some tariqas have become controversial due to their social and political influence.

[7]   A system of governance in the Islamic world that served as both a religious and political leadership following the death of Prophet Muhammad. The caliphs were responsible for ruling the Islamic state and implementing Sharia law. It was officially abolished in 1924 by the Republic of Turkey.

Hagia Sophia[8], which our ancestors sacrificed hundreds of thousands of lives to conquer, is closed to worship, a handful of mujahideen who are ready to shed their blood for the sake of Allah have started the great jihad to raise the flag of the caliphate on the blessed city of Istanbul, as heralded by our Prophet. Many of our brothers have been martyred in this cause. The treacherous unbelievers infiltrated our tariqa, and there were betrayals. Our precious Hadji Halit Nurullah was treacherously martyred. That man, who endured countless hardships and torments for our holy cause, was lost to the Islamic world. This unbeliever system's murders, which began with Mr. Ali Shukru, have martyred many of our great masters and warriors. But as long as they cannot tear this faith from the hearts of the people, mothers will give birth to many more Ali Shukru, many more Hadji Halits."

Imam Sait was on the verge of tears. He took out a handkerchief from his robe and wiped his eyes, swollen from lack of sleep. The murder of his comrade of 30 years and the betrayal he sensed had increased his anger and sorrow.

"Brothers, you have all been part of the community for years. I sense something strange behind this murder," Imam said, hinting at a question. A slightly overweight man with almond-shaped mustaches, wearing a black jacket and a collarless shirt, sitting on one of the cushions, spoke:

"You are right, teacher. The Black Shrouds haven't killed anyone for three years. Moreover, our group is not known within the community. Only those in this room and Allah know about our goals and objectives."

The Imam took the floor again.

"Brothers, Hadji Halit was a modest tradesman. His activities within the community were not significant enough to disturb the Black Shrouds. Only we knew his role in the secret operations. It's unlikely that the unbelievers killed him without learning something. If they had, they wouldn't just have attacked him, but many of us."

---

[8]   Located in Istanbul, it was built as a church in 537 by Byzantine Emperor Justinian I. After the Ottoman conquest in 1453, it was converted into a mosque and later became a museum in 1935. In 2020, it was reopened as a mosque. Hagia Sophia is a significant cultural heritage site that showcases both Byzantine and Ottoman architectural and artistic elements.

Another member continued the conversation.

"Hodja, could someone else have done it?"

"No, it was the Black Shrouds. The abduction, the removal from Konya, the murder... The crime was executed so skillfully that only the Black Shrouds could have committed it."

Another member spoke.

"And who else would want to kill Halit?"

Chapter

4

Assembly

Raindrops were falling like a torrent, beating against the windows with the wind's help. Cihangir Demirkaplan drew back the curtain and wiped the steam off the window with his hand to watch the rain and the city view. A slight smile appeared on his lips. He had loved the rain since he was a child.

Cihangir Demirkaplan, the head of the distinguished Demirkaplan family, was a short, dark-skinned, quite obese man. His cheeks were chubby, and his neck was rather prominent. He looked to be in his sixties, and most of his hair had fallen out.

He saw that the time was 6:30 PM. The meeting was at 7:30 PM. "With the rain and traffic..." he muttered.

He left the hotel with his bodyguards. Just a few steps towards the waiting car, one of the bodyguards opened an umbrella. Mr. Cihangir pushed the umbrella away with his hand. The bodyguard, accustomed to this, did not find it strange.

He got into his specially made armored vehicle. One bodyguard sat in the front seat while the others split into two black SUVs, four in each.

Mercedeses, BMWs, SUVs, and many other vehicles were gathered in Comson Holding's parking lot. The parking lot looked like an auto show. Among the luxury cars, a Renault-19 stood out.

Around the conference table, nearly twenty middle-aged men were seated. At the head of the table, Cihangir Demirkaplan was chatting with those next to him. Imam Sait sat at the far end, counting his prayer

18

beads and looking down. Most of the attendees were clean-shaven and in suits. Only the Imam wore his usual attire of hair, beard, turban, and robe.

The members were talking about investments, new cars, and their children's education abroad. Imam Sait increasingly felt disgusted and sickened. He wanted to spit in each of their faces one by one.

The attendees were quieted by the voice of Cihangir Demirkaplan.

"We have buried a very dear brother. My condolences to our entire community and to you, esteemed members of the Council of the Exalted."

The members continued to listen in silence.

"And especially, my condolences to our brother Sait Nurani."

The Imam placed his hand over his heart and said, "Thank you. May Allah be pleased with you."

Demirkaplan, with a fake expression of sorrow, continued to speak.

"Halit Nurullah made great contributions to our cause. With his activities within the community, he earned everyone's admiration and respect. We will never forget that noble person. May his grave be light upon him. A Fatiha[9] for his soul!"

Everyone recited the Fatiha and then, wiping their faces[10], said, "Amen!" Demirkaplan continued:

"This heinous murder shows that we must act very carefully and avoid individual actions. We must remain calm and conduct all our activities with great caution."

Most of the members were uninterested in the conversation. Except for one or two who were listening attentively, the majority were playing with their pens and papers. Twisting his beard slightly, Imam Sait was becoming more and more furious.

---

9 The Fatiha Prayer is the opening chapter of the Quran, containing praise to God, a plea for mercy, and a request for guidance on the right path. It is a central prayer recited in every Muslim prayer ritual.

10 This practice is seen as a symbolic gesture to "receive" the blessings and mercy that one has prayed for. By wiping their hands over their face, believers express their hope that God's blessings will be bestowed upon them, as if metaphorically "embracing" the blessings that have been sought in the prayer. It's a tradition rooted in the belief that the hands raised in supplication are blessed, and touching the face is a way to transfer that blessing.

Demirkaplan, after taking a few sips of water, continued his speech.

"The Black Shrouds have been silent for three years. But what happened to Hadji Halit indicates that these killers are still active."

Demirkaplan scanned the members with his eyes.

"Each of you must manage your respective groups with the utmost secrecy. In this complex period, we need to be more careful than ever," he said. Imam Sait thought about the major changes the community had undergone. He looked at the luxury of the hall, the chairs they were sitting on, the table, and the attire of the members. He thought about the expensive cars in the garage. He felt disgusted by the casual chatter following the murder of a great mujahid[11]. They should be grieving, mourning, making vows of revenge, not behaving like this, he thought.

Faruk Altan, responsible for finance and a former MP, spoke up.

"The community has grown so large. We are not fully aware of all activities. This leads to significant problems. We need to prevent unauthorized formations."

Many members of the Council of the Exalted nodded in agreement with Faruk Altan. Osman Karahan, responsible for education, put down the pen he was holding and said, "The loss we have suffered shows that we need to strengthen central authority. No activity should be carried out without the approval of the Council of the Exalted. The late Hadji Halit was opening numerous Quran courses and engaging with students in various formations. Neither I, as the community's nor the education group's leader, had any knowledge of these activities."

Unable to contain his anger, the Imam said, "Was Halit Nurullah killed for opening a few Quran courses and giving scholarships to poor students?" His deep voice filled the hall.

Imam Sait rarely spoke at meetings. He usually prearranged with Halit what he wanted to say, and Hadji Halit would speak at the meeting. But now, he was alone. His mysterious demeanor always gave members the chills. There was a brief silence due to the unfamiliarity with his speaking. Imam Sait continued:

---

[11]   In Islamic belief, a person who strives to defend their faith and fights in the path of God. The term is often used to refer to those who participate in jihad, meaning a sacred struggle or effort.

"If engaging in educational activities is so dangerous, why aren't the Black Shrouds bothering you with your 500 private schools and hundreds of other institutions?"

Osman Karahan, nervously twirling the pen on the table, replied, "I am not saying it is dangerous to engage in educational activities. I am talking about acting without the knowledge of the community, in unknown ways!"

The Imam looked at Karahan with great hatred. Cihangir Demirkaplan, in a soft tone, said, "Esteemed friends, in this time of sorrow, we must seek unity, not discord."

Taking courage from Demirkaplan's words, Osman Karahan added, "And to unify, we must refrain from acting without the knowledge of the Council of the Exalted, sir."

"Certainly!"

Others also spoke, voicing the importance of centralization, of consolidating all efforts under one command. The Imam listened to these speeches with deep- seated hatred and disgust, his greatest ire provoked by Faruk Altan's smug declaration, "Well, this is how it's done!"

"Any action taken outside the Council endangers both our cause and the individual themselves. A wolf will seize the stray from the flock."

The Imam could not hold back any longer.

"I wonder, Mr. Ramazan, who told the wolves that Halit Nurullah had strayed from the flock?"

Sensing that the conversation was about to turn hostile, Cihangir Demirkaplan quickly intervened. With a few neutral words aimed at preserving peace, he promptly adjourned the meeting, attempting to leave no side inflamed.

Chapter

5

Ali Fuat

The sun's rays seeped through the gap in the curtain, entering the bedroom in a thin beam. Ali Fuat's right eye was exposed to the first light of the day as he lay on his left shoulder and ear.

He sat up. The strip of light coming through the window was about six or seven centimeters wide and, by luck, it passed right over his pillow. He cursed with slurred words in his drowsy state. He turned to the other side and lay down again, nuzzling his face into his wife's shoulders and planting kisses. Sliding his hand under the duvet, he embraced her and began to caress her full breasts. Selin responded by wiggling her buttocks. Ali Fuat parted his wife's delicate brown and yellow mixed hair with his face and began kissing her neck and nape.

Selin tensed up, tickled. She giggled like a mischievous little girl, "Good morning, darling," she said. Ali Fuat , with a voice full of lust, replied, "It wasn't a good morning kiss!"

"Oh, what was it then?"

"I have bad intentions!"

"Hmm, what are those?" Her words came out in a soft, inviting tone. They started kissing. Selin's smooth, fair body melded with Ali Fuat 's dark and formidable frame.

Their sweet lovemaking, adorned with exciting jokes, ended in disappointment once again, without giving Selin time to release that energy inside her.

"Oh dear, not this little again... At least don't finish early!" she thought. She felt like punching him in the face. Though she often played the role of a satisfied woman, this time she was very annoyed. Her loins were still tense.

Ali Fuat felt like a defeated Roman general. He was exhausted and humiliated, exiled from his own bed. He cracked the bathroom door open and looked at his face in the mirror. Seeing the medicine cabinet, he thought of his urologist. "Son of a bitch," he whispered. "It's psychological, is it? I can overcome it by myself, can I? If I could do it on my own, why would I come to you? Just prescribe some proper meds, you animal. All you do is give advice, you jerk. If I don't put a grenade in your yap and pull the pin..." He was muttering and cursing under the shower. Channeling his hatred towards the doctor's imaginary figure helped him regain some composure and shed his defeated, crushed spirit a bit.

He dried off and put on his bathrobe before leaving the bathroom. When he entered the bedroom, Selin was dressed. She gave her husband a forced smile. "Enjoy your shower, darling."

"Thank you, dear," said Ali Fuat, without looking at his wife's face. He opened the wardrobe, took out his clothes, and then opened the large bottom drawer to get his underwear. Selin, sensing that their daughter had woken up, said, "I'll go check on Ece," and left the room.

After getting dressed, he went back to the bathroom. He turned on the hairdryer briefly, then decided to comb his hair. The comb was on top of the washing machine, but Selin had moved it, along with the cream and nail clippers, to the bathroom cabinet with a lot of grumbling. He opened the cabinet and took the comb. He combed his straight black hair, which he kept in a military cut. He never used gel or pomade, although occasional white hairs were visible.

As he always did, he tossed the comb on the washing machine, but immediately afterward, he picked it up and put it back in the cabinet. He couldn't understand why he had done that. Perhaps the lingering humiliation from the earlier bed scene was still affecting him. When he left the bathroom, he saw that his daughter had woken up. With her floral pajamas, shoulder-length blonde hair, green eyes, and perfectly drawn nose, she was the spitting image of her mother. She squinted her half-asleep eyes and pouted her lips adorably.

"Daddy, are you leaving?" Her words sounded as if she was saying, "Don't go." In the mornings, her father's suit and tie indicated to her that he was leaving.

"Oh, look at that adorable little pout! Those sweet lips are just too cute when they're all puckered up. Are you trying to catch some kisses with that face?" he said, picking her up. Ece seemed tiny in her father's 1.90-meter frame, broad shoulders, and long arms. She wrapped her arms around his neck.

"Daddy, I waited so long last night. I missed you so much."

"I'll come home early tonight, my little bird."

Selin intervened. "Honey, don't promise the child. You can't always make it."

"This time, her daddy will come home," he said, kissing his daughter's nose while she giggled. "What should I bring my princess when I come home? A toy, chocolate, whatever you wish, my princess?"

"Uncle Serkan brought chocolate. Bring me a toy, daddy."

The playful expression on his face disappeared instantly.

He looked at Selin.

"Honey, he just dropped by to see how we were doing.

He brought some chocolate for Ece."

"Daddy, he brought me a big chocolate. Mommy also made tea."

"Out of the mouths of baby…" He struggled to avoid cursing in front of his daughter. Selin, as always, said, "Come on, little lamb. Let's get you dressed. You'll catch a cold."

Ali Fuat never cursed, shouted, or spoke harshly in front of his daughter. Struggling to control his voice, he said, "What was that guy doing here…?" His anger was getting the better of him; he couldn't find the words.

Selin focused all her attention on dressing Ece slowly and gently. She was using her daughter as a shield. "Honey, there's nothing going on. He's just a neighbor," she said, swallowing nervously.

"Daddy, are you going to get me the car like Duygu's?"

Ali Fuat 's heart melted at the sound of his daughter's voice. He glared at Selin, as if to say, 'We'll talk later,' then turned back to his daughter with a fake smile. Ali Fuat's brother Feridun, a military judge, had a daughter Ece's age. During a family visit, Ece had seen her cousin's battery- operated car and loved it. She had said, "I want one too," but Ali Fuat had never gotten around to it. Ece hadn't mentioned it again.

"Okay, my little sunshine." He approached and bent down, hugging and kissing her affectionately. "My sweet girl. My one and only," he said. He had never said 'my one and only' with such emphasis before.

Leaving the house, he started down the stairs. As he passed by the door of the apartment of Serkan Cenet, a financial inspector, he cursed under his breath. He stepped out of the building and walked towards his car. The air was a bit chilly, with a gentle sun.

He got into his car.

Chapter

6

Black Shrouds

The headquarters of the Black Shrouds, a company disguised as "Agricultural Machinery Import Export Inc." resembled a failing business with its seven-story nondescript building. As Ali Fuat entered, he locked eyes with the guards at the door. Despite recognizing his vehicle, their rigorous training required them to stay vigilant.

Today, he was early. The Black Shrouds had unique working conditions- they could come at irregular hours, sometimes staying until midnight, other times not coming at all. Spring was in the air, and the flowers in the garden absorbed some of the negative energy from the unpleasant start to his day, providing him with a bit of relief.

He ascended to the fourth floor where the operations unit was located. Beside the large steel door, a security mechanism the size of a television was installed on the wall. He passed his special ID through the device like a credit card through a POS machine. The red light on the small button above the machine turned off, and the yellow light next to it lit up. Following the yellow light's instructions, he bent down and brought his right eye close to the screen. A powerful beam of light started at his eyebrows, scanned his eyes for a retina check, and vanished with a 'beep.' The yellow light turned off, and the green light came on. The door opened.

Once inside, Ali Fuat walked briskly to his office. The door automatically closed behind him. As he walked, he greeted his fellow guards. He placed his thumb on the small box next to his office door.

After a two-second fingerprint scan, a 'beep' sounded, and the door to his office opened. He entered and first opened the windows. The fresh air hitting his face made him realize how stuffy the room had been. He turned on the kettle and sat down to open his computer.

Once the water boiled, he made himself a cup of sage tea. He took out the pastries he had brought. Usually, he had breakfast at home, but after the morning's disaster, he had wanted to leave immediately. He added one sugar cube, stirred it, and took a bite of the pastry. He noticed the message he had been waiting for had arrived. He clicked on the email titled "Dr. Shanli."

"Dear Ali Fuat,

What you described is very intriguing. It stretches the boundaries of imagination to think that a sixty- kilogram, frail old man could lift and throw a one- hundred-forty-kilogram man, who you say is specially trained and a very good fighter. According to the scenario you presented, this has nothing to do with the psychological effects of fear. 'Fear' does not give someone such power, but it can provide certain motivation. 'A person chased by a dog runs faster,' but this ordinary person being chased by a dog cannot break the 100-meter Olympic record.

The case you mentioned of the old man beating the other person could have a different reason. However, it is clear that this is not related to fear. It could be something like bioenergy, which science has not yet fully explained. To provide a more accurate answer, I would need to meet the person in question.

Best regards,
Prof. Dr. Mustafa Shanli"

As Ali Fuat read the letter, he had finished one pastry and started on the second. Mustafa Shanli was a professor in the psychology department at Istanbul University. Ali Fuat often asked the professor questions about the psychology of religious communities and the psychological effects of religion on organizations. This time was a bit different. He had asked about the Halit Nurullah incident without naming names.

The response did not surprise him. He had given the execution order for many people before. They had also been afraid, but none had managed to break their handcuffs. Moreover, how could a frail old man lift and throw Arab Zekeriya? What made Halit Nurullah different?

He was deep in thought, buried in files, when the door suddenly opened. Colonel Zeki, the commander of the intelligence unit of the Black Shrouds, entered. Ali Fuat immediately stood up.

"Sit, sit," Colonel said.

"Yes, sir," replied Ali Fuat. Colonel Zeki got straight to the point.

"Fuat, I am leaving. I came to say goodbye."

Ali Fuat didn't respond. He was surprised. This decision was probably related to the reprimand from Pasha Vefik.

"Commander, I wish you hadn't acted in anger," he managed to say.

"Anger? If it were anger, I should have smashed that bastard's face right there."

"First Commander Tuncay, now you. There's no experienced commander left in the organization."

"Good, now that bastard can play his games without interruption."

"I wish you had reconsidered this decision."

"There's nothing to reconsider, Fuat. There are a thousand ways to tell someone to 'get lost.' The man doesn't want us."

No matter how much he pleaded, he couldn't convince him. After Tuncay Sipahi, the Black Shrouds were losing another valuable commander to Pasha Vefik's whims or deliberate policies. Ali Fuat couldn't decide if it was due to frayed nerves over the years or a different agenda. He couldn't make up his mind…

Chapter

7

Yasin 's Secret Chamber

After performing the morning prayer, Yasin continued to sleep until around ten o'clock when he was awakened by his mother's voice.

"Wake up, my dear. You need time to get ready."

Groggy, Yasin opened his eyes and sat up slightly. He looked at the watch he had taken off and placed beside his pillow before going to bed. It was three minutes past ten. He stretched while staring at the ceiling. Rolling to the left side of his bed, he reached down and grabbed his phone from the floor. He looked at the wide screen of his cell phone. There were no calls. Who would call me anyway, he thought.

After his two older sisters got married, he moved into their spacious room. The bed was pushed against the wall, with a wardrobe opposite it and a small desk with a laptop on top. A large table was placed in front of the window, which offered a beautiful view of the forest when the curtains were open.

After washing his face and hands, he returned to his room and opened the window to check the weather. As he had expected, it was cool outside. He was getting dressed when the room echoed with the sound of a message notification. This was a rare occurrence. He quickly reached for his phone.

"Peace be upon you. We'll be a bit late. Save us a spot, we don't want to be left outside and get soaked!"

The message was from Salih, one of Yasin's few friends. Every Friday, they went to Ulu Mosque for prayers. Afterward, they would wander around and usually head to Green, where they would have tea or coffee at Hunkâr Tea Garden. Yasin lived in the dormitories at Gorukle Campus, while his friends stayed at the sect's house in Yavuz Selim Neighborhood on the other side of Bursa.

After reading the message, he tossed the phone onto his bed. Getting a message once in a blue moon filled him with hope, but after reading it, he would feel disappointed and frustrated. He knew he was getting angry for no reason. He had a few friends, all male and from the sect. He had no idea how to break out of his shell. The image of Imam Sait flashed before his eyes, and he felt a chill of fear.

Suddenly, he shivered. Wearing just an undershirt, he felt cold. He took out his sweaters from the wardrobe and put on the brown one.

In the kitchen, his mother, Neriman, who had placed a few breakfast items on the round table, was peeling a boiled egg. When she saw her son, she smiled. "Don't overheat in that turtleneck sweater," she said.

"I looked out the window; it seems cold," Yasin replied as he sat at the table. His mother, slicing the egg, said, "Son, you'll get hot in the mosque. Why don't you wear your cream-colored sweater instead?"

As he poured tea into his glass, Yasin responded, "That one doesn't match my pants!"

Placing the egg on the plate and pouring olive oil over it. Neriman said, "It doesn't matter, son. You're going to the mosque. As long as you're clean, what difference does it make?"

Yasin grimaced. It was this mentality that had caused his best years to pass by so uneventfully. "Put some thyme on the egg, Mom," he said. He stirred his tea and started his breakfast.

Mrs. Omen poured herself some tea and sat at the table. Yasin looked into his mother's hazel eyes. "Mom, I'll stay at the place tonight, alright?" he said.

She was used to Yasin spending two or three nights a week at the sect's house. "Alright, son. Just don't forget to close the window before you go to bed, okay?"

Yasin changed his sweater, slung his bag across his shoulder, and placed his phone, handkerchief, and wallet inside. He left the house.

He walked down from the dormitories of the Dormitories Institution, passed the girls' blocks, and arrived at the administrative building. He greeted the staff with "Peace be upon you" and asked how they were doing. He went up to his father's office.

"Peace be upon you, Dad."

"And peace be upon you. Come, have a seat!"

Ilyas Omen, the deputy director of the Gorukle Dormitories Institution, had a short stature, a hooked nose, a bald head, and a belly that complemented the profile of an old-fashioned manager. His neatly trimmed mustache above his lips also completed his political image. He was a neatly dressed, respectable man. He performed the small tasks assigned by the sect and lived peacefully, believing he was serving a great cause on the path of Allah.

Yasin glanced at the clock. It was a quarter to eleven. "Dad, let me check your computer... Salih and the others will be a bit late, so I'll go and save us a spot."

"You go ahead, son; it might take a while. You can check it later," said Mr. Ilyas, who had mentioned that his computer had broken down the day before.

"No, Dad, it won't take long."

Mr. Ilyas stood up from his office chair and offered it to Yasin . Out of respect, Yasin didn't sit in his father's chair. Instead, he began to check the computer. After a quick investigation, he realized that one of the system files had been deleted. Smiling, he opened the recycle bin and restored the system file.

"We never learned how to use these blessed things, son. Maybe I should have taken lessons from those infidels too," Mr. Ilyas said with a laugh.

Yasin couldn't help but laugh. The 'infidels' his father referred to were some of the world's greatest programmers and hackers, like Kevin Mitnick and Johan Helsingius. The sect had paid each of them six hundred thousand dollars for a four-month course. Yasin, who had been secretly trained by Turkey's best experts with bags of money, had taken his final lessons from these two wizards and had become a computer genius, adding his own exceptional intellect to the mix.

After fixing the computer, Yasin hurried out.

Yasin and his friends performed the Friday prayers at Ulu Mosque. They wandered around the Tophane hills, enjoying the view of Bursa. They walked to Setbashi and then to Green.

They arrived at the Guney Apartments in Yavuz Selim Neighborhood. Although the building belonged to the sect, only apartments eight and nine were actively used, with the others rented out to devout families to create the appearance of an ordinary apartment building. The goal was not rental income but to obscure the activities in apartment nine, where Yasin operated.

Yasin and his friends prepared the meal and set the table. The meal prayer was recited by Davut Buyukdere, who was the eldest among the students both in age and sect rank.

After the meal, Yasin asked for permission to go to his apartment. Only Yasin and, when he was there, Imam Sait were allowed into this apartment.

Yasin arrived at the apartment door. He unlocked the upper and lower locks of the steel door and entered a small two-square-meter area. There were walls on both sides and a custom-made door in front of him. He inserted and turned the key in the small slot next to the door. The lights on the security panel lit up. He entered the code '1453,' unlocking part of the lock mechanism. A "beep" sound came from the small box in front of him. The beeping continued like the ticking of a time bomb. Yasin counted, and after the ninth beep, he brought his mouth close to the parabolic microphone and said, "Peace be upon you." The frequency concentrations in his voice were verified by the system, and the security locks of the door were released. He stepped inside, reciting a prayer.

As soon as he entered, he began reciting Ayat al-Kursi. He turned on the lights and went to the kitchen. He lowered the door of the old dishwasher all the way down. Taking a crawling position, he entered inside. Pushing the inner surface of the machine, the opposite side opened similarly downward. He moved into the pitch-dark space beyond.

The hidden room in the house was quite spacious. One wall was lined with an extensive computer system, featuring four computers side by side, each with a case three to four times the normal size. However, the case of the fourth computer was unusually large, almost the size of a refrigerator. This system, equipped with one of the world's most powerful processors, had been purchased from the Russian mafia. Originally designed for space science and nuclear research, the processor was now used by Yasin's skilled hands for decrypting codes.

The opposite wall was arranged as a library, with shelves holding hundreds of books, mostly focusing on Abjad, Kabbalah, and Cifr. There were handwritten works by medieval scholars "Muhyiddin Arabi[12], who had delved into huddam (the practice of summoning and controlling spirits)" A large Star of David on the ceiling was surrounded by Hebrew inscriptions, with hooks attached to each of its six points and one in the center. Chains extended down from these hooks, with bowls hanging at approximately waist height. The bowls contained a mixture of the fat from a sacrificial camel and the baptismal water of a Christian child. The wicks were made from the threads of a rabbi's kippah from a synagogue in Jerusalem. These ancient bowls were inscribed with Aramaic prayers meant to burn away evil spirits.

Below the chain hanging from the center of the Star of David was a low table covered with various books. The five chains and bowls surrounding the star encircled this table.

Yasin individually powered up each computer. He lit the wicks in the six bowls hanging from the ceiling and the bowl on the table. A cold, pale flame flickered faintly, almost as if it wouldn't burn if touched.

The melody from his phone, inside his bag, began to play. It was probably Imam Sait, who always called knowing the Friday schedule.

"Yes, hodja..." "..."

"Yes, I've arrived..." "..."

"Alright, hodja."

He ended the call. They rarely spoke on the phone for long, knowing it could be overheard. They usually communicated over the internet. Yasin had written a special program. This program sent messages as 120,000 different pieces of content, making it nearly impossible to intercept the correct one. Imam Sait 's computer, equipped with the program, would extract the correct message. Likewise, when Imam sent

12   A renowned Islamic scholar and mystic born in Al-Andalus, who lived between 1165 and 1240. Known as the "Greatest Master," he pioneered the concept of Wahdat al-Wujud (Unity of Being).

a message to Yasin, it arrived as 120,000 different letter combinations. Anyone hacking in would see millions of messages, unable to determine which corresponded to which.

The first messages were typical greetings and well- wishes. Imam Sait knew a very special task was at hand today. To boost morale, he began the conversation.

"With Allah's permission, you will break the codes of three spirits today, won't you, my son?"

"Inshallah, hodja. I've been working for a month, and I'm now at the final stages. I should complete it today or tomorrow."

"You know Hadji Halit was martyred. We must speed up our work, my son. The great day is approaching."

"Inshallah, hodja."

"The infidels are doing everything they can to thwart our jihad. Be very careful. Don't leave the house unnecessarily."

'Just once, tell me to go out,' Yasin thought. He had become a homebound bird.

"Okay, hodja," he typed.

"May Allah be with you, my son."

"May Allah be pleased with you, hodja."

Yes, today was going to be very important. For a month, he had eliminated almost all possibilities. What he sought must be among the remaining ones...

He got to work feverishly. First, he connected the four computers to a network running a common program called GEMETRIA. The screens were split in two, with Arabic texts scrolling on one side and various numbers appearing and disappearing on the other. Occasionally, a number would light up and be transferred to the laptop along with a short Arabic sentence. This program decoded sacred texts written in Arabic, Hebrew, Chaldean, and Aramaic using the Abjad and Cifr methods. Words or sentences with specific numerical values were matched with others of the same value to check for connections. Once relationships between the numerical values were identified by the scanner, this information was stored.

After a considerable amount of time, the four computers, with a "clack, clack" sound, established a connection and sent a file with related sentences and numbers to the laptop. Yasin printed the incoming information and began to analyze it.

The book indicated by the computer was the "Buni Treatise." Ebul Abbas Ahmed bin Ali bin Yusuf Al-Qurayshi Al-Buni, a legendary figure in the world of magic who died in 1225, had compiled all his works into a 1208-page book. Yasin took the thick book in his hands. It was as heavy as lead. The legend of the magical world, Al-Buni, must have assigned a djinn to protect his book against the ravages of time. It was as clean and new as a middle school math book belonging to a lazy student. It was covered in a thin layer of leather, coated with a shiny oil resembling today's laminates, gleaming like glass.

Yasin removed his shirt and donned the djinn armor. He crouched at the table he had set on the floor.

He looked at the words and sentences on the pages identified by the computer. He wrote down the indicated sentences on a clean sheet of paper, noting the page numbers and arranging them from top to bottom. Each sentence consisted of five words, and there were a total of five sentences. Every sentence began with 'he' and ended with 'nun.' In the Abjad system, 'he' corresponds to 5 and 'nun' to 50. He underlined the 'he' and 'nun' letters and wrote their numerical values next to them. The total Abjad value of the sentences should be 19 or multiples of 19. The Quran presents a mystery with the verse "Over it are nineteen." Dr. Rashad Khalifa, the renowned Egyptian chemist known for his work on the "19 miracle," never fully understood its true secret. The verse "Over it are nineteen" was used in creating coded prayers to summon and command the guardians hidden in the scriptures of the four religions. When creating these prayers, the Abjad and Cifr values had to be 19 or multiples thereof. This was the consensus among the greatest magicians and summoners throughout history. In their books, they cryptically advised future generations interested in summoning to use the 19 framework. Yasin had been very excited when he first discovered the "19 framework" method. He considered himself luckier than the old scholars. He didn't need years to calculate probabilities based on a single verse; he could do it in a few minutes with a computer.

Yasin calculated the total values of the sentences he obtained. He encountered the number 1007. Being a product of 19 x 53, this number fit within the framework of 19, confirming that the sentences complied. Having passed the first stage, he began to examine the meanings. What could Al-Buni be indicating with these sentences? There was no apparent connection between the five sentences. One said, "Melted copper flowed like a river." Another stated, "There is no doubt unless behind strength." The remaining three sentences also lacked coherence both internally and with each other. Yasin turned the paper over and over. He rearranged the words but reached no conclusion. He set it aside for later destruction and rose from the floor table, careful not to bump into the hanging bowls. He glanced at the streaming numbers on the screen and waited for a new connection to be made.

The "clack, clack" sounds signaled that the computer had discovered a new connection. Yasin printed out the information sent to the laptop and applied the 19 framework. The initial stages presented no issues.

He began reading the Arabic sentences. Al-Buni had written the book in the Egyptian dialect of Arabic, which Yasin knew well. The sentences indicated that a prayer named Ahdname should be recited seven times, specifying which words to add to the prayer. The instructions stated that while reciting the prayer, one should write the first seven sentences of the Torah's Ahdname prayer on a piece of paper and burn it. It explained that this prayer existed in the original Torah, making it a divine prayer, and that the Quran had hidden the djinn in this part. Yasin crawled out from under the hanging bowls, stood up, and retrieved the Torah from the shelf. He returned to the floor table, opened to the indicated prayer, and took a piece of light yellow papyrus- like paper. Dipping his quill into a ginger root dye mixed with the blood of three orphan children from Christian, Muslim, and Jewish backgrounds, he began writing the first seven sentences of the indicated prayer. Hebrew words flowed quickly onto the paper.

The writing process finally complete, he looked at the bowl in the center of the table. The dim flame inside flickered. He was excited. He began reciting the Ahdname. By the fifth recitation, as he started the sixth, he placed the paper flat over the flame in the bowl. The pale flame gradually illuminated the light yellow papyrus-like paper. Within a few seconds, the prayer-inscribed paper covering the bowl began to glow as if lit by a projector. Strangely, the flame did not or could not burn the paper. It was so colorless and pale that it lacked the strength to burn the paper. As he began the seventh recitation of the Ahdname, the Hebrew words on the paper started to disintegrate, the ink writhing like tiny worms. Each letter separated from its word and sentence, losing its shape and morphing into small lines darting back and forth.

Even after completing the seventh recitation, no definitive result had been achieved. The djinn within the prayer should emerge from the fire's burning effect and the prayers Yasin recited, entering the paper inscribed with its name on the table. Only then would the djinn be under Yasin's command.

The yellow color of the paper, shining like the sun, filled the room. The dispersed letters were slowly reassembling and merging. If the prayer was correctly formed, the codes of the Zamradun djinn would have been broken. Yasin focused on the paper, trying to discern the form of Zamradun. From the center of the illuminated paper, an image began to appear—first, three heads connected to the same neck, then a body with six arms. Yes, this was Zamradun, matching the mythological description exactly. In each hand, it held a sword, a bow, a pitcher, a rebab, a shield, and a mace. The room's temperature began to rise. The paper darkened from the center—where the fire touched it. Agonized screams filled the air. The darkened spot expanded, and the pale flame started to consume the entire paper. The heat was becoming unbearable. Yasin was drenched in sweat. The image on the paper, screaming, began to rise. The Zamradun djinn had freed itself from the prayer-inscribed paper where it had been confined. Disturbed, it was furious. However, Yasin had accounted for all dangers and taken precautions. The djinn could not return to its paper, for it was burning. It could not escape to another place because it was surrounded by Aramaic bowls. It could not attack Yasin because he wore a protective djinn armor with prayers. It could not just stay there, as it would burn when the paper was consumed. It had to be bound to another prayer. Everything was going as Yasin planned. The Zamradun djinn had risen halfway when Yasin placed three pre-prepared papers on the table. The edges of the papers were adorned with summoning prayers. This was the djinn's only salvation. It left the burning paper and entered the three new papers. The heat instantly dropped, and the room returned to its normal temperature.

Months of work had finally paid off. The Zamradun djinn was now under his command. He placed the papers containing the djinn in a book. He needed to deliver the good news to Imam Sait as soon as possible.

Chapter

8

The Stench of Betrayal

The clock showed 11:30 PM. "I'm late again; the kid must be asleep," he thought. As soon as he entered the complex in Atasehir, he parked his car and quickly began climbing the stairs. He never took the elevator, finding it unsafe. When he reached the second floor, the light went out. He pressed the phosphorescent button to turn it back on and saw the name Serkan Cenet on the door. As always, he cursed and continued up the stairs.

Selin deleted the message she was typing when she heard the door open. She turned off her phone and placed it beside the couch.

"Welcome, darling." "Thanks."

Selin took the bag from her husband's hand.

"You're late, honey. Ece has been waiting for you," she said, smiling. She had a beautiful face and a sweet smile.

"She was on my mind even while I was on the road, but today was full of issues again. I couldn't find the time."

They went to the bedroom. Ali Fuat was undressing. Selin mimicked her husband, deepening her voice, "Full of issues again," and hugged him as he was taking off his clothes. "Are you very tired?"

Ali Fuat sat on the bed and pulled Selin onto his lap. Her blond hair cascaded over her shoulders, her green eyes twinkled, and she pouted like a little girl. Looking at her made his heart flutter. He gave her a kiss on the lips. He loved his wife very much.

Selin was looking into his eyes, her hands wrapped around his neck. She rubbed her small nose against his, moving her head side to side.

"Wow, you're busier than the Prime Minister, darling." She grinned mischievously. Ali Fuat began to laugh too.

"Don't tease me," he said, giving her a playful slap on the bottom.

Their breaths mingled as they adorned the moment with small kisses.

"We thank our dear daddy very much," she kissed him, "we really like our electric car."

"I was going to ask about that. I sent it with the store's car because it wouldn't fit in ours. Was there any problem when they delivered it?"

"No, darling, there were no problems."

"Was Ece happy?"

"She was overjoyed. I wish you were here to see how excited she was, how adorable she acted."

"She's asleep now, right?"

"She's been asleep for a while, love."

Selin got up from Ali Fuat's lap.

"Come on, love, put on your sweatpants and let's watch some TV," she said.

Ali Fuat hadn't planned on that. "I have a couple of files to review," he said.

Selin tensed up.

"What files, honey? You're already not home until midnight."

Selin went into the living room and sat on the couch. She turned on the TV and started flipping through channels. Ali Fuatjoined her and lay his head on her lap.

"Darling, put on the news; let's see what's happening."

"Oh, what could it be? Accidents, murders, fires... It's like a horror movie!" She switched to a gossip program. Ali Fuat didn't object. The program was full of sensational news. As he watched indifferently, two names suddenly caught his attention.

"The famous playboy Alp Demirkaplan, Horasanli Holding's heir Shuvaip Horasanli, and nightlife's new regular Murat

Sancaktar were caught by our cameras leaving the club with their companions. Here are the moments of their panic..."

What was this? He was stunned. Wasn't Murat Sancaktar Pasha Vefik's son? What kind of friendship could he have with Alp Demirkaplan? His wife's question broke his surprise.

"Fuat, what are we going to do about Ece's daycare?"

Ece was unhappy at her kindergarten. She would pretend to be asleep when the school bus arrived or claim she needed to use the bathroom just as they were about to leave and stay there for a long time. Selin and Ali Fuat wanted to enroll her in a different daycare, but Ali Fuat was too busy to look into it.

"Honey, I'll check in a couple of days."

"There's a kindergarten nearby. They say it's nice. They have English teachers who speak English with the children all the time."

"Alright, let's enroll her then. Did you check it out? How much is it?"

Selin hesitated. There was a look of unease on her face.

"The neighbors checked it out."

Ali Fuat was startled.

"Which neighbors?" he asked, his voice no longer calm. "Which neighbors, dear?"

Selin didn't answer. She was looking at the TV with a tense expression. Ali Fuat got angry. "Is it that guy downstairs?" he said. Selin suddenly switched to the offensive.

"Darling, that's not the point now. We're talking about our child's education."

His hand began to tremble. His eyes grew larger. "Why is this man so involved with my family?"

"Darling, don't get upset. I mentioned once in passing that our child wasn't happy at her kindergarten. He went and checked it out, that's all. Do we always have to assume bad intentions?"

"He shouldn't be checking. Is it his business?"

He stood up and lit a cigarette. For a moment, he wanted to grab his gun and go downstairs to empty it into Serkan Cenet's head.

"Please, darling. We already barely see you. Let's not fight when you're home."

He didn't reply. Taking a few more puffs from his cigarette, he went to his study room and closed the door. They would go to the supermarket together. He would bring chocolate to his child. He would take care of household chores. Was all this happening because he didn't spend enough time at home, or was there something between him and Selin? Sometimes he thought about kidnapping and killing the man. He was a principled and honest person. He didn't want to take the wrong step. Was he overreacting? Serkan Cenet was also very friendly with the other neighbors. Was this just his personality? Did he have no bad intentions? He couldn't decide.

Chapter

9

New Recruit

The Black Shrouds' first and second ring guards had taken their places in the meeting room. The seat at the head of the table was empty. To the right of the empty seat, in the first position, sat the Operations Unit Commander, Ali Fuat. The others were seated according to their rank and seniority. The only person there who didn't belong was Arab Zekeriya, who was watching for Pasha's arrival at the door. His position didn't warrant participation in the meeting.

Arab Zekeriya had been recruited into the organization in an unusual manner. The Black Shrouds utilized many people: journalists, doctors, professors, law enforcement officers, politicians, members and leaders of terrorist organizations, prostitutes, artists, athletes... But there was a crucial point. Those who were used did not know the structure of the guards, not even their name. Only people of a certain lineage could know the Black Shrouds. Very rarely were outsiders taken in, and even then, they were never given classified information or the organization's history. These individuals had no access to archives, could not attend any meetings, and could never become leaders. Arab Zekeriya was one of them. He was inside the organization but also an outsider.

The organization discovered Zekeriya when he was 19 years old. He was from the Rahmanlar district of Hatay, an Arab and an Alawite. He had killed three people in a blood feud. The police had been unable to catch him for days. During interrogation, he didn't utter a single word, nor did he flinch under beatings and torture. Even in prison, he didn't leave his enemies alone. They tried to stab him in the toilet, but he beat the hired killer to death against the walls. The Black Shrouds saw potential in Zekeriya and moved in. His prison record was altered to show he had died, and he was recruited into the Black Shrouds as a living dead. These methods were part of the guards' history and had now been used for Zekeriya. From that moment on, he was under the command of Ali Fuat and began participating in operations. His boldness, recklessness, strength, ruthlessness, and loyalty earned everyone's admiration. Fourteen years passed like this. Ali Fuat was now thirty-six, and Zekeriya was thirty-four. Zekeriya was a peculiar man. He rarely spoke. If asked a question, he might respond. No one had seen him joke or laugh. He had a strong memory, remembering everything he saw and heard very well.

Ali Fuat glanced at the door. It was four minutes past nine. Pasha Vefik was four minutes late. He thought about how much Pasha had changed. The legendary guard Vefik Sancaktar was gone, replaced by a cranky old man giving orders, whether relevant or not. Ali couldn't understand this change in Pasha Vefik. As a result of his erratic behavior, Colonel Zeki and Colonel Tuncay had become disillusioned with the organization and left. The guards had lost their former dynamic structure.

Ali Fuat's thoughts were interrupted by Arab Zekeriya's shout. "ATTENTION!" All the guards at the meeting table stood up. Pasha entered and said, "Good morning, friends."

"Thank you, sir!" they responded in unison. As Pasha sat in his seat, the others also sat down. Zekeriya closed the door from the outside. Accompanying Pasha was a tall, fair- skinned young man with black curly hair and blue eyes. The slightly overweight young man with a somewhat large rear was very excited. Pasha said, "Aydin, you sit here as well."

The round-faced young man, with excitement in his eyes behind his thin, frameless glasses, looked at Pasha Vefik and said, "Yes, sir." He sat in the indicated seat. There was a faint smile on Pasha's face.

"There are two reasons for today's meeting," he said. He opened the water bottle in front of him and filled half of his glass.

"First, we have a new member joining us," he said, indicating Aydin. Gathering the attention on him, Aydin stood up and, with a forced expression that didn't suit his boyish face, said, "Aydin Sipahi, at your command, sir."

"You may sit down, Aydin," said Pasha.

Ali Fuat looked at the young man with a seriousness he hadn't shown before. The surname 'Sipahi' had caught his attention. Pasha continued his speech.

"Aydin is the son of Tuncay Sipahi, one of the esteemed guards of the Black Shrouds. He has successfully completed his training and will now be with us."

Indeed, he was the son of Tuncay Sipahi, the former operations unit commander. He was the son of Colonel Tuncay, Ali Fuat's mentor and esteemed commander. Pasha said, "I wish you success in your new position." Aydin Sipahi responded loudly, "Thank you." Pasha took a few sips of water. He opened the blue box he had brought with him. Inside was a white gold ring, consisting of seven interlocking squares that grew smaller and rose like a pyramid. At the top, the letters BS were engraved. Pasha handed this ring, the insignia of the Black Shrouds, to Aydin Sipahi. Although Aydin didn't know it, he was in the first circle of the Black Shrouds. He wore the ring with great pride. Pasha then gave a speech about the importance of the republic and the revolutions.

"Our other topic concerns the intelligence unit," he said. After swallowing once or twice, he continued, "As you know, with Colonel Zeki's 'retirement,' a new commander is needed for the unit. Until a new commander is trained, this unit will also be under Ali Fuat's command." He looked at Ali Fuat, who was seated immediately to his right. "I wish you success," he said, continuing his speech.

Ali Fuat was deep in thought. Two important units had been assigned to him at a young age. He was the most authoritative commander after Pasha in the Black Shrouds. He didn't know whether to be happy or sad. What was Pasha Vefik planning? What was his goal in driving away experienced commanders?

After finishing his long speech, Pasha looked at Aydin and asked, "Who will be Aydin's mentor?"

Without hesitation, Ali Fuat raised his hand. Pasha smiled and said, "Alright, let's go with that. Tuncay was your mentor; now you're repaying the favor."

Mentors were responsible for the education and loyalty of the young recruits they took under their wing. Initially, general information about the Black Shrouds was given, and later, depending on their success, they were informed about the history and activities of the guards.

At the end of the meeting, while the guards returned to their duties, Pasha Vefik spent some time in his office before leaving the headquarters. Ali Fuat and the other guards thought their commander had gone to his son's workplace again. For the past few years, Pasha had been overly involved in his son's business, neglecting the Black Shrouds.

Ali Fuat took Aydin to his office.

"Aydin, what would you like to drink, buddy?"

"Please, commander, no need to trouble yourself, I can make it."

Ali Fuat smiled. "It's no trouble. Tell me, what would you like to drink?"

Aydin hesitated, "Coffee," he said.

Ali Fuat prepared coffee for Aydin and tea for himself. He brought them to the table and sat in his chair. Aydin took his coffee and placed it on the small table in front of him.

"Commander, isn't there a tea station here?"

"There is, but access to this section with the archives is prohibited. Because all our secrets are hidden in this section. Not only the tea station, but they can't enter even for cleaning. We do everything ourselves. Only guards from the first three rings can enter here."

Aydin imagined Ali Fuat cleaning windows. The thought of such a charismatic man cleaning with a cloth amused Aydin, but he didn't laugh. He maintained his seriousness.

"Commander, isn't it difficult?"

Yes, the training was beginning. Aydin would ask, and his mentor would answer. In time, there would be nothing left to learn.

"It is, but for security reasons, it has to be this way. Even a single document taken from here could throw Turkey into chaos. The discovery of the Black Shrouds' existence would put the state in a very difficult position. The European Union would give us a hard time. All human rights organizations in the world would be up in arms."

As Aydin sipped his coffee, he listened to Ali Fuat. The steam from the coffee fogged up his glasses. He took them off and placed them on the table. He thought about how charismatic Ali Fuat looked, especially his eyes. When he looked into his eyes, he felt the presence of a scorpion ready to strike.

Ali Fuat continued his talk about security. "The first thing you need to learn is this: you will not mention the existence of the Black Shrouds to anyone. You work at Agricultural Machinery Import Export Inc. That's what everyone will know. Your father was also a member of the Black Shrouds, and so was your grandfather. But did your mother, your siblings, or anyone else ever find out?"

"No, commander," said Aydin, adding with a smile, "During the February 28 process[13] my father didn't come home for several days a week. He often fought with my mother. The poor woman thought he was cheating on her."

Ali Fuat laughed, having similar memories.

"Don't ask, this job has its dirty sides..." He glanced at Aydin's fingers. "I guess you're not married?"

"No, commander," said Aydin. Was there time to get married, for God's sake? He was still thinking about the security matter. Didn't everyone here know what was going on? Were there layers within their own ranks too? He asked about these things.

---

[13] The February 28 Incident, also known as the "post-modern coup," refers to the events in Turkey in 1997 when the military exerted pressure on the government led by Prime Minister Necmettin Erbakan, resulting in his resignation. The National Security Council issued a series of recommendations on February 28, 1997, aimed at curbing the rise of political Islam and maintaining Turkey's secular principles. These measures included restrictions on religious education and the wearing of headscarves in public institutions. The military's influence during this period did not involve direct intervention but utilized political and social pressure to ensure the government's compliance with secularist policies. This period significantly impacted Turkish politics, leading to the closure of several Islamic-oriented political parties and reshaping the country's political landscape.

"Yes, there are. The Black Shrouds consist of seven layers. I will explain what these layers are as the time comes. Of course, people within our ranks know what we do. But they don't need to know everything. For example, we wouldn't explain our political role during the February 28 process to the cafeteria staff here. Anyway, such staff are usually selected from people who are not very literate, don't think much, are ignorant and elderly. They clean our offices, brew our tea, and cook our meals. If you asked them where they work, they would barely be able to tell you the name of the company. There are many poor neighborhoods close to our area. We know very well who is who now. We carefully select those who will do the menial tasks. Many of them have been working here for years. For example, the gardeners, they are all relatives. First, their fathers started, then their uncles, brothers, and so on. Neither do we hire outsiders nor do they let outsiders in. But even they don't have access to very special areas."

"Commander, wouldn't it be better if the organization's own members did these tasks?"

"Think about it! If we told a young person, trained in secret services, for example, you, to go and dig in the garden or wash the dishes, how would you feel?"

"I understand."

Aydin was trying to form some thoughts in his head. "There is much you need to learn."

They didn't speak for a few minutes. Aydin broke the silence.

"Commander, where are you from?" he asked. Ali Fuat smiled. "We're from the same place."

Aydin asked in surprise, "Are you from Giresun[14]?"

Ali Fuat nodded. "Ninety percent of the Black Shrouds are from Giresun. Because the Black Shrouds are an organization founded by people from Giresun, our ancestors. You will learn everything in time. I've already given you too much information, but it's alright. You are the son of the esteemed commander Tuncay Sipahi."

The door was knocked and Kenan Ferit entered. He greeted those inside. "Come in, Kenan, have a seat," said Ali Fuat.

---

[14] Giresun is a city located in the Black Sea Region of Turkey. It has been used as a settlement since ancient times.

The handsome guard of the Black Shrouds, Kenan Ferit , looked at Aydin and said, "Welcome. I wish you success in your new position." Aydin Sipahi thanked him.

Kenan Ferit turned to Ali Fuat and said, "Commander, I also wish you success in your new position." Aydin thought to himself, 'Damn, I forgot!' and quickly said, "Commander, I also wish you success. I got caught up in our conversation and forgot to say it earlier, I apologize."

"Thank you both."

The conversation continued about Tuncay Sipahi. Ali Fuat asked how his former commander was doing. Aydin listened with interest. He took down his address. Maybe he would pay a surprise visit one day.

"Aydin, go to the intelligence unit now. Get to know your colleagues."

Aydin stood up immediately and said, "Yes, commander." Following military protocol, he asked, "Do you have any other orders, commander?"

"No, thank you."

Aydin saluted and left the room.

Both of their facial expressions were tense from discussing such an important topic.

"As we suspected, he couldn't appoint a new head to the intelligence unit. He assigned it to me. What is this man trying to do?"

"Does he want to burden you with too much responsibility and make you ineffective?"

"I don't think he considers me. He is the great Pasha Vefik, and I am just a youngster compared to him. He has served this organization for as many years as we have been alive. Pasha's problem isn't with me. There is something else. He is driving away all the experienced names. He is being cranky, insulting them, and eventually forcing them to leave the organization. What's the underlying reason for all this?"

"Our operational capability has weakened, commander. We are not as active as we used to be. We will be putting on weight soon."

"You're right. If it weren't for the recent incident, we would have turned into desk officers."

"The recent incident was a bundle of oddities, commander."

"Yes, it's still hard to believe, but we didn't all have the same hallucination, did we?"

"Isn't it strange that he brought this new guy in too, commander?"

"Indeed. He drives Tuncay Sipahi out of the organization and then takes his son in. Pasha Vefik is doing things that defy logic." Ali Fuat sipped his nearly finished tea.

Kenan noticed the newspaper in his hand.

"What's that, Kenan?" he asked. Kenan opened the relevant page of the newspaper and pointed with his finger, saying, "Look at this news, commander."

"Is it in the paper too? I saw it on a gossip program yesterday," he said. Then, feeling the need to explain, he added, "I mean, Selin was watching, and I saw it by chance."

"Our little prince is advancing, commander. Look at this, models, rich friends..."

"More importantly, the man next to him is Alp Demirkaplan. Isn't he the son of Cihangir Demirkaplan? The son of the leader of the sect and the son of the leader of the Black Shrouds are partying together. What's going on, Kenan?"

"Something's happening, but... we'll find out soon enough."

Ali Fuat's cell phone started ringing. He looked at the screen. It was his brother, Feridun, calling. He answered...

Chapter

10

Poison

They had worked together for years. They had been involved in numerous dangerous operations, been injured, and narrowly escaped death many times. They had dismantled many sects that wanted to overthrow the Republic and its revolutions. Not once, not even for a moment, had he felt fear in any operation or difficulty. It was unknown how fear would look on Ali Fuat's face. Excitement, sadness, grief, pain, anger, tension – all had visited his face, but fear had never made an appearance. Kenan Ferit was in a state of mixed shock and sorrow. He had tried to say many things to comfort him along the way, but none had worked. Ali Fuat was plainly terrified, horribly so. He had not even dared to drive the car. "You drive," he had said.

While driving, he talked to Ali Fuat. "Commander, don't worry so much. They must have pumped her stomach. She'll be fine."

He said 'don't worry,' but it was clear that the expression on the Commander's face was not one of mere worry. After entering the hospital and parking their vehicle, they learned from the reception at the emergency entrance how to find Selin Sezgin, who had been brought in with a poisoning case.

Her stomach had been pumped, and she had been placed in a room. When Ali Fuat reached the door, he hesitated for a moment. His heart was pounding wildly. Kenan Ferit couldn't understand these behaviors of Ali Fuat. "Commander, let's go inside," he said. Ali Fuat stepped in with fear.

One of her arms was outstretched with an IV attached. Her brother, the military judge Feridun Sezgin, was there. His wife was also present. He glanced at them briefly and said nothing, then knelt beside Selin.

"My love."

He wanted to say, 'My love, how are you, are you okay?' but could only say 'my love.' He remained like that. Selin's face was swollen. She smiled. "My dear, I'm fine, there's nothing to worry about," she said, as if she could read everything from her husband's face.

Feridun said, "She's fine, brother. They pumped her stomach."

"Hey, everyone. I'm sorry, I couldn't pull myself together for a moment."

"Oh, brother?" said Feridun, with his wife supporting him. Feridun took his brother outside and briefly summarized the situation: "She ate some wild mushrooms she bought, felt sick afterward, and vomited. Ece screamed, and neighbors came over. The initial intervention was done by the doctor in Atasehir, then they brought her here by ambulance."

"How did she come across wild mushrooms?" "She bought them from the market, brother." "What market in Atasehir?"

"Not in Atasehir. She got them from a neighborhood market in Yeni Camlica."

"What was she doing at a neighborhood market? Why did she go there?"

"A neighbor told her there were leaves for wrapping, so she went for that. She saw the wild mushrooms and bought some. The result is obvious."

The conversation continued for a while longer. Ali Fuat had him recount the same things a few times. Feridun wanted to talk about something else.

"Brother, Selin is fine. There's a more important issue."

Ali Fuat's heart was about to burst out of his chest. Kenan Ferit was also excited. What did 'a more important issue' mean? Was something wrong with Ece?

"Ece," he said. His heart was about to stop. He was on the verge of tears. He couldn't control himself.

Feridun felt sorry for his brother's state. He thought he needed to be firm.

"Brother, pull yourself together. We already have enough problems; don't let us have to deal with you too."

Using his professional experience, he scolded him gently but firmly.

"You need to see the hospital's doctor. Ece has had a trauma. They gave her a sedative. She's okay now."

They went to the doctor's office together. Ali Fuat entered and introduced himself.

"Mr. Sezgin, your daughter is in good health now, but there's a significant issue." The doctor opened the file in front of her. She had forgotten the girl's name. She looked at the name on the patient tracking card and continued talking. "Ece was in severe shock when she was brought here. The intense fear she experienced over her mother's potential death caused her to lose physical control quickly. We gave her a sedative. I believe your daughter has obsessive concerns about her mother. Her reaction was disproportionate. There's something abnormal here.

Ali Fuat didn't understand much. What kind of obsessions? In what way?

"Your daughter has a different bond with her mother. She's afraid she might die. This fear has deeply settled in her young mind. I don't know what caused it, of course." The doctor thought for a moment.

"Has Ece ever witnessed someone's death before? It could be a traffic accident, for example. She might have watched an injured person being carried into an ambulance. Do you recall anything like that?"

"No. We've seen cars that crashed during our travels, and Ece looked at them, but I don't remember seeing any scenes of dead or injured people."

"Don't just think of it as a traffic accident. Has she encountered such an event in general?"

Without much thought, Ali Fuat remembered such an event and started explaining.

"She witnessed her grandmother's death."

The doctor nodded in an understanding manner and asked for more details.

"My mother-in-law had heart disease. There was an emergency, and we took her to the hospital. They took her into surgery, but she couldn't be saved. When we got the news of her death, my wife cried a lot. Then Ece started crying too. I immediately took her outside." Ali Fuat thought for a moment. "I mean, it wasn't that bad. She cried, but nothing else happened."

"This incident could be the cause, Mr. Sezgin. We need to conduct a comprehensive evaluation. I'll give you the address of a friend who specializes in child psychology. Dr. Levent Taner. He's a bit expensive. Since he's in private practice, your insurance won't cover it, but he's the best in his field. There aren't many doctors specializing in child psychology anyway."

Ali Fuat took the address written by the doctor.

Chapter

11

Vengeance Starts

Faruk Altan, the head of the financial department of the sect, sat on his bed with delight. He was wearing a robe de chambre. Taking a sip from his whiskey, he placed the glass on the nightstand. He was a fifty-four-year-old, slender, and average-height man. Because he dyed his hair and mustache, he looked younger. He had served two terms as a parliamentarian. He was a figure who drew the media's attention with his super-luxurious lifestyle.

The guest who was getting ready in the bathroom would join him soon. He was in good spirits. "It's not every day you get a virgin girl. It was a good thing I came to Konya," he thought. He had been in Konya for two days due to Hadji Halit's funeral and the subsequent meeting. His men, knowing their boss's special tastes, had scouted the market.

The fifteen-year-old, short, fair-skinned girl saw her chin trembling slightly as she looked in the mirror. Her hands were shaking too. She was very scared. She wanted to escape. She thought of Esad. "If you run, I'll dunk your face in boiling water, you won't be able to show your face to anyone," he had said. They had sold her to a man before, but she had escaped then. Her stepbrother Esad had to return the money and then beat her severely. Unable to contain his anger, he had stripped and, holding his genitals, said, "Is this what you're running from? Is this what you're running from?" and tried to force it into her mouth. When he failed, he beat her until he was exhausted, leaving her semi-conscious, and then sodomized her. As the girl lay in a wretched state, Esad dressed and cursed at her. "Have you gotten used to it now, you bitch? Will you run again? If you do, I'll shove a hot iron into you, you whore." All of this flashed before her eyes like a movie reel. She was afraid to go inside. She was afraid to run away. She didn't know what to do.

Mr. Altan had gotten used to the timid state of young girls after many experiences. Especially the virgins, who were very scared; they trembled at his touch. He went to the bathroom, brought the girl to the bed, and undressed her with his hands. He undressed himself completely. The girl was too ashamed to lift her head.

"My dear, why are you so timid?" he said, while stroking her hair. "I gave your brother six thousand dollars. Come on, please me, and I'll secretly give you five thousand dollars too. Without your brother knowing." Faruk Altan knew that not a single penny of the money given to the pimp of these girls ever reached their hands. That's why he tried different methods to increase their motivation. The girl gave no response. He moved his mustache and lips over her young body. And…

It should have happened much later... After walking hand in hand with a lover, running in the rain to avoid getting wet, watching the sunrise, crying for each other... After longing, kissing in secluded places, saying it couldn't happen before marriage... After making tea for him, opening his surprise gift, strolling together, going to the cinema...

It should have been much later, much...

It should have been with a lover. With someone very different... She had lost the only thing she felt was innocent in her disgusting environment, filled with her nonexistent family, poverty, cruel stepbrother, beatings, lack of education, and insignificance, and having told life to fuck off. The man who was the age of her father, hairy, growling like an animal, covered in sweat, spewing saliva from his rotten teeth and dirty mustache as he hovered over her... Her hopes were shattered…

Three young men entered the royal suite. With large amulets around their necks, black clothes, long coats, and expressionless eyes, they were copies of each other. Their faces were very peculiar. It was as if they weren't alive. They didn't breathe, they didn't look, they didn't see. Not a single muscle on their faces moved. No expression, no words...

One of the young men moved quickly amidst Faruk Altan's stunned gaze and, with the same expressionless face, lifted Faruk Altan and carried him towards the window. He opened the curtain. The huge window offered a 15th-floor view of Konya. The city lay beneath them. They forced him to look out the window. Blended with the darkness outside, the silhouette of Imam Sait Nurani appeared in the window. He was staring at him with great hatred in his eyes. Faruk Altan began to struggle madly. He wanted to scream, but no sound came out, and he couldn't escape the young man's grip.

The young men worked like a well-oiled machine. One of them took two bags out of his coat. The bags contained meters of chains. They took out the chains and tightly handcuffed Faruk Altan's arms. Another young man astonishingly pulled two steel cases from inside his coat. The cases were filled with mercury, each weighing one hundred and fifty kilograms. They attached the other end of the chains to the cases. They propped Faruk Altan against the wall between the two windows. Two young men took the cases and simultaneously threw one out of one window and the other out of the other window. The cases shattered the windows and began to fall rapidly. The chains stretched simultaneously, and his arms were torn off, causing blood to spurt everywhere. Mr. Altan collapsed to the ground in agony. He was writhing in indescribable pain. Blood covered everywhere. The three young men were about to leave when they heard a voice.

"Please, kill me too."

It was the girl's voice. She was naked on the bed, with blood stains on her legs and the sheets. One of the young men approached her. He grabbed her head and quickly twisted it.

Chapter

12

Zamradun the Djinn

Ten minutes after the three young men left the hotel in Konya, they were in Bursa. They arrived in front of a large mansion. Approaching the gate, they climbed over it right in front of the guards who were looking around. They walked through the magnificent garden and soon entered the house. Despite the pitch darkness inside, they walked confidently. They reached the bedroom.

Osman Karahan, who was at the helm of Turkey's largest educational community with five hundred prep schools, hundreds of private schools, two universities, and dormitories, was sleeping with his wife.

The young men turned on the light. One of them blew into the sleeping woman's face. They woke Osman Karahan. He was terrified of these devilish-looking young men and wanted to scream, but no sound came out.

One of the young men opened his palm and poured gasoline from a small canister he took out of his coat. As he lit it, a fireball formed. The other young men forced Osman Karahan to look at the fireball. Within the fire, Imam Sait Nurani appeared, his face filled with scorn and intense hatred.

They forcibly placed a funnel in his mouth, with the tube going down his throat. They poured gasoline into it and forced him to drink. One of the young men drew a sword from his coat. In a swift motion, he slashed Osman Karahan's abdomen. The gasoline that had entered his mouth began to flow out from his stomach mixed with blood.

The silhouette of Imam Sait , appearing in the fire in the young man's hand, swiftly attacked Osman Karahan. The gasoline ignited fiercely.

The young men left the room. As Osman Karahan burned to death internally, the flames and smoke triggered the fire alarm. The ceiling-mounted sprinkler system began to pour water profusely. The fire on the furniture was quickly extinguished. The flames on Osman Karahan's burning clothes, hair, and body were also put out, but his insides were still ablaze.

While Mrs. Karahan slept, her husband had stopped struggling and, under the influence of the water pouring over him, had turned into a large cloud of steam.

The three young men had interrupted Osman Karahan's sleep when they entered. But it didn't matter... Now he was sleeping again, this time never to be woken...

Chapter

13

Imam Sait Nurani

The strong light from the street lamps illuminated the narrow road lined with two- and three-story houses in Husrevaga Neighborhood. None of the houses, which were interlocked like a spider web, showed any light.

Three young men appeared at the end of the road. They wore coats, large amulets around their necks, and had a terrifyingly expressionless look on their faces. They walked with confident steps.

Imam Sait Nurani was sitting cross-legged in the basement of his house. He wore a green robe and a white skullcap. In front of him was a small wooden table resembling the low tables Anatolian women use for rolling out dough. On the table was a thick, old-looking book. There were three pieces of paper on the table with Arabic writing on them. The papers looked very old and had burnt edges.

Two elderly disciples sat cross-legged on either side of the Imam, reciting the Quran loudly. The sound echoed in the empty room.

The three young men entered the room. They stood side by side in front of Imam Sait. Following them, eight or nine more disciples entered and stood behind the young men.

Imam Sait, with a contented smile hidden in his long beard and mustache, slowly stood up. He walked to the first young man, reciting prayers. Those reading the Quran raised their voices, and the disciples between the young men also joined in loudly.

The Imam reached for the young man's amulet and began to recite the Covenant prayer. In his deep voice, he said, "Bismillahirrahmanirrahim[15]." The disciples were highly excited. The Imam pulled on the amulet with a "Ya Allah" and as the cord snapped, a strong wind blew past the Imam's robe and entered one of the papers on the table. The paper twitched for a few seconds. The young man collapsed to the ground as if his skeleton had disappeared.

The Imam performed the same ritual on the other two young men. The collapsed young men were carried out of the room one by one by the disciples. The Imam picked up the twitching papers from the table, reciting Ayat al-Kursi[16], and carefully placed them into the thick book with burnt edges. He placed the amulets on the table.

The young men, carried out by the disciples, re-entered with their hands clasped respectfully over their stomachs.

"Peace be upon you."

Everyone in the room responded in unison: "And peace be upon you."

The Imam was smiling. The young men came and kissed his hand. The Imam embraced each of them and said,

"Oh lions of Muhammad[17], may Allah be pleased with you."

The young men were extremely pleased to hear this. They bowed their heads in modesty.

The Imam patted their heads in a fatherly manner. He was very happy.

"My brave ones, my heroes, the Caliphate State will be established on your shoulders. May Allah forgive your sins as heavy as this burden upon you. May our Lord grant you the honor of being neighbors to Muhammad Mustafa S.A.V. in paradise..."

The young men sincerely said 'amen'. The Imam led them out of the room and commanded them to go rest.

---

[15] An Islamic phrase that means "In the name of Allah, the Most Compassionate, the Most Merciful.

[16] It is considered one of the most powerful verses, highlighting God's sovereignty, knowledge, and limitless authority. Muslims often recite it for protection and peace.

[17] Muslims regard him as the messenger of God, through whom the Quran was revealed.

Imam Sait returned to the room and motioned for the two elderly disciples, who were standing, to sit. He sat down next to them.

"By Allah's will, our Movement has started successfully." The elderly men were exhausted from reading the Quran. They nodded in approval of the Imam.

"The infidels who used the money of thousands of Muslims not for our cause, but to violate young girls, and to acquire luxury cars, yachts, and mansions, could not escape the grasp of divine justice."

The long-bearded disciple with bulging eyes interrupted. "We must crush the head of the real snake, hodja." Imam Sait 's eyes narrowed.

"That too will happen, with Allah's permission."

Chapter

14

The Media is in an Uproar

The media was in a frenzy on the night of March 23rd, leading into the 24th. Agencies were sending the incoming news to all their affiliated radio and television stations with a 'flash' code.

Televisions and radios interrupted their broadcasts to deliver the news to their audiences, while newspapers stopped the presses in a rush to add the latest update.

The novice news anchors on the night shift presented the news with astonished expressions on their faces.

"Turkey is shaken by news of two major murders. Green capital barons Faruk Altan and Osman Karahan have been killed by unidentified person or persons."

All television channels were delivering similar news. They spoke of Faruk Altan's large finance companies and his past as a former parliamentarian, and of Osman Karahan's educational institutions. Allegations that they were involved in a sect were once again being brought to the forefront.

Chapter

15

Meeting Awaits Ali Fuat

They arrived home around eleven at night. Selin was feeling a bit better. Ece, however, had not fully shaken off the effects of the sedative. She was looking around with drunken eyes. The doorbell rang. It was their upstairs neighbors. They had come down after hearing Ece's screams and had possibly saved Selin from death. Ali Fuat invited the guests inside. They talked everything over again from the beginning.

Despite Ali Fuat's insistence, the neighbors did not stay long. Ece had fallen asleep in her mother's arms. Ali Fuat carefully picked up his daughter to avoid waking her. Her blonde hair, like strands of silk, hung down his arm. He gently laid her in bed.

"If I put her pajamas on, she'll wake up, what should I do?" he thought. After a brief hesitation, he decided to put on her pajamas.

The hands that turned ruthless when holding a gun were now touching his daughter with a delicate gentleness, as if afraid. He slowly unbuttoned her clothes. Seeing his daughter like this brought back memories. He remembered how he and Selin would bathe her. Ece loved water and would smile with joy. That smile was the most beautiful thing he had ever seen.

With trembling hands, he stroked his daughter's hair. Suddenly, he jerked back. She'll get cold, he thought. He immediately started looking for the pajamas. He rummaged through a couple of drawers but couldn't find them. He became increasingly flustered. I'll just tuck her into bed so she doesn't get cold, he thought. He moved Ece from the middle of the bed to the side and pulled back the blanket.

The pajamas were folded under the blanket. He was delighted to see them. He quickly took them and began dressing her. As he did, he said, "I've been away from home for too long." He realized he needed to spend more time with his daughter.

As he put on her nightclothes, Ece woke up. She looked at her father with half-closed eyes for a few seconds, then closed them again. Ali Fuat smiled and kissed his daughter. He laid her down and carefully tucked in the blanket. He turned off the light and went to the living room. Selin had fallen asleep while watching TV. He leaned over the side of the sofa.

"My love." Selin started to wake. "You fell asleep, let's go to the bedroom."

"Where's Ece?"

"I put her to bed. I undressed her and put on her pajamas."

Selin smiled. She closed her eyes and rested her head back on the small pillow of the sofa. "Will you put me to bed too, my love? But you'll have to undress me and put on my pajamas," she said.

Ali Fuat smiled too. "Of course, I will."

He kissed his wife's cheek. "I'll put you to bed and undress you, but I don't know if I'll put on your nightgown," he said, grinning mischievously. Selin opened her eyes and sat up. There was a sweet smile on her lips.

"I almost died, and look where your mind is!" After the fear-filled hours, Ali Fuat was slightly cheered up.

He had been cold and distant in their relationship before marriage. Their marriage, which happened after a brief acquaintance with Selin, had changed this serious man somewhat. He no longer minded jokes and sometimes even made his own. In the first few years, this change was limited to home, but later he also stopped being so strict with his colleagues at work. This change didn't happen overnight, but those who had known Ali Fuat for many years noticed it. He loved his wife very much and held her in high regard.

Selin said, "Take off your clothes, my love. You're squatting; they'll get wrinkled."

He hadn't had the chance, or it hadn't crossed his mind. Whatever the reason, he was still in his everyday clothes. The surprises of the tense time for Ali Fuat were not over yet. His cellphone began to ring. He quickly moved to prevent it from waking the child and answered it without looking at who was calling. The call was from the Black Shrouds. It was past midnight. The guard on the phone summarized the situation. Osman Karahan and Faruk Altan had been killed, and Pasha Vefik had immediately ordered a "meeting."

"Okay," he said, ending the call.

"What happened, dear? Is it bad news?" "Unfortunately, I have to go."

Selin was used to these situations. She sensed that her husband was part of a secret organization working for the state. But she couldn't guess much more. Ali Fuat was also very secretive about this.

"Okay, my love. What can we do?"

Ali Fuat felt sad. His wife had recovered, but he still didn't want to leave her alone. He sat next to her on the sofa. "How are you? If you want, I can call Feridun and his family. They can stay with us tonight," he said. Feridun's house was very close. In such situations, the brothers helped each other. Usually, it was Feridun who helped his brother.

"No need," said Selin. "Let's not disturb them at this hour, and I'm fine."

Ali Fuat hesitated, saying nothing. Two senior figures of the sect had been killed. He urgently wanted to learn the details and examine the crime scenes. But he also didn't want to leave his wife in this state. Selin understood her husband's thoughtful expression and said, "It's okay, my love. If you have to go, you must go. I'm fine, don't worry."

They talked for a while. Selin asked about the child's condition, and Ali Fuat explained briefly. "They gave her a sedative injection while they were pumping her stomach," he said.

Selin saw her husband off. She turned on her cellphone...

Chapter

16

Panic at the Mansion

The Fevzipasha Mansion, overlooking the Bosphorus, was a scene of great commotion. In Istanbul, a city known for its convoluted politics, rebellions, coups, dictatorships, ultimatums, and uprisings, these historical mansions and waterfront houses had witnessed many escapes. When the Committee of Union and Progress stormed Babiali[18], the pashas close to power hastily gathered their belongings and fled; during reactionary uprisings, the reformist pashas escaped; when the Janissaries[19] rebelled, pashas who feared being targeted fled, and when the Ottomans conquered Istanbul, the Byzantine nobles fled as well... This pattern of escape continued, and continued...

He was on edge. Running back and forth in the bedroom, he was saying something to his wife who was getting dressed, giving orders to his men in the mansion's living room, and then quickly returning to the bedroom to hurry his wife. His heart was pounding faster than ever before.

---

[18] It was synonymous with the Ottoman government and its bureaucracy. Today, the term symbolically represents the government or bureaucracy.

[19] An elite military corps of the Ottoman Empire, established in the 14th century. Comprised mainly of young Christian boys taken through the devshirme system and converted to Islam, they were known for their loyalty and discipline. They were a key part of the Ottoman army until they were disbanded by Sultan Mahmud II in the 19th century.

With his wife, he got into the armored Mercedes waiting at the door. He had taken along a driver and a security chief. No one else would know where they were going.

They were heading to a house he had bought for use in tough times. "Did you call the child, Cihangir?" asked Mrs. Demirkaplan. Cihangir Demirkaplan had no idea what he was doing. The Angel of Death was breathing down his neck. His body, exhausted from running around, was drenched in sweat. The salty water running down his forehead trickled down his cheeks and gathered on his chubby chin before dripping off. The head of the illustrious Demirkaplan family was huddled on the back seat of his car, looking miserable.

"Is Alp coming? Answer me, Cihangir?" she repeated. She knew all about her husband's activities. Feyza was the granddaughter of Halim Pasha, the Finance Minister during the reign of Sultan Abdulhamid II. When Abdulhamid fell, the Pasha had immediately sent his son and daughter-in-law to France. Feyza was born in Paris years later. She received an excellent education at the most prestigious schools. She was raised by her family as a true Ottoman lady. She was married to Cihangir, a member of the Demirkaplan family with whom her father had political and business connections, through an arranged marriage.

Since her husband became the head of the family, Feyza had been involved in the business, trying to maintain control. The idealistic policies the Demirkaplan family had upheld for years were softening and changing shape under Mrs. Demirkaplan's influence.

"Yes, I called him," said Cihangir.

When his phone rang, he was watching a movie, snuggled up with his girlfriend. They hadn't gone out that evening.

When he saw it was his father calling, he answered. "Yes, Father?"

"Where are you, son?"

Alp Demirkaplan sensed the excitement in his father's voice. "I'm at home, Father. What's wrong?"

"Leave the house immediately. Go to the villa in Tarabya that I showed you before. Do you understand, son? Leave the house right now. Immediately."

"What's going on, Father?"

"I'm telling you to leave, son, don't stay there for even a second. Don't tell anyone where you're going. Don't waste any time, leave quickly!"

His father had mentioned this villa before, explaining that they would use it in difficult times, and had taken him there once for a tour.

As soon as he pulled the phone from his ear, his girlfriend, who had been listening intently to the short phone conversation, immediately asked,

"Sweetheart, what's happening?"

Alp, looking puzzled, said, "Something's happening, but I don't understand either. I think I need to go home. You can stay here if you want. Or don't, I don't know, I'm confused."

"It's okay, sweetheart. You go. I'll go to my place." Alp got into his red Ferrari and drove off quickly.

For a moment, a glimmer of hope appeared on the tired faces of Mr. and Mrs. Demirkaplan. Their son was safely with them.

"Thank God you're here, son!" Mr. Demirkaplan sighed deeply.

"Is everything okay, Father? Hopefully, nothing bad happened?" Alp didn't like the state his parents were in.

"What's going on? Why do you look like this?" He was very confused. Feyza got up from her chair, took her son's hand, and they sat on the couch together. She gestured for him to watch the TV directly across from them. Alp hadn't noticed that the TV was on. It was showing news footage of a burned man, with a reporter speaking excitedly.

"...and they entered without forcing the door. Initial impressions indicate that the murder was committed by people who knew the house and the Karahan family very well, as the complex nature of the murder suggests..."

Mrs. Demirkaplan managed to compose herself enough to explain.

"Son, your uncles Osman and Faruk," she gulped, "have been killed."

Alp was very saddened. He loved them both like his own uncles. They watched the news in silence for a long time.

The silence was broken by Alp's phone, which rang louder than the TV. It was his girlfriend calling. He declined the call and quickly sent a message telling her not to worry, then turned off his phone.

Cihangir and and his wife Feyza gathered themselves a bit. The security chief brought tea. There were no servants in the house. Although all the personnel and close security guards they employed were very trustworthy, only the security chief and the driver knew about this house.

Chapter

17

Stormy Meeting

They held a stormy meeting. The laziness that had come with the calm working order of the last three or four years had dissipated overnight. The murders of Osman Karahan and Faruk Altan had been like a tonic. The seriousness mask they wore during the meeting was inadequate to conceal the joy in their souls.

Faruk and Osman were among the few known top figures of the sect. It was decided to prepare a team to investigate the murder scene and to obtain information from the police examining the site. The task was given to Ali Fuat by Pasha Vefik, who then left the meeting.

Ali Fuat ordered the intelligence unit to investigate all aspects of the incident, closely monitor the sect, and have the analyst guards prepare reports based on the incoming information. Ali Fuat was issuing various orders, but this was nothing more than a verbal repetition of what the guards would already do. With their professional staff and years of accumulated work traditions, the Black Shrouds could understand what needed to be done without being told. Ali Fuat was aware of this too, but the issue was very different. He was excited. In recent years, there had been no sound from the sect. They hadn't conducted a proper operation in a long time, except for the last mystery. They had been preoccupied with their internal affairs. One pasha had said this, someone else had resigned... This gift from the sect greatly pleased the Black Shrouds.

Aydin followed the meeting with his blue eyes behind his thin glasses, in astonishment. He knew Osman Karahan and Faruk Altan from the media. He knew both were very wealthy and close to Islamic ideas. In other words, he knew as much as Turkey knew. Now, he had learned many things during the meeting. It turned out that these two men were at the very top of a Sharia organization. "What a strange working order these Black Shrouds have," he thought. He had become a member. He was now a guard. He attended the meetings. He wore the BS ring. But he knew nothing.

Chapter

18

The Sacred History of The Sect

Alp was aware of the turmoil they were in. He looked at his father, who was sipping his tea, and turned down the volume of the TV.

"Father!"

"Yes!"

"If you feel up to it, can we talk for a bit?"

"Of course, son, let's talk," said Mr. Demirkaplan. Mrs. Demirkaplan also joined the conversation.

"We should tell the child everything, Cihangir. He should know too." Mr. Demirkaplan shot a disapproving glance at his wife sitting next to his son, as if to say, 'What's the relevance?'

"My dear, are we saying he shouldn't know? Fine, let's tell him. If he had been paying attention to the business instead of mingling with models, he would have learned it all by now."

"Please, father, let's not argue about this." Alp was a bit annoyed.

Alp Demirkaplan's bohemian lifestyle, frequently featured in gossip columns, was putting Mr. Demirkaplan in a very difficult position. Hadji Halit often criticized this situation. Though he spoke little, it was clear that Imam Sait was also disgusted by Alp's lifestyle. In the Council of the Exalted, aside from Imam Sait and Haci Halit, other members did not meddle much in this matter because they had vested interests with Mr. Demirkaplan. They were living in opulence with fortunes that were not rightfully theirs.

Mr. Demirkaplan had spoken to his son many times but had never received a serious answer beyond "Okay, father, I'll be careful." His wife was also largely to blame. "Don't interfere with my son, let him live his life," she would say. Alp took his mother's side, and while he acted cautiously to avoid upsetting his father, he continued doing what he wanted.

Mr. Demirkaplan always insisted that his son was not the person the media portrayed. "He does it deliberately," he said. "He's camouflaging the family, creating the impression that we are secular, republican. Otherwise, my son wouldn't be involved in such things. He is trying to conceal that we are a caliphate-supporting family!"

After a brief period of unpleasantness, Mrs. Demirkaplan placed her hand on her son's knee and began to speak.

"My son, there are problems within the community. There has been – she paused, searching for the right word – a sort of rebellion against your father."

Alp looked at his father's face, then turned to his mother again.

"What rebellion, mother? Our grandfathers founded this community. Many of our relatives hold very influential positions. How could there be a rebellion?"

Mr. Demirkaplan interjected:

"Yes, son, you're right. There is no problem with the community as a whole. It's a small group, they are the problem."

"Get rid of the troublemakers, father."

"This time, it's not that simple! Look at what happened to Faruk and Osman . If we are not careful, they will get rid of us."

"Who are these men?"

"It's a long story, but let me put it this way. You know the community was established to bring back the caliphate. However, the collapse of the Soviets, the events of September 11, and the February 28 process in our country changed the perception of Islamic organizations negatively. The community reached a point where it could no longer achieve its founding purpose, the caliphate."

He took a few sips from his almost empty tea and asked his wife to refill it.

"The upper management of the community realized that it is no longer possible to bring the caliphate to Turkey. But they act as if they are not aware of it."

"Why?"

"Why? Son, the community has turned into a giant holding company. Should we dismantle such a large organization? Then how would we live in this mansion? How would you drive your fancy sports cars?"

"So, how do you keep it together, without a goal?"

"They act as if there is a goal. It's already a closed structure. The sub-organizations don't know us well. We continued economic activities by pretending there was a goal, without engaging in serious actions or disturbing certain state units."

Mrs. Demirkaplan brought the tea. She placed it on the small table in front of her husband and sat down to listen carefully.

"But father, is it that easy? Don't people question?"

Taking advantage of her husband sipping his tea, Mrs. Demirkaplan quickly interjected:

"The majority do not question. This community benefits many people, not just us. From the bottom to the top, many people have great economic interests according to their positions. There are commercial connections."

Alp cut off his mother.

"Is this the Istanbul Chamber of Commerce? We are talking about a secret organization."

Mr. Demirkaplan replied. "Of course, it's a chamber of commerce, son. But not just Istanbul, it's the Turkey Chamber of Commerce. In fact, if we called it the World Chamber of Commerce, we wouldn't be exaggerating."

Mrs. Demirkaplan continued her husband's words:

"To make a long story short, the community is no longer the one your grandfathers founded. Your father is also not of the same mindset as your grandfathers. Most importantly, Turkey is no longer the same. When it was first established, during the revolutions, when the call to prayer was recited in Turkish, and the caliphate family was still alive, everything was different. There was a stronger excitement. There was great opposition to the republic and the revolutions. It was very different back then, but now? Engaging in activities with militaristic elements and radical rhetoric now only brings destruction. To prevent the established order from being disrupted and to avoid the community from disbanding, your father and I followed a different policy. We cleansed the community of its radical elements. Of course, it wasn't completely successful, but we shaped the majority as we wanted."

Alp was trying to form a picture in his mind.

Mr. Demirkaplan continued:

"Pour me another tea, dear. Tell the manager to get something from outside; I need to take my medicine, my blood pressure is all over the place."

"Alright, dear." Mrs. Demirkaplan did as she was told and returned.

"Son, as your mother said, all Islamic organizations in Turkey faced a strong wind. The orders, communities, and sheikhs who couldn't position themselves against the wind disappeared, scattered everywhere. But those who adjusted their course to the wind progressed faster than ever."

"Didn't anyone object to this change?"

"They did, but the majority eventually accepted it. And what could they do if they didn't accept it? Life is hard, and no one wanted to disrupt the established order. The schools, financial companies, and holdings we established for years to bring the caliphate didn't bring the caliphate but brought in sacks of money. So, at this point, is there any reason to throw a wrench in the works?"

"I understand, economic interests made the change easier than you expected."

"Exactly. Especially after the September 11 attacks in America, what we did became even more legitimized. We softened the community just in time. If we had remained the same as before during September 11; if we were like the Kaplancilar, Bin Laden supporters, with connections everywhere trying to take over the country from within, the Black Shrouds would have cut us all down."

"Hmmm, and then there were the Black Shrouds, right?" "Yes, son."

"So what happened now to cause such turmoil?"

"Did you understand everything up to this point, son?"

"I did."

"Now, let's get to the other side of the coin. We created a significant change, and although the community accepted the change, some dissenting voices did emerge!"

"From whom?"

"Two buddies named Imam Sait and Hadji Halit – Mr. Demirkaplan cursed inwardly – in their thirties, they started getting involved in sciences like abjad, geomancy, numerology, occultism, and kabbalah."

Alp interrupted his father.

"What are those, father?" Mrs. Demirkaplan chimed in:

"Mystic sciences, my dear. They believe that through certain methods, you can activate and control entities like djinn."

Seeing her son shiver, Mrs. Demirkaplan thought it best not to go into too much detail. Mr. Demirkaplan also noticed the situation.

"As your mother said, they started getting involved in such sciences. It was around seventy-five or seventy-six, I think, we were in our thirties. The work they did caught the attention of the community. The leader of the community was my great uncle. Even though my uncle didn't value it much, the young people admired the work. I was very interested too, but my uncle and father never allowed me to engage with the lower levels of the community. This movement was immediately accepted by the most radical faction of the community."

Mrs. Demirkaplan went to the kitchen, thinking the water was boiling.

"When my uncle passed away, my father took over. He was also against these practices but he couldn't control the administration as much as my uncle did. Imam Sait and Halit continued their activities in the hidden houses of the order, in obscure corners, along with their sympathizers. The half-witted disciples of the community wouldn't miss their talks. In no time, a group of maniacs who would slit throats without blinking formed around them. They used a street in the Husrevaga neighborhood of Konya, and the whole street belonged to this new group. They were called the 'Huddam' within the community. Over the years, they continued their work without interruption and became very powerful. They hadn't found anything related to mystical powers, but they had created fanatics who had turned into killing machines."

"What was the purpose of these men?"

Mrs. Demirkaplan was bringing the tea, one with lemon. "Take the one with lemon, dear. It will lower your blood pressure."

"I'll take my medicine when the food arrives." "No, dear, have some lemon tea as well."

Mr. Demirkaplan added sugar and lemon to his tea and continued talking.

"Their goal was to decipher some codes from the holy books to activate great powers and establish a sharia state and raise the banner of the caliphate. In other words, a complete fantasy!"

He drank some of his tea and, after taking a deep breath, continued.

"They didn't achieve anything from their studies, but their fantasy world won them hundreds of militants. The most fanatical and murderous members of the community gathered around Imam and Halit. This was a very serious power. After my father's death, they became even more audacious. Until then, they were only introverted. The community had these fanatic youths do their dirty work. This was also a reason why Imam and Halit's activities weren't severely hindered because they motivated these killers. But over time, the Huddam turned into an uncontrollable monster. Now, they were taking some of the smart kids we trained to become governors, district governors, police chiefs, and judges, and inducting them into their ranks. They started training a brain team alongside the killers. The February 28 process halted this trajectory. The Black Shrouds and the Western Working Group cleaned many of them out. Imam and Halit were ineffective for a long time. That's when I implemented the reforms I mentioned. As a formality, I included both of them in the Council of the Exalted. I tried to moderate them, but while I succeeded in many areas, some things went wrong. They started their old activities again. Just when I had brought the community into the order I wanted, they were going to train a bunch of fanatics again. Now, there is no structure in Turkey that can carry radical Islam. This would be the end of the community. Something had to be done, and during this time, Halit Nurullah died. I thought this would weaken them or even stop them completely, but," pointing to the TV, "you saw the news."

Mr. Demirkaplan drank his lemon tea. He leaned back in his chair. The security chief had arrived with various dishes. They nibbled lightly. He took his blood pressure medicine. They were silent for a while after the meal. The silence was broken by Alp's question.

"Father, were these men you mentioned the ones who killed Uncle Osman and Faruk?"

"Most likely."

"Could it have been the Black Shrouds?"

Mr. Demirkaplan thought for a moment. "There's no reason for them to do that," he said.

"How can there be no reason? Weren't these men killers? They had killed many people from the Demirkaplan family and the community."

"Of course, they are killers, but the guards are not a sadistic organization; they don't kill for pleasure. They commit murders for a specific purpose: to protect the secular system and the reforms."

Alp jumped in as if he had solved the puzzle:

"Exactly, you are the head of a sharia organization, so couldn't they have killed for that reason?"

Mr. Demirkaplan spread his hands slightly to both sides and said, "Oh, what have I been explaining to you all along, son!" in his usual gentle and calm manner.

Mrs. Demirkaplan chimed in this time:

"The guards no longer have an issue with us. The community has changed significantly. It no longer has any structure that poses a threat to the secular system. In fact, the existence of the community has become one of the guarantees of the secular system."

"The guarantee of secularism?"What does that mean now? He understood nothing. His mother and father's sentences were writhing like little worms in his brain. Mrs. Demirkaplan felt the need to explain:

"The masters of the secular system knew that a rebellion would arise. You cannot prevent the birth of a reaction, but you can prevent it from reaching its conclusion. That is, you cannot prevent the formation of a sharia organization, as many have been established. But you can prevent them from reaching their goal, which is to overthrow secularism and replace it with sharia. They have already done so; no community or order has succeeded. For example, if a movement is going to start against you, would you prefer it to be led by bloodthirsty, militant, killer-minded people, or by calm individuals?"

Alp responded, "Of course, the latter."

Mrs. Demirkaplan nodded approvingly, "Good," she said, and continued: "Now think about all this from the perspective of the guards. Would they prefer the movements against secularism to be led by radicals like Hezbollah and the Kaplancilar, or by people like your father and Uncle Osman and Faruk?"

Alp nodded, starting to understand the situation. After his wife's explanation, Mr. Demirkaplan wanted to give an example:

"Do you know Hamas in Palestine, son?"

"Yes."

"What would you say if I told you that Mossad played a role in shaping the dynamics of Hamas in its early days?"

Alp remained silent for a short while, thinking deeply. He did not immediately oppose the idea, trying to find the reasoning behind it. Mr. Demirkaplan continued:

"Israel has always sought stability and security in the region. Given the persistent conflict and tensions, especially considering the hatred that Muslims have towards Jews and Israel, it was inevitable that some form of anti-Israel would emerge within Palestinian territories. Right?"

"Yes."

"Good. Since opposition was unavoidable, Israel had to consider how best to manage it. Would it be better for Israel to deal with a radical, militant organization that posed a direct and immediate security threat, or with a more structured movement that could be engaged with diplomatically when necessary?"

Alp frowned. "But Hamas isn't exactly soft, Father."

"That's true but they have carried out attacks, they set off a suicide bomb every three to four months. Yet their potential for destruction could have been far greater. Without any containment, terrorist activity against Israel might have escalated unchecked. By understanding and indirectly influencing the landscape of Palestinian factions, Israel ensured that it was dealing with a group that, while hostile, was at least somewhat predictable and manageable."

"Manageable? But they still carry out attacks."

"Yes, but imagine if there were multiple splinter groups, all more extreme, all completely uncontrollable. Back in the 1960s, in the very poor areas of Palestine, there were Zakat

Committees. Around 1967. These committees were supported by Israel.

They played a role similar to the Trojan Horse. This removed the Palestine Liberation Organization (PLO), which had been the dominant force in Palestinian politics, as the sole address for the cause. Thus, the people's power was divided, and the hate that had been solely directed at Israel weakened. Internal conflict began within the Palestinians themselves. Prisoners were divided into PLO supporters and Islamists. Islamist prisoners stopped participating in hunger strikes, saying they would only observe the fasts prescribed by their religion. Naturally, prison authorities provided these prisoners with a more livable environment. At universities, Islamist and PLO students clashed. Israel achieved its goal. It divided the movement started by Arafat. However, over the years, Hamas evolved beyond its origins and became what it is today—an extremist organization that prioritizes conflict over governance."

Alp raised an eyebrow. "So Israel actually help Hamas grow? Created them?"

"Not in the way conspiracy theorists like to claim. Israel never 'created' Hamas but made strategic decisions to manage threats in a way that aligned with its security interests. The real issue is that, like many political and militant movements, Hamas evolved beyond its original framework. What started as a counterbalance became an independent force, one that no longer serves the interests of peace or stability."

"Now Hamas is very prominent."

"Yes, that's how these things go. You can help them, you can direct them, but only to a point. They can get out of your influence. At some point, you might lose control."

Alp thought for a moment. "So, is there no way to control them now?"

"At a certain point, no external actor can fully control a terror organization like Hamas. Israel has had to adapt its strategy repeatedly as Hamas shifted its goals and tactics. That's the challenge of security in a volatile region—you can influence events, but you can't dictate their long-term trajectory.

Alp thought for a while.

"So, did the Black Shrouds establish the community?"

"Your grandfathers established it. The Demirkaplan family established it. In its early years, it had a radical structure. It was militant. This structure continued for many years. However, our method was not to set off bombs or engage in armed struggle. It's impossible to overthrow the super-equipped Turkish army of one million people with armed struggle. Moreover, that's not the only problem. In Turkey, secularism is a system based on the people. Among the people, there are millions who would fight to protect this system, including the rich, the poor, officers, civil servants, journalists, and students. The difference between Mustafa Kemal Pasha and leaders like Shah Reza Pahlavi or Afghan King Amanullah Khan, who wanted to bring a secular democratic system to their countries, lies here. Mustafa Kemal Pasha acted very cleverly and spread the revolutions among the people. Other leaders could only convey their thoughts to the elite at the top of the pyramid. As a result, they were overthrown by popular movements with a sharia structure. In Turkey, a movement like Khomeini's would not emerge. Because here, secularism is based on the grassroots. In Afghanistan and Iran, the secularists had vested interests because they were generals or high-level bureaucrats. But in Turkey, even a half-starved university student might take up arms and head to the mountains against a sharia state."

Mr. Demirkaplan realized he had strayed from his son's question.

"It would be wrong to say that the Black Shrouds established us like Mossad did with Hamas. But after February 28, the community came to the structure they wanted. This situation pleased them, of course. That's what your mother meant. A sharia movement is inevitable. You can't prevent its birth. It's better for calm people like me, Faruk, and Osman to lead it rather than fanatical radicals. That's why the guards wouldn't kill Faruk and Osman."

"So, do you have an agreement or some kind of relationship with them?" He asked this question fearfully, not wanting to offend his father.

Mr. Demirkaplan thought for a moment. There were things to explain, but he decided to leave them for later.

"We'll have many opportunities to talk. I want you to be directly involved in the work now because you can't stay away even if you want to. You are an Demirkaplan. You are probably on these djinn-summoners' hit list too."

Upon hearing this, Mrs. Demirkaplan sighed, "God forbid." Knowing this reality, hearing it from her husband's mouth terrified her.

Mr. Demirkaplan saw his wife's tearful state. Alp was the only weak point of this resilient woman. He was born after a long treatment process. She couldn't bear anything happening to him.

Chapter

19

Murder Investigation

When they arrived in Konya, it was 4:30. During the journey, they thoroughly discussed the incident in Bursa. There were many oddities. The security guards at the mansion's entrance gate claimed they hadn't seen anyone, but the cameras had captured three people. Although the steel door of the house was locked, it had been opened without any force. The footprints led straight to the bedroom. This meant the killers knew the house. The strangest thing was that Osman Karahan's wife hadn't woken up while he was being killed. Even after the fire suppression system was activated, she hadn't woken up. They thought the killers might have used ether or a spray on her. Nothing had been stolen from the house, despite there being many valuable items. Osman Karahan had been murdered with a rare brutality. The manner of his death indicated that the killers harbored great anger towards him.

During the helicopter journey, Zekeriya didn't join the conversation. After the vomiting incident, Aydin couldn't lift his head. A proper agent wouldn't act like that... How could the deep state ride in such a car... What kind of secret organization was this... He felt ashamed because of all these thoughts. He criticized others, but he had stumbled on his first task. Thankfully, the issue wasn't brought up in the helicopter.

They arrived at the hotel where Faruk Altan was killed. The homicide detectives had collected all the evidence. Ali Fuat and his team took a cursory look at the crime scene and then went to the Black

Shrouds farmhouse in Konya. They set their phones for nine o'clock and went to bed.

When they woke up in the morning, Zekeriya was the first to get ready and go down for breakfast. The others came a few minutes later. Kenan still looked groggy. Aydin had quickly pulled himself together after waking up. Ali Fuat looked alert. They glanced at the newspapers. All of them had the murders on the front page.

They left their headquarters. Their first task was to visit the Konya Police Department. Zekeriya was driving. Since he had been to Konya a few times, he remembered the roads. Ali Fuat and Kenan Ferit had also been there before, but they had forgotten the details. Aydin, who had never been to Konya before, watched the surroundings with curiosity.

When they arrived at the police department, they immediately requested all the information related to the murder. They didn't forget to mention that they were endowed with unlimited authority and handed over a document stamped 'top secret.'

When the police chief saw the president's signature, he straightened up. He called the head of the homicide division and ordered him to provide all necessary information.

There was an hour left until lunch. Ali Fuat was chatting with Inspector Salih from the homicide division.

"Who was the girl killed in this room?"

"Call girl," said Inspector Salih. After thinking for a few seconds, he felt the need to clarify.

"Actually, not exactly..."

"What do you mean?"

"Well, it was her first job. We investigated, and her stepbrother was her pimp. That night, they had agreed on six thousand dollars. According to her brother, the girl was a virgin. She was only fifteen years old. The autopsy found sperm and blood belonging to Faruk Altan. The doctor said the tear in her hymen was recent. There were fibers and skin fragments under her nails. There were also scratches on the victim's back. They must have occurred during the struggle."

Ali Fuat's eyes widened with anger. He wanted to kill Faruk Altan with his own hands. Kenan Ferit asked, "How many people committed the murder?"

"Three people. There's an interesting situation, though. The camera captured them, but no one saw them." He took a CD and put it into the computer. He fast-forwarded the footage. Three people were entering through the door. The four staff members at the hotel reception were busy with something. They looked at the newcomers and suddenly snapped to attention like soldiers seeing a general. They straightened up. The three young men approached the receptionists and asked something. Then they walked towards the elevator. The elevator operator also snapped to attention when he saw them. They got into the elevator...

Ali Fuat and his men watched attentively. They followed the three young men through the elevator camera until they reached Faruk Altan's room. They went inside. Since there were no cameras in the rooms, the footage they could watch ended there. Inspector Salih began to explain.

"These three men committed the murder. We are trying to identify them. However, their faces are very peculiar, almost as if they weren't human. We don't know if they underwent some medical procedure or used makeup. An even more intriguing point is that the four receptionists claimed that the three men in coats, who asked for Faruk Altan's room number, were the hotel manager and the assistant managers. We took them into custody. However, neither the manager nor the assistants resemble the men in the footage. Moreover, all of them were at home with their families at the time of the incident. The police officers went to their homes to pick them up. I showed the receptionists the footage. They were very surprised and couldn't believe it. Despite everything, they didn't change their statements. They said they didn't see those people. The elevator operator gave the same statement.

Ali Fuat requested copies of all the evidence and reports related to the case. Inspector Salih said he could have them ready by the afternoon.

Ali Fuat couldn't understand the reason for the girl's murder. Normally, professional killers would only kill the target.

"Inspector, can I see the stepbrother?" He couldn't find an answer. Zekeriya's threatening gaze made him uneasy.

"Of course. We questioned him; he was scared out of his wits, but if you want, you can question him too," he said.

"That would be good. Let's see this son of a bitch."

All five of them entered the interrogation room. Esad looked quite exhausted. It was clear from his appearance that he was a delinquent. His arms were covered in razor blade scars. He had both elbows on the table and his head hanging down. He would have fallen asleep right there if allowed.

"Lift your head," said Ali Fuat. "What's your name?" "Sir, I... um..."

A slap landed on his face like lightning. "I asked your name, you bastard!"

"Esad."

He was crying.

"Did you kill the girl?"

"What killing, sir! She was my sister."

Another slap landed.

"If she was your sister, why were you selling her?" "Sir, she wanted it herself!"

This time, the slap was even harder.

Esad would have fallen off the chair, but Aydin, who was right behind him, caught him. His mouth was full of blood. Inspector Salih wanted to intervene. He reached out to stop Ali Fuat, but suddenly he felt his wrist being gripped like a vice. With surprising agility for his large frame, Zekeriya had grabbed Inspector Salih's outstretched hand. In a firm tone, Kenan Ferit said, "Don't interfere. If necessary, we'll say he couldn't bear his sister's death and bashed his head in to commit suicide. We'll take full responsibility," he added. Inspector Salih couldn't find an answer. Zekeriya's threatening gaze made him shudder.

Chapter

20

Turn to Selin

When they took the reports and set off for Bursa, it was 2:30 PM. They received the report prepared for them by the Bursa police and immediately headed to Istanbul. They arrived in Istanbul around 9:00 PM. They were sleepless and exhausted. They parted ways, agreeing to meet in the morning. Despite being very tired, Aydin didn't go straight home. He reviewed the work Black Shrouds had done regarding the murders.

Ali Fuat drove his car home with bloodshot eyes. He had a slight headache. Before going up to his apartment, he thought of stopping by the site clinic to get a painkiller.

When he entered, the on-duty doctor folded the page of the book he was reading and set it aside. After a brief dialogue, he gave him a painkiller. Opening the notebook where he recorded the medications, he asked, "Can I have your name and last name?"

"Ali Fuat Sezgin."

As the doctor wrote it down, he pondered the surname Sezgin.

"C-2 block, apartment 8"

"Of course, of course. The place where the woman who was brought in with poisoning the other day lives."

"Are you related to Selin Sezgin?" the doctor asked. Ali Fuat felt a mix of curiosity and anxiety. "Is there something wrong?" he asked.

After all, he had called and spoken with his wife, and she sounded fine. Had she suddenly fallen ill?

The young doctor sensed the anxiety on Ali Fuat's face.

"She was poisoned, right? I just wanted to ask how she was doing. I did the initial treatment and then we sent her to the hospital."

Ohh... For a moment, he had thought something bad had happened. "She's fine now," he said. "They pumped her stomach. You did your part, thank you."

The doctor smiled, "It's my duty," he said. His large glasses and acne-ridden face gave the impression of someone who had spent his educational years buried in books. Ali Fuat was about to get up when the doctor asked another question.

"Did they get the mushrooms from the same place as the other person?"

Ali Fuat didn't fully grasp the question. "What do you mean by 'other person'?" he asked, confused.

"The other person who was poisoned," The doctor said.

The pain in Ali Fuat's head intensified. "Who?" he managed to say.

"I don't remember the name, but it should be in the records." The doctor thought for a moment, "Was he a financial advisor or an inspector, something like that," he said, opening the record book. Ali Fuat realized who he was talking about. It felt like bombs were going off in his head. The pain became unbearable. He asked for a glass of water and took one of the pills. His temples were throbbing.

The doctor found the name in the book. "Yes, Inspector Serkan Cenet. He was also poisoned by mushrooms. Did they perhaps get them from the same place?" he asked.

"How should I know?"

Ali Fuat's voice came out much harsher than usual. The doctor immediately noticed the change.

"When was he poisoned?"

"He came in half an hour after we sent Mrs Sezgin to the hospital." The doctor's voice was nervous. His face had fallen. "He vomited at home, drank a lot of water and vomited again, then ate yogurt. After that, he came here."

After leaving the clinic, he looked around. He didn't want to go home immediately. It was cold outside. The medicine hadn't yet taken effect and his intense headache persisted. Realizing his hands were shaking, he took a rubber ball out of his coat pocket and started squeezing it. He couldn't decide what to do.

A few of the security guards in the area were looking at him. It was best to head to the car. He walked quickly. He opened the door and got inside. He reclined the seat back and stretched out his legs. He took out a cigarette and cracked the window. He lit the cigarette and took a deep drag. Again, 'Serkan Cenet,' again 'Serkan Cenet'...

Selin had said she bought the mushrooms at the market. Had they bought them together? Had they gone to the market together? Or was it a coincidence? Did he also get them from the same place? It could be a coincidence. After all, how many places sell mushrooms at the market? Clearly, that bastard bought them from the same place.

But what if they went together... He flicked the ash from his cigarette into the car ashtray. He noticed his hands then. He looked at the rubber ball he had been squeezing. "You're useless too," he said, tossing it onto the passenger seat.

Suddenly, a deeply troubling thought occurred to him. What if they had gone together as neighbors do? Let's say they bought them together. Did they decide to cook them at the same time? Or did Selin cook them and they ate together? He cursed loudly.

If they ate together, why did he get poisoned half an hour later? He didn't understand what was happening, or perhaps he didn't want to understand. He tried to calm down. He didn't want to delve deeper. He didn't have the courage to face the 'possible outcome.' Ali Fuat had solved many complex cases, and he had the country's most secret intelligence agency at his command. If he wanted, he could find out in two seconds. He could plant a listening device at home, put his men on her trail; he had a thousand methods. They tracked government officials and dangerous killers when necessary, knowing their every move. Couldn't they track Selin? That would be easy. But what would be the result? No, no... And why track her, really? Is there anything to track?

He reached for his cigarette; he smoked it with a mix of urgency and hesitation. He didn't know what to do. Selin's sweet smile flashed before his eyes. He saw Ece. A picture of his family appeared on the windshield. And then, a surge of anger... A surge of rage... The picture faded, and the pitch-black darkness beyond the glass hit him in the face.

No, no... He didn't want the darkness, he didn't want the loneliness. He quickly opened the door. The security guards' eyes were on him.

Selin opened the door with a smile. "Welcome, my love!"

"Thank you," Ali Fuat said with a frown. "Is my dear husband very tired?"

As he took off his shoes and headed to the bedroom, he said, "I am exhausted." He took off his coat and hung it behind the door. He began to undress. Selin followed him immediately.

"Shall I tire you out a bit more, my love?"

She embraced him, starting to caress and kiss him. "Sweetheart, don't... I'm sweaty. I need to take a shower."

After laying Ali Fuat on the bed and climbing on top of him, Selin whispered, "Then we'll take one together." They started kissing. Ali Fuat had missed her very much. The resentment only lasted for a second. Selin's warm body shattered his walls...

Chapter

21

Cihangir Demirkaplan

After that long night, they stayed one more day at the villa. The head of security was in constant contact with the security team at the mansion. There was nothing unusual.

They left the villa and returned to Fevzipasha Mansion. Cihangir Demirkaplan was considering holding a meeting with the upper management of the community to assess the recent events. He called many members of the Council of the Exalted. He couldn't reach any of them—neither at home, work, nor on their mobile phones.

Each member of the council was the head of a group. Finance, education, propaganda, industry, foreign relations... They were like government ministries. When Mr. Demirkaplan couldn't reach them through any number, he called the groups they headed.

He couldn't get through to anyone. Apparently, the members who received the news of the murder had vanished without a trace."Seems our nobles have quite delicate lives," he muttered to himself. He thought about the transformation the community had undergone. If these events had occurred during his father's, uncle's, or grandfather's time, they would have gathered that night to discuss how to take revenge and what actions to take. The community's enforcers would have been specially prepared to punish the culprits. But now... starting with himself, every member had scattered.

The funerals of Faruk Altan and Osman Karahan were neglected. There were thousands of people from their families and the community, but none of the Council of the Exalted members were present. Mr. Demirkaplan also learned about the funerals from the television. It pained him. He took his son with him. Their first stop was the finance group, followed by the education group. The general managers of all the companies affiliated with these two groups met the new chairman: Alp Demirkaplan.

The general managers, who knew him from his glamorous life in the tabloids and thought his only interests were cars and models, chuckled under their breath at the appointment of this young man as the group chairman.

Ali Fuat went to headquarters early in the morning and examined the evidence until noon. There was a meeting scheduled for the evening, which Pasha Vefik would also attend. He decided to take Ece to a psychologist before the meeting.

He called his brother Feridun Sezgin, wanting him to come along. First, he picked up his brother with his car and then went home. Selin wasn't fully aware of their daughter's condition. Ali Fuat hadn't informed his wife about it. Selin found it strange that her husband came home at noon with Feridun to take Ece. Ali Fuat gave a casual explanation: "Ece was very scared that day. The psychologist wants to check her out. It's nothing serious." Selin wanted to join them, but they said it wasn't necessary. They told her to stay home, prepare dinner, and that they would be back in the evening.

Ece was very happy to go out with her father and uncle. She was smiling joyfully. Occasionally, she asked, "Why didn't mom come?"

They decided to eat fish by the Bosphorus. Ece was constantly teasing her uncle, wanting to eat his fish, mixing the salad and yogurt, and being mischievous. Feridun was more of a child than Ece. He tried to get her to drink his raki[20]. The girl almost threw up.

"Feridun, you're worse than a child."

"Come on, bro, don't interfere," Feridun laughed. "What's wrong, sweetie, didn't you like raki?"

Ece scrunched up her face, "It's awful."

Ece wanted to feed the restaurant's cat some fish. The pampered cat ate the fish and walked away without even a thank you. No rubbing, no meowing. With aristocratic grace, it disappeared into the restaurant, flicking its long fur.

The customers in the restaurant were smiling at Ece. She stared after the cat. The elderly restaurant manager brought the white cat back to her.

Ece's healthy state made her father happy. Ali Fuat felt a bit relieved from his stress. His joy would vanish when his daughter picked up his cell phone from the table.

"Daddy, I want to talk to mom."

Feridun and Ali Fuat exchanged glances. Ali Fuat took the phone from his daughter and called his wife. Ece talked to her mother at length.

The psychologist was as expensive as the doctor at the hospital had mentioned. He charged 450 TL for a one-hour session. Ali Fuat explained the situation first. Then the psychologist had a one-on-one session with Ece.

Feridun and Ali Fuat waited in the lounge. Other parents who brought their children were also waiting there. From their attire and conversations, it was clear they belonged to the elite class. The waiting lounge was furnished with ultra- luxury. Even though Ali Fuat wasn't interested in art, he could tell the paintings on the wall were expensive.

Ece walked in, holding the hand of Dr. Taner, who had a childlike appearance with his colorful shirt, smiling. It was as if God had specially created the psychologist for this job. His chubby face, the dimples

---

[20] An anise-flavored alcoholic drink popular in Turkey. It's a clear spirit that turns cloudy when mixed with water, earning it the nickname "lion's milk". Typically served with ice and water.

that appeared when he smiled, and his childlike voice. He couldn't pronounce the 'r' sounds, which added a unique charm to him.

Ece had also taken a liking to the doctor uncle. She was giggling. Ali Fuat and Feridun stood up immediately when they saw Ece. It was as if the psychologist had come out of a life-saving surgery and had saved Ece, now presenting her in a cheerful state to them.

Feridun picked up his niece. Ali Fuat, on the other hand, went with the psychologist to a separate room.

Ece's constant laughter in his arms made Feridun curious. "Sweetie, what did you do inside?"

"Uncle, there were big fish, and we looked at them. And then I held a baby rabbit in my hands. Its tummy was going up and down, up and down." She described the excitement she felt when holding the rabbit as if she was experiencing it right now.

"Was there a baby rabbit, too?"

"Yes, its tummy was going up and down, uncle." She was very cheerful.

Feridun noticed the joy in his niece's eyes. "Did you love the rabbit very much, sweetie? Shall we get you one?"

Ece hugged him tightly and kissed him. "Let's get one, uncle," she said.

Feridun laughed. "Okay, sweetie, I promise. So, what else did you do?"

Upon her uncle's question, she quickly raised her left arm and showed a bracelet made of evil eye beads. "This was behind my ear. The doctor uncle found it and gave it to me." Feridun realized that the psychologist had performed a small magic trick. He thought the psychologist was very skilled at communicating with children. "Did you say thank you, sweetie?" "Uh-huh," Ece nodded.

The conversation between the uncle and niece caught the attention of everyone in the waiting room. The positive impact the psychologist had on this child pleased the parents. They thought they had chosen the right person.

Ali Fuat watched in amazement as the psychologist's facial expression changed suddenly. The childlike, friendly man who had just held his daughter's hand and brought her into the room was gone, replaced by a serious man who occasionally glanced at the papers in front of him while carefully scrutinizing Ali Fuat. There was an air in his gaze that seemed to say, "I'm in charge here, and you will treat your daughter as I direct." Of course, Ali Fuat didn't feel intimidated by this gaze. He was an intelligence officer, trained in body language and other such skills. The psychologist played his role so well that even though Ali Fuat wasn't influenced by him, he couldn't help but watch with admiration.

He thought the psychologist probably used this technique to ensure the parents took him seriously. When he had entered the waiting room with such a childlike expression, it made people want to pinch his cheeks rather than have a serious conversation with him. Clearly, he applied different strategies for children and parents.

Ali Fuat had shared many things. He mentioned that he worked at Agriculture Machinery Import Export Inc., that he was very busy because of some joint projects his company had with the state, that he couldn't pay enough attention to home, Ece's problems at kindergarten, Selin's poisoning, and then Ece's subsequent shock. He recounted what the hospital doctor had said... He had shared many things, except for private matters. He said there was no abnormality between him and his wife. Dr. Taner seemed to sense something and asked question after question on this topic. Ali Fuat became anxious that his secrets might be exposed. With every question, thoughts of his small penis and Serkan Cenet came to his mind. He tried not to show it, but he was getting tense.

Dr. Taner realized that Ali Fuat was uncomfortable with the questions about his wife. When he first arrived, these topics had been discussed with Ali Fuat. Then, Dr. Taner had focused on Ece, and now Ali Fuat was back in front of him. What the little girl had shared strengthened Dr. Taner's suspicion that Ali Fuat was hiding something. This was a common situation. Many parents didn't mention certain things about themselves or their spouses when discussing their child's problems. Yet, these hidden details could be fundamental elements in the onset of the child's issues or crucial for solving the problem. Dr. Taner had some methods to deal with parents. Over one or two sessions, he would meet separately with the mother, father, and the troubled child, and if there were other children in the family, he would compare the information he gathered.

He would take each one into separate rooms and ask them to write a general account of their lives. People could lie when speaking, but interestingly, this tendency decreased when they were writing. Those who wrote the truth wrote briefly and clearly, while those who lied wrote longer, more complex, and inconsistent accounts.

Dr. Taner's goal was to tire the brain of the person he was talking to by asking questions in a consistent manner. Because there was a correct answer to the questions, the truth was always before the person's eyes while they were giving a false answer, which disturbed their psychology.

Dr. Taner thought Ali Fuat was a difficult person to get information from. He could skillfully handle the questions. Ali Fuat professionally dealt with questions that were subconscious prompts or probed specific points. This skill could only be acquired through training. What was Ali Fuat's profession? 'Agriculture'... Pfft, nonsense. He could swear this man was an intelligence officer. Well, early diagnosis wasn't very accurate anyway.

He thought Ali Fuat had problems with his wife. Of course, he couldn't connect his assumptions to the child's issues, but there was something there. Perhaps something the mother had done had instilled this fear in the girl.

Dr. Taner didn't know where to start or which technique to apply. He was tired; how many sessions had he had since morning? He decided to describe his observations about Ece in simple terms and observe the father's reactions.

"Yes, Mr. Sezgin."

"Yes, doctor, I'm listening to you."

"How would you prefer me to address you?"

Actually, he wouldn't usually ask this question. This question gave the other person the authority to exercise some initiative over him. "I prefer you call me by my second name." Though it seemed like a small detail, it was a significant matter. The last thing Dr. Taner wanted was to lose control during a conversation with a parent. So why had he asked this question now? He didn't know. Maybe his uncertainty about which technique to use had affected his psychology.

"As you wish," said Ali Fuat. His tone was respectful. "Well then, I prefer to call you Mr. Ali."

"Very well. Go ahead, I'm listening to you."

Dr. Taner interpreted Ali Fuat's repeated "Go ahead, I'm listening to you" as a signal that he wanted him to start talking about his daughter.

"Although it's too early to make a full diagnosis, I can share some initial observations with you."

Ali Fuat listened intently.

"The diagnoses of the hospital doctor are partly correct. Yes, your daughter is afraid that her mother, Mrs. Sezgin , will die. However, this fear of death is not as straightforward as it might seem from the first session."

"What kind of death are we talking about?"

Ali Fuat's serious demeanor faltered. Dr. Taner continued, "Your daughter doesn't think her mother will die in a car accident or by falling from a balcony. She thinks her mother will be killed by a third party."

He asked excitedly, "Who is this third party?"

"We don't know yet. It might be that this third party isn't a living person or even a human at all."

"What do we need to do for a definitive result?"

"Long sessions with your daughter and with you, and of course with her mother as well."

Ali Fuat was silent for a few seconds. He hadn't brought up the issue with Selin and didn't want to explain it to her.

"Is it necessary to speak with my wife or me?"

"Yes."

"But why is that necessary?"

"Allow me to be the judge of that, Mr. Ali." Ali Fuat realized he was being disrespectful.

"Sorry, of course, you will decide," he said.

Dr. Taner continued to explain his observations about Ece.

"Your daughter's extreme reaction to the poisoning incident is actually a minor response. It's just the tip of the iceberg. Even though your wife has recovered, her fear persists. Something is keeping that fear alive, but what?"

Every word the psychologist uttered increased Ali Fuat's distress.

"What will we do?" There was helplessness in his voice.

"At this moment, we can't take any steps. It's still too early. But you can get some pets to distract her. It might help divert her attention from her mother a bit."

"Of course, of course, we'll do whatever is necessary." The sharpness in Ali Fuat's eyes had disappeared. Dr. Taner noticed this. If they had a bit more time, they would have reached a point where they could gather complete information, but...

"Mr. Ali, our time is almost up. Please schedule another appointment as soon as possible, and come alone this time."

They shook hands. Feridun was waiting eagerly for his brother. Ece had been talking on the phone the whole time her father was inside. She had called her mother and told her about the rabbit.

Chapter

22

Alp Demirkaplan

Alp Demirkaplan quickly adapted to his role as the boss. After the introductory meeting, he requested activity reports from all the companies under his control. He appointed the advisors of Faruk Altan and Osman Karahan as his own advisors. He had a one-month program prepared to personally inspect all companies under the education and finance groups. The advisors informed the companies of the dates for the inspections.

He asked all the general managers to rate their employees. He indicated that the number of employees was too high and that there might be mass layoffs. He didn't forget to add that inefficient companies would be completely shut down.

By noon, the Demirkaplan tsunami had struck, leaving the education and finance groups in ruins. Rumors about company closures and mass layoffs spread quickly from person to person. Preparations for the inspections had already begun.

The new chairman had slammed his fist on the table. Fear spread like waves in the sea.

Alp realized how wise it was to follow his father's instructions to the letter. Any potential insubordination or lack of seriousness due to his youth was nipped in the bud from day one.

He felt more powerful than ever.

Cihangir Demirkaplan had left his son early and returned to his mansion, which he used as a sort of presidential palace. He continued to reach out to members of the Council of the Exalted. After much effort, each reachable member was informed of a meeting to be held the following evening.

He discussed the day's developments with his wife.

Chapter

23

Ece

After leaving the Psychotherapy Center, they went to a market that sold all kinds of animals. Feridun bought two baby rabbits. One was black and white, and the other was completely white-both adorable.

Ali Fuat couldn't make up his mind. He had thought the place would only have birds and fish, but it was like Noah's Ark. There were crocodiles, spiders, snakes, and a variety of tropical animals.

As they looked around, they decided to buy a parrot. They paid $750 for a beautiful, talking parrot. Ali Fuat had no problem affording it, but he still found such a purchase strange. If it weren't for his daughter's health, he wouldn't have spent that much money. Paying so much for a bird seemed nonsensical in a poor country like Turkey.

Ece wanted a big aquarium and a variety of fish. Her father and uncle immediately fulfilled this request. They put the purchases in the car and went back. Feridun said, "I should get something for my daughter too." He was right. During a family visit, his daughter might go mad with jealousy upon seeing her cousin's pets. Ali Fuat, feeling more and more annoyed by what he considered a "silly environment," was eager to leave. Ece, meanwhile, was watching everything with her uncle. She saw a large fish in an aquarium. The fish was truly striking with its colors, and she insisted on getting it.

Ali Fuat stood by the aquarium and called into the shop without feeling the need to enter.

"Hey, how much is that big fish?"

The seller, whose appearance suggested he was from the east, was tired of countless people being fascinated by the fish's colorful appearance, asking the price, and then not buying it. He no longer paid much attention to those who asked. From inside the shop, he replied half-heartedly, "480."

"What?" "What?"

The seller, still indifferent, repeated, "I said 480."

His voice was barely audible, but this time Ali Fuat paid close attention.

"Hey, come here and answer properly." "480, are you deaf?"

Ali Fuat's hands began to tremble. He rushed into the shop.

"How dare you talk like that!" "How dare you talk to me like that!"

"Idiot, am I going to learn how to talk from you?" he said, his chin trembling. With his scythe-like arms, he landed two punches, leaving the young man's face covered in blood.

The shopkeepers rushed to the shop. Feridun met the crowd, showing his ID and saying he was a military judge. His hand was also on his belt. Ali Fuat snapped at the onlookers, "What are you staring at?"

Not a peep was heard.

Ali Fuat wanted to call the police and have the young man arrested, but the older shopkeepers begged him to drop it. Feridun also didn't want the situation to escalate. Besides, Ece was on the verge of tears due to the commotion.

They bought a beautiful parrot for Ece's cousin as well and returned to their car.

When they got home, Selin greeted them with a carefully prepared table. While they weren't too surprised by the feast, Selin was very surprised by the animals they had brought.

Feridun gave a brief explanation. "The psychologist suggested this method to prevent the child from focusing on a specific point and to develop a sense of responsibility," he said. He even mentioned that he had bought a parrot for his own daughter as well.

While they were eating, Selin and Feridun chatted. Ali Fuat, however, was silent and thoughtful. Ece's parrot occasionally made random noises, drawing everyone's attention to see if it was talking.

Since they had eaten fish a few hours earlier, they weren't very hungry. The meal didn't last long.

As Feridun left to go home, Ali Fuat started getting ready by putting on his brown suit. He mentioned that he had an important meeting in the evening and had to leave. Although Selin was used to it, Ece was disappointed when she saw her father in his suit, realizing he was going out, just as she was trying to get her parrot to talk.

Ali Fuat left the house.

Chapter

24

The Headquarters of the Black Shrouds

Ali Fuat arrived at Agriculture Machinery Import and Export Inc. and parked his car. As he walked toward the building, he spotted Aydin in the spacious garden by chance. Aydin had also arrived early. Ali Fuat called out to him, and they began walking together. It was getting dark. The guard at the front of the building adjusted his stance and grip on his weapon. They entered without paying much attention to the meticulously prepared guard.

They took the elevator to the fourth floor and went to Ali Fuat's office. They didn't talk much until the meeting time. Ali Fuat didn't know what to focus on -his daughter, his wife, the murders, or Inspector Serkan Cenet. Amid all these complex thoughts, his daughter weighed heaviest. He couldn't make sense of what the psychologist had said. "She's afraid her mother will be killed..." He couldn't get past this sentence.

There was a knock at the door. They were told the meeting would start in ten minutes. They hadn't realized how time had flown. They got up and went to the meeting room.

Zekeriya's loud "Attention!" signaled that Pasha Vefik was about to enter the room. The Pasha greeted with a "Hello, friends," and quickly took his place.

A special setup had been prepared for a simulation presentation. A guard started the presentation. The details of Osman Karahan's villa and the hotel where Faruk Altan was murdered were explained. Various images of the villa and the hotel were shown. The presenting guard highlighted how well-protected both locations were.

The bodies were shown repeatedly from various angles: Osman Karahan's charred head and Faruk Altan's severed arms. The guard described the sequence of the murders.

Photos of three young men appeared on the screen. Dressed in long black coats and large amulets around their necks, their outfits were coordinated. The expressionlessness on the young men's faces caught everyone's attention.

The security cameras of the hotel and the villa had recorded how the killers entered these places and what they did. The only missing footage was of the actual murders because the hotel rooms, considered private areas, had no cameras. Similarly, despite many cameras in the villa, there was none in the bedroom for the same reason.

The presentation continued with the villa's camera footage. The screen showed a long iron gate and a guardhouse on the right. The inside of the guardhouse was illuminated, with strong light streaming out from the large windows. The presenting guard froze the image and pointed to a spot.

"This is the entrance gate of the villa. The killers will enter shortly. But first, let's note the camera's recording date and time."

The date was 24.03.2013, and the time was 01:03. The attendees noted the time.

The three young men arrived at the gate. The guard froze the footage again. "Watch this part very carefully." The three young men approached the large iron gate, grabbed the bars, and started climbing up. The gate rattled loudly. Two men armed with guns immediately came out of the guardhouse. The three young men jumped into the villa's garden. The fact that the armed guards didn't see the three individuals right in front of them had previously astonished the Black Shrouds who had watched this footage. The presenting guard froze the footage.

"As you can see, this is an interesting situation. The three killers climb the iron gate right in front of the security guards, who come out armed but look around without intervening. It's as if they can't see them..."

Ali Fuat interjected:

"Maybe they really can't see them."

The Pasha objected:

"The distance between them is less than a meter. How could they not see them?"

"I don't know, Commander. I can't find a logical explanation right now, but the two security guards definitely don't see them."

Since Ali Fuat had seen the crime scene and examined all the evidence before, he had a broader perspective.

Pasha Vefik asked about the possibility of the security guards being in collusion with the killers.

One of the guards in the meeting spoke up.

"Commander, we know both of them well. They've been part of the community since childhood. The community arranged their marriages, gave them jobs, and provided houses. One of them even named his child Osman, born two years ago. The likelihood of their betrayal is almost nonexistent."

The guards had a strong database concerning the community.

Ali Fuat said, "I agree that the likelihood of betrayal is low. Besides, even if they did betray, they wouldn't choose such a method. 'You come, jump over the gate into the garden, and we'll ignore you.' It's too stupid."

The presenting guard brought up the security camera footage from the hotel in Konya.

"This is the reception of the hotel where Faruk Altan was murdered." Four people were standing at the reception, all busy with something. Occasionally, guests came and went, some checking in or out. Everything seemed normal.

When there were no guests, they chatted among themselves. The three young men entered. The guard immediately paused the footage.

"Let's check the camera's date and time," he said.

The date was 24.03.2013, and the time was 00:48. The officers were astonished. If the killers were the same people, they had traveled from Konya to Bursa[21] in fifteen minutes. This couldn't be done with any vehicle. They would have had to board an F-16 in front of the hotel and land in front of the villa. Even then, it would take more than fifteen minutes."

---

[21]   The distance between these two cities are 362 miles.

The Pasha asked a question.

"Could the perpetrators be individuals who look very similar and wore the same clothes?"

"We initially considered that, Commander, but the fingerprints and shoe prints taken show that the three people at the hotel and the ones at the villa are the same individuals."

The Black Shrouds couldn't explain this situation. The guard also showed the oddities at the reception. "As you can see, wherever the three killers go in the hotel, the staff immediately straighten up."

The attendees were attentive. Ali Fuat had seen these parts before and was looking on routinely.

One of the guards spoke up.

"Could it be that the killers tampered with the cameras at the villa and the hotel? Something like photomontage?"

"Yes, we considered that possibility. We sent the cameras and recordings to forensics. The footage was examined, and it was confirmed that there was no tampering."

The Pasha interrupted.

"Could the camera times have been adjusted?"

"Technically, it could be done, Commander. But finding the recording centers of the villa and the hotel, getting past all the staff, and cracking the computer passwords is not easy."

Ali Fuat interjected.

"Even if the camera times were changed, it doesn't matter to us. We can determine the times of the murders from other sources. Faruk Altan checked into the room at 23:08. This is recorded in the hotel logbook. The girl was brought to the room around 00:10. This is confirmed by the testimonies of the bodyguards and the girl's brother. So, no murder had taken place by 00:10. He had intercourse with the girl. The discovery of the murder and the report to the police happened around 01:15. As for Osman Karahan, we can determine the time of death independently of the cameras, as the fire suppression system activated right after he was burned, and the guards rushed into the house."

The Pasha acknowledged with a nod.

As the presentation was ending, Ali Fuat realized there was an unexplained point and spoke up.

"The brutality of the murders is noteworthy." Upon hearing Ali Fuat's words, the presenting guard pressed a few keys on the computer and brought up the photos of the bodies on the large screen of the simulation. Osman Karahan's naked body in the fetal position, with his head and abdomen charred from the fire, and Faruk Altan's body without arms, with the area turned into a pool of blood...

Ali Fuat's words about the brutality carried a weight far stronger than just words. He was pleased with the display of the photos on the screen and continued speaking. "Professional killers don't use such methods. They just kill. It's clear that the killers harbored a deep hatred for the victims. Such brutality can only be carried out with a long-nurtured and deeply rooted desire for revenge."

Aydin gathered all his courage and spoke up.

"The killers didn't attempt any theft, nor did they interrogate the victims to obtain any information. Their sole apparent purpose was to kill."

Everyone looked at Aydin with approving eyes, and he felt a sense of inner satisfaction from those looks.

Pasha Vefik smiled.

"Well done, Aydin. That's how it should be. Keep your eyes open and pay attention to everything, understand?"

"Yes, Commander."

Pasha Vefik made the closing remarks.

"Friends, it's been a long time since there have been disturbances among the radical Islamist factions. The Black Shrouds have managed to curb the Islamic factions with timely and skillful maneuvers. Radical Islamist groups are no longer as radical as they used to be. As Black Shrouds, we must maintain this situation. The Republic of Turkey needs stability. Chaos and murders will turn the factions that have moved from illegality to legality back into monsters. We cannot allow the peace we have established in recent years to be disrupted. The murder of two prominent community leaders cannot be explained by theft, psychopathy, or any other reason. The only explanation is a political power struggle. Identify which group initiated this struggle immediately. Although the infighting among the country's Islamists might seem beneficial to us, it actually disrupts stability and harms the economy. These two murders could lead to more. We must absolutely prevent this. We are entering a period full of operations. Command is under Ali Fuat Sezgin."

Ali Fuat responded, "Yes, Commander."

Pasha ordered the preparation of continuous reports on the progress of the operations and then left the meeting.

After Pasha Vefik departed, the guards continued their conversation among themselves. The upcoming operations brought a hidden joy among them. They definitely didn't agree with Pasha Vefik's praise for the years of inactivity. In their view, the duty of the Black Shrouds was not to maintain stability but to protect the secular Republic of Turkey and its reforms. And what was the economy to them anyway? Were they economists, they wondered.

Chapter

25

Alp Demirkapan with his Girlfriend

Alp Demirkaplan thought the stern boss image he had created had penetrated all his employees to their very core. He felt as if he had won a great battle.

He walked out of the company with prideful steps. The smile on his face was meaningful.

He got into his car and started driving fast. He called the number saved under the name "My Love." On the other end was the curious voice of his girlfriend.

"Honey, where have you been?" This was the start of a long conversation, but Alp cut it short.

"Come over tonight. I miss you."

"I'd love to, sweetheart, but where have you been? I've been trying to reach you all morning…"

"We'll talk when you get here."

As Alp Demirkaplan continued driving, he called his father. He told him that he wouldn't be coming to the mansion tonight and would stay at his own house.

Cihangir Demirkaplan sensed the determination in his son's voice. Although he allowed it, he didn't forget to send a twelve-person security team to the villa, urged by his wife's persuasion.

When Alp parked his car and saw his girlfriend's SUV, he knew she was home. He quickly went inside. The girl heard the key in the door and walked towards it. They met in the long, narrow hallway.

"Honey, what happened? I was dying of curiosity!"

They hugged and started kissing. After a short kissing session, the girl thought they would talk, but every question she asked was answered with a kiss, a caress, or the removal of some piece of clothing. Once they were both completely naked, she abandoned her questions and got lost in the magic of their lovemaking. Alp was rougher than ever before, making love as if he were beating her. It was as if he was trying to inflict pain.

Chapter

26

Feyza Demirkaplan

Feyza had sent a small army of bodyguards, but she barely made it through the night. She was up by 7:30 AM. Knowing her son's habit of going to bed at dawn, she thought he would be asleep at this hour. "If I call now, I'll wake him up. I better call the bodyguards," she said to herself. The chief bodyguard answered his ringing phone and assured her that everything was fine, mentioning that Alp and his girlfriend were having breakfast. She was surprised he was up at this hour. She then called her son's cell phone.

"Yes, Mom?"

"Sweetheart, are you awake?"

"No, Mom, I'm talking to you in my dream," he laughed. Feyza laughed as well.

"How was I supposed to know? Our Alp usually sleeps until noon..."

"Not anymore, Mom. He's working. He has responsibilities. He's a chairman now," he emphasized the last sentence.

"I'm proud of my handsome son. Your father told me. Don't overwork yourself in the first few days."

"I won't get tired, Mom. I'll call you later. I'm having breakfast and don't want to be late for work."

Cihangir Demirkapan woke up to the sound of Feyza's voice.

"What's going on, dear? Why are you up so early?"

"Nothing, dear. I was just worried about our boy and thought I'd call."

He propped himself up slightly in bed and put a hand on his stomach with a sour expression.

"Is he awake at this hour?"

"I was surprised too. He's up. He's having breakfast with that model girl. He's going to work!"

"Good for him. He adapted immediately."

"Is everything okay? You're holding your stomach." Cihangir responded with a laugh.

"There's a burning sensation in my stomach, but hopefully, it's a sign of good things to come."

They laughed. As they prepared for breakfast, they talked about their son's swift entry into the business world. Cihangir Demirkapan was very happy that his son was working with him. Finance and education were very important groups, and these two fundamental institutions needed to be in reliable hands.

After the deaths of Osman Karahan and Faruk Altan, the members of the Council of the Exalted had scattered like frightened birds. It had taken Cihangir Demirkapan a long time to reach them. He was so angry that he cursed the very reforms he had implemented within the community. Murders had been committed, delivering a major blow to the community, and yet they were only able to gather three days later.

The stress Mr. Demirkapan experienced and his nostalgic longing for some aspects of the past, along with questioning his current actions, didn't last long thanks to his wife's timely intervention and reassurances.

After breakfast, he sat down with his wife. They began discussing the evening's meeting in great detail. They exchanged ideas about what needed to be done and the stance that should be taken.

Chapter

27

There is a Big Surprise at the Meeting

The Council of the Exalted convened at the headquarters of Kaviyan Holding in Mecidiyekoy. Kaviyan Holding was one of the smallest companies within the community. Its commercial activities and profit margins were modest and inconspicuous. It was a very clean group, lacking the characteristic work style of Islamic organizations. The company featured women in miniskirts, men with nightlife, a small minority of young men wearing earrings, a very modern and European-looking middle management, and a top management that was entirely loyal to the community but concealed this from everyone, including the employees. Kaviyan Holding was a very special company for the Community because of its donations to Kemalist associations and its selection of all employees, except for the top management, especially from Kemalist and democratic youth. They took their appearance so seriously that, just to reinforce the Kemalist[22] image, they hired a retired general as the public relations manager with a salary of thousands of dollars. The general's sole duty was to attend Ataturk-themed dinners and seminars organized by various associations on behalf of the company.

The surface of the dark brown walnut meeting table shone brilliantly thanks to the high-quality varnish used. This valuable table, costing

---

[22] Refers to individuals who adhere to the principles and reforms of Mustafa Kemal Ataturk, the founder of the Republic of Turkey, embracing values such as secularism, modernization, national sovereignty, and republicanism.

more than a government employee's retirement bonus, was surrounded by 'fairweather Islamists' lounging in their comfortable leather chairs.

For the sake of the supreme interests of the Islamic world, the Council of the Exalted reached a consensus regarding this deviant faction of the community.

"He must be killed..."

To formalize the general opinion about Imam Sait and to issue the fatwa of "his execution is to be obligatory," President Cihangir Demirkaplan began his speech in his capacity as the "Deputy of the Caliph."

Mr. Demirkaplan began his speech, knowing it would end in a fatwa, and the members listened attentively. They were relieved that they would finally get rid of this troublesome "imam" who threatened their lives. Mr. Demirkaplan gave a long speech and prepared his final sentences to deliver the ultimate command.

"The killing of these two mujahid brothers by Imam Sait and his deviant followers..."

His words hung in the air. He was staring at the door. Everyone in the meeting room who looked at the door was frozen, hypnotized.

The wide meeting room door was half-open. Standing there was Imam Sait, with his long robe, thin imamah -headwrap, white cloth covering the sides of his face like a turban, and a smile cleverly hidden in his long beard. No one understood how he had gotten wind of the meeting, found the location, or bypassed all the security. The images of Osman and Faruk's corpses flashed before their eyes. For a moment, they thought their end had come. Now the Imam would step aside, and dozens of fanatic militants would storm in and slaughter them like chickens. When the Imam moved his lips, the fear in the room peaked. The members thought the words from the Imam's mouth would be the last they ever heard.

"Peace be upon you," said the Imam.

"Peace be upon you" was a phrase the members had used for years. They had heard it thousands of times.

It was one of the words they used most frequently. Now, however, it felt very unfamiliar; they couldn't recognize what "Peace be upon you" meant for a moment. This was not the phrase they expected from the Imam. They thought he would utter a command to have them killed.

None of them could say, "And upon you be peace." With a significant smile on his face, the Imam approached the table. He pulled one of the leather chairs, carefully spreading his robe so it wouldn't wrinkle, and sat down.

"Sorry for being late," he said. "The child who informed me about the meeting gave the wrong time," he continued with a mocking expression. "However, meeting times should be communicated to the Council of the Exalted members more seriously. Isn't that right, Mr. President?"

Mr. Demirkaplan could only manage to say, "Yes, you are right," half-heartedly. The Imam turned his gaze to Alp.

Alp's elegant suit was drenched in sweat. He was trying to avoid eye contact with the Imam. After a brief look, the Imam turned his eyes back to Mr. Demirkaplan and said, "Your son, I presume?"

"Yes," Mr. Demirkaplan replied. He felt the need to explain:

"My son was appointed head of the education and finance groups by the decision of the Council of the Exalted."

"How nice. How nice. May God grant him success. Of course, it's important to value the youth. If I had arrived earlier, I would have voted in that direction too." Contrary to the tension in the room, the Imam had a great sense of ease on his face.

"So, what are the other agenda items for the meeting?"

"Actually, we were just about to adjourn. The meeting was over."

"Really... So, we have been struggling in vain. We only managed to catch the end of it." There was an indescribable laugh in his voice. They all sensed the subtle mockery.

"Well then, I will take my leave. You know, I have a long way to go." The Imam got up from his chair and walked out of the room with slow steps. None of them could distinguish whether what they had seen was a dream or reality.

Chapter

28

The Deep Knowledge of the Community

Mrs. Demirkaplan was watching the rain from the large window overlooking the garden of the mansion. The garden was adorned with lighting fixtures shaped like ship lanterns, placed on two-meter-tall thin poles. Despite the brightness of the garden, the only place where the raindrops could be clearly seen was around the lights.

Mrs. Demirkaplan noticed that the iron gate at the end was opening. Cars, whose headlights were the only visible part, entered. The vehicles traveling down the wide path approached the building. Mrs. Demirkaplan saw her husband and son get out of the car. Bodyguards getting out of the other cars opened their umbrellas and held them over her husband and son. They started walking towards the house. Knowing how much her husband loved the rain, Mrs. Demirkaplan thought, "He will now ask the bodyguard to remove the umbrella," and smiled. However, Mr. Demirkaplan neither paid attention to the umbrella nor the rain during the fifteen to twenty steps it took to enter the house.

Mrs. Demirkaplan also came down from the third-floor room of the mansion. Fear had created a harmony in her husband and son's facial features. This sight instantly shifted her mood from the sentimentality of the rain to tension.

"What happened? Alp, what happened? Cihangir... Cihangir, what happened?"

She couldn't maintain her composure when it came to her family. She was excited again. After changing their clothes, Mr. Demirkaplan explained what had happened at the meeting. He tried to express their astonishment when Imam Sait appeared and then left.

Mrs. Demirkaplan's first reaction was, "How did he get past the security?"

"No one saw him."

Mrs. Demirkaplan listened to her husband with eyes that screamed, 'I don't understand.' Mr. Demirkaplan also explained the oddities in the murders.

The Imam had to be killed.

Now Mr. Demirkaplan was discussing methods with his wife and son. The Imam was very powerful in his region in Konya. How should they proceed? What needed to be done?

Alp was trying to think of something. He felt more stuck than ever before. "Maybe," he said. His parents' eyes were on him, but he couldn't continue. "Maybe a hitman or something?"

Mr. Demirkaplan thought he should explain some things about the sect.

"Their lifestyle is very different. Capturing the Imam is difficult. His followers believe he is a sacred person. With his perverse ideas and some superstitions, he has turned them all into killing machines. Many of them are capable of killing with just one order. There's a wall of flesh around him. It's nearly impossible to infiltrate with an agent or leak information."

"You said they all live together, right, Dad?"

"Yes, most of them live together. In the Husrevaga neighborhood of Konya. Of course, they have houses in many places, but this is their center. They don't sell or rent houses to strangers."

They even pay a lot of attention to people passing by on the street. They have young people assigned for this job. If a stranger is seen there a few times, they're in trouble. They'll likely get a clean beating from the locals. I tried to buy a house by sending an elderly couple they didn't know at all. The man had a beard and turban, and the woman wore a black chador, perfectly fitting the neighborhood's structure. But despite offering prices above their value, no one wanted to sell their house."

"So, what did you do? Couldn't you find any way to monitor them?"

"There was a small plot of land owned by the municipality in that neighborhood. I managed to get a decision to sell it from the council. They are so well organized in the municipality that I had a lot of difficulty with this too. I eventually bought the land under a cover construction company. I sent men to start the construction, and the locals sent them all to the hospital. They had children under eighteen set the vehicles on fire. One of the young kids shot the team leader with a hail of bullets. I don't remember exactly, but he had ten or twelve bullets in his body and died right there. The police conducted an operation and caught the boy. Actually, it's more accurate to say they handed the boy over to the police."

Alp listened in amazement.

"So, they didn't hide the kid?"

"No, son, why would they hide him? He was out a month later."

"Did he escape?"

"No. It turns out these people operate in a very planned and organized manner. They start training orphans and particularly brave children from their dormitories in firearms from the age of 12-13. They also take them to both state and private hospitals, pretending they have psychological issues."

"What kind of treatment?"

"They take the chosen kids to a psychologist, saying, "This is a relative of mine, he's been acting erratically since his parents died, attacking people, trying to burn the house down. They put them in sessions for a year or two and then get a certificate saying they're insane."

"Don't the psychologists realize they're normal?"

"They're not normal anyway, son. Those deviant activities involving djinn and devils have probably messed up their heads. Plus, the sect probably gives the children suggestions on how to behave with the psychologists. For instance, 'Go there and don't say anything, or cry, curse, attack... I don't know, they must be giving such suggestions. These kids are not normal, they live in a world of superstitions and fantasies."

"So, in the future, if they need to shoot someone, they're raising killers who won't face any punishment."

"Yes, unfortunately, son."

"In the end, you couldn't do anything with that plot of land."

"Was it possible? The shooting incident wasn't the end of it. That day, hundreds of people protested in front of the municipality building, claiming 'The sale of the land is illegal. The building was stoned. The police couldn't control the crowd. Everyone was baffled by the events caused by the sale of a small plot of land. The mayor met with the angry crowd and announced the immediate cancellation of the land sale. After all these incidents, it was impossible to build anything there. Imam and Halit made a grand display of power and declared their rule in that area."

"So, you couldn't monitor them in any way?"

"I tried to infiltrate spies. Some believed in the activities and defected to them, even betraying their comrades. Of course, we never heard from the men we sent again. But we kept trying. We sent them again. We sent people who didn't know each other, and in the same way, some joined them. We did receive some information, but we couldn't obtain anything very important. They have an interesting structure. Cells don't know what each other is doing."

"Dad, while these people are harboring so many killers, didn't you do anything? At least some kind of tight security measures?"

"Every member of the council is protected by highly trained individuals. We have people in the police force and many other places. The community-trained state officials and the community's special intelligence unit ensure our security. However, all these seem to be insufficient."

There was a brief silence.

"Dad, you mentioned that these people deal with djinn and such. Do you know what kind of dealings these are?"

"Well, I know the general outlines."

Alp was curious about what the men his father called 'huddam' were involved in. His curiosity was further piqued by the fact that the spies had defected to their side. Could these men have formed an organization like the Hashshashins[23]? How could they bind people to themselves so tightly and brainwash them?

Mr. Demirkaplan didn't want what he was about to explain to scare his son. He thought about how he could explain it in the mildest way possible.

"Yes, son. Now, what are these men dealing with?" He paused a bit, then continued. "Let's start with huddam. Huddam refers to the use of djinn as servants. It's a practice that has existed since the birth of Islam," he paused a little, "or rather, let's say it's an area of study. They say certain verses in the Quran are hidden with djinn. Using abjad and cifir, these djinn can be summoned. If one can summon the djinn, they can command it."

Alp listened with great curiosity. His first question was about 'abjad' and 'cifir.' Mr. Demirkaplan explained:

"Abjad is a calculation method based on the hidden numbers each letter gives and the numerical value each letter holds. In Arabic, letters are also numbers. Meanings are tried to be derived from the numerical values of words and sentences using abjad. Cifir is a step beyond that. It's based on more advanced mathematical theories. Huddam, through these activities, supposedly come into contact with djinn or it's believed they do. Many people have been involved in this for centuries, but we don't know how successful they've been. In the Middle Ages, Arabs intensely engaged in these activities. Notable researchers like Muhyiddin Arabi emerged. However, the state has always been cold towards these practices; for example, Muhyiddin Arabi was executed."

Mr. Demirkaplan observed his son while talking, checking for any signs of discomfort or fear. Seeing Alp's curiosity, he relaxed and continued.

"They used to talk about these in our youth. There were books written in this field, and even Imam Ja'far al-Sadiq, one of the Prophet's

---

[23] A secret sect founded in the 11th century by Hasan-i Sabbah, affiliated with the Ismaili branch of Shia Islam. The Hashashins were known in the medieval period for their assassinations and covert operations, particularly in Syria and Persia. The name is believed to originate from the use of hashish by its members before missions. Historically, they were renowned for their discipline, secrecy, and loyalty.

grandsons, wrote a book on these topics. Inspired by him, many people in the Arab world began engaging in these practices. Various significant works were produced at different times. Back then, Halit and the Imam believed that these books were lost and that if they could be found, they could decode the secrets and command the djinn. They obtained some works but couldn't find the three main books they were looking for. While these studies were ongoing, as I mentioned before, my uncle banned both of their activities. It was like this in the early years, but now we don't really know what they are doing."

"Is the matter of commanding djinn real?"

Mr. Demirkaplan opened the palm of one hand and pursed his lips as he sat silently for a moment.

"Djinn exist, but how realistic it is to command them, I don't know."

"If these men don't have supernatural powers, how do they deceive so many people? Even the spies you sent?"

"You don't need to show supernatural powers to influence people, son. Look at me, I'm also a community leader with thousands of members. Governors, district governors, and judges come and kiss my hand, they show deep respect for me. Am I a supernatural person? No, it's a psychological phenomenon."

"But do you have followers like theirs, who are always ready to sacrifice themselves?"

Mr. Demirkaplan laughed. "Of course, son. The number is very small because I've reformed, but they still exist. In your grandfathers' time, the structure of the Community was more radical. Creating martyrs within a group is easier than you think. You don't necessarily need religious indoctrination for it. For example, nationalist organizations and radical leftist groups also have such martyrs. It's not much related to religious motivation. It's a different psychology..."

Alp agreed with his father.

The Imam and his followers were tough nuts to crack...

Chapter

29

Raki

Dr. Taner had insisted, "Make an appointment for the earliest possible date," so he made an appointment for two days later. He came to the session alone. They talked for a long time.

Dr. Taner constantly delved into the topic of his relationship with his wife. Although Ali Fuat skillfully handled all the questions, he couldn't stop thinking about his concerns regarding his small penis and premature ejaculation. Serkan Cenet kept appearing in his mind. Dr. Taner, without showing any signs of weariness, kept asking the same questions over and over again.

Ali Fuat made another appointment for a week later as he was leaving. He then went to a tavern in Kadikoy. He sat at a table overlooking the sea and ordered raki and meze[24]. The sky was slowly darkening. He gazed at the unique scenery created by the last rays of the setting sun. He took his first sip without thinking about anything.

After the first glass, Selin appeared in the raki glass. "Think of me first," she seemed to say. Was his wife cheating on him? How could Serkan Cenet's poisoning from mushrooms be a coincidence?

He took a big gulp of the raki. His throat burned because he had added too little water. He popped a few pieces of fruit into his mouth.

---

[24] Small dishes served as appetizers or accompaniments, especially with raki. These can include a variety of cold and hot items such as: olives, cheese, stuffed grape leaves (dolma), grilled vegetables, seafood dishes, meatballs (kofte). Meze is meant to be shared and enjoyed slowly alongside drinks and conversation.

Obviously, they had eaten the mushrooms together. This thought created a different kind of fragility in his heart, beyond anger. Cooking for each other, eating together, the man bringing chocolate to Ece, Selin offering him tea, and taking care of his daughter's school problems... If it was just about sex, why bother with all that? They could have made love when he wasn't around —which was often enough. But whatever was between them wasn't just meaningless sexuality. What if they loved each other?

He drank the rest of his glass in one go.

No, no...

It couldn't be! Selin loved him. They were very happy. They had a sweet little girl. He became tearful. He remembered his daughter's morning words, "Daddy, are you leaving?" How sweetly she said it. No, it was impossible. Besides, she was like an angel. She was the best person in the world. While he was a grumpy person, Selin always managed to be cheerful. She had changed him. She had taught him to smile. She had never made an issue of his sexual problems or the intensity of his job. Anyone else would have left the house long ago, but she was different. She was playful, loving, and pure-hearted. Yes, purehearted. Pure heart...

He finished his raki.

Of course...

That bastard had taken advantage of his wife's good nature. His intention was to approach her sneakily under the guise of a friend. Of course, his angelic wife hadn't understood the intentions of this 'bastard.' She had only tried of the food she had cooked.

He refilled his raki. He reassured himself. His wife wasn't cheating on him.

He needed to deal with the Serkan Cenet matter. He could kill him if he wanted, but would that be right? Ali Fuat was an honorable man. That punishment would be too harsh. The best thing was to let it go, he thought to himself.

It was now completely dark. The sea view was no longer visible. The bright lights of the frequently passing ships and ferries added a unique beauty to the night's darkness. He remembered what Aydin had said in the helicopter and smiled. "The boy was right; it really does look like a star..." he said to himself.

He didn't get in his car. He hailed a taxi instead.

Chapter

30

Ali Fuat at Home

When he opened his eyes in the morning, he was in pain. He moved slightly and looked around, trying to recognize his own bedroom. He stared blankly at the wardrobe, the windows, and the ceiling. The headache continued with full force.

He saw a glass of water and aspirin on the nightstand. He took a pill, drank half the water, and lay back down. While rubbing his forehead with his fingers, he kept looking at the ceiling. The headache wasn't going away.

Selin entered the bedroom, wearing a black tank top that clung to her body and highlighted her large breasts. Her golden blonde hair and tan skin created a sexy look in her black outfit. She sat down next to the bed and placed her hands on her husband's bare, hairy chest. She leaned in and kissed his lips. Selin's blonde hair fell over Ali Fuat's face.

"Did you wake up, my love?"

Ali Fuat looked into his wife's green eyes and saw the smile on her face. He had missed her as if they had been apart for a long time. Selin glanced at the glass on the nightstand. "I thought you'd wake up with a headache this morning. You came home very drunk last night."

Ali Fuat held his wife's hands that were resting on his chest. In a low voice, he said, "Was I very drunk?"

"Yes, my love, you were drunk. Who did you drink so much with?" Selin's loving smile continued with all its charm.

"Alone."

Selin leaned in, their noses touching. "Wouldn't a man take his wife with him?" she said, planting a few small kisses on his lips.

"Sure, honey. Let's go together next time," said Ali Fuat. He hugged her and pulled her down next to him. Her sexy outfit had stirred his feelings.

"Honey, did you buy these recently?"

They were wrapped around each other. As they kissed, Selin briefly paused to ask, "Do you like them?" They continued kissing...

He hadn't planned on making love. Seeing his wife in her new nightgown had aroused him. As their bodies heated up, Selin mentioned, "I had prepared breakfast, my love, if you want..." But her words were lost in the heat of their passionate lovemaking.

Ali Fuat had taken longer to get an erection. He thought it might be due to the alcohol. He climbed on top of her with his large body. Selin was buried under her husband's massive frame. She tried to hold back, to not enjoy it. When her desires soared but couldn't reach full satisfaction, her psyche got disturbed. She thought he would finish quickly anyway.

This time, Ali Fuat surprised both himself and Selin. It was an incredible lovemaking session. It was one of the rare moments in their marriage. He didn't ejaculate for a long time, or couldn't. Selin was amazed. The lovemaking that she had thought would end quickly made every point on her body tremble and took her breath away. Her eyes were smiling.

After their previous lovemaking sessions, Ali Fuat would hang his head and head for the bathroom. Out of habit, he was getting up to go to the bathroom again when Selin, although she hadn't asked in previous times, said, "Where are you going, my love?"

"To the bathroom!"

"Don't go right away, honey," she said, laying him on his back and climbing on top of him...

After the bathroom, Ali Fuat put on his suit. His daughter was awake too. They had breakfast together. Selin was a sight to behold. All thirty-two of her teeth were visible. Ece couldn't make sense of her mother's joy so early in the morning.

"Mommy, are we going out?" she asked with her child's mind. No...

They weren't going out. Her father hadn't bought her mother a gift either. So, what was going on? She didn't understand anything. She left her breakfast half-finished and ran to her parrot.

Ali Fuat spent some time with his daughter and the parrot.

Before leaving the house, Selin found an opportunity to kiss her husband for a long time. "Come home early tonight," she said. Her tone and the way she said it left no need for further explanation.

He went to the headquarters. He couldn't decide what to do about Serkan. Should he shoot him in the head? It wasn't something he hadn't done before. No one would question him, but...

He ordered his men to investigate Serkan.

Chapter

31

Retaliation in Progress

The Council of the Exalted, stunned by Imam Sait's surprise, asked the guards at the door, "How did this man get in?" The guards responded that they hadn't seen anyone entering or exiting except for the tea server.

Mr. Demirkaplan understood the gravity of the situation very well by the end of the meeting. He thought he wouldn't see the Council members for a long time. Now, each of them would run off somewhere. Mrs. Demirkaplan agreed. There was no use for the Council of the Exalted anymore. While not officially dissolved, the council had effectively disbanded itself.

Mr. Demirkaplan, with his wife's approval, decided to handle this matter personally. He would deal with the problem using the community's intelligence organization, and once the job was done, he would put the Council of the Exalted through a major overhaul. He now wanted men who were tightly loyal to him and a bit more courageous.

Cihangir Demirkaplan initiated the operations. As a first step, everyone identified as connected to Imam Sait's group was marked. Those working in the community's companies were immediately dismissed. During this process, Alp played an active role.

The intelligence group began simultaneous operations in Bursa and Konya. They carried out significant work based on information received from community-affiliated police officers within the security forces.

The community's intelligence agents suspected that two guards assigned to Osman Karahan's villa had been bribed. It was impossible not to notice three assassins passing a meter away from them. There could only be one explanation for this incident! They decided to kill both guards. This would declare to everyone that the community did not leave treachery unpunished. Initially, Mr. Demirkaplan opposed this. He couldn't believe the guards were traitors. The only oddity in the murders wasn't just the guards failing to see the killers passing right under their noses. There were many peculiarities. However, the intelligence group insisted that both guards needed to be killed.

The community's intelligence agents received the approval they were waiting for from Mrs. Demirkaplan.

"Cihangir, you know the guards aren't traitors, but hundreds of thousands of people in the community don't. Try to put yourself in the public's shoes. You learn about the murders from television and newspapers. The news tells you, 'Osman Karahan and Faruk Altan were killed. Although the Karahan villa was well-protected, it appears the killers entered through the front door. The guards at the door are suspected of negligence...'" Mrs. Demirkaplan mimicked a news anchor reporting the murders. "Haven't we heard similar things on TV? Now, if you were an ordinary person and didn't know about the peculiarities of the murder, what would you think?"

Mr. Demirkaplan needed no further explanation. He fully understood the situation. To indicate he understood, he cut his wife off with a small addition.

"Prestige..."

"Exactly."

He had to make this decision, difficult as it was. He was saddened. The gears of the system turned mercilessly.

One of the guards was shot while walking from Fomara Square to the Covered Bazaar in Bursa. At the same time, the other guard was gunned down by someone from a white minibus as he was exiting Kucuk Sanayi through the Besevler gate.

Both murders made headlines in the media. The media speculated that the guards had been killed for revenge. Writers and commentators developed their own conspiracy theories. Some even linked the events to the CIA and MOSSAD.

Except for close friends who knew how honest and loyal the two murdered guards were, organized Islamists in the country greeted these killings with the satisfying smile of revenge.

The community's intelligence agents had done their homework well. They embarked on extensive activities to identify Imam Sait's contact in Bursa. All signs pointed to the same place: Yavuz Selim Neighborhood. Known for its reputation in Sharia law, this neighborhood was the center of dozens of small and large sects. Using their connections within these sects, the community began investigating Imam Sait's group in Bursa. They quickly identified and researched the prominent figures and well-informed individuals in Yavuz Selim Neighborhood. They singled out those with weaknesses for money and women and offered large bribes. They brought in well-known models from Istanbul, paid them thousands of dollars, and had them perform temporary marriages[25] with the neighborhood's womanizing hajjis and hodjas. After spending the night with their supposed spouses, the hajjis divorced them by saying, "I divorce you, I divorce you, I divorce you," and the models returned to their colorful lives in Istanbul, unaware of the need for such games but happy with the large sums they had received.

The intelligence group finally identified the name they sought: Davut Buyukdere. This 27-year-old man, who managed all of Imam Sait's operations in Bursa, was an assistant at the Bursa Faculty of Theology. He was kidnapped in a midnight operation and taken to a farmhouse in Soganli Village. They asked him questions about the

---

[25] Muta nikah, also known as nikah mut'ah, is a type of marriage contract in Shi'a Islam for legitimate fulfillment of sexual needs. It's a temporary union with a predetermined duration, ranging from hours to years. The couple agrees on the length of the marriage and any financial arrangements at the outset. This practice is accepted by Shi'a Muslims but is generally not recognized by Sunni Islam.

murders. What were Imam Sait's intentions? Who were the perpetrators of the murders? Initially, the young man answered all questions with "I don't know." After a moderate beating, he mentioned that there were a few radical sects and a very small number of university students loyal to the Imam. He also mentioned the Imam's apartment, where he stayed in one of the flats when he visited. However, these answers were unsatisfactory. They wanted more information, but the young man insisted, "That's all I know."

After each slap, beating, and punch, they repeated their questions, but the "I don't know" response remained unchanged. The only difference was that the initial plain "I don't know" was replaced with "Brother, I swear I don't know," "I swear I don't know," "Oh, ah, God, I don't know." As the torture continued, the "I don't know" responses became raspy and guttural. Soon, the young man was unable to speak. The community's enforcers realized that the young man truly knew nothing. After killing him, they burned his body in the farmhouse's inner yard to prevent identification. The corpse was taken that same night and dumped in a garbage container near the Ilgar Mansion in Muradiye.

Chapter

32

Imam Sait Nurani

He rarely watched this devilish invention, this unclean device. Especially in his youth, he was completely against it. He would get angry if anyone watched it. But the media had become so influential that not watching the news could be considered a significant loss.

He had been following the disturbances in Bursa as much from his own men as from the media. The murder of Davut Buyukdere following the killings of Osman Karahan's two guards had stirred up Bursa. The police, MIT, and most importantly, the Black Shrouds were searching every nook and cranny, trying to find connections to the murders.

After the news ended, the Imam turned off the television. All the news, including local Bursa channels, had the same message: 'Despite the police's intense efforts, the murders remain unsolved...'

He got up from the cushion where he had been sitting cross-legged in front of the TV. He left his room and started pacing in the wide hall of the dergah[26] (Dervish Lodge). The turmoil in Bursa was troubling the Imam.

---

[26] Nowadays, the term dergah is commonly used to describe places where people interested in Sufism gather for spiritual discussions, remembrance (dhikr), and teachings. Traditionally, these were spaces where dervishes were trained, secluded, and underwent spiritual maturation. However, today, dergahs are more focused on preserving the Sufi heritage, offering spiritual guidance, and fostering social cohesion.

Yasin being arrested or taken in for questioning would destroy the Imam. Though there was no reason for his arrest, the Black Shrouds didn't care about justice, law, or regulations. Another danger was the possibility that those who killed Davut Buyukdere might link the crime to Yasin. Any disruption in Yasin's encryption work or his inability to continue could hinder the sect's goal of establishing a 'Caliphate State. He needed to keep Yasin away from the chaos in Bursa, but how?

Bringing him to Konya would attract attention. He couldn't send him to sect members in Istanbul or Sakarya either. The Black Shrouds and the community were conducting extensive profiling.

As Imam Sait continued his walk without straining his elderly body, he was also fingering his prayer beads and stroking his beard. Actually, the safest place was by his side. No one could touch Yasin in Konya, but this would bring another problem. Bringing Yasin to Konya could undermine Imam Sait's authority within the sect. Most of the codebreaking involving djinn was done by Yasin. However, the sect believed that Imam Sait was responsible for all this work.

He realized he had walked too much without noticing. He pulled back to a corner and sat on the cushions. He was sweating. He took out his handkerchief from his robe pocket. After wiping his face, he carefully folded it and put it back in his pocket.

He thought about Yasin's longing for university. How wonderful it would be to enroll Yasin in a university in Istanbul now. And if they rented a house away from prying eyes, Yasin could comfortably continue his work on the codes.

He got up from the cushion he had been sitting crosslegged on. With his head down, he started walking again in the wide hall, looking at the floor. The idea of university made sense to him, but how would it be possible? It was April. Enrollment had long ended. Moreover, to register, one needed to have taken and passed the university entrance exam.

University enrollment seemed impossible at the moment. In that case, sending him as a student preparing for university was the most reasonable idea.

Chapter

33

The Tide is Turning for Yasin

Ilyas Omen, in his room at the Dormitories Institution, hung up the phone in astonishment. The caller was Imam Sait Nurani. To fully comprehend what he had heard, he leaned back in his chair and began to think. He tried to recall every word: "Yasin will prepare for the university entrance exams," "He will attend a preparatory course in Istanbul," "We will rent a house there," "The sect will cover all the expenses!"

He was surprised.

Imam Sait had personally obstructed Yasin's university entrance before, and now he wanted him to prepare for the exam. What had changed? And why did he need to prepare in Istanbul? "Aren't there any prep courses in Bursa?" he thought. Moreover, if he was going to a prep course in Istanbul, why did they need to rent a house? The sect had plenty of houses and dormitories... Due to his strict adherence to the sect hierarchy, Mr. Omen didn't oppose the Sheikh, Imam Sait, and simply said, "Okay," but it gnawed at him inside. The thought of Yasin leaving home deeply saddened him.

He didn't eat much at dinner that evening. He moved a few stuffed grape leaves around on his plate with a fork, then nibbled on a bit of yogurt before getting up from the table. He went to the living room and turned on the television. Mrs. Neriman, feeling uneasy, left her halffinished meal and went to the bedroom.

"What's wrong, Ilyas? You didn't eat anything. Didn't you like the food?" Ilyas replied with a sour expression:

"Don't talk nonsense, Neriman. Have you ever heard me complain about the food in 38 years?"

"Heavens, no, Ilyas. I never have. But seeing you so out of sorts…"

"My mood isn't about the food, woman. It's about Yasin."

Neriman became anxious.

"Oh God, protect us. What happened to Yasin?"

"Nothing has happened. Don't get worked up over nothing."

"Then tell me, for heaven's sake."

Mr. Omen called Yasin and recounted what Imam Sait had told him.

Yasin's face lit up with joy. Going to university was his biggest dream. The exam was two months away, but that didn't matter. There was no question that he would pass the exam. He went to his room and took his university preparation books off the shelf. Physics, math, chemistry, biology, literature, he knew all these subjects at an excellent level. Physics and math, in particular, were Yasin's hobbies. He followed many scientific publications and journals, constantly improving himself. His interest in abjad, cifir, and huddam also required a good knowledge of physics and math. He was already confident he would pass the exam.

That night, Yasin went to bed dreaming of studying computer engineering at Bogazici University. He would soon have co-ed environments and friends. He tossed and turned several times, unable to sleep, dreaming of the colorful life awaiting him in Istanbul.

Neriman and Ilyas lay with their backs turned to each other, both unable to sleep. Neriman worried about what her son would eat and drink alone in Istanbul. The separation was already breaking her heart. Despite not being able to oppose the Imam, Ilyas couldn't make sense of the Istanbul plan either.

Ilyas didn't sleep all night. After performing the morning prayer, he went to the living room. He sat in a chair without turning on the lights. Even while praying, his mind was preoccupied with his son. He couldn't focus on his prayer. "God, please accept it," he thought. If his son had to go to Istanbul, "At least I could request a transfer and take my wife with me," he thought. After all, what ties did they have in Bursa? He had married off his two daughters. If the transfer didn't work out, he could even consider retirement. With the comfort of having partially solved the problem, he fell asleep on the chair.

Chapter

34

Securing a Spot for Yasin

Mr. Omen leaned back in his office chair after hanging up the phone. He had called Imam Sait as soon as he arrived at work. He had shared his idea of going to Istanbul with Yasin. However, the Imam insisted that Yasin must go alone. He wouldn't be able to conduct his encryption work comfortably in a family environment. These tasks required a specially consecrated room protected by prayers. If Mrs. Omen entered the room while cleaning and started to meddle with things, it could activate the djinn. These uncontrolled entities could harm Neriman or cause difficulties for Yasin in subsequent work. The Imam did not accept Mr. Omen's proposal. Instead, he suggested finding a relative or compatriot in Istanbul.

Mr. Omen, still leaning back in his chair, pondered over the conversation. He started thinking about who they knew in Istanbul as friends or fellow townsmen.

Yasin woke up with great joy. It felt like he had had the best sleep of his life. He opened the curtains to see the view of the forest. He wiped the foggy glass with his hand. Dark clouds covered the sky, making the weather look pale and gloomy. A light drizzle was falling. Yasin felt as happy as if he were looking at the Bosphorus view from

Galata Tower[27] on a sunny July day. When he squinted and looked to the left side of the forested area, he saw the endless shores of Cuba. Chocolate-colored, big-bottomed mixed-race girls were lying around sunbathing, swimming, and joking with each other. The setting seemed to be waiting for Yasin.

He had gotten out of his warm bed and shivered. He put on the cardigan he had hung on the chair the night before. He went to the kitchen. His mother was preparing breakfast. She seemed as happy as when she had held her first grandchild. Although there was no smile on her lips, the lines on her face were more pronounced, her eyes were watery, and her cheeks were gaunt. Despite all this, he felt that his mother was happy.

"Good morning, mom," he said. He poured himself some tea and sat at the breakfast table. He hadn't called her "mom" since he was a child.

After finishing his breakfast, Yasin went to his room. He opened his laptop and sat down. He typed "Istanbul" into the Google search engine. He started opening the top results from the millions that appeared. He then typed "Bogazici University" and searched again. He entered the university's official website. He was trying to familiarize himself with his future university by looking at the photos. He examined the graduation pictures and looked at the students throwing their caps into the air.

Mr. Omen's mind was so preoccupied with his son that he forgot many tasks he was supposed to do that day. He was pondering how to solve the "relative" issue. Most of the relatives were in Sakarya. Among those in Istanbul, no suitable name came to mind. Most were elderly, people who Yasin needed was a young companion. He thought hard. To ensure he didn't forget anyone, he opened his phone book and looked through the names one by one.

---

[27]   A historic tower located in Istanbul's Galata district, built by the Genoese in the 14th century. It is one of the city's iconic landmarks, offering panoramic views of Istanbul. Over the centuries, it has served as a fire watchtower and a prison.

While flipping through the phone book, he saw "Veysel Kurak/ Shoe Repair" written down. The name of his childhood friend, the shoe repairman from Sakarya, sparked something. Of course! Veysel's son had gotten into Kabatas Boys' High School in middle school. Back then, he had helped them with dormitory arrangements. What happened to that boy afterward? He strained his memory. What was his name again? Yes, Erkan! The boy's name was Erkan. "I'd better call Veysel," he thought. He dialed the numbers.

———m———

At dinner, Mr. Omen was recounting the day's developments to his wife and son:

"Honey, do you remember Veysel, the shoe repairman?"

"How could I forget? Sebahat's husband."

"I don't know his wife's name."

"So, what happened?"

"Veysel had a son. Remember, he got into a school in Istanbul and asked us for help with the dormitory? Do you remember?"

"For God's sake, Ilyas, are you going to keep asking if I remember? Just tell me what happened."

"Lord, grant me patience! I'm telling you, Neriman. After finishing high school in Istanbul, Veysel's son got into literature teaching. He used to stay with his aunt. Now, he's living with a friend. I told Veysel about our son's situation. God bless him, he was very concerned. He immediately called his son. The boy said he would help, but there are no rental apartments in the building. There is one, but it's for sale. Anyway, I got the boy's address and phone number. Then I called Imam Sait and explained the situation. The Imam said, 'No problem.' "Tomorrow, we'll buy the apartment, furnish it, and settle Yasin there,' he said."

Chapter

35

Student House

After finishing his morning workout, Erkan took a shower. Wrapping a towel around his waist, he stood in front of the mirror and began to dry his hair. His long, wavy hair, which had started to show streaks of white, looked perfect with gel but was just as bad without it. While drying his hair, he also admired his muscles. He wasn't a bulky bodybuilder, but he wasn't bad either. Tossing the towel aside, he put on his boxer shorts with the "Tasmanian Devil" picture on them. Smiling softly, he murmured, "Oh, my divine love..." The first day he wore those boxers, Bahar had said, "Let me stay with you," and didn't return to her apartment upstairs. Another of their frequent lovemaking sessions ensued. After long kisses and whispered 'I love you's into each other's ears, Bahar had burst into laughter when she saw Erkan's "Tasmanian Devil" boxers as she undid his shorts.

"Do you like it, my love? I just bought it."

"Oh, I love it... i!"

"Isn't it nice, my love?"

"Nice, nice, hahaha!"

That day, they both had a lot of fun. It had been an event that made their routine lovemaking different. Erkan put on his black sleeveless shirt. He picked up his phone and called the number saved under the nickname 'kardelen'. Bahar's sleepy voice answered on the other end.

"I'm preparing breakfast, come over." Their relationship had been going on for three years. Erkan was in his third year of literature, and

Bahar was in her fourth year of physics. They understood and loved each other very much. Bahar was staying with her school friends Melisa and Pelin. Erkan shared the same apartment with his classmate Can. Just like Erkan and Bahar, Melisa and Can were also a couple. Even though they lived in separate apartments, they were often together. Erkan was a semi-professional chef. He had learned the trade while staying with his aunt during his high school years. His aunt was a chef at Dedeman in Taksim[28]. Erkan would come home immediately after school and not go anywhere else. Perhaps due to the intimidation of the big city, he was very shy and didn't wander around outside. His aunt would take him to the hotel so he wouldn't get bored at home. Over time, all the staff in the hotel's kitchen embraced this cute boy. Within a year or two, Erkan had mastered the job. He prayed for his aunt whenever he thought of those days. He owed his current financial comfort to her. By working two days a week, he earned enough money to cover all his expenses. If he could increase what he earned from cooking, he would buy musical instruments online. He would later sell the guitars, amps, and pedals he bought at bargain prices for good prices. He also played acoustic guitar himself.

They were continuing their breakfast when Can walked into the kitchen, still half-asleep. He was blinking, yawning, and stretching. "Good morning," he mumbled.

"Dude, what's up? Did you see the time wrong? It's not even noon yet!" Erkan teased his housemate's habit of oversleeping.

Can poured a cup of tea, spilling some over the edge.

"Seriously, why are you up early? Are you sick? Do you have an exam?"

"For heaven's sake," said Can, stretching out the words irritably.

"I'm really curious. Tell me! It's like a panda mating event for you to get up early!" This time, Bahar couldn't hold back her laughter. Can stared at them with sleepy eyes and said, "I got up because of some jerk."

"Who is this jerk?"

---

[28]   The Dedeman Istanbul Hotel is a 5-star establishment in Taksim, a central district of Istanbul. Located near Taksim Square, it offers modern amenities and Bosphorus views. Its prime location provides easy access to major attractions, making it popular among tourists and business travelers alike.

"Erkan, give it a rest. I'm already off balance, I'm not myself. Don't make me swear in front of the girl."

"Go back to bed, who's stopping you?"

"Damn it, don't you have a court hearing today?"

"Shit!"

"Yeah, shit. I would be sleeping now if I hadn't witnessed a jerk like you." Erkan and Bahar had gotten serious.

"Is it today, are you sure?"

"Of course, it is. I had saved the date on my phone."

Two years ago, during the harshest days of winter. A young manager in his 30s, hurrying to escape the morning chill, entered the business building and took the elevator. Just as the doors were closing, a figure with a long, thin coat, leather gloves, and a helmet managed to squeeze inside. The young manager, standing by the control panel of the spacious elevator, asked politely before pressing his floor, "Which floor?" At that moment, he received a violent punch to the face. The elevator camera showed the helmeted man cornering the young manager in a suit and headbutting him. The young man's face was covered in blood. The impact of the helmet had broken his nose, jaw, teeth, and cut his eyebrows. Within a few seconds, the attacker finished his job and exited the elevator. Before security noticed, he sped away on a motorcycle with a mud-covered license plate.

The court case was opened based on these images. The young manager's family claimed that the person who brutally beat their son was Erkan. Their son had previously dated Erkan's aunt's daughter. After their relationship ended, the girl attempted suicide, and Erkan, blaming their son, sought revenge. However, they couldn't prove it. The person's face wasn't visible in the cameras, and there were no fingerprints due to the gloves.

Erkan listed Bahar and Can as witnesses. In his statement to the court, he claimed he was at home that morning, sleeping with his girlfriend! They had woken up around noon and went to university with Can. They attended a 2PM class, and their signatures were on the attendance sheet. The last part of the statement was indeed true. Erkan had planned everything perfectly. He came home and told Bahar and Can about the incident. He also mentioned that he would likely be interrogated. He made them memorize what to tell the police. While taking Can to school, he asked Bahar to prepare a breakfast for three and leave the table as if it had been eaten.

Erkan who was fond of detective novels, had arranged everything flawlessly. After overcoming the initial shock, Can and Bahar were very angry. But Erkan believed he had done the right thing.

This wasn't his first incident. Once, he had followed the Principle who had slapped Can in public and hit him hard with a knuckleduster in the bathroom. The Principle almost died.

After that incident, Can and Bahar decided not to tell Erkan about any problems they faced. They also tried hard to persuade him to abandon his vengeful nature. The fact that the Principle nearly died in the last incident caused Yasin to feel guilty.

After finishing their breakfast, they left. They were waiting for their turn in the courtroom. There was a brief silence. To break the boring silence, Bahar said, "The kid who bought the top apartment is from your hometown!"

"Yes, he is preparing for university. He is going to attend a prep school." Can joined the conversation. "Isn't there a prep school where he came from?"

"People's actions are hard to understand. With two months left for the exam, they come and rent a house." Bahar corrected her boyfriend's mistake. "They didn't rent it, love, they bought it."

"Yeah, they bought it. Just to be close to me. I don't get it. I told his father, if he is only staying for two months, don't rent a house, he can stay with us, but..." Can speculated, "Could it be for a transfer? Prep schools in Istanbul buy students who can become national top scorers."

"Maybe. His father is a public servant; he can't just come and buy a $150,000 apartment like that."

As Erkan, Can, and Bahar continued chatting about Yasin, the court usher called out the name "Erkan Kurak" from the list in his hand.

Chapter

36

The House is Ready

It looked like a wealthy student's house, but this was not a problem from the Imam's perspective. The concern was that the house might appear to be a sect house. The Imam had a long talk with Yasin. He advised Yasin not to meet with anyone from the community or the sect, not to make friends with Islamists, and not to go to the mosque, including for Friday prayers. He also warned Yasin not to become too close with the kid from his hometown and not to let him into his study room.

Yasin was enrolled in a major prep school's Bakirkoy branch. The teachers at the prep school were astonished by this 'super' student who arrived just two months before the exam. In the placement test, he solved physics, math, geometry, and Turkish with 100% accuracy. He had one mistake in chemistry and three in biology. The prep school administrators placed Yasin in a special class. This class, called the project class, consisted of elite students aiming for the top rank in the country. Among these students, who were brought in from various places with big gifts and money, Yasin was the only one who came on his own.

He didn't like his new class at all. It was full of people who constantly solved questions and didn't chat outside of lessons. However, the lively students and girls he saw in the cafeteria... That's what he had come to Istanbul for. He didn't need a prep school to get into university. He was upset about being placed in such an unappealing class. Girls who didn't wear makeup to save time, boys who didn't use gel in their hair, people who studied even during breaks, and asked each other math puzzles – they were all colorless and unpleasant. Yasin was tired of living as one of them for years.

He thought about talking to the administration to change his class but didn't have the courage.

He was comfortable at home. He started decorating his room according to his own taste. First, he bought a poster of the movie "The Sixth Sense" and hung it in his room. He bought a poster of the movie "The Others" and hung that too. He fortified the inside of the house, especially his study room, with protective walls.

He didn't know anyone in the apartment except Erkan. He had only met him twice anyway.

He continued his cipher work at full speed. He had all his books brought from Bursa. Although everything was better compared to Bursa, he couldn't capture the atmosphere he wanted. He hoped the future would be better.

Chapter

37

Meeting New Friends

After boiling the broccoli, he chopped it and added it to the now-cooked onions. He sautéed it a bit and then cracked two eggs. He mixed the broccoli with eggs and the previously boiled pasta. After placing it in a large dish, he poured his special sauce over it.

Bahar had brought down the mushroom salad she prepared at her place. All the preparations were for Yasin. Erkan planned to introduce Yasin to his friends over a dinner party.

"Love, let's call everyone now."

Bahar called the girls and asked them to come downstairs. Erkan also called Yasin. Shortly after, Can arrived, having gone to the market to buy red wine.

After the introductions and some chit-chat, they started eating. Without asking, Can poured wine for everyone. While eating, Yasin looked at the wine in front of him. It seemed like the key to a secret door, one that would pull him out of the sect world and into a colorful life. The three beautiful girls at the table seemed to be signs of this. Should he drink it? He kept thinking about this while eating. Imam Sait appeared in his mind. Then he thought of his father. He saw the glass as a step towards approaching the girls. It was like an elixir, it would change him. It had been placed before him without being asked, just like other stages of his life. At those times, it was the Imam who placed the glasses... A voice from the past scratched his ear:

"We will get you a computer course,"

"You will specialize in mathematics and physics!"

"You will not go to university!"

"You will move to Bursa!"

"You will have no friends other than those we choose!"

"You will solve the ciphers!"

"You will go to Istanbul!"

Now there was another glass. He wanted to reach for the wine. He wanted to take a sip. Again, the silhouette of the Imam appeared, looking at him with all his anger. Then his father appeared, standing behind the Imam, supporting him.

No one could understand why Yasin was sweating profusely. The house wasn't that hot. They couldn't understand the internal struggle Yasin was experiencing.

He wanted to try one more time. He wanted to reach for his freedom. Move his hand... He experienced deep darkness inside. He heard the closing of prison doors.

"Yasin... Yasin... Shhh Yasin. Are you sleeping? Eat your food."

He was startled. It was Bahar's voice. After swallowing, he looked up. With her black hair and blue eyes, she was right in front of him. There was a faint anger on her face.

The others were also looking at him. Sweat dripped from his nose, chin, and cheeks onto the table.

"Careful, idiot, your sweat is dripping," said Bahar. The other girls also supported her. "Fool! Erkan, where did you find this guy?" they said. Yasin couldn't respond, couldn't look any of them in the eye.

"Why didn't you drink the wine, man? We offered it to you, even if it was poison, you should drink it." This time it was Can. Erkan grabbed his arm. He probably was going to say, "You have no place in our world, buddy," and kick him out.

Yasin... He felt shaken.

"Are you sick, what's wrong?"

"Are you okay? Let's wash your face."

Erkan helped him up from the table. Was he going to throw him out? For a moment, he wanted to beg. He wanted to look at the girls. It was the first time he sat at the same table with girls who weren't his relatives. They had said "Hello" and shook his hand. He wanted to say,

"Please don't throw me out, brother Erkan," but the words wouldn't come out of his mouth.

The water from the tap hit the sink. As a wet hand caressed his face, he noticed his reflection in the mirror. Erkan was beside him, splashing water on his face.

"Brother, what happened?"

"I don't know, buddy, you suddenly got ill. You lost yourself."

They returned to the meal. Those at the table were looking at Erkan, expecting an explanation. Without Yasin noticing, Erkan looked at them and shrugged as if to say, "I don't understand."

The meal continued. Despite losing his appetite, he tried to finish what was on his plate. The only thing he didn't touch was the wine.

After the meal, they moved to the TV. They turned on Dream TV. Erkan liked the music programs there.

"What will you apply for, Yasin?" asked Melisa.

"Hopefully, Bogazici University Computer Engineering."

Melisa, who was studying Art Education at Istanbul University, chuckled under her breath.

"Hopefully, Yasin. But you know, these things don't happen just with hope."

"Good," he said, gathering some courage, "Very good."

Yasin's shyness caught everyone's attention. "If you struggle with anything in physics, let me know," said Bahar.

"God bless you," said Yasin. Then he regretted it. It was a habit. He wished he had said, "Thanks." Thinking he might not be too late, he added, "Thanks." He had messed everything up. He kept looking at his hands. He checked his nails. They were clean. He thought, "I hope my feet don't smell." He had washed and put on clean socks before coming. Normally, they didn't smell anyway.

The girls found Yasin's state quite endearing. Shy, honorable, pure Anatolian boy...

"How many correct answers did you get in physics in the last trial exam?" Bahar asked, wanting to know his weak points and help him.

"I got them all right," said Yasin. For a brief moment, he looked up at Bahar and Pelin, who was sitting next to her. Then he started looking at his hands again. He interlocked his fingers and occasionally tapped his knee rhythmically.

Erkan and Can were engrossed in their backgammon game. Bahar was amazed that Yasin was so good at physics. "Your physics teacher must be very good?" she asked. "Good," said Yasin. Then he felt the need to explain briefly. "He's very inadequate on topics like astrophysics and black holes. In fact, he knows nothing about them," he said. Bahar was surprised. These were topics that even physics professors struggled with. They were newly developing fields. There was no way a prep school physics teacher could know these.

"Do you know the topics you mentioned?" she asked.

"Yes, I know them very well," said Yasin. He rubbed his toes together, watching from the corner of his eye.

"Can you explain black holes? I'd like to learn."

"Sure." Yasin said. He wanted to say, "Sure, but it would take at least a month," but could only manage to say, "Sure." Bahar brought a notebook and pen and sat next to Yasin, with Melisa on his other side. Pelin, taking advantage of her small size, sat on Melisa's lap. She didn't want to miss a single moment. Erkan and Can couldn't understand the sudden activity in the room. They looked for a moment and then continued with their game.

Yasin felt like he was about to suffocate. He took the pen with trembling hands. Melisa's shoulder was touching his. He felt her breath on his cheek.

He gave a short, roughly twenty-minute introduction. He drew shapes and wrote some formulas. He used a heavy language. Bahar was stunned. This kid was a genius. While Bahar could grasp bits and pieces of what he was talking about, the others understood nothing. Only Pelin, who studied mathematics, realized that Yasin was also a highlevel mathematician.

Yasin had relaxed a bit while teaching. When he stopped to take a break, he noticed the girls had spread out quite a bit. Their arms, legs, and shoulders were touching his body. He shivered with a mix of excitement and anxiety.

After the teaching session, the girls went back to their seats. Bahar carefully folded Yasin's notes and placed them on the table.

Everyone in the room looked at Yasin with respect. Erkan and Can had finished their game. It wasn't clear from their faces who had won.

The soft sound of Duman[29]'s "Maybe I need to get used to it" started playing on the TV. Erkan turned up the volume. He liked the band and the song. The room filled with the beautiful melody of the guitar and the raspy voice of the vocalist.

Pelin wondered what kind of music this "superior human" listened to.

"What kind of music do you listen to?" she asked. Yasin didn't have a specific type. In Konya, he was made to listen to religious hymns. His friends in Bursa listened to instrumental music. Other than religious hymns, music with human voices was not allowed. Yasin didn't like hymns or instrumental music. He couldn't decide what to say. If he mentioned folk, rock, pop, or rap, they might ask, "Which band do you listen to?" After a brief indecision, he said, "Instrumental music."

She was a petite and cute girl, Pelin. Her height and age were just right. These features caught the attention of others too. The conversation seemed to continue over music.

Erkan wondered if the prodigy child played any instruments.

"No," replied Yasin. He didn't know how to play any instrument. For a moment, those in the room imagined he might pull out a harmonica from his pocket and start playing blues pieces, or go up to his apartment to fetch his saxophone and play jazz pieces they had never heard before.

Erkan got up to brew some tea. From above, he noticed Yasin sitting hunched in the middle of the three-seater sofa.

"Is the house cold? If you're cold, I can turn up the thermostat," he said. Yasin wasn't cold. The temperature of the house was quite good.

Erkan went to the kitchen to put on the tea, and Can went to his room to get the photos he thought of showing the girls. They both returned promptly. The girls were joyfully examining the photos, while Erkan, having already seen them, was not interested.

The girls really liked the computer-printed photos. In one, Hitler was saluting the Nazi troops, and next to him was Can. He had edited

---

[29] Duman is a popular Turkish rock band formed in 1999 in Istanbul. The band's name means "smoke" in Turkish. They are known for their alternative rock sound and poetic lyrics. Duman has been one of the most influential and successful rock bands in Turkey over the past two decades.

his face onto the officer next to Hitler. In another photo, he had put Bahar's face in place of an astronaut's face going into space. They laughed a lot at the last photo, where a beautiful girl was reading the 'Kadınca[30]' magazine. On the magazine cover was Erkan's photo with the headline 'Women Desire Erkan' in big letters.

Can had also prepared a surprise for his girlfriend Melisa. He had edited the faces of a couple at a wedding table and placed himself and his girlfriend. The girls really liked this picture.

Pelin asked, "How do you do these?" Before Can could answer, Melisa interjected, "There's a program for it, it's very easy." Can continued explaining.

"In fact, they can even edit a character in a movie. For example, they can replace an actor's face with yours and make it look like you are acting in the film. It's not very realistic, but it's still fun."

Pelin smiled. "Do it, let's watch."

They were all laughing and having fun. Erkan said, "Bro, seriously, do it, it'll be hilarious." Can said the program was on a U.S.-based website and that the site required membership. Yasin, in a low voice, joined the conversation from where he was sitting. "Do you want me to hack the site and download the program?" He was a bit shy. Suddenly, everyone in the room paid attention. So, he understood computers too. Just as Bahar got excited about physics, now Can was excited.

"Honestly, man, we've tried a lot, but give it a go," he said. They all got up and went to Can's room. Erkan went to the kitchen, brewed the boiling water, and turned down the stove.

Yasin sat at the computer. First, he checked the power, speed, and capacity. Compared to his own computers, this was like a Tetris game. He examined the programs Can used for hacking. They were all amateur programs. "These programs can't break the passwords of strong sites," he said. He asked for the name of the site. He examined the site thoroughly. It was impossible with this computer and these programs. But with his own computer, he could easily handle it. He said he was sorry and explained the situation.

Can really wanted this program. At that moment, he made an offer that had never crossed Yasin's mind. "No problem. Let's go to your

---

30   Womanly

place, download the program, and load it onto a CD," he said. Yasin couldn't respond. The Imam had said not to bring strangers into the room. Although Erkan intervened by saying, "Forget it, the tea is ready. Let's drink it first and then you can handle it," Can was insistent.

"Bro, you guys drink. Let's just go out for a couple of minutes and handle this, right Yasin?" said Can.

"Sure," was all Yasin could say.

The girls insisted on coming along too. They were curious about his house and wanted to see his performance on the computer.

Yasin felt alone.

"Erkan, you come too."

He was surprised he could say that. A smile appeared on his face. The Imam had said, "Don't bring anyone into the house." Even though his heart was heavy, he was proud of himself.

They all went out together.

The living room furniture, the television, and the carpets were all very nice. When they entered Yasin's study room, everyone was amazed. Hundreds of books, four computers, and movie posters on the walls; it didn't resemble a typical study room they were used to seeing. Although there were two more rooms available in the house, Yasin had made the largest room his study and placed his bed there too. He didn't feel the need for a separate bedroom.

Can said, "Bro, what is all this? It looks like an internet cafe." Melisa looked at the original posters of THE SIXTH SENSE, WHAT DREAMS MAY COME, and GHOST. "Where did you find these? Did you bring them from Europe?" she asked. "No, I got them from here," said Yasin.

A strange figure drawn on papyrus caught Bahar's attention. It had 'YHVH' written underneath. She asked its meaning. She couldn't make sense of it. Yasin couldn't explain it. Even if he did, he didn't think Bahar would understand. "An old Jewish ritual," he said.

Erkan entered the room with a tray in his hand, having taken the teapot to the kitchen to get it ready for serving. "Your kitchen is very nice," he said. He was about to say it was quite a rich kitchen for a student, but he forgot the kitchen when he saw the study room. After distributing the tea, he started looking at the books. He couldn't understand the language of many of them; they were old books. This piqued his curiosity. Yasin was uncomfortable with Erkan touching his books, but he couldn't say anything. Erkan pulled a book called 'Kenzul Havas' from the shelf. It was written in a language he guessed was Arabic. "What's this?" he asked. Yasin started to sweat. Erkan was straining his mind. He remembered the name Havas from somewhere but couldn't quite place it. "What does Havas mean?" he asked, lifting his head from the book and looking at Yasin. His facial expressions were screaming that he was uncomfortable. Erkan interpreted this expression as 'he doesn't like his books being handled' and put the book back.

Can wanted Yasin to get on the computer as soon as possible. "Come on, man," he said. Yasin broke the security codes and downloaded the program Can wanted.

Can watched in amazement as the site they had struggled to break for so long was cracked within a few minutes.

As Erkan observed the surroundings, he saw a book titled 'Kabbalah'. Considering Yasin's previous state, he didn't pick up the book. If he remembered correctly, Kabbalah was a heretical ideology practiced by Jews. What were such books doing in the house?

Once they finished the computer-related tasks, each of them sat in a corner. Yasin sat on his bed. Pelin, although there was a chair she could sit on, moved next to Yasin.

After finishing their tea, they went down to Erkan's place. Can immediately sat at his computer and started installing the program. He wanted to see what it was like.

The others moved to the living room. The girls were asking many questions. Where did you learn physics? How can you use a computer so well? Which high school did you graduate from? Which foreign languages do you know?

Yasin gave short answers. That evening, there were two questions that took his breath away. One came from Pelin. "Do you have a girlfriend?" It was the first time Yasin had faced such a question. He didn't know what to say. "No," he managed to say with difficulty. Pelin was embarrassed too. She had asked the question suddenly. Melisa and Bahar laughed quietly.

These dialogues didn't catch Erkan's attention at all. His mind was still on the books. The second question that troubled his heart came from Erkan. "What are Kenzul Havas and Kabbalah about? Your bookshelf was filled with these kinds of old books. What are all these?"

Yasin didn't know how to explain. He was already flustered by Pelin's question.

"Kabbalah is Jewish mysticism. It has been around for two thousand years," he said. After swallowing, he continued. "In Hebrew and Chaldean, there are no separate numerical characters other than letters. Therefore, every number is a word, and every word is a number. Kabbalah studies these relationships." These words caught the attention of Erkan and the girls.

Erkan asked if Kabbalah was a heretical ideology. "Definitely not," said Yasin.

"It's a completely consistent and logical science."

Erkan, thinking that the concept of Havas was related to djinn, asked about it. This question made the girls uneasy.

Yasin's answer would make them even more nervous.

"Yes, it's a book about djinn. Havas and hoodoo are the arts of controlling djinn," he said. Everyone in the room was attentive. Erkan, thinking the book was written in Arabic or a similar alphabet, asked if Yasin could read it.

Yasin said, "I know Hebrew, Chaldean, Aramaic, Arabic, and almost all their dialects very well. The book is in Arabic." Actually, he shouldn't have given this information, but the girls were looking into his eyes. What else could he talk about? He knew nothing about sports, music, or gossip. These were the topics he could discuss, and he felt the girls were impressed. "Oh well, what would the Imam know?" he thought to himself.

The parts about djinn caught the girls' interest.

"How do you control djinn?" they asked. Yasin felt he needed to give a brief explanation. Maybe he shouldn't take the conversation to this level. But the girls, especially Pelin, were looking into his mouth.

"Some prayers have a guardian or servant. If recited correctly, it is possible to command that servant. Havas deals with these," he said.

The girls were looking as if they were mesmerized. Erkan was uneasy. What could a student in his twenties, preparing for university, have to do with such topics?

Pelin asked, "Do you know how to summon spirits?" Melisa and Bahar confirmed the question with their looks.

"There is no such thing as summoning spirits," said Yasin. After thinking for a while about how to express it, he said, "What is known as spirit summoning among the public is actually very dangerous. Because the thing that comes is not a spirit."

"Then what is it?" they asked.

"A djinn, a demon."

The girls' hair stood on end. Melisa asked, "What do you mean?"

They were both scared and wanted to talk about this topic. Erkan noticed the girls were scared. He wanted to intervene, to cut it off. He mentioned coffee, but the girls shut him up. All three were focused on Yasin.

"A spirit cannot come to this world after passing into eternity."

"The entities that can cross from their dimension to ours are djinn. What we call Spiritualism or spirit summoning is very dangerous. If the summoned djinn is malevolent, it can bring various calamities upon the people present."

"Are there good djinn too?" Bahar asked.

Before Yasin could answer, Erkan jumped in, "Or should we ask this way: Do djinn exist?"

Yasin found Erkan's question odd. There was a verse in the Quran. Could Erkan not be a Muslim? How could he ask such a question?

"Yes," Yasin said. "Djinn exist." He thought for a while. "It's a long topic, but let me put it this way: there are good and bad djinn. They live in their own dimension. If a bad djinn is summoned and we don't know how to protect ourselves, we can face all kinds of dangers, including death," he said. The girls thought of spirit summoning as a social amusement. They didn't fully accept what Yasin said. They believed that the entity summoned was a spirit, not a djinn.

Melisa said, "But dear Yasin, I participated a couple of times. The spirit of the person summoned came and knew many things. It recognized the people there. It talked about old events it had experienced. It didn't harm anyone."

After listening to Melisa, Yasin thought about how to give an example for better understanding. "It's possible," he said. He paused for a moment. "The entity that knows all these things is not a spirit but a djinn," he said. Actually, he was just giving headlines. He needed to talk at length about every sentence he said. "Djinn live for about 1000 to 1400 years. They never forget. Their concepts of time and space are very different from ours. They can know the details of a person's life. The fact that the djinn summoned during a spirit summoning didn't harm anyone is purely coincidental. I'm not saying all djinn are bad; there are good ones too. But it's a risk. Let me give an example."

The girls were listening with curiosity. Erkan wished this topic would close as soon as possible. Yasin shaped the example in his mind. The usually reserved Yasin, who spoke only when asked and gave short answers, had suddenly transformed. He was speaking like a flowing river. He had changed his timid sitting posture, at least a bit. He could look at the girls while talking now.

"Imagine you entered a dormitory room at midnight. There are a few people sleeping, but you don't know any of them. You randomly wake one person up and pull them out of bed. The person you wake up will ask why you woke them up. Of course, you have no answer. From that point on, the person will react according to their personality. If they are irritable, they will likely yell and kick you out of the room. If they have a vengeful, psychopathic nature, they will harm you physically. If they are mild-mannered, they will endure it and try to go back to sleep. It's all up to chance... Spirit summoning is exactly like this. The entity you think you are summoning is a djinn. If this djinn is a good djinn, there's not much of a problem; if it's a bad djinn and you don't know the protective prayers..."

They were all affected. Yasin seemed knowledgeable on this topic and had a lot more to say.

"Do you know the protective prayers? Can you summon a djinn and then send it away?" Melisa asked. That was nothing compared to what Yasin knew. "Of course," Yasin replied. He was pleased with the girls' interest. Talking about a subject he was proficient in had boosted his confidence.

Imam Sait came to his mind. He had warned him hundreds of times not to discuss these topics with anyone. Although he felt he had somewhat escaped the Imam's psychological pressure, he thought that the girls' curiosity and desires were endless.

Suddenly, the door opened. The girls jumped in their seats. It was Can who had come in. "Hey, man, thanks! The program is awesome!" he said. The topic in the room had changed so much that they couldn't comprehend what was being said for a moment.

"No problem."

It was good that the topic had changed. Thinking "Enough of this," he excused himself.

When he reached his apartment door and took out his key to open it, he saw Pelin quietly coming up the stairs. He smiled slightly. He was surprised but maintained his confident demeanor. He knew he had made Pelin fall for him, drawn into his charisma. She had a cellphone in her hand.

"Sweetheart, you forgot your phone," Pelin said, trying to use all her charm. She had unbuttoned one more button on her shirt. She wasn't like that a while ago. Her chest was quite visible. "Thanks, darling," Yasin said. As he took the phone, he held her hand. They looked at each other for a while. With their petite frames, they were very compatible. Yasin slowly approached. They started kissing. Pelin wrapped her arms around his neck. Yasin held her waist.

When the neighbor across the hall heard footsteps, she became curious and started watching through the peephole. She saw the new kid. He was standing right in front of the door across the hall with a key in his hand. The apartment's automatic light had gone out. A small beam of light from the portable fluorescent lamp placed on each floor for power outages was filtering through the corner. The woman could see that Yasin was still standing. Was he sick? Trusting that her husband was at home, she opened the door. The light from her house illuminated Yasin a bit, but he wasn't moving.

"Son, are you sick?" she asked. Yasin didn't hear. "Are you sick, my boy?" she shouted.

Suddenly, Pelin disappeared. Yasin turned to look at the woman. He glared with anger. He quickly opened his door and entered his apartment.

Chapter

38

Serkan Cenet is Sick

Ali Fuat lit a cigarette. His men had conducted extensive research on Serkan Cenet. He took the file and began flipping through the pages.

He was exhausted. He couldn't believe that his wife was cheating on him, that she loved someone else. He couldn't bear it. In a moment of rage, he feared he might go downstairs and empty the magazine into his own head. He had to do something. Should he send her to another city? Or should he just pull the trigger on himself?

The intelligence report in his hand delivered a surprising piece of news. He couldn't decide whether it was something to be happy about or saddened by. Inspector Serkan Cenet had cancer. He was undergoing treatment.

He had carried out the investigation with entirely different intentions. Among the possibilities were kidnapping and even killing him, but... Now everything had changed dimensions. He needed to say hello to the Serkan Cenet issue once again, from scratch.

He wasn't the type to revel in others' misfortune; he was an honest, principled man, but it was as if a part of his heart was secretly smiling.

Chapter

39

Meeting with the Psychologist

They had booked a two-hour appointment for that day. Dr. Taner wanted to spend an hour with Ece and another hour with Selin. He thought the information provided by her mother would be crucial in resolving Ece's fears. Dr. Taner first took Selin into the consultation room. While Selin sat across from him, he was seriously flipping through the file in front of him. He had made some personal notes about Ece. He pulled out that paper and began to review it. With many patients, he could forget the details. Reviewing the relevant person's file before the session was helpful.

After reading all the notes about Ece, he looked up at Selin with the same seriousness. He thought she was a beautiful woman, though a bit short.

Dr. Taner started talking to Selin about trivial matters to help her relax. Gradually, he moved on to Ece's issues. "Your husband has told you about your daughter's fears, right?" he asked. Yes, Ali Fuat had told her before they came. Actually, he had planned not to, but when the psychologist requested a session with Selin, he had no choice.

"He did," Selin replied.

Dr. Taner briefly mentioned Ece's problems. "To solve this, we need the information you and your husband can provide," he said.

Dr. Taner asked many questions. He had Selin talk about her life before marriage, discussed family and relative relationships, and probed her relationship with her husband. Up until this point, Selin had given quite normal answers, but when it came to her relationship with her husband, she got excited. She started giving panicked answers like "Very good," "Very, very good," "No problems at all." Dr. Taner didn't miss this part. Also, Ali Fuat had been uneasy when discussing his relationship with his wife.

Dr. Taner felt he needed to focus on this issue. He had ruled out many other factors. The family's financial situation was good. They had no chronic health issues. There were no problems with their relatives or parents. He also didn't think there was domestic violence. There were no signs of a lack of love or communication between them. He crossed these off.

The first problem was in Selin and Ali Fuat's relationship. Since this fee problem hadn't been disclosed to him, it was most likely related to sexuality, as he had seen in many cases. Discussing sexual issues often made women uncomfortable. To eliminate this discomfort and increase the likelihood of honest answers, he used written explanations.

Dr. Taner quickly wrote down questions on a blank sheet of paper. Among them were irrelevant questions like who their neighbors were and where they shopped, as well as questions probing their sexual relationship.

He handed her the paper and said, "Please answer these. I'll be outside for about 15 minutes." Then he went to the adjacent room. By pressing a few keys on the computer, he brought Selin's image up on the screen. There was a hidden camera in his office.

Selin looked distressed. After writing a few sentences, she would lift her head and sigh. He had deliberately given her a pencil and eraser. The subconscious possibility of erasing what she had written could make her write a few truthful words before lying. He could read the erased parts by shining horizontal light through the back of the paper.

Seeing from the footage that Selin had stopped writing and was leaning back in her chair for a long time, he thought she had finished. Just as he was about to return to the room, he saw her pick up the paper again. Selin was reading what she had written. She held the paper to her chest and thought for a while. Then she brought it back in front of her and continued reading. He felt that Selin was reassessing what she had written. A few seconds later, he realized he wasn't wrong. Selin took the eraser and erased something she had written. Dr. Taner thought the erased part was quite important. After watching for a while, he returned to the room. He didn't pay any attention to the paper. "I'll look at this later," he said.

After the session with Selin, Dr. Taner rested for a short while. Next in line was Ece. He needed to prepare himself psychologically for the session. First, he changed his clothes. He took off his brown suit, which gave him a serious look, and put on colorful, childlike clothes.

Selin threw herself onto the waiting room couch, feeling quite tense. She noticed her husband's curious gaze but wasn't in a state to talk. About five minutes had passed when she saw a man enter the waiting room, whom Ece ran to and hugged joyfully. Selin was shocked. The man who had looked as serious as the Secretary General of the Warsaw Pact a while ago had turned into a clown. He was in colorful clothes, with a big smile on his face.

Ece and Dr. Taner, hugging each other, went into the consultation room. Ece was talking about her parrot and rabbit, even claiming that her rabbit was prettier than the Psychologist's rabbit.

After a cheerful fifty-minute session, Dr. Taner held Ece's hand and handed her over to her parents. He asked Ali Fuat to schedule another appointment for a few days later.

Chapter

40

Cemetery

It was time to avenge the murder of Davut Buyukdere. After arduous efforts, Yasin had deciphered the codes in the book "Davetname (The invitation)" by Uzun Firdevsi, a djinn scholar from the 15th century.

The Imam and his followers gathered at the Christian Cemetery in Konya. The disciples wore large amulets around their necks. The full moon illuminated the sky. A disciple, clutching a Quran tightly, approached Imam Sait. "Hodja, the graves are ready," he said.

They had dug in front of the Christian graves. The Imam glanced at the pits. There were exactly thirteen, just as he wanted. He ordered those around him, "Write the names." With white chalk, the names of the thirteen members of the Council of the Exalted were written on the stones of the Christian graves with pits in front of them. Each pit had a large jar in front and two men standing guard. Disciples in white clothes poured salty water and vinegar into the jars they had brought. With each action, they recited the prayers commanded by the Imam. When these strange prayers, composed of unfamiliar words, were finished, the command "Bring the dogs" echoed.

The disciples worked like the cogs of a machine. Thirteen mongrel puppies were taken out of several sacks and brought next to the pits. An old shroud was divided into thirteen pieces and distributed. The disciples tied the dogs' mouths tightly with the prayers taught by the Imam. They tied them so tightly that the dogs' jaws were locked together. With a gesture from Imam Sait, the dogs were simultaneously placed into the jars. The dogs, whose eyes burned from the salty water and vinegar, howled in pain. The jars were sealed and placed in the pits at the same time. The pits were then covered with earth.

The Imam, sensing the final moments approaching, looked at the paper he had taken out of his robe. He didn't want to make any mistakes. He examined the paper with the codes Yasin had sent. Yes, the final moment was near. The howling from beneath the earth ceased. The puppies had died. At the Imam's signal, thirteen roosters were brought in. The disciples laid the roosters directly on top of the pits filled with earth. They pressed razor-sharp knives against their necks.

Imam Sait began to recite the Arabic prayer sent by Yasin. A great heat and foul smell rose from the pits. As the Imam's prayer progressed, the heat and smell intensified.

"Oh angel Zamradun, destroy our enemies."

The heat and stench had reached unbearable levels. The cold night air had vanished, replaced by the heat of a desert. All eyes were on the Imam.

The Imam took out a cloth. It bore a depiction of the djinn Zamradun. Holding the cloth by its edges, he shouted, "Oh Zamradun," and flung it into the air and began reading the "Ahdname (The Covenant)" The rising hot air was so intense that the cloth began to ripple in midair.

As soon as the prayer ended, the cloth caught fire. The Imam said to himself, "Now." It was the moment to give the order. With a gesture indicating the disciples should finish off the roosters, the thirteen disciples, their eyes fixed on the Imam, swiftly drew the knives across the roosters' throats from below upwards. The blood of the roosters spurted onto the pits filled with earth.

Simultaneously, in Bursa, Izmit, Sivas, Germany, Iran, Hatay, Istanbul, and Syria, twelve more people; in their beds, while sleeping, talking to their spouses, watching TV, or drinking tea, began to bleed from their throats. A great heat and foul smell filled the places where they were.

In the cemetery, the foul stench and hellish heat disappeared instantly. They were replaced by the smell of earth and the chill of the night. The disciples, drenched in sweat, were suddenly paralyzed by the cold. The Imam commanded them to prepare for departure.

Chapter

41

The Wave of Fear Spreads

Cihangir Demirkaplan was pacing back and forth in the large living room of the mansion. He was wearing his robe. He kept rushing to the window to look outside, glancing at the television, and looking at the paper he held tightly. The paper listed nine names, all members of the Council of the Exalted. As he received the news of each death, he noted it down on the paper.

The death news was coming in waves from Bursa, Hatay, Izmit, and Istanbul. Cihangir wanted to immediately take his family and escape to the villa in Tarabya[31], but the head of security had prevented him. "The villa may have been compromised, sir. They could ambush us on the way. The safest place is here. We have a heavily armed security team of 60 people. The entire place is surrounded by cameras and electrified barbed wire," he had said.

Still, he was afraid, afraid for himself, his wife, and his son. He looked at the paper again. It was one of the most terrifying nights he had ever experienced. After four in the morning, he received the news of a friend's death every fifteen to twenty minutes. Was his turn next? It felt like a fiery oil well was burning inside his stomach.

Alp, who was sitting on the couch with his mother, listened intently to the news anchor.

---

[31]   A prestigious neighborhood located in the Sariyer district of Istanbul, along the Bosphorus

"Another link has been added to the chain of murders that started at midnight. The common feature of the deceased is that they are known as prominent merchants and industrialists with Islamic views. The latest news comes from Iran. One of our country's leading textile magnates, Mehmet Poyraz, was killed in his villa in Tehran. For details of the news, we are connecting with Ihlas News Agency's Tehran correspondent Ekrem Erhan. Ekrem, over to you..."

"Yes, Asli, we are currently in front of a large villa near Tehran. The Iranian police are conducting an investigation. According to the information we have obtained, Mehmet Poyraz was killed by having his throat slit in his bed at midnight. The Tehran police chief is here, as are officials from our embassy. No one is making a statement. Known for his Islamic views, Poyraz became a target of which power centers in Iran, we are trying to understand this..."

With trembling hands, Mr. Demirkaplan wrote down the name Mehmet Poyraz. Like the others, he had been killed by having his throat slit at midnight. A large bead of sweat rolled down Mr. Demirkaplan's neck and started to slide down his back. He had just learned that his forty-year-old friend Mehmet had a house in Tehran. How could the killers reach all the way to Tehran?

The eleventh murder report came from Germany. Mr. Demirkaplan's cheek started to twitch. He couldn't control himself. He dropped the paper he was holding. His body began to tremble and slowly curl up. "Dad... Dad..." shouted Alp. Mrs. Demirkaplan ran to the bedroom to get his sublingual tablet.

The head of security remained calm. Knowing his boss's heart condition, he always carried a box of his medication. He placed the sublingual tablet in Mr. Demirkaplan's mouth.

Mrs. Demirkaplan also entered the living room with the medication box in hand. "I gave it to him, ma'am. Don't worry," he said.

The head of security called the mansion's medical cabin and requested an ambulance to be prepared.

During this commotion, the news anchor reported the 12th murder. It was another strange death. According to the victim's wife's statement, they were chatting in bed when suddenly blood started gushing from her husband's throat. With this murder, only three members of the Council of the Exalted remained alive: Mr. Demirkaplan, Alp, and the Imam.

Chapter

42

Black Shrouds Assess the Murders

Ali Fuat, Kenan Ferit, and Aydin started their morning shift by reviewing the murder files. The victims were the cornerstones of the religious sect structure in Turkey.

There were more strange aspects to the case. The first thing that caught their eye was that all 12 individuals had been killed by having their throats slit. However, no one had seen who did it.

"What kind of murders are these?" said Ali Fuat.

"Look, according to the information from Hatay police, the guy was returning from a party with his friends, and suddenly blood started gushing from his throat while he was in the car. No one understood what happened."

Aydin, wanting to support, mentioned another case. "The one in Germany is just as interesting, commander. He was with his wife, and suddenly blood started gushing from his throat."

Kenan Ferit looked at the situation from a different perspective. "In Hatay, Istanbul, Germany, Iran, and many other places, 12 people are slaughtered like chickens, but there are no arrests, no witnesses, and no murder weapons. What are we dealing with?"

Ali Fuat angrily threw the file in the middle of the table. They were facing things that defied the limits of logic.

"We're stuck, Kenan."

"There's no one to confront, commander. If we knew who did it, we'd be on top of them immediately, but..."

Despite the Black Shrouds' investigation, they couldn't reach any conclusions. The series of strange events that started with Hadji Halit Nurullah continued like a twilight zone.

The tense atmosphere caused by the Bursa murders had escalated into a political crisis with the recent events. Opposition party MPs were submitting questions to the Ministry of Interior and the Ministry of Justice. Civil society organizations, the media, and the public wanted the murders solved as soon as possible.

Pasha Vefik ordered an urgent meeting. In a short time, the guards had taken their places in the meeting room. General Vefik was tense. In front of him were reports related to the murders. He took a sip of water.

"Team, days have passed since the murders of Faruk Altan and Osman Karahan. We still haven't lifted the fog. The subsequent Bursa murders remain unsolved. As if that weren't enough, we now have these 12 murders. What is happening?" After his last words, he looked at his men. Ali Fuat thought to himself, "You should be the one to explain what happened. Why did you kill Halit Nurullah?"

"It's very clear that there is a reckoning within the Islamist structure. All the victims belonged to various sects. Why can't we reach any perpetrators starting from this point? What is the problem, team?" The general's attempt to start calmly was raising his anger with every word. He scanned his guards with eyes that demanded answers.

"The peace we have had in recent years has brought many benefits to the country. However, the extraordinary events we have experienced in the past few weeks suggest that everything will be turned upside down. The only necessary element for our country is stability. We cannot allow any radical religious formations to disrupt this stability. It is our primary duty to eliminate these formations by any means necessary."

Those in the meeting listened to a tedious speech. Pasha Vefik was not giving his usual dynamic talks. He was using arguments about stability, the economy, things the Black Shrouds were not used to hearing. Ali Fuat cursed under his breath repeatedly.

Chapter

43

The Djinns of Yasin

The evening news had ended. He turned off the TV and tossed the remote to the side of the couch. He had done it. The news was reporting that twelve people had been killed in different places in the same manner. This meant he had deciphered the codes correctly. For a brief moment, he thought, "But why twelve?" It was supposed to be thirteen. Who hadn't been killed?

He now understood the encryption method Uzun Firdevsi used in the "Davetname." These news reports were proof of his scientific success. He would also decipher YHVH. Then, all the power would be his.

He went to his room and looked at the YHVH figure drawn on papyrus paper. "One day, yes, one day, I will solve you too. You may be the world's greatest secret, but..."

He wondered what the Imam was doing. As the congregation was gradually being taken over step by step with the codes Yasin had deciphered, what was he telling those around him? Yasin was very curious. "He must be claiming that he solved the codes himself," he thought. This was the reason for his removal from Konya, not being sent to university, and suddenly being sent to Istanbul when Bursa became dangerous.

Seeing the concrete success of his codes boosted his confidence.

His cell phone rang. It was Bahar calling.

"Yasin, my friends are here. Come down now." "Okay," Yasin replied. Bahar, Pelin, and Melisa had insisted that he summon a spirit. They had told their school friends about Yasin's mystical side and brought a curious group. The girls were very insistent. Yasin had now become "dear Yasin."

The stories he told about djinn, Kabbalah, Cifir, Havas, and Huddamlik caught the girls' attention. He had never thought of something like this. He used to think that to impress girls, one had to be talented in music or sports.

He imagined himself as a witty, funny guy. He thought that was when beautiful girls would fall in love with him. It had never crossed his mind that they would be interested in or impressed by his knowledge of Huddamlik, Kabbalah, and djinn.

They were waiting for him to summon a spirit. Imam Sait's orders came to his mind: "You will not speak of our secrets to anyone. Not even your family will know. You will remain hidden until we reach our goal."

If the Imam knew what he was about to do, he would probably kill him. But he couldn't kill him either. He was the one deciphering all the codes; what would the Imam do without him? "Now I am powerful too," he said to himself. For the first time, he was admitting to himself the power he had held for years.

"Sorry, dear Imam," he said with a sarcastic smile. He turned on the bathroom light and looked in the mirror. His straight, reddish-blond hair had grown a bit. It looked nice. "I wonder how it would look if I grew it out like Erkan's. Would it suit me?" he thought.

His phone buzzed with a message. The girls were saying "come on." He put on his protective shirt, donned his amulet, grabbed his prayer beads, and headed down to Erkan's place.

The household was waiting in excitement. There were five girls and two boys he didn't know. He was introduced to all of them. The shirt covered in Quranic writings and strange symbols, the amulet around his neck, and the large prayer beads in his hand made everyone shiver. The excitement was palpable.

The newcomers were trying to decipher Yasin with looks filled with curiosity and mystery.

The only uneasy person was Erkan. He had been against this from the beginning. He was scared something might happen to his girlfriend and friends. Finding an opportunity, he pulled Yasin aside with an angry expression, "Listen, Yasin. Don't let any trouble arise," he said.

Yasin was very relaxed and confident. "Everything is under control. There's nothing to fear, brother. I'll just do a small demonstration."

"Didn't you say that spirits don't come, but djinn do?"

"I did."

"And didn't you say if a djinn comes, it can cause harm? Didn't you say that if you enter a dorm room and wake someone up, you'll be in trouble?"

"But that was for you. It doesn't apply to me. It depends on who gets woken up."

"What do you mean?"

"Think about it, brother. If you or Can were the ones to wake up the guy in the dorm, he might beat you up. Just saying... But if Don Carlone woke him up, the guy wouldn't do anything because he would be scared and powerless."

"What does that mean?"

"It means I am the Don Carlone of the djinn world. So, don't worry unnecessarily."

"Yasin, if anyone gets hurt, I'll cut your ear off, just so you know."

Despite Erkan's anger, Yasin always gave positive answers. He was completely confident.

They gathered in the living room. He made everyone perform ablutions. He pasted prayers written on paper in all four corners of the room. He had an aluminum tray brought and placed it on the carpet. He asked everyone to pluck three strands of hair and throw them into the tray. The people in the room felt like they were performing legendary Masonic rituals they had heard of for years. Even Erkan, who initially refused to pluck his hair, had to comply under his girlfriend's insistence. Yasin distributed papers and asked them to write down their sins that troubled them the most. They were to crumple the paper and throw it into the tray. One by one, papers started being thrown into the tray.

Yasin saw that the excitement had reached its peak. He began reciting his prayer beads, uttering a coded prayer for each bead. He turned off the light.

He was nearing the end of the prayer beads. The room was filled with intense heat. The students were looking at each other. As his fingertips touched the last bead, he glanced around the room in the dim light. The girls were holding onto each other, and the boys were sunk into their seats. The only one maintaining his composure was Erkan.

He recited the last prayer. Dropping the bead from his hand, he said, "Oh Azazel djinn, manifest with your smokeless fire." He said this part in Turkish so those in the room would understand. Immediately after, he said in the coded Chaldean language, "Azazel machezi nuschezi nl." As soon as he finished speaking, a fire rose from the tray to the ceiling.

The fire was smokeless. It didn't burn the room but flooded it with heat and light. It wasn't like any fire they knew; it was a different element. It burned more fiercely than anything they had ever seen, and its redness was more vivid than any fire.

The people in the room were paralyzed with fear. Yasin stood next to the fire that rose like an electric pole in the middle of the room. Thinking that a few seconds of this display were enough, he began to recite prayers. As the fire weakened, the scream of a dying entity filled the room.

When they later discussed the event, they could find no description for this sound. It was a terrifying noise unlike anything else. The way it reached their ears indicated that the source of the sound was in a very unpleasant state. It was dying.

The people in the room couldn't control their limbs. Their hands and jaws were trembling uncontrollably. As the fire vanished and the screams reached their peak and then stopped, the room plunged into darkness. This only added to their fear. Some of the girls started crying. Yasin turned on the lights and then opened the windows. As the cool air hit their faces, they began to recover.

Chapter

44

Psychologist and Selin

Dr. Taner examined the paper Selin had written on. He was certain there was a problem in their sexual relationship. But he couldn't pinpoint what it was. His experience had taught him many things; he had seen various cases, but he couldn't determine which applied here. The most common cases he encountered were those of unwilling marriages. In marriages arranged by family pressure or for wealth, sexual problems often arose. In such situations, women were reluctant but couldn't say anything to their husbands. They often felt as if they were being raped. Sexual problems were key factors in infidelity and various disturbances. Indirectly, this also affected the children.

He was using various eliminations to find the sexual problem he believed existed between Ali Fuat and Selin. He considered the possibility that Selin might have lesbian tendencies. If so, the sexual relationship with her husband would seem burdensome to her. Unable to speak about it, she would leave the bed each time with psychological distress. But he had not encountered any signs that would indicate lesbianism.

Ece's fear was entirely focused on her mother. However, there was nothing in their lifestyle to warrant this fear. They lived in a well-protected, elite community. Their relationships with neighbors, relatives, and friends were quite civilized.

If Ali Fuat were beating his wife and the child witnessed it, she might fear that her mother could be killed by her father. But there were no signs of this. He could easily detect domestic violence.

Dr. Taner let out a deep sigh. He closed the Ece Sezgin file and tossed his pen onto the table. He leaned back in his chair. Despite considering all possibilities, he hadn't identified the problem. The best course was to investigate further. He decided to request all the drawings Ece had made at her kindergarten. He could also have a brief conversation with her teacher.

He was about to take another patient's file when he recalled the moment Selin had erased something on her interview paper. He took the paper and inserted it into a device the size of a photocopier. The machine scanned the paper with horizontal light, capturing the indentations in the paper fibers. He retrieved the A4-sized photograph from the output tray. The erased part was near the question about neighbors: "Who are your neighbors, and what are your relationships like?" Selin had listed many names in response to this warming-up question and then erased one. The indentations showed that the erased name was "Serkan Cenet."

"What's special about this neighbor?" he wondered. Why was the name first written and then erased? As he was about to close the file, new thoughts began to form in his mind, leaving him indecisive. He should review the files of the other patients as well. After noting down the name "Serkan Cenet," he closed the file and opened the file of a six-yearold boy who wanted to harm his newborn sibling.

His mind was still on 'Serkan Cenet'.

Chapter

45

Ali Fuat Lost in Deep Thoughts

Pasha Vefik's words were ringing in his ears. Five minutes after crushing his third cigarette into the ashtray, he had lit his fourth.

Leaving the window slightly open had not prevented the room from becoming smoke-filled. Ali Fuat was sitting as if sunk into his chair.

He was thinking it over thoroughly, but he still couldn't find a solution to the Serkan Cenet issue. Maybe he had exaggerated a bit. Yes, yes, he had exaggerated. "The man has only a few days left, and here we are, thinking all sorts of things," he said to himself. True, there were many signs, but that mushroom incident and all. No, no, it's impossible, it couldn't be! The man was going to die...

Did Selin know? Maybe that's why she was showing so much closeness. "My compassionate wife," he said, as if speaking to Selin who was in front of him. But if she knew, why hadn't she mentioned it at all? You'd think she would have mentioned it in passing. "Maybe it just didn't come up, or she didn't find the opportunity," he answered himself.

"God! There's not just one problem." he thought. Pasha Vefik had almost cursed their mothers. They were facing strange murders of a kind they hadn't seen in years.

Blood was flowing like a river. "What kind of organization is this, leaving no trace?" he asked himself. How could they carry out such well-organized murders? Even the CIA or Mossad couldn't plan murders of this scale. How could they kill twelve men, each with 6-7 heavily armed bodyguards, in different cities, even different countries, at the

175

same time, in the same way, without leaving any trace? Surely someone would be caught, some trace would be left. Moreover, the bodyguards were either relatives or compatriots of the victims. This weakened the possibility of betrayal. Even if they did betray, it wouldn't happen all at once. "12 times 6 makes 72," he calculated in his mind. Bribing 72 people at once, against their own relatives... It didn't make sense. Another factor that made the murders impossible was that they were committed in different countries. Conducting a clean operation without any intelligence service noticing was very difficult. Evading the secret services of Germany, Iran, and Syria all at once was no easy task. "Let's say the killers made a deal with these countries, that doesn't make sense either," he said to himself. What kind of power could persuade countries with such different policies, friends, and enemies as Germany, Iran, and Syria all at once?

Outside of all this, another thing that troubled his mind was the fact that the murders were committed using the most difficult method. No bombs, no sniper rifles, no guns; none of these required as much expertise as using a knife. The knife required being the closest to the victim to commit the murder. Overcoming the bodyguards and leaving no trace... Doing this with a knife was very difficult. Committing twelve murders at once with a knife was beyond reason and logic.

He extinguished his cigarette, now down to the filter. "With bombs and snipers available, why use a knife..." he murmured.

Chapter

46

Feyza Takes the Reins

Feyza had been keeping a close eye on her husband for the past two days. The heart attack had been mild, thanks to the intervention of the head of security.

The problem was now beyond control. Those who could kill 12 members could reach them as well. She wanted to speak with her husband and determine the community's strategy as soon as possible. She decided that two days of rest were enough.

Mr. Demirkaplan, who was seated on the cushions in the eastern corner of the mansion reading his newspaper, put it down and turned his attention to his wife as she called to him.

Feyza thought it was time to gradually bring up the subject.

"Cihangir, what does the newspaper say? Is there any news about the murders?"

Mr. Demirkaplan inwardly smiled. Yes, he felt it was time to talk. He also knew that he had to take the first step.

"Come here, dear. Sit down. I'm fine, we can talk about everything. I know you haven't brought up any topics for the past two days to avoid stressing me out."

"Cihangir," Feyza said. She paused for a few seconds, not knowing where to start. "What are we going to do? Have you thought of anything?" she asked, passing the ball to her husband.

"I've thought about it, but I haven't come up with a reasonable plan."

"Cihangir, this situation is very delicate this time. You're the only surviving member, and..." She scrunched up her face as if she had seen something disgusting, "...that infidel Sait."

"And then there's our son. We made him a member at the last meeting, remember?"

"God forbid," said Feyza. The thought of her son being associated with the Council of the Exalted, whose members were being killed one by one, sent shivers down her spine. Even though they didn't know where to start the conversation, they had found the topic. The first problem was Alp's situation.

"Cihangir, let's get the boy away from here immediately," she said, her voice filled with great concern. "Let's send him to Europe or America."

Mr. Demirkaplan had thought about this idea too over the past two days, but... Some of the Twelve Murders had been committed abroad. This meant the killers had long arms.

"Sending him abroad isn't the solution," he said. There was a moment of silence.

"What can we do?" asked Feyza, breaking the silence.

Mr. Demirkaplan took a deep breath.

"Look, dear. You have as much life experience as I do. Just as you think calmly and act coolly in other matters, please do the same in this one. I know our son is your weakest point. But Feyza, you know very well that hiding Alp isn't the solution. Those who could kill 12 people despite their good protection and very secret hiding places..."

He swallowed. Feyza had turned pale. Mr. Demirkaplan didn't finish the sentence, but it wasn't necessary. Feyza's expression resembled that of a person who had been slapped by the harsh truth.

"Hiding him. Sending him to Europe would work if it were the solution, I wouldn't hesitate for a second. But that might be a wrong decision. The safest place right now is the mansion."

Feyza agreed with her husband. But what were they going to do? Were they going to keep their beloved child in this circle of fire?

"What are we going to do?" she asked helplessly.

"Feyza, we can't run away anywhere. This won't end without quelling the rebellion and killing Imam Sait. I think the thing we need to discuss is how to carry out this purge."

Chapter

47

Yasin in Taksim[32]

After Yasin's little show, they couldn't recover for a long time. The screams that filled the room for a few seconds echoed in their ears all night. They thought the blazing fire had vanished instantly, but as their eyelids fell, the curtain of fire rose. Couples who slept together felt luckier. They clung tightly to each other. Those who slept alone faced the toughest sleep process of their lives. The pillows they rested their heads on, the blankets covering them, their pajamas, the room's carpet; everything was suspicious. When they closed their eyes, there was a blazing fire; when they opened them, there was a terrifying darkness.

Despite shivering to their bones, the first thing they did when they got up was to tell their friends about the mysterious event in a hushed voice. They felt privileged, as if witnessing such an event made them different. The children of the barren lands of the West, stripped of mysticism, saw Yasin as an oasis filled with spiritual material. Seeing the blazing fire rise to the sky felt like drinking a cup of water from this oasis.

The uproar caused by Bahar and her crew deeply affected their circle of friends. Yasin Omen's name was now at the top of the list of most curious subjects.

---

[32] Taksim Square is a major public space and tourist attraction in Istanbul, Turkey. It's known for its vibrant atmosphere, significant cultural events, and bustling shops, restaurants, and hotels. It also serves as a hub for public transportation and is the site of many historical and political gatherings.

Within a day or two, the legend of Yasin had reached its peak. Students were begging, "Introduce us too." Pelin was annoyed by the requests from her girlfriends to meet Yasin.

The curious youth who wanted to meet Yasin turned to Bahar and Melisa after receiving cold responses from Pelin. Pelin's excuse of "I don't know, he's a bit shy, and he's busy preparing for university," was refuted by Bahar's explanation: "Girl, does he need to prepare for the exam? The kid is beyond prepared."

Bahar, calling Yasin on her cell phone, said, "We're hanging out in Taksim tonight, will you join us, dear Yasin?" Her friends, who were eagerly waiting for the answer, rejoiced at his affirmative response, while Pelin went into a fit of jealousy.

The cool air that caressed their faces at noon seemed to have gotten angry, as if someone had said something bad. Despite the wind, Yasin kept turning his head left and right, scanning the surroundings with curious eyes. The strong gusts of wind had driven away the usual crowd of Istiklal Street[33]. On both sides of the tramway-split street, the quickpaced, shivering people with their hands in their pockets and the older generation dressed warmly, deceived by the midday sun, walked with heavy, proud, and happy expressions. Groups of friends moved more slowly compared to individuals or pairs walking alone. Every two or three shops, someone in the group would stop to comment, "Oh, look at that guitar," "Oh, what a nice shirt," "Is this Ahmet Umit's new book?" "I can't believe it, I've been looking for this hat," slowing down the group's pace even more. The person who had just stopped their friends a moment ago would get annoyed when another friend stopped to look at a shop window a few steps later. The pitch-black sky lit up as it approached the street, engaged in an interesting battle with the inviting lights of the shop windows. The darkness, which seemed to lose the battle on Istiklal Street, had absolute dominance in the alleys leading to Cihangir and Tarlabasi. The low-quality paving stones laid by municipalities that thought municipal work was limited to providing iftar[34] meals during Ramadan trembled despite the tram's gentleness.

---

[33] A historic and iconic pedestrian street located in Istanbul's Beyoğlu district.
[34] "Iftar" is the meal eaten by Muslims after sunset to break their fast during the holy month of Ramadan.

They trembled with the wind, with the tram, and when stepped on, the muddy water accumulated under the broken ones prepared unpleasant surprises for shoes and pant legs. The ill-timed, unplanned wind caused those who had taken no precautions to shiver, while those who were well-prepared looked like terrorists with scarves and shawls covering their faces. Yasin observed with fascination the pessimistic faces of smokers with cigarettes fixed to their mouths, the disgusting men who wanted to spit out the filth of their souls, the prostitutes and transvestites preserving their provocative outfits despite the cold, the pimps with open collars, yellow teeth, and dirty mustaches hoping to be called "master" or "sir" soon, the dignified-looking gay men in suits watching handsome men with envy, the one-million-lira kebab sellers, the guards of the inns with wide mustaches who thought they knew all the secrets of life from a few offices closing down or a couple of scandals, the university students in green parkas calling for revolution, the constantly smiling Japanese tourists returning to their hotels, the astonished homeless people labeled as a different species, the grandeur of Galatasaray High School's gates, the solemnity of the consulate buildings, the child beggars introduced to the harshness of life too early, the old women selling tissues with theatrical sadness. Despite the gloom, sorrow, pain, cold, filth, and unhappiness, he looked at every corner of Taksim with joy. He was happy! Because he was experiencing this beauty for the first time. Yes, for the first time, he was out with a mixed group of friends. There were girls interested in him, asking him questions. Oh my God, what a big dream was this? Or... Or was it a dream? He was scared! He was afraid that the girls who were asking him questions, trying to learn the general outlines of his life, Bahar, Melisa, and Pelin, who never left his side, would disappear.

Bahar was steering the group towards a jazz bar. For Erkan, the only good thing about this meaningless evening meeting, which he wouldn't have joined if not for his girlfriend's request, was the jazz bar. The others didn't care much where they were going. After all, the point of the night was Yasin. Maybe they wanted to ask him to do a small show, or see the same show Bahar and her friends had witnessed.

In the bar, cheap Chinese-made candles in glass lanterns were placed on the tables, creating an authentic atmosphere. The sound of the electric guitar and drums was distinctly filling the hall. With the addition of the saxophone, the band started a new piece.

In the overly musical atmosphere that was a bit too loud for conversation, the efforts to get to know Yasin continued with all their difficulty. As the topic revolved around spirit summoning and djinn, none of Yasin's scientific evaluations or philosophical approaches were being listened to. In fact, words, phrases, and sentences had no meaning. Yasin was caught in the webs of postmodernity. Because for the new generation, it wasn't the newspaper but live television; not the novel, but the film. Not hide-and-seek or tops, but PlayStation. It was action, movement, and visuality. They insisted on seeing the fire and screams too.

Yasin was pleased with the attention. "Okay, but not here," he said. What harm could another small show do? He looked at the couples making out at the nearby tables and sighed.

Aydin Sipahi

He took off his glasses and placed them next to the table so he could wipe his nose comfortably. Aydin Sipahi redirected his observant gaze from the surroundings back to his computer. Grabbing the mouse, he began scrolling down. The screen moved to lower pages. He started following the statistics with his tired eyes. Every second, the work seemed to get heavier. Realizing he was seeing the numbers blurred, he remembered he hadn't put on his glasses. He picked up his glasses next to the keyboard. Instead of immediately putting them on and continuing his work, he leaned back and stared at the ceiling of the room. This second interruption after wiping his nose completely broke his concentration.

After putting on his glasses, he grabbed a tissue and stood up. There was an imprint of his seat on the chair. After experiencing a brief back strain and taking a few steps, he began walking briskly.

The steam from the coffee opened his nostrils. As he slowly sipped, he thought about how much he knew about the Black Shrouds. Well, he had learned some things but it wasn't enough. Most importantly, he didn't know the history. Who founded it and when? What were their activities?

They were working to prevent Sharia law, but he didn't know the details.

"This won't do!" he thought. He needed to learn some things now. How could he solve all these murders without even knowing his own organization?

With his muscular body, full lips, and all his handsomeness, Kenan Ferit entered. "Hello, Aydin," he said, smiling.

"Hello, Brother." Aydin replied. He wasn't in a good mood.

"Haven't you recovered yet?" Kenan Ferit asked. After getting himself a chamomile tea, he sat next to Aydin. The cafeteria was empty. Aydin didn't hear the question. He was fixated on another point.

"Brother, when will I fully understand the Black Shrouds?" he said with a submissive look. The pleading in his voice was noticeable.

"There's nothing I can do. Your acting teacher is Ali Fuat Sezgin. The command is with him."

"When do you think he'll tell me?" he asked, his voice trembling.

Kenan looked into Aydin's blue eyes before lowering his head. He filled his nose with the pleasant scent of the chamomile tea's steam and took a small sip.

"Aydin, it's best to talk openly with the commander. I'm sure he'll realize he's delayed it. He's a bit stressed these days. He may have forgotten he's your acting teacher."

"But, brother..." he wanted to speak but was also scared.

"Shouldn't we be careful not to get scolded?" he said with a timid look.

"No, don't worry. He's strict but also very fair."

Aydin wasn't convinced at all. The scolding he received on the helicopter for 'nothing,' the way he was stared at like a scorpion after vomiting in Bursa, and slapping the kid in Konya just because he was annoyed... These all flashed through his mind. He couldn't muster the courage.

Chapter

49

Psychologist's Office

Dr. Taner, sitting diagonally from his laptop, thought the next appointment would be sufficient. He picked up the phone and dialed 12. The worker of the clinic, Safiye, who only had an elementary school education, answered the phone. "Cafeteria, at your service," she said in a Central Anatolian accent. He was a bit hungry. A coffee and some cookies would be nice.

"Safiye, are there any cookies left?"

"They're almost gone, doctor. I put two trays of pastry in the oven, but the guests ate them all. I took another plate, and they asked for more. I saved a few slices from that."

"Then prepare something with a coffee. Don't put too much, save some for yourself."

He knew Safiye took the leftover cookies and pastries home. He was also aware that sometimes she made extra to take more home. But considering her difficult circumstances, and knowing that her grown, lazy sons still relied on their mother, he didn't say anything.

Safiye was one of those self-sacrificing, troubled women who had never seen the bright side of life in Anatolia. Looking at her made him think psychologists should come down from their ivory towers and conduct fieldwork on these people. These types of people were so similar to each other.

They had forgotten how to smile, love, and be cheerful. Smiling seemed like a memory from childhood or something that only belonged to children and wealthy people on TV. The fabric life had woven for them was made of beatings, poverty, lack of education, their children dying as martyrs in the military, or becoming thieves and vagrants. If they were lucky, they could become janitors or laborers. Life for them was being grateful for a loaf of bread, a piece of cheese, and a couple of black olives, not expecting a flower from a spouse, a word of love, or a gift from their children on Mother's Day.

The dark side of life pressed down on them so intensely that eyes that hadn't seen light for a long time mistook darkness for brightness. The brain, after dealing with all the bitter aspects of life and eliminating familiar joys and happiness, created new codings, producing new joys and happiness.

Less painful things were good, moderate pains were normal, and severe pains were bad. That's why forgetting an anniversary might be a reason for divorce for some, causing them to be devastated by unhappiness, while others didn't even have such a concept of unhappiness coded in their brains. An anniversary was as meaningless as the pi number to Safiyes.

The rare moment when her husband, in his anger, forgot to beat her was something to be happy about. Sociologists and psychologists should study these lives, but the lack of financial gain and state support for such research made these studies impossible.

Sometimes he thought about taking a few idealist colleagues and going to Anatolia, but... leaving this clinic that minted money every minute... What would his dear wife and kids say? They'd probably think the psychologist had lost his mind. Whenever he thought of Safiye, his strict socialist ideas from university came to mind. How far he had come... Now he was serving to upper class.

There was a knock at the door. Safiye's 14-year-old daughter, Semiha, entered with a tray. Semiha worked in the cafeteria with her mother. She carefully placed two slices of pastry and cookies, arranged on a glass plate, on the desk. While setting the plate on the table, Dr. Taner took the coffee she was balancing in her other hand. Smiling, she left the room. Dr. Taner noticed that her breasts seemed larger than usual. Who was here today? Oh, of course! It was the appointment of Mr. Ekrem's handsome 17-year-old son. The secretary and Semiha had been tracking that boy's session days. On those days, they all dressed up a little more. Semiha hoped to fall in love with and marry one of the wealthy kids from these families, and not live the same fate as her mother. The other staff were not much different. Except for the married accountant, the secretary and the hostess girls all hoped to catch the eye of middle-aged or wealthy peers. They wanted to experience even a sliver of the glamorous life while they were still young. Semiha, despite her age, was following the example of the secretary and hostess girls. In fact, in many ways, she surpassed them because she was the poorest and most desperate to escape the life she was living.

Dr. Taner recalled the day he took all the staff to the islands. Makeup-free faces, hair messed up by the sea, and breasts free from padding... He smiled to himself.

He enjoyed swallowing the particles of the half-eaten cookie mixed with his coffee. He opened the "Ece Sezgin" file. Although he remembered all the details, he preferred to take another look as a matter of principle. As he opened the file, he popped a piece of water pastry into his mouth.

He had colorful photocopies of the drawings Ece had made since kindergarten. He pulled out the notes he had taken about the drawings from the file. Among the seventeen drawings, two were particularly noteworthy. One depicted a large face, likely her own, because the hair was long and dyed blonde. The eyes were colored green. What broke the ordinariness of the drawing was a large cross over the mouth. While the eyebrows, eyes, nose, and ears were drawn, there was a cross over the mouth. This could mean several things. First, the kindergarten teachers might be scolding the children to "be quiet, don't talk." He found this unlikely.

The kindergarten Ece attended was a high-quality and expensive place. Another meaning of the cross over her mouth could be that our little girl was in love with a cute boy in her kindergarten. Of course, he didn't know how accurate it was to call feelings at that age 'love,' but it was common for 5-6-year-old children to develop crushes on each other. Ece might have liked one of her classmates a lot, and maybe the boy liked her too, and perhaps they had kissed while playing. He noted this possibility down. Another meaning of the cross over the mouth could be that Ece knew a 'secret' she was afraid to tell or forbidden to speak of.

The third possibility nagged at him. A 'secret'... What could it be?

The other drawing that caught his interest was a rectangle with two green eyes inside. At first glance, nothing could be made out from the drawing. However, the note written by the teacher under the drawing made this otherwise meaningless picture interesting for Dr. Taner. "Rectangle=door, Ece's eyes behind it," was written. The teacher had probably asked about the drawing when she couldn't make sense of it and noted down Ece's response. A door and Ece's eyes behind it... This was the second drawing that had puzzled Dr. Taner the day before when he reviewed the drawings. Trying to remember 'yesterday' by looking at his notes, he thought about what the meaning of the drawing could be. The first thing that came to mind was that Ece might have accidentally seen something she shouldn't have. He found this possibility too vague and set it aside, then tried to think of other possibilities but nothing came to mind. The only theory he could come up with regarding the eyes looking from behind the door was that 'Ece had seen something.' But what could it be?

He read the notes in his hand, trying to remember the previous day. The coffee and cookies were finished. He thought about brushing his teeth and putting on his colorful clothes for his session with Ece.

He put on his green shirt with daisy patterns. He wore a tie featuring 'Tweety' and 'Tom.' He put on baggy pants like hip-hop artists and placed his parrot 'Mistik' on his shoulder before heading to the waiting room. Ece greeted Dr. Taner with great joy again. She tried to get Mistik to talk. After shaking hands with Ali Fuat and Selin, Dr. Taner said he wanted to have the first session with Ece and took her to his office.

Ece became uneasy after separating from her parents. Dr. Taner turned on the TV in his office to show Selin and Ali Fuat sitting in the waiting room. "Sweetie, look, your mom and dad are here waiting for you. They haven't gone anywhere," he said. Like all children, Ece was surprised to see her parents on TV. This made her smile and relieved her tension. She kept glancing at the TV. Dr. Taner laid out the seventeen drawings Ece had made on the table. He sat down next to her. "Sweetie, do you remember drawing these pictures?" he asked.

"Uh-huh," giggled Ece. She sneaked a smiley glance at the TV. Her parents were reading newspapers.

Pointing to a landscape drawing, Dr. Taner asked, "Why are there so many birds in this picture? Do you love birds a lot?"

"Yes," said Ece.

After discussing a few more drawings, he asked about the picture with the cross over the mouth. Ece turned to the TV. She acted as if she didn't understand the question. She started talking about the birds in the first picture again. Dr. Taner listened patiently.

He asked again about the picture with the cross over the mouth. Ece talked about her cousin, the rabbit at home, and the battery-operated car her father had bought. She rambled on, glancing at the screen every few seconds.

Dr. Taner asked relaxing questions about other drawings. The little girl tried to answer all the questions as best as she could. Feeling that she had calmed down a bit, Dr. Taner showed the drawing with the door and green eyes behind it. "Sweetie, can you tell me what you drew here?" he asked.

Despite being shown the door drawing, Ece pointed to the flower drawing beneath it and asked, "This one?"

Dr. Taner responded, "Yes, sweetie." Clearly, she didn't want to say anything about the drawing. She talked at length about the flower drawing. He listened to all her chatter attentively. Then he placed his finger on the drawing and asked, "What did you draw in this picture?"

There was a noticeable look of distress on Ece's face. She sought refuge in the TV with furtive glances.

"Sweetie, who is behind this door?"

Ece pursed her lips, started swaying slightly, and tugged at her clothes' buttons. Dr. Taner thought Ece was torn between telling and not telling. In a soft tone, he said:

"Are the green eyes behind this door yours?" he asked.

"Yes," said Ece, continuing to shake her head slightly and avoiding Dr. Taner's gaze.

"So, where is that door? Is it in the kindergarten?"

"No. It's the room's door."

Dr. Taner became excited. "Which room, sweetie? Did you see something there? Would you like to tell me?" Ece was tugging at her button as if to tear it off. It was clear she was very uncomfortable. He thought this state was an internal struggle. It would be resolved soon. He began to wait patiently.

Ece glanced at the TV and couldn't see her mother in the overhead camera view of the waiting room. Her father was sitting there, and the seat next to him was empty. "Where's my mom?" she asked, almost in tears. Dr. Taner looked at the TV and cursed internally. Selin had probably gone to the restroom. Ece started crying and headed towards the door. From this point on, it was impossible to get the child to focus on the drawings. He followed Ece.

Ali Fuat stood up in surprise when he saw his daughter enter the room crying. "What happened, sweetheart?" he asked, taking Ece in his arms and looking at Dr. Taner for an explanation. As the psychologist began to explain what had happened, Selin entered the room. Ece threw herself towards her mother, trying to break free from her father's arms. Selin took her daughter into her arms, looking bewildered.

Dr. Taner invited Ali Fuat into the consultation room, and they went inside together. Starting with the drawings on the table, Dr. Taner explained everything that had happened. Ali Fuat took the two drawings his daughter had made and leaned back in his chair, studying them for a long time. They were indeed interesting.

"So, doctor, in summary, are you saying that Ece has a secret and she's not sharing it with us?"

"I think so!"

"What could it be?"

"I don't know, but whatever this secret is, I believe it's related to Ece's fears."

"What did she mean by the door to a room?" asked Ali Fuat, still looking at the drawing in his hand.

"We were just about to find out when... you know what happened," said Dr. Taner, referring to Ece running out of the room crying. Ali Fuat directed his sharp gaze at his daughter's drawings, searching for some 'thing.' He didn't even know what he was looking for. He was caught in a tremendous confusion. What secret could his five-year-old daughter know? "Doctor, what kind of 'secret' can a fiveyear-old child know?" he said, almost talking to himself. "Five years old is not an age to be underestimated, Mr. Ali. Remember, children's perception is open even when they are in the womb."

"Do you think her fear that her mother might be killed is related to this?"

Dr. Taner had been thinking about this point constantly. Yes, there was definitely a connection, but how?

They chatted for a while longer. Dr. Taner took out the note he had written under the heading 'Topics to be discussed with Mr. Ali' for today's session.

1) His sexual relationship with his wife

2) Serkan Cenet

He decided not to bring up the topic of sexuality now. He chose to talk about the mysterious neighbor Selin had mentioned before writing and then erasing.

"Mr. Ali, what kind of people are your neighbors? Are there any problematic ones?" he asked generally.

The moment he heard the word 'neighbors', Serkan Cenet's name popped into his mind. He didn't know how to respond.

"Good..." he said.

"Who lives there, what kind of people are they?" he repeated his question.

"I don't know much. But people with good financial status live there. It's an expensive neighborhood," said Ali Fuat. He wanted to close the topic as soon as possible.

"So, do you have any neighbors you don't like or have conflicts with?"

Serkan kept coming to his mind.

Dr. Taner noticed that Ali Fuat was getting uncomfortable with the topic of 'neighbors.' There might be something here. He decided to push further.

"If you have a neighbor you've argued with, your daughter might be affected by this," he said, renewing his question and subtly implying, "You have to answer for your daughter's health."

"We don't have conflicts with anyone."

"Is there a neighbor your family dislikes or hates? Do you discuss this at home, in front of your daughter?"

For a moment, he thought about telling everything to relieve himself, but he didn't have the courage. He had to answer the question. What was he going to say?

"There are people I don't like, of course, but I don't think this has anything to do with Ece... I mean..." he made a gesture with his hands indicating 'I don't know' or 'it's not related.' Dr. Taner clearly understood that Ali Fuat wanted to avoid the topic. Most likely, the person he was uncomfortable with was Serkan Cenet, whose name Selin had erased. Now it was time to bring up this name. He couldn't say, 'Your wife wrote this name down and then erased it.' The best approach was to use Ece.

"Mr. Ali, when I talked to Ece, she frequently mentioned someone named uncle Serkan." Dr. Taner saw Ali Fuat's face turn pale after he said this. Yes, there was something about this name. "Who is this Uncle Serkan? Is he someone your daughter likes or a family friend?" he asked, passing the ball to Ali Fuat.

"Yes, there is such a person," he said. He paused for a while. During this time, Dr. Taner felt that Ali Fuat was having an internal struggle. "But he is not a family friend," he said sharply.

"So, do you have a problem with this man?"

"No. I don't see him much; I don't like him." Dr. Taner thought, 'Well, that's interesting. No problem, but you don't like him. How does that work?"

"Doesn't Ece dislike this person? And your wife too, of course."

He was getting increasingly uncomfortable. He glanced at the door, waiting for the session to end.

"No," he answered. "I don't think Ece dislikes him. In fact, she might even like him; he buys her chocolates sometimes," he said.

Yes, this point was important for Dr. Taner. "And doesn't your wife dislike this person?" he asked, trying to delve deeper.

He expected an answer like, "Yes, she doesn't like him."

Maybe this man was a secret lover or a clingy pervert. He was bothering Selin, and Ece knew this, which is why she feared for her mother's life... All these possibilities hinged on the answer, "Yes, Selin doesn't like him either."

When he answered, "Selin and he get along fairly well," Dr. Taner's reasoning collapsed.

Selin and Ece had a fondness for Serkan Cenet, or at least they didn't hate him, but Ali Fuat didn't like this person. In light of all this, he tried to reanalyze the situation. Was there jealousy involved? Dr. Taner preferred to ask openly.

"So, while your wife and daughter have sympathy for this person, why don't you... Is it jealousy?"

It was a troubling question.

"Nothing important. A couple of chocolates he bought for my daughter or his polite conversations with my wife are not things to be jealous of," said Ali Fuat. Dr. Taner sensed that Ali Fuat was not being sincere.

"He's going to..." Ali Fuat started. He was going to say, "He's going to die soon," but he couldn't use the word 'die.'

"I mean, he has cancer. He's sick," he said. Dr. Taner understood that Ali Fuat meant to say, "He's going to die soon." Talking about a cancer patient as "going to die soon" was either typical for doctors who were used to delivering bad news or someone who really disliked the person. Since Ali Fuat was not a doctor, his current state of mind was shouting that he hated Serkan Cenet. It was necessary to delve into the reasons for this hatred, but Dr. Taner felt that Ali Fuat was becoming increasingly tense. He decided to end the session here and talk to Selin.

When he brought Selin into the room after sending Ali Fuat out, he had already gathered all the drawings from the table. Using the same tactic he had with Ali Fuat, he said, "Ece mentioned a name. It seems he's your neighbor," and asked about Serkan Cenet.

"He's just an ordinary neighbor," said Selin. She had started off just like Ali Fuat.

He needed to ask a well-structured question to prevent her from lying or hiding information.

"We talked at length with your daughter and Ali about this. They detailed your relationship with Serkan Cenet, but I'd like to hear it from you as well."

"Well, he's like the other neighbors," she said, pausing as if to think. "There's nothing special about him. And my husband has already mentioned..."

Clear lines had formed on her beautiful face. She was tense. Dr. Taner felt he was on the right track. Selin wanted to close the topic as quickly as possible, knowing she couldn't lie.

"Does your husband get jealous of Serkan Cenet?" he asked, probing deeper into the matter.

Selin was overly demoralized. She kept playing with her fingers and avoided looking at Dr. Taner.

"Yes, my husband is jealous of Serkan... Mr. Cenet." Her switch from "Serkan" to "Mr. Cenet" caught his attention.

"Mr. Cenet is a good person who cares about all the neighbors, helps them with their problems. He also cares about me and Ece within the boundaries of being neighbors," she said. She paused for a moment, gathering her words. "Mr. Serkan is truly a considerate and sensitive person. Everyone in the building likes him. My husband's jealousy is related to being a typical Anatolian man. Like most men, he doesn't believe that a man and a woman can just be friends."

"Could it be that everyone's affection for him is partly out of pity because he's sick?"

"What do you mean by sickness?" There was curiosity and concern on Selin's face. Dr. Taner couldn't make sense of this. Ali Fuat had said that Serkan Cenet had cancer. If it were true, how could Selin not know about it? Or how did Ali Fuat know?

"Didn't you know?"

"Know what?" Selin replied, her eyes alert.

"Your husband said that Serkan Cenet has cancer. I thought you knew too."

"I didn't know," she managed to say with difficulty. Her chin was trembling. The reaction she showed, or rather tried to hide, made Dr. Taner think.

Could there be an affair? There was another problem. If Serkan Cenet really had cancer, how did Ali Fuat know? If Serkan himself had told, why hadn't he told Selin? If he hadn't told, which seemed likely, then how did Ali Fuat find out? Dr. Taner had suspected from the beginning that Ali Fuat was not an ordinary person. This incident had increased his suspicions.

He felt he was close to the end. Thinking that Selin was getting worn out, he ended the session.

Ece's drawings and the Serkan Cenet case... Dr. Taner smiled. He took out his file and noted down the main topics and his thoughts from the session.

50

Djinn of Love

The love djinn was working to bring Ishtarel under its control. In his work, Davetname (Invocation), Uzun Firdevsi provided a lot of information, but he did not specify how many times a prayer should be recited or what should be written on the paper to be burned in the fire. That was the main issue.

Yasin was going to use his conjuring abilities for his own benefit for the first time.

Accompanied by the sounds of "Klak", "Klak", a new connection was discovered. He printed out the information sent to the computer. He applied the frame of 19. There was no problem. He wrote down the sentences he obtained. He began to check if they were related to each other.

Although he wasn't entirely sure, he thought he might have cracked the code. He took the papyrus he had written for Ishtarel. He filled its surroundings with the codes he had deciphered. He placed the paper directly on the Aramaic bowl in the floor setting. The pale-colored flame was flickering from below.

The color of the paper, shining like the sun, filled the room. The letters were slowly scattering. The lines, merging within themselves, began to gather at the point where the flame shone from below. A face was forming. He carefully watched the merging letters and the face forming.

Suddenly, he flinched and threw himself back. The face formed by thin lines had turned into a terrifying demon. It had a disgusting appearance with its eyes red with rage and pus flowing from them. Despite wearing his protective shirt and talisman, coming face to face with the demon made him shiver. The room was filled with intense heat and screams.

The paper on which the demon's face appeared was slowly burning. The weak flame of the bowl had finally managed to pierce through the paper and rise up. The screams were getting louder. A body with melting flesh was emerging from the burning paper, screaming. It wanted to escape the paper but couldn't get past the flames hanging down from the bowl. The demon was dying amidst screams.

Yasin closed his eyes; the sight had become unbearable. He waited for the paper to burn and the demon to die as soon as possible. The heat and the foul smell disappeared. The paper was completely burnt. The demon was dead.

He sighed deeply. So, the code he found wasn't Ishtarel's code. It was a demon placed by Uzun Firdevsi to destroy those trying to capture the djinn.

He stood up, careful not to hit his head. He felt that the moment to bring Ishtarel under his control was approaching. He took a tissue and wiped his face. His phone started ringing. From the melody, he understood that it was Imam Sait calling.

Even though his name didn't scare him as much as before, his heart still raced. "Why is he calling?" he thought. Had he sensed that he was trying to summon Ishtarel? No way... How could he sense it?

The phone was still ringing.

"Yes?"

"Peace be upon you, son."

"And upon you, Imam."

"Log on to the internet, let's talk, my child."

"Imam, I'm running scans on all four computers."

Yasin couldn't log on to the internet. All the power was being used for the program scanning the sacred books. The Imam understood that Yasin was working on something. He wanted to get information about the progress.

"Son, have you cracked the code, have you captured the Zamradun djinn?" He was very excited. A few days ago, he had called and asked for all efforts to be focused on the Zamradun djinn. This djinn was the strongest in its realm. Anyone who wanted to establish a state would surely succeed if they could bring Zamradun under their control.

Finding this secret had been the dream of all wizard scholars. It had been solved once in history. That was during the Crusaders' occupation of Jerusalem and the days that brought suffering to the Islamic world.

The wizard scholars who came together to summon the djinn and put it in the service of the rising commander, Saladin, achieved this.

Young Saladin, who established his state, became anxious when a wizard who envied his fame among the people said, "We made him." Fearing that he would lose all his prestige with the revelation of the truth, he had all the wizards who summoned Zamradun arrested in a midnight operation. The charge was "spying for the Pope and secretly converting to Christianity." The next day, they were tried in a military court and executed for "treason."

This incident had buried Zamradun's code in the depths of history forever, but a coded note left by one of the wizards had fallen into Uzun Firdevsi's hands, and only years later, the secret of that day had been uncovered.

The Imam believed they would reach the final point with Zamradun. Since Yasin didn't respond, he repeated his question:

"Did you solve the code, my child?"

'Yes, damn it, I did,' he thought to himself. As if only his work was important. Did you solve this, did you solve that?

'Is this a solution center, you bastard,' he wanted to say. He used to get angry with the Imam before, but he never thought of cursing him. He would immediately repent and blush to himself. Now he was getting really irritated. To brush him off, "Yes, Imam, I'm working on Zamradun, but I haven't solved it yet," he said.

Imam Sait was disappointed; for a moment, he had thought the code was cracked. "Alright, my child, continue with your work," he said.

After entrusting Yasin to Allah, he hung up the phone. Yasin was about to turn to his computer when the phone rang again with a different melody. It was Pelin calling.

"If you're not busy, why don't you come over?" she said. He actually had a lot of work, but this offer was hard to refuse.

Chapter

51

Bahar

As Bahar sipped her tea, she noticed that the boy in the back corner of the café was still staring at her. She looked at the time in frustration.

"Where are you, my love?" she muttered. Her eyes involuntarily drifted back to the table in the corner. The boy with thick eyebrows and a wide grin fixed his gaze on her as if he had been waiting for this moment.

"Ugh, what an ugly creep, he's lucky to have a girlfriend and yet he's staring at me!"

Bahar guessed that the girl with curly hair, sitting with her back to her, was the unibrow boy's girlfriend. She was most annoyed by these types. If you have a girlfriend, why don't you pay attention to her? What greed! What rudeness!

She had seen all kinds. There were the timid types who looked around as if they weren't interested, only to steal a glance at her in a split second; the mysterious types who, upon realizing a beautiful and lonely girl was nearby, would change their posture, stroke their goatees, and cast deep, philosophical looks around, often lighting a cigarette – probably social science students; the leering monkeys with silly grins; the boorish types who stared like they'd never seen a girl in their life; those who would focus on one point and mutter to themselves as if reciting poetry, trying to project an air of mysticism to impress her; the ones who unnecessarily fiddled with their latest model cell phones, glancing sideways to see if she was looking; and those who, when their eyes met hers, would smile as if they were the most serene, joy-filled person in the world, adopting an air of a wise man who had renounced worldly pleasures.

Erkan climbed directly to the second floor of the café without looking at the first. That's what they had agreed upon. He scanned the tables. He saw his girlfriend, her face glowing like moonlight in the dim atmosphere of the café. Bahar saw him too and smiled. As he approached the table, his weariness was evident in his tone,

"Did I keep you waiting, my love?" he asked. Bahar glanced at the unibrow boy at the back table before kissing Erkan on the lips and saying, "It's okay, my love."

Erkan carefully leaned his 1.5-meter-long rectangular case against the wall.

"Did you get a guitar, my love?" Bahar asked. Ercan had found a second-hand guitar and bought it after some tough bargaining.

"Yes, my dear, it's a good one and will bring in a nice profit. Do you want to see it?"

Their conversation continued about the guitar for a while. Eventually, the topic turned to 'Yasin and his djinn.' Erkan was uneasy. Bahar saw the topic as a bit of fun between friends and didn't see any danger.

"My love, something bad is going to happen. Don't mess with djinn and spirits. This kid scares me, is he a cultist, an agent, or what? Don't get so close to him, my love. Honestly, if I had known, I wouldn't have brought him to us."

"You're exaggerating, my love. We're just having fun among friends."

Erkan couldn't convince his girlfriend.

"Honey, why don't you want to understand?" Erkan was pleading. "These are dangerous things. Look at the guy's library, it's full of books on magic. The pentagram on the ceiling, the hanging chains with weird charms at the ends…" For a moment, he didn't know what to say. "Do you think it's normal? Is it normal for him to make fire appear on a tray?"

Bahar maintained her relaxed demeanor. "Yasin just has strong bioenergy, that's all. There are many examples of this in the world."

No…

No matter what he said, he couldn't convince her. Bahar kept saying 'No' and refused to believe. Erkan couldn't trust Yasin at all. It was as if there was a wolf hidden under the guise of a lamb.

"I wish that guy would take his exam and leave already..." he thought.

Chapter

52

Plans are Being Made

It had been over a week since Alp last left the mansion. He was bored out of his mind. His rapid start as the head of the education and finance group had practically come to an end. He couldn't focus on work. During their days spent at the mansion, Mr. Demirkaplan and Feyza had plenty of conversations. After long discussions, they settled on two plans.

Both plans had the same goal: to kill the Imam. However, they could have dangerous implications and severe consequences. They needed to think carefully. They had discussed it many times.

"Cihangir, it's best to inform the Pasha. You can transfer a large sum of money to his son's company, and they can handle this just like they did with Halit Nurullah."

"Money isn't an issue, Feyza. We can give it, but…"

"But what?"

"Well, Feyza, what I mean is, after all, this man isn't a hired killer. He's a high-ranking Pasha!"

"When he killed Halit, we purchased materials worth millions of dollars from his son's construction company at three to four times the market price. Isn't that essentially hiring a killer?"

"I don't know, Feyza, I'm confused. What if any businessman came along and offered the same amount, or even more, to get someone killed?"

"Cihangir, what's confusing you?"

"Pasha Vefik has been our enemy for years as the commander of the Black Shrouds. Although we didn't know him personally, he knew the Demirkaplan family. One day, he suddenly appeared before us and introduced himself as the commander of the Black Shrouds. Until that day, we knew of the Black Shrouds's existence but didn't know a single member. When did this man come forward and introduce himself?"

Cihangir looked at his wife.

"When we were implementing the softening policy and dismantling the militant structure of the community," Feyza answered.

"Yes. He said we needed to continue these policies. He even said he could help us. Of course, he didn't forget to mention that his son was involved in the construction business."

"..."

"So what did we do? We had Halit Nurullah killed to silence his strong opposition within the community and curb his growing power."

Feyza nodded in agreement.

"Perhaps both of us made a mistake. We only associated the Pasha's contact with us with money, overlooking an important point. When did he approach us?" Cihangir answered his own question, "When the community softened. So why not before? The Turkish intelligence had known for years that the Demirkaplan family managed the community. What changed?"

After swallowing, Cihangir continued.

"I think it's the policy of the Black Shrouds. They also want to neutralize radical religious elements. That's why they support my policy of aligning with the system."

Feyza couldn't understand what her husband was getting at. "We already know all this. We even explained it to Alp. Why are you repeating it?"

"Because we overlooked one point, Feyza."

"What point?"

"There have been many murders. Turkey is in chaos. Even the world media is closely following the developments. We've portrayed all these events as if they're related to us. The Black Shrouds believed this. If we now come out and say all the murders are being committed by a deviant sect trying to take over the community, the reputation of the Demirkaplan family would be in shambles."

"So..."

"So, we can't call the Pasha and tell him to kill Imam Sait. If we do, Pasha Vefik will think we've failed to cleanse the community of radical elements."

"But aren't we calling him because we can't manage it?"

"No, no. That's not what I mean. The point at which Pasha Vefik will think we've failed isn't that we can't kill Imam Sait."

"Then what is it?"

"Pasha Vefik will think we've failed in our mission to moderate the community. If he gets that idea, he might clean out the Demirkaplan family and hand the contract to another family."

Feyza tried to understand the logic her husband was presenting.

"Couldn't the guards find out that the chaos and murders are because we can't control the community?"

"I don't think so. If they thought it was related to us, they would have said something by now."

Turning the matter over to the Black Shrouds didn't seem very consistent. They began discussing Plan B.

Chapter

53

The History of the Black Shrouds

Aydin gathered all his courage. He furrowed his brows and began talking to himself. "Of course, one would want to learn about the structure of the institution they work for," "If you're going to tell, just tell already..." No... It wasn't working. Neither furrowing his brows, nor banging his fist on the table, nor talking to himself was helping him get motivated. He just couldn't muster the courage to speak to Ali Fuat. The commander's recent behavior had played a big part in this. He was irritable and sullen. He only spoke to Kenan Ferit and no one else.

Aydin stood up from his desk. He needed to speak up now. Waiting to be motivated was pointless. He started walking. With every step he took towards Ali Fuat's office, his heart pounded harder. He took a deep breath, knocked on the door, and entered when he heard the "Come in."

Ali Fuat was sitting hunched over, with his elbows on the desk. His daughter's drawings, the psychologist mentioning Serkan Cenet, Pasha Vefik's reprimand at the meeting; their inability to solve the murders, and the baffling incidents... His mind was cluttered with various thoughts, blending into a stifling mood.

Aydin explained the situation.

There was a long silence. Ali Fuat lit another cigarette; he had been smoking more lately. "We've forgotten we are the boy's guardian," he thought to himself. He could imagine how curious Aydin was.

"Let's talk, then."

Aydin felt relieved. He had prepared himself for a negative response.

"What have you learned so far? Tell me. I'll fill in the gaps."

Aydin shared everything he had learned about the guards since joining. He mentioned their efforts to prevent Sharia rule and their secrecy.

The commander listened patiently. Smiling, he said, "You've learned everything already!" The joke scared Aydin. "Is he not going to tell me?" he wondered.

Ali Fuat extinguished his cigarette. He opened the window to air out the room.

"Shall we drink something?" he asked.

"I won't drink, commander. But if you'd like, I'll prepare something for you."

"Make us some tea," he said. While Aydin prepared the tea, Ali Fuat organized his thoughts.

As he sipped his tea, he began speaking slowly and clearly.

"Let's start with the history." Ali Fuat began like a gust of wind blowing from the dark recesses of history.

"Our organization was founded in the 1920s under the name Black Shrouds." He took a deep breath and continued, "Black Shrouds was a Kuva-yi Milliye[35] gang founded in Giresun. At that time, they were engaged in guerrilla warfare against the occupations. The gang's leader was Topal Osman[36]." Ali Fuat paused. He directed his vacant gaze towards Aydin and asked, "Have you ever heard of Topal Osman?"

"Yes, commander."

"What do you know about Topal Osman?"

"He was a great Kuva-yi Milliye fighter, later commanded Mustafa Kemal Pasha's Guard Regiment, and was executed for a crime," Aydin listed what he knew about Topal Osman.

---

[35] Kuva-yi Milliye (National Forces) refers to the local resistance forces formed during the Turkish War of Independence (1919-1922). Emerged spontaneously in response to post-World War I occupations. Structure is irregular armed units composed of civilian volunteers.

[36] "Topal" is a Turkish word meaning "lame" or "crippled," and it's used as a nickname or descriptor.

"Yes. All of that is correct, no mistakes." Ali Fuat blew on his steaming tea and took a few more sips. Then he began speaking again, vaguely looking at Aydin, who was listening intently.

"Topal Osman participated in the Balkan Wars[37] and subsequently fought against the Greek gangs in the Black Sea, gaining significant experience and skill as a warrior. The brave men from Giresun under his command were both well-trained and courageous. Let me also mention that Topal Osman was an excellent intelligence officer. He undertook important roles within Teskilat-i Mahsusa[38] in various positions. He met Mustafa Kemal Pasha through Teskilat-I Mahsusa. Topal Osman and Pasha were very close and trusted each other completely. When M. Kemal Pasha needed a guard regiment while serving as the president of the assembly, he chose one of his most trusted comrades, Topal Osman, for the job. The Black Shrouds, brought from Giresun, started serving as Kemal Pasha's close guards."

Ali Fuat swallowed and continued after taking another sip of his tea.

"While Topal Osman was in Ankara, he used his intelligence experience to make numerous observations and realized that while the nation would be saved and cleansed of the enemy, the reforms that Pasha had secretly spoken to him about would never be implemented. This was because groups, especially Islamists and members of the Committee of Union and Progress, who saw the nation's liberation was near, were working frantically. Secret organizations were forming, and plans to seize power were being made. Everyone was waiting for the war to end, and it was the calm before the storm. Once the enemy was driven out of the country, there would be chaos."

He sipped his tea.

"Topal Osman, having made all these analyses, decided to form a secret society. The society, established under the name 'Black Shrouds,' took shape as a cell organization consisting of eight young men and Osman. From that day on, Black Shrouds began profiling all groups

---

[37] The Balkan Wars were two conflicts that took place in 1912-1913 in the Balkan Peninsula.

[38] Teskilat-i Mahsusa was a secret paramilitary intelligence organization of the Ottoman Empire. Founded in 1911 by the Committee of Union and Progress (CUP).

that could obstruct Mustafa Kemal Pasha's reforms. They encountered a significant problem early on. Mr. Ali Sukru, the Trabzon[39] deputy and leader of the second group in parliament, was conducting such harsh opposition during the country's most tumultuous period that it threatened parliamentary unity. Mr. Ali Sukru, operating entirely on Islamic principles and the caliphate axis, was increasing his power in parliament and was also involved in some activities outside of parliament, which were identified by Topal Osman's Black Shrouds. Topal Osman was caught in a great dilemma. He needed to stop him, but on the other hand, he faced the problem of his organization being exposed. Because they were still very new, they had not yet become a full-fledged intelligence organization. Think about it, Aydin; we are currently completely behind the scenes, right? No one knows us, no one knows who our commander is. Back then, Topal Osman had a problem with popularity. All of Ankara knew him as the commander of Mustafa Kemal Pasha's guard regiment."

Ali Fuat took the last sip from his cup and asked Aydin to refill it. He continued to talk while Aydin prepared the tea.

"Topal Osman discussed the situation with General Ismail Hakki, the commander of the Ankara army units. They decided that Ali Sukru needed to be dealt with, no matter the cost. A plan was made. Prisons were searched, and a man resembling Topal Osman was found. He was made to grow a mustache in the same way and dressed in the same clothes. This man was imprisoned at Topal Osman's farm. Several tall and robust young prisoners were placed alongside him, and a tunnel was dug from inside the farmhouse to the reeds 100 meters away after intense activity."

Ali Fuat observed the astonished expression on Aydin's face while he stirred his tea and took a sip.

---

[39] Trabzon is a significant city located on the northeastern coast of Turkey, bordering the Black Sea. Known for its rich history and cultural heritage, Trabzon has been an important port and trading center for millennia. Founded in the 8th century BCE, Trabzon has been ruled by various empires, including the Greeks, Romans, and Byzantines. It was also the capital of the Empire of Trebizond from 1204 to 1461.

"Once the tunnel was finished, they decided to implement the plan. Topal Osman invited Ali Sukru to his farm for coffee. Seeing no harm, Ali Sukru accepted the invitation from his fellow Black Sea countryman and was strangled while drinking his coffee. From that day on, the Black Shrouds gave death orders with the code 'have coffee.' Then they deliberately left the body in a field next to his house, even though they had the opportunity to bury him where no one would see."

"Why, commander?"

"We'll get to that," Ali Fuat said. After swallowing, he continued, "Ali Sukru's absence was felt within a few days. The second group deputies launched a verbal attack on the government and gave accusatory, harsh speeches from the parliament's rostrum. Everyone expressed the need to find Ali Sukru as soon as possible. Units under the command of General Ismail Hakki supposedly found Ali Sukru's body by coincidence and, after an investigation, claimed that he was killed by Topal Osman. General Ismail Hakki surrounded Topal Osman's farm, refusing to surrender. Of course, leaving the area with the reeds open."

Topal Osman and his men were fired upon, but they responded with such a fierce barrage, including machine guns, that the general's army couldn't even lift their heads from the trenches. The general ordered his soldiers to be very careful, explaining how dangerous the killers inside were. He commanded that anyone seen should be killed and that even their bodies should be shot to ensure they were dead. Naturally, the soldiers' fear intensified. Meanwhile, the Black Shrouds brought out the prisoners who resembled them and lined them up in front of the farmhouse's exterior door. Topal Osman lit a pre-prepared stove, causing smoke to rise from the chimney. Seeing the smoke, the general immediately ordered an assault. The prisoners, who had been kept in the basement for days and had lost their ability to comprehend what was happening, tried to make sense of the situation. Topal Osman handed each a dummy rifle and threw them out of the house. The prisoners, in their excitement to escape, ran quickly from the house. Seeing Topal Osman and his men running towards them from the door, the soldiers fired. The prisoners were killed on the spot by dozens of bullets. Topal Osman and his men escaped through the tunnel to the reeds. The general, witnessing the events before five hundred soldiers and dozens of officers, took the unrecognizable bodies and displayed them to the public. Of course, the soldiers, experiencing the excitement and fear of death, were convinced that those who came out of the farmhouse were Topal Osman and his men. Hence, the public did not suspect either."

Ali Fuat took another sip of his tea to soothe his throat.

"After that day, the Black Shrouds operated completely behind the scenes, becoming an organization known only to a few pashas, not even the highest-ranking officials of the state. The plan was executed so perfectly that there were grand laments for Topal Osman in Giresun. The entire city shed tears and couldn't accept that the heroic Kuva-yi Milliye fighter who had protected their honor against Greek gangs for years, Topal Osman, and the Black Shrouds had been killed by the state. Giresun elders still remember Topal Osman. They tell their children and grandchildren about his heroism. The plan was carried out so flawlessly that neither Topal Osman nor the eight Black Shrouds members ever revealed themselves. They never visited their tearful parents to say, 'We're actually alive.'

After that incident, the Black Shrouds cleaned out anyone who posed a threat to the regime. Former members of the Committee of Union and Progress who tried to form organizations to overthrow the regime were killed one by one. The Black Shrouds became increasingly professional over time. New young members were recruited from Giresun to replace those who had died or grown old.

As the Republic was established and reforms began, opposition to the regime reached its peak. The Black Shrouds took on a new identity: no longer just an elite force loyal to the state, but also a shadow organization dedicated to eradicating radical threats that exploited religion for political gain. They began targeting all identified members of religious sects and Sharia supporters who threatened the secular foundations of the young Republic. The Black Shrouds, true to their name, operated in the shadows, striking with precision and ruthlessness to protect the nation from internal threats, much like they had done against foreign invaders in their early days. The "black shroud" now symbolized their resolve to lift the veil of extremism and prevent any darkness from overtaking the country.

Naturally, the opposition also woke up. They started forming secret societies and sects, adopting covert operations. The public was incited. The underground activities of the opposition became untraceable after a while. During this period, the Menemen Incident, which unfolded, was also a significant source of tension for the organization. When the responsible parties were gathered and interrogated, the existence of a secret sect, tariqa, behind these activities was discovered. That is, the very community that threatens us today!

Aydin posed a question, "What happened to Topal Osman, Commander?"

"He fell ill with a severe disease in 1928 and unfortunately didn't recover."

"Who is aware of our existence now, Commander?"

"Yes, this is important. Firstly, as the head of the state, the President, then the Chief of General Staff, the force commanders, and naturally, the members of the Black Shrouds."

"Do the Prime Minister or ministers know?"

"No, they don't. As a principle, the Prime Minister is not informed because the Prime Minister's office is a political position; it exists today but may not tomorrow. We can't fully trust them. There was even a President who wasn't informed due to his conflict with the military. Of course, it's not a rule that no Prime Minister knows about the Black Shrouds."

"How do we make this distinction, Commander?"

"Over time, you will develop an intuition about this. The important thing to remember is that we are a military organization. This country was founded by soldiers. Soldiers have always ensured peace, tranquility, and order. The country has often been turned into a battleground by politicians. The most honest institution is the military. Politicians can't be trusted."

"Commander, is the group responsible for the Menemen incident the same as the community we are currently tracking?"

"Yes, it dates back to the political formation responsible for the 31 March Incident. After the 31 March Incident was suppressed by the Committee of Union and Progress, they withdrew for a while. The foundation of the community was laid by the Demirkaplan Family.

Many members of the family held significant positions during the reign of Sultan Abdulhamid II. They are a wealthy and influential family. They advocate Pan-Islamism, which was Sultan Abdulhamid's official policy. When the Committee of Union and Progress took power, strong families like the Demirkaplan Family were marginalized. These families, wanting to restore Sharia and regain their former political influence, incited the public to a major rebellion. After the Action Army suppressed the rebellion, the Union and Progress Retribution Brigades began eliminating the leaders of the rebellion one by one. Faced with this wave of violence, the Sharia supporters retreated into their shells. The seeds of the community were sown during this period. The Demirkaplan Family, engaged in trade, saw that openly fighting the Union and Progress was difficult and dangerous, so they decided to form a secret community, much like the Union and Progress."

Ali Fuat paused and took a sip of his nearly finished tea. The tea had grown cold. He placed the cup on the edge of the table, declining Aydin's offer to refill it with a hand gesture.

"The community expanded discreetly, recruiting people in high positions. After World War I, when the Union and Progress cadres left the country, the community intensified its efforts to seize power. However, this time they faced pro-British state officials. The most prominent among them was Damat Ferit Pasha. Damat Ferit Pasha envisioned a pro-British liberal government, aligned with Prince Sabahattin's views. Thus, he opposed the community's proposal to establish an Islamic model. Essentially, two treacherous groups clashed. The Union and Progress adopted a very harsh policy against those who did not accept their political dominance, especially those wanting to establish a Sharia regime. They conducted systematic purges. Leading figures were eliminated through various assassinations.

Damat Ferit Pasha's efforts to block them were weak because he didn't have a strong cadre or execution squads supporting him. His only power was his ability to command the state apparatus as the Grand Vizier, which wasn't very significant. The state authority was on the verge of collapse. No one was listening to the central government. The community saw there was no longer a threatening environment like before. They decided to bring their secret activities into the open

212

and established the Teali Islam Society. You must have read about the activities of the Teali Islam Society in history books. They organized many rebellions. The Grand National Assembly was weakened against the enemy because it had to deal with these uprisings. After the rebellions, which were suppressed with great difficulty, severe measures were taken against the Teali Islam Society. Many of its prominent members either fled the country or were killed.

Of course, these measures were not enough to stop the Sharia movement. There was a need for a dynamic organization to watch them at all times and to conduct operations when necessary. The establishment of the Black Shrouds, as I mentioned earlier, coincides with those days. The social structure at that time was not very promising. Apart from a handful of intellectuals, the majority favored fanaticism. It was such a delicate situation that a small spark could destroy the Republic and replace it with a Sharia state. The purpose of the two institutions was revealed here. The community tried to ignite that spark with all its might, while the Black Shrouds tried to prevent it."

"Commander, does the community still have power that could be considered a threat?"

"They are very strong economically. They have hundreds of thousands of sympathizers. But they can't take action. They operate like an ordinary holding company."

"Why, Commander?"

"The community was established to bring back the caliphate. They worked towards this goal until February 28. Now they have no activities; I don't understand what they are planning."

"Could the recent murders be related to this inactivity?"

"I don't know, I haven't thought about it." Aydin's casual question started to gnaw at Ali Fuat's mind.

54

Psychologist Investigating

Dr. Taner looked at the address in his hand once more while waiting at a red light in his black Jaguar. As the light turned yellow, the car in front of him sped off like an arrow. Dr. Taner slowly lifted his foot off the brake and gently pressed the gas pedal.

He was nearing the end of Ece's case file. The upcoming meeting could be the final piece of the puzzle. Elements that seemed unrelated were actually small parts of a larger whole. Ece's drawings had a unifying effect, especially her interpretation of "the eyes behind the door" as the door to the room, which clarified many points.

The love between Selin and Ali Fuat, the sexual issues he suspected between them, the name Serkan Cenet, which was written and then erased, Ali Fuat's dark personality... All these key points passed through his mind. He had almost created the whole scenario. The only mystery that remained was the nature of the sexual issues between Selin and Ali Fuat.

Due to Ali Fuat's knowledge of interrogation techniques, he had decided to investigate the sexual problem using a different method. He used his friendship with the President of the Istanbul Medical Association to send an email to all urologists, asking if there was any record for a patient named Ali Fuat Sezgin. He received a positive response from a private medical center.

Leaving his car running, he handed the keys to the parking attendant, who eagerly sat in the driver's seat of the brand-new Jaguar.

Dr. Taner took a brief look at his car before asking the parking lot's mustachioed manager for directions to the urologist's office. The elderly manager, with a pleasant accent, provided detailed instructions, "Well, father, after entering the building, take the elevator to the 4th floor. You'll see the sign, there's a big doorbell, press it, and the nurse will open the door." Dr. Taner smiled as he started walking. He thought about people who took such ordinary questions seriously and answered them with great effort.

The old manager seemed to exude a sense of satisfaction, as if he had been there before and found a solution to his problem. 'You should go too,' he seemed to be saying. 'If you press the bell, the nurse will open the door,' positioning the establishment as a place where problems were solved and those who came found healing. Since he had been treated, anyone who went would have the doors open for them and receive treatment. Dr. Taner thought that his assessment was 95% correct. He even decided to test the manager on his way back.

After reaching the fourth floor, he informed the receptionist that he had an appointment with Urologist Dr. Tolga. Dr. Tolga was expecting him. Dr. Taner talked about young Ece's fears and explained that to solve these issues, it was necessary to uncover the family's psychological state. He mentioned that he needed medical information about Ali Fuat Sezgin, as the individual in question had been reluctant to provide it.

"Under normal circumstances, I wouldn't disclose any patient's information, but considering the request from the President, we can make an exception. However, I also have a request."

"Of course, I'm listening."

"If you need a report, I ask that the information be officially requested by the Medical Association. If only verbal information is sufficient, I can provide it without any official procedures, as long as you forget you got this information from me. The choice is yours."

The urologist didn't want to fall out of favor with the Medical Association, but also didn't want to engage in conduct that could be legally proven to be unlawful.

"Just tell me what Ali Fuat's issue is. I don't need a report. No one will know I got this information from you. Please, don't worry."

Dr. Tolga accessed the archives on his computer and verbally relayed the medical results related to Ali Fuat.

The scenario was now complete. A small penis, premature ejaculation, and an obsessive concern about it... He had solved one of the most interesting cases of his career. Now, he had to sit down and talk with Ali Fuat. It would be a difficult and possibly harsh conversation, but it was necessary.

When he returned to the parking lot, the attendant ran to the Jaguar as soon as he got the keys. While waiting for his car, Dr. Taner went to the manager to pay and, with a smile, said, "This psychologist is very talented!" The message reached the mustachioed manager, who grinned and, looking around to ensure only Dr. Taner could hear, said, "He really made me feel young again." He laughed heartily.

Dr. Taner smiled as he got into his car and tipped the attendant.

Chapter

55

Bomb

The truck, along with the car in front of it, entered Husrevaga neighborhood. Both vehicles, under suspicious gazes, turned onto the street where Imam Sait's house was located.

After the morning prayer, Imam Sait had retreated to a well-lit corner of the basement's large hall, poring over his books. The first light of the day made the ink on the yellowed papers glisten. His mind was on Yasin. Had he managed to decipher the codes and create the prayer?

The car, which was moving slowly through the narrow street where all the houses looked alike, finally came to a stop. The freckle-faced man in the driver's seat said, "I think this is the house." The chubby man sitting next to him did a quick calculation in his head.

"'Think' won't do; we need to be sure."

The freckle-faced man, unable to control his nerves due to the tense moments he was experiencing, snapped, "How can 'think' not do? We'll just go in and ask, 'Does the Imam live here?'" The chubby man, not wanting to escalate the situation, kept silent.

Imam Sait lit the wick in the vessel. A weak, colorless flame rose from the Aramaic bowl covered with various symbols. Before him were an open Quran and a book by an ancient scholar. He took his prayer beads and began reciting the first prayer for the mental exercise he tried to do every morning. Suddenly, the large hall filled with an intense heat wave. After finishing the prayer, he blew into the bowl about a meter and a half in front of him. The lifeless flame suddenly grew wild and rose toward the ceiling. A scream, reminiscent of death, filled the space. He moved the beads and recited another prayer, blowing into the bowl again, but the feeble flame did not change. Realizing he had made an error in the prayer, he opened the special notebook containing the codes Yasin had deciphered. Flipping through the pages, he found the prayer he had just recited. Indeed, he had made a mistake in the final part. Correcting the mistake, he recited the prayer again. Upon blowing, the spirit freed by the prayer was consumed by flames. The fire shot up to the ceiling.

The occupants of the car continued to scrutinize the house in front of them, trying to determine if it matched the description. Suspicious eyes behind the curtains had been watching the two stationary vehicles for a few minutes. The number of peeking curtains increased as members of the community signaled each other by ringing their phones. A hidden wave of anger began to ripple through the street.

As the men in the car couldn't decide what to do, they began to worry the men in the truck as well.

"What are they waiting for?"

The truck driver dialed the freckle-faced man's number. "Should we activate the mechanism? A couple of curtains have moved. We need to hurry."

The freckle-faced man was indecisive. The houses all looked very similar. None of them had numbers. The colors were almost identical. Based on the wall and the number of floors described, this had to be Imam Sait's house. There was no point in waiting any longer. "Activate the mechanism," he said. The driver and his companion, who had started the countdown, got out of the truck and began walking towards the car in front. The two personnel from the truck had only taken a few steps when the iron gates of the surrounding houses opened. Young men, who all looked very similar, began to emerge. They were wearing long white nightgowns. Many wore prayer caps. They were carrying various weapons—cleavers, big knives, Kalashnikovs, pistols, clubs. Whatever they had grabbed in the moment. The narrow street suddenly filled with over forty people. The men who had gotten out of the truck and the two in the car were at a loss for what to do. Everything had happened so quickly that within ten seconds, they were surrounded. No matter which way they turned, there was a young man in white. A man with a graying beard stepped forward, his face a mixture of anger and impatience, and barked, "Who are you?" The words spat like venom. The countdown in the truck continued.

"What are you doing, standing in the middle of the street?"

"Car... broke..." they stammered. Despite their professionalism, the cold face of death hindered their ability to think clearly. Ignoring the responses, the leader sharply moved his head. Chaos ensued. The two men who reached for their weapons were quickly subdued by blows to their heads and shoulders from hatchets and cleavers. The men in the car, facing pistols and Kalashnikovs, helplessly got out. Their hands were tied and they were dragged into a building. The leader ordered the two men, whose heads had been bashed open, staining the street with their blood, to be taken to the basement as well. He also ordered a group of disciples to search the vehicles.

The two men taken from the car were seated and bound to chairs in the basement. Their weapons had been confiscated. Seeing the weapons, the bearded leader grew even more furious. "Who are these for, you infidel dogs?" He was so enraged that he couldn't string words together coherently. "Who are they for, huh? Who are these weapons for?" Suddenly struck by a thought, he became even more enraged. This time, his anger was different, each beard hair turning into a spear. In a low voice, he said, "Did you come here to harm the blessed life of Imam Sait?" He ordered one of the young disciples to bring a screwdriver. It was brought within seconds.

"You filthy infidels!"

The two men remained silent, on the verge of death from fear. The people before them seemed like psychopaths straight out of a movie. They had brutally killed their two friends without so much as a word.

"I asked you if you came here to kill Imam Sait," the leader said, turning to the chubby man. "Who are you?"

The chubby man couldn't speak. The leader moved behind the chair and tightly grabbed the chubby man's neck with his arm. He began pushing the screwdriver into his right ear. The chubby man's screams echoed throughout the building as the screwdriver tore through the inner ear, causing blood to gush out. The chair shook violently as the chubby man's eyes bulged in pain, and despite being tightly held, his head thrashed from side to side. The leader, unable to control him, removed the screwdriver. Half of the metal was covered in blood. The leader held his nose, the light blow making his eyes water.

"Gag him."

The disciples stuffed cloth pieces into the chubby man's mouth. Now his screams came out as muffled groans.

"Why did you come here, whose men are you?"

The freckle-faced man, his jaw trembling, tried to speak but could only manage a few words. "Ci... ci... ci... Cihangir... Cihangir Demirkaplan," he stammered.

The name froze his blood. He immediately ordered one of the disciples to inform Imam Sait of the situation. He thought about striking the freckle-faced man with the cleaver but restrained himself. "Imam Sait might want to interrogate this infidel," he thought. Overcome with rage, he slapped the man hard. Unsatisfied, he hit him again.

The freckle-faced man thought he was going to be killed. There was no way out. In a few moments, they would take his life. He was making a desperate attempt to wish for the opposite. As if by saying it, the opposite would come true, and he wouldn't be killed. But... the thought that came to his mind... "Damn it!" he said. They had activated the mechanism. Nothing could save him now.

Unaware of what was happening, Imam Sait continued reciting prayers. He began reciting a prayer to summon another of the spirits under his control. The room's temperature rose once more. With the final words of the prayer, the heat became unbearable. The breath he exhaled into the bowl mingled with the flame.

The disciple hurried past the two cars parked in the middle of the street. After passing twelve or thirteen houses, he began knocking on an iron gate. Knock knock...

The 'bip bip bip bip' from the car's alarm joined the knocking. 'Knock knock knock' and 'bip bip' sounds mingled together. The knocking became faster as the young disciple grew impatient. The 'bip bip' sounds also sped up.

The door opened.

"Bip!"

"Yes, my child."

"Bip!"

"Biiiiip!"

Chapter

56

The Men Are Not Returning

It was a moment of horror. A scene where even birds hesitated to land. Everything had been leveled, as if an atomic bomb had been dropped. Like a mischievous child knocking down sandcastles on the beach, everything was obliterated in one fell swoop. The rising wave of fire, accompanied by a long beep, had scorched even the white clouds in the sky, painting them an ashy hue. The sound waves spreading across the flat plains had awakened the entire city of Konya.

The first local reporter on the scene remarked, "There's a strong smell of ammonia everywhere," bringing Al-Qaeda to mind. Speculations followed. Although national channels did not rush to the scene to inhale the ammonia scent themselves, they followed the local reporter's lead and embraced the ammonia narrative. The international media also reported with headlines like "The city of Rumi, Konya, engulfed in a strong smell of ammonia." They discussed how gasoline poured on fertilizer and compressed ammonia could achieve high destructive power, emphasizing that this method was frequently used by Al-Qaeda.

The ammonia smell narrative ended when bomb experts from the police department examined the scene and declared the bomb was TNT. The origin of the mysterious ammonia smell remained unknown, but ammonia is not used in TNT explosives.

Civil defense teams and various special search and rescue units were at the scene. Burnt bodies were being extracted, and the injured were rushed to hospitals. The attack was perceived as radical Islamic terrorism. While the world offered condolences to the Republic of Turkey, it condemned terrorism.

The Demirkaplan family was following the developments from their mansion. They were quite satisfied with the results; a weight had been lifted off their shoulders. They paid close attention to the names of the dead and injured on television, looking for the name Sait Nurani.

The head of security grew suspicious. His four men had not returned yet. They were supposed to activate the mechanism and return by car. Had something gone wrong? Had they been caught? Or had they been unable to escape and perished as well? If he had to choose, he preferred them to be dead. Dead men couldn't talk.

Mrs. Demirkaplan and Mr. Demirkaplan were pleased with the comments on television. Assigning the blame to Al-Qaeda mitigated any potentially severe repercussions for the community. Writers who acted as the community's mouthpieces had been briefed before the operation, each handsomely paid off. The Al-Qaeda paranoia prevented people from thinking differently. Even without any evidence, suggesting that the bomb wasn't set off by Al-Qaeda seemed almost unscientific.

"Do you think they might suspect us?" asked Alp.

"There have been some very strange murders. Maybe they'll consider this bomb as one of them," said Mr. Demirkaplan.

"What kind of problem would it be if they suspected us?"

"The Black Shrouds would take very harsh measures. They would eliminate the Demirkaplan family and find another family to manage the community more smoothly," replied Mrs. Demirkaplan, answering her son's question.

Alp couldn't fully grasp this part of the issue.

"Did they bring our family to the head of the community, and now they can bring someone else?"

"Of course, they didn't bring us, but times have changed."

As they conversed, their eyes remained on the list of the dead and injured. More names were being added every moment. The name they were waiting for still hadn't appeared.

Chapter

57

Pasha Vefik

The General sat in the back seat of his official vehicle, deep in thought as he made his way to headquarters. This bomb was the last straw. He didn't believe the nonsense about Al-Qaeda on TV. The final act of the power struggle within the community was playing out. He could no longer allow Turkey to be turned into a battleground.

The melody from his cell phone, signaling a call from the highest levels of the state, interrupted his thoughts. The massacre of the 12 and the recent Konya incident had infuriated the powers that be. With a stern tone, they demanded to know what was going on. "Why haven't you identified the responsible parties? What's with the recent incompetence of the Black Shrouds?"

For Pasha Vefik, it was a deeply frustrating call.

Upon arriving at headquarters, he hurried to his office. He took off his hat, placed his elbows on the desk, and rubbed his temples with his thumbs. The day had started with an overwhelming amount of stress. It was time to call Cihangir Demirkaplan. He dialed the number.

Mr. Demirkaplan saw that the caller ID read 'Pasha'. Realizing he had no choice, he answered, "Yes, Pasha?"

Pasha didn't bother with pleasantries and launched into a long speech, using indirect threats. Mr. Demirkaplan listened patiently.

"We had nothing to do with it, Pasha. We don't know who did it. According to our intelligence, there was a conflict between the Turkish branch of Al-Qaeda and a radical sect in the area where the bomb exploded!"

"Which radical sect?" Pasha Vefik asked.

"We're not sure, but it could be remnants of Halit Nurullah's group."

"That's impossible, Mr. Demirkaplan! Al-Qaeda's presence in Turkey is very weak. We have them all under surveillance. They are still in their formation stage and would not engage in such a conflict with any sect. Something else is going on here, and you're not telling me. Remember, there was no dialogue between the community and the guards for 80 years, and many people died. For the past five years, we've acted wisely, and everyone has benefited. Burning bridges now won't help either of us. But if I must, I will, and I'll start with you."

"Let's keep the bridges intact, General. We'll still have a lot of back-and-forth over those bridges, to secure a bright future for your son and to hand over a smoothly running community to my son. General, I understand you very well. These are the most critical hours. Maybe our leaders are urging you to swiftly eliminate the culprits. If absolutely necessary, I can have a four or five-man team prepared and set up a house to look like an Al-Qaeda cell. I can plant some broadcasts and materials—these were already prepared anyway—and you can capture them with official forces so that the public and our leaders are reassured that the culprits have been found."

"Did you set off that bomb?"

"No, General. But believe me, whoever did it, though it has put you in a difficult position for now, has done something that will ease things in the future. Those who died there were the most radical group in Turkey."

"Mr. Demirkaplan, I reached out to you because I believe that mass killings will not solve this issue. I don't care about the benefit that bomb might bring. If I needed such a thing, I would have done it myself. I believe this came from your side. You made a huge mistake."

Mr. Demirkaplan realized the conversation was heading in a dangerous direction. He jumped in to calm the Pasha.

"Please, Pasha. Believe me, we both want the same thing! We can resolve this issue. Trust me, we've removed the last thorn from the rose garden. What remains is a Turkey free from problematic Islamic structures. Please, Pasha, don't burn the bridges. That bomb toppled the sect that has recently bathed Turkey in blood. The 12 murders and all the previous ones were the work of this sect, General. Their goal was to take over the community and use its vast resources to control Turkey. The two people leading this group were, as I previously informed you, Hadji Halit Nurullah. When he died, I thought the group would disband, but Sait Nurani turned out to be even worse. But now it's all over. We tried to resolve this in different ways but failed. Instead, he took a step closer each day to taking over the community. The knife had reached the bone, Pasha."

"If there were such major disturbances, why didn't you inform me? Had you done so in time, things wouldn't have escalated to this point."

"You're right, but there were no indications that things would escalate to this extent. I still can't comprehend many aspects of what's happening. The strange circumstances of Faruk and Osman's murders, the peculiarities of the 12 murders, I still haven't figured them out."

"How do you know about the peculiarities of the murders?"

"Come on, Pasha, you know we have ways to find out," said Mr. Demirkaplan, unable to directly state, 'We have a lot of men in the police force.' After all, he was talking to the commander of the group aiming to neutralize his own group.

Pasha Vefik understood the implication.

"That bomb has put me in a very difficult position, Mr. Demirkaplan. If you had problems you couldn't solve, we could have dealt with them together."

"You're right, General, but you have to understand my position. We didn't have this level of dialogue between us. When I told you about Halit Nurullah, I had to twist my words, struggle immensely. I managed to tell you with great difficulty. You also pretended not to hear."

"Yes, I remember."

"So, why did we behave that way, General? Because the groups we lead had been at each other's throats for years. After all that enmity, we had a forced marriage, but we couldn't quickly move to a more intimate level. Look, have we ever had such an advanced conversation before now?"

"No."

"But the extraordinary morning we're experiencing has pushed us to this level of discussion."

"You have valid points."

Mr. Demirkaplan relaxed a little. His entire body was drenched in sweat.

"Pasha, I sent some of our tight-lipped men to a prepared safe house. They're aware of the situation. I'll give you the address, you can capture them, and the world will see that the perpetrators have been caught. My men will testify that they are Al-Qaeda members. Believe me, peaceful days are ahead of us."

Pasha Vefik felt an urge to grab a big stick and crack Mr. Demirkaplan's head. However, he decided to act calmly. After discussing the details, he ended the call.

Mr. Demirkaplan signaled the household, who were watching with curiosity, to wait. He wanted to shake off the stress of the conversation. He handed the phone to the head of security and leaned back. Closing his eyes, he took deep breaths. The household grew more curious. He opened his eyes for a moment and sat up. Just as they thought he was about to start explaining, he asked, "Has Sait Nurani's name come up yet?"

"No, sir," the head of security replied.

Pasha Vefik paced back and forth in his spacious office, randomly flipping through books on the bookshelf. He pulled back the curtain and looked outside, fidgeting with various objects. He pondered deeply. Had he been making mistakes from the very beginning? The bomb had been planted by the community. The reason was internal strife, as he had suspected. Was this bomb truly aimed at the opposition? Or was the Demirkaplan family playing a game? He couldn't decide.

If there was a scheme involved, he would kill Cihangir Demirkaplan with his own hands. He looked at the address written on the small piece of paper. Could the entire process he was living through be a conspiracy? Now, it seemed to be concluding with the capture of these individuals. He felt increasingly suffocated. There seemed to be no other choice but to implement Mr. Demirkaplan's plan.

He called for an urgent meeting of the Black Shrouds.

Pasha Vefik entered the meeting swiftly. He handed the address to the intelligence unit and instructed them to immediately forward it to the Istanbul Police Department. He wanted the arrest to be conducted by official authorities and the incident to be reported in the media.

The guards passed the specified address to the police. Five militants were arrested on charges of being Al-Qaeda members and detonating the bomb in Konya. The suspects confessed to their crimes during interrogation.

The capture of the perpetrators brought some relief to the public. The Prime Minister, standing before the cameras, thanked the police. "We are examining the incidents from every angle. Whoever is behind this will face the strongest response from the Turkish nation," he said, appealing to national pride.

The arrests once again interrupted the media's programming. Commentators appeared on various channels, boasting about how accurate their assessments on Al-Qaeda had been.

Mr. Demirkaplan was also pleased with the execution of his plan. The capture of the supposed culprits saved his family from serious danger.

Pasha Vefik, too, felt a sense of relief. The fabricated scheme he was a part of was progressing smoothly. He needed calm days ahead. He thought about taking radical decisions concerning the community and the Demirkaplan family.

The only one not feeling at ease was Ali Fuat. It was peculiar that the intelligence unit directly under his command had no information, yet the General suddenly provided the names and addresses of the culprits. Were those apprehended truly guilty? If so, how did the General know? Something was happening, but what?

Chapter

58

The Psychologist's Office

Dr. Taner had taken a prominent place in his professional life. It was the most complex, challenging, and exciting case he had ever worked on, involving Ali Fuat, Selin, and Ece, like a puzzle. Of course, let's not forget Serkan Cenet. His name was like the end of a thread. Once he started pulling it, the rest unraveled like a ball of yarn.

It wouldn't be easy to explain everything to Ali Fuat, but it had to be done. He would be devastated, hurt, and possibly angry, but the truth had to come out, no matter how painful. It would also provide the necessary environment for Ece's treatment.

As Dr. Taner waited in his office, Ali Fuat was driving with Zekeriya, Aydin and Kenan Ferit. They had just picked up the interrogation records of the bombers from the Police Department. They wanted to interrogate them personally, but Pasha Vefik had given strict orders. "The Black Shrouds will not interfere; official authorities will handle this," he had said.

Dealing with family issues amid all this tension had further strained Ali Fuat. He considered telling Dr. Taner that he was not available today, but when would he ever be available? With the recent events, his sense of time and place had become completely disoriented. "Okay," he said. After leaving the police station, he decided to stop by for half an hour before returning to headquarters.

When they left the car in the parking lot, Kenan Ferit said, "We'll wait here." He was aware of Ali Fuat's personal issues and thought he might feel uncomfortable with them around.

"Come on, you can have some tea."

They all went up to Dr. Taner's office. After a short wait, Dr. Taner, dressed in a black suit, arrived. After greeting everyone, he went into his office with Ali Fuat.

"How are you, Mr. Ali?"

"Not great."

"We've finally developed a theory regarding your daughter's condition."

Their conversation was interrupted by the phone ringing. He had repeatedly instructed his secretary not to forward calls unless it was extremely important. Annoyed, he picked up the receiver. "Yes," he said, and his face immediately changed.

"Tell them I'm in a meeting right now, have them come later, or make an appointment!"

He was anxious. He debated whether to call the police. He hadn't expected them to show up at his office.

Ali Fuat noticed Dr. Taner's distress. "What's wrong, doctor? Bad news?" Dr. Taner, contemplating whether to call the police, decided to briefly explain the situation to Ali Fuat.

"I have a large property in Pendik. Some mafia-type guys are pressuring me to sell it for much less than it's worth," he summarized. Dealing with the mafia was not his forte.

"Who are these people? Let's see them," Ali Fuat suggested.

"Let's not get sidetracked. I already told the secretary that I didn't want to see them."

Dr. Taner wanted to stay focused, but the visitors had no intention of waiting. After all, they were men of Erzurumlu Kemikci Cemal, who could dare tell them to wait? The secretary couldn't even say, "The doctor is not available right now," before they barged in.

Dr. Taner looked at them with fearful eyes, but Ali Fuat remained calm and composed. The two thugs in striped suits and no ties didn't faze him at all.

"Who do you think you are making wait?" one of the thugs barked.

Before he could finish, the door was flung open again. Zekeriya burst in with a pump-action shotgun, followed by Kenan Ferit and Aydin with their pistols drawn. Seeing the thugs arguing with the secretary and heading toward Ali Fuat's office, they had immediately thought their commander might be in danger and acted quickly.

The thugs, who had been shouting moments before, deflated at the sight of the weapons. Their bravado was replaced with fear and surprise. Their 'Brother Cemal' had never mentioned such a scenario. He had described Dr. Taner as a wealthy and mild-mannered man. Where did these armed men come from?

Kenan Ferit, with a quick glance, checked that Ali Fuat was unharmed and focused back on the two thugs. "Is there a problem, or did we misunderstand, Commander?" he asked, ready to fire if necessary.

"We don't know yet, Kenan. These boys haven't explained themselves."

Ali Fuat took out a cigarette and lit it. "Well, go on, tell us what you want," he said, turning his swivel chair to face them and crossing his legs. He blew a large cloud of smoke in their direction, his mocking smile combined with his bulging eyes creating a menacing effect.

One of the thugs, summoning his courage, asked, "Who are you?" He was scared, but after all, they were Erzurumlu Kemikci Cemal's men. He thought of this and tried to find courage. His tone was the first act of the last struggles of his bravado.

Ali Fuat, blowing out smoke, greeted the question with a smile. "Do you not know the people whose office you've barged into?"

One of the thugs said proudly, "We're Kemikci Cemal's men." His voice was filled with confidence.

"What does this Kemikci Cemal do? Does he sell meat?"

The thug puffed out his chest and replied, "He breaks bones."

"Oh, so he breaks bones…"

He drew his gun. "Handcuff them, and if anyone talks too much, gag them," he ordered.

Aydin immediately obeyed the command. He stripped the talkative thug and gagged him with his own shirt. Then, he handcuffed both of them with their hands behind their backs. Meanwhile, Ali Fuat was busy attaching a silencer to his gun.

"So he breaks bones, huh?" he muttered to himself. He aimed at the thug's kneecap and pulled the trigger. The muffled 'thwip' sound was followed by the bullet shattering the thug's kneecap.

Choosing the kneecap was intentional because it was the most painful spot on the body. The thug writhed in pain, and his muffled screams filled the room. He couldn't gather himself and started choking on the shirt gagging him. Kenan Ferit held him and turned him face down, carefully pulling the shirt to free his breathing while avoiding being bitten. To reduce blood loss, he tied a belt around the thug's leg, tightened it to the maximum, and cut a hole in the belt with his knife, securing the buckle.

The other thug, now drenched in sweat, couldn't speak. His eyes darted around the room, looking for where the next bullet might come from.

Ali Fuat stood up and walked over to the trembling thug. "Do you have a car?"

The mafia member, seeing his friend's shattered knee and fearing he might experience the same, looked at Ali Fuat's gun with terror.

"Do you have a car?" Ali Fuat shouted, growing impatient.

The thug couldn't take his eyes off the gun, his mind swinging back and forth between the gun in Ali Fuat's right hand and his friend's mangled knee.

A sharp slap echoed through the room. The thug, snapping back to reality, managed to say, "Yes, we have a car, sir."

After a brief pause, Ali Fuat continued, "First, tell us where we can find this 'Kemikci' or whatever that scumbag calls himself, and then take this piece of trash to the hospital."

The thug, understanding the situation perfectly, quickly betrayed his boss. Ali Fuat called the central office, providing the address and identity of Cemal Inceefe, aka Erzurumlu Kemikci Cemal, and ordered his immediate arrest and transfer to a safe house for a good beating. After hanging up, he turned to Dr. Taner with a smile.

"Let our guys rough him up a bit. Then I'll go in and add the finishing touches. After that, he won't even dream of bothering you again," he said.

Just as they were about to take the injured thug and the other one outside, Ali Fuat called out to Zekeriya, "This kid seems quite talented. He can drive with one hand."

Zekeriya's cold eyes fixed on the thug. He grabbed him and began breaking his fingers one by one.

Dr. Taner couldn't believe what was happening. Ali Fuat had coldly shattered a man's kneecap and ordered the illegal arrest of another without bothering to hear the other side. He was as calm as a carpenter hammering nails when he drew his gun and fired. He belonged to an organization capable of kidnapping and torturing people. Dr. Taner's brief observations led him to deep thoughts, concocting countless intricate scenarios, all ending in blood, murder, and massacre. He didn't know what to do. The Ece Sezgin case had been solved, and he needed to tell the father, but Ali Fuat's recent actions indicated how he might react to the news about his daughter.

Ali Fuat noticed the psychologist's shock and thought, "Probably the first time he's seen someone get shot." People often said things like "I'll shoot, I'll cut, I'll break, I'll destroy," but actually doing it or even watching it happen was a different story altogether.

"Aydin, clean up the place!" he ordered.

"Yes, Commander," Aydin responded.

Turning to Dr. Taner standing behind his desk, Ali Fuat said, "Doc, let the boys clean up here, and then we can continue from where we left off."

Dr. Taner had no intention of continuing. He wanted to collapse into his chair as soon as possible. Moreover, he didn't know what to say. He needed to rethink and replan everything from scratch. He needed time.

Chapter

59

Terror of the Djinn

Can slowly started to get frustrated. Despite all his efforts, he couldn't download the graphics program. He tried various methods but couldn't get past the site's firewalls.

"No way... This won't work with our old junk," he muttered, giving the monitor a resigned slap.

"If Yasin were here, he would handle it, my love," said Pelin.

"If I had his computer, I could do it too."

There was a short silence. Both were thinking the same thing.

"Yasin left the key with Erkan. Would it be inappropriate if we just went and downloaded the program for a couple of minutes?" Can asked.

Pelin shrugged. "I don't know, love. Probably not."

"Of course not! If he didn't want anyone entering his place, why would he leave the key?"

They took the key from the sugar bowl where Erkan always left his keys and spare change.

Together, they went to Yasin's mysterious house. They slipped inside quietly. Despite talking about how natural their actions were, they were far from comfortable. They kept expecting one of the room doors to open, and Yasin to raise his usually downward-looking eyes and ask, "What are you doing here?"

They entered the room with the computer. The star of David drawn on the ceiling, the chains hanging down, the thick books on the floor

233

table, the bowls at the ends of the chains, and the movie posters on the walls made the room eerie.

Can sat down at the computer next to the bed, turned it on, and waited for it to boot up. Melisa examined the Aramaic bowls hanging from the chains.

"Love, these bowls are also candles…"

"Don't touch anything."

"What's the harm? We can blow it out immediately."

Melisa took out her lighter and lit the wick of the bowl on the table. After observing it for a few seconds, she turned her attention to the books and began to browse through them. Can was inserting a CD while trying to access the site to download the program.

Everything went smoothly for about ten minutes. Can was busy downloading the program, and Pelin was engrossed in Yasin's books. A doorbell rang, making them jump. They looked at each other in panic.

As Can moved to look through the peephole, the "dingdong" sound repeated, startling him again. He cautiously looked through the peephole and saw an elderly woman with large glasses and a white scarf.

"Who is it, love?" Melisa asked.

Instead of answering, Can opened the door.

Melisa was surprised to see the old woman peering at them curiously from behind her large glasses.

The old woman spoke first. "Are you Hacer's children?"

"No, grandma," Can replied. "You've come to the wrong place."

"Isn't this Hacer's house?"

"No, grandma."

"Hmm…"

"No, I said, it's not."

"Hacer's not here?"

"No, grandma. You've got the wrong place."

The old woman looked at them with disbelief, but at that moment, the door across the hall opened. A woman in her fifties, wearing a headscarf - probably Hacer - called out, "Sister Hidayet, you've got the wrong door, our flat is over here."

"Why didn't you tell me Hacer lives across the hall?" the old woman scolded them before heading to the neighbor's flat.

Melisa burst into laughter at the old woman's aggressiveness, and Can couldn't help but laugh too. They returned to the room.

Can started the installation process for the program he had downloaded from the internet. However, the computer gave a warning indicating that the CD was full.

"That's strange, it should be empty. What's on it?"

When Can opened the CD, he saw a file named "Ipek Tasci" and smirked.

"What's 'Ipek Tasci'?"

"Never mind..."

"No, really, tell me, I'm curious."

"It's a video of a famous model having dinner with a man."

"Dinner? You mean porn?"

"Yes."

"Is it really Ipek Tasci?"

"I don't know, that's what they say."

"Wow! Let's watch it," Pelin urged.

Can thought about suggesting they watch it downstairs but changed his mind. The forbidden nature of their actions excited him.

When the video started, a woman who looked very much like Ipek Tasci appeared and began to have sex with a man.

"Oh, it really is her!"

"I don't see the resemblance."

As they commented, the video progressed, and the characters engaged in various positions, their moans filling the room. The scenes aroused both Can and Melisa. Melisa climbed onto Can's lap. As the video progressed, they began kissing.

They quickly moved from romance to erotica and then to pornography. They found themselves in bed. The deep breaths of Can and Pelin mixed with the moans from the computer. Yasin's bed was witnessing its first act of intimacy beyond imagination.

They started undressing each other rapidly. It felt as if they were having sex for the first time. Each piece of clothing revealed a familiar body they knew by heart but felt like they were seeing for the first time. In the back of their minds, they knew time was a factor. Yasin or someone else could walk in at any moment. They had to hurry. As they kissed and bit each other, Melisa removed Can's last piece of clothing, his underwear. He, in turn, tore at her bra and panties like a madman, throwing them aside. Melisa's panties floated through the air, avoiding the chains and bowls, and landed right on the table, on top of the thick spell books. The air current from the panties caused a papyrus between the pages of an open book to shift a few inches.

The papyrus came into contact with the cold-looking, lifeless flame from the Aramaic bowl. Though the flame appeared weak, it managed to ignite the yellow papyrus. The fire, which seemed as feeble as a dying patient, began to consume the paper. As Can and Melisa's passionate union continued at full speed, the fire slowly progressed, eating away at the writings on the paper. Arabic prayers and calligraphy figures started moving, gathering in the center of the paper. Gradually, a face began to form. The first features to become clear were the eyes—angry, large eyes that seemed ready to burst from their sockets.

The room's temperature rose. As the fire took over the center of the paper, guttural growls began to emerge. Can, still lying on top of Pelin and waiting for the trembling in his body to subside, turned his head toward the sound. When he saw the creature with rotting flesh rising slowly from the table, he threw himself against the wall in fear.

Now, Melisa was closer to the table. "What's happening?" she asked, only to answer her question with a scream. As deathly screams filled the room, the enraged eyes of the djinn from the paper were fixed on Can and Melisa. The two clung to the wall in their naked state. An air current started to fill the room, forcing air into their eyes. Both tried to cover their eyes with their hands but couldn't. Their facial skin began to tear and peel toward their cheeks. They screamed madly. As their lips tore along with the peeling skin, their ears fell off, exposing their jugular veins, which pulsed rapidly. The air moved from their eyes to their hair, lifting and splitting the scalp lengthwise. The room filled with blood and screams, leaving no space for anything else. Can and Melisa were unrecognizable. Their skin had peeled off completely, hair, lips, and ears gone, exposing the nose bone and teeth. The djinn didn't kill them, only tortured them. The air current started entering through their toenails, which fell off one by one. Their skin was boiling from within. Suddenly, it began to tear, and with a burst of blood, the skin on their legs started to separate. Their screams echoed throughout the building.

The building residents, unable to bear it any longer, decided to call the police. Bahar, too, had stopped studying to try to understand what was happening.

Two officers got out of the police car with reluctance, expecting another routine noise complaint about noisy university students and complaining neighbors. But what they saw was so horrific that it would later require psychological treatment. Two young people had been skinned from head to neck, from feet to waist, like sacrificial lambs. The room was so mysterious it put horror movies to shame. The star of David on the ceiling, the hanging chains, hundreds of books, the posters on the walls...

The police officers' radio call put the Istanbul police on high alert. Dozens of officials from the police department arrived at the scene immediately. The news of the two skinned university students spread by word of mouth throughout the city. The police placed the building under surveillance and prohibited entry or exit until further notice from the prosecutor. Permission to search all apartments was granted at lightning speed. As their identities were confirmed, Bahar, Pelin and Erkan, as housemates of the victims, and Yasin, as the owner of the apartment where the crime was committed, were detained by order of the public prosecutor.

Chapter

60

Yasin and Erkan

After the investigation concluded that Yasin, Erkan, Bahar, and Pelin had no involvement in the incident, they were immediately released.

Bahar and Pelin's families had rushed to Istanbul as soon as they heard the news. Erkan and Yasin, on the other hand, had informed no one. They left the police station, bewildered and silent. For a long while, they didn't speak; they just walked. Finally, Erkan broke the silence:

"What is going on?" he asked.

Yasin, though unsure of the exact details, had a pretty good idea. Somehow, Can and Melisa had managed to unleash the djinn. If the photos with prayers written around them were still in the room, the djinn might target and Bahar as well. Pelin and Bahar were in danger. But how could he explain all this to Erkan?

"I don't know," Yasin replied.

They walked aimlessly for a while longer. Erkan tried to piece things together, crafting various scenarios in his head. Yasin, on the other hand, was pondering the potential consequences of the incident. Would the djinn go after Bahar and Pelin? Would the police find anything in the house? Would the Black Shrouds get involved? The mere thought of this legendary assassin organization constantly mentioned within the cult terrified him. He needed to retrieve his spell books and computer from his room, but how? He was also afraid of the cult. Although he hadn't spoken to Imam Sait since the big explosion in Konya, and Sait was probably dead, if he wasn't, Yasin was in serious trouble. He didn't know what to do.

Erkan, lost in thought, couldn't make sense of it all. He grabbed Yasin by the arm, his patience wearing thin, and with furrowed brows, asked:

"What is going on?"

Yasin, with a helpless expression, replied, "Brother, how should I know? Wasn't I with you guys?"

"How can you not know?" Erkan shouted, squeezing Yasin's arm harder. It hurt. "What is all this? Who are you?"

"Brother, get a grip!"

"Who are you?"

"Brother..."

Before he could finish his sentence, Erkan slapped him hard. Yasin winced in pain. As Erkan raised his hand to strike again, he noticed Yasin muttering something under his breath in that split second, and then brought his hand down. This time, it felt like he had hit concrete, his hand stinging as if he had struck an iron anvil. In desperation, he threw a punch, but it felt like his fingers were about to break. Yasin's face seemed made of steel. Tears of frustration welled up in Erkan's eyes, and he crouched down, sobbing.

Yasin stopped reciting his protective prayer. Erkan no longer seemed dangerous. He waited beside him for a while.

The Black Shrouds, reviewing the flow of information within the police and intelligence services, took note of the news about the two young people skinned alive. Ali Fuat, considering the potential connection to the strange murders committed in the past three months, deemed this case significant and ordered a detailed report.

Pelin and Bahar, feeling secure with their families by their side, had let themselves go completely and were constantly crying. They were placed under observation, and the hospital's psychologist had given them sedatives after speaking with both.

Their families wanted to take them home after obtaining a report from the school, but neither Bahar nor Pelin was willing. With finals approaching, they argued that they wouldn't be able to study if they went back home.

Their friends visited them, offering their condolences. One of them asked if they would be able to stay in the same building. The thought of returning to that building was horrifying to both of them. "Come to the dorms," one student suggested. As they discussed whether it would be possible, they realized it wasn't such a bad idea after all. Being in a crowded place would make them feel safer.

Yasin was far from being at ease. He couldn't enter his apartment. A police officer standing guard at the door showed him a court order stating that the apartment would be under investigation for 48 hours. The area had been secured to prevent tampering with evidence. Yasin knew he could get in if he wanted, but all his books had probably been taken by now.

Erkan's apartment had also been thoroughly searched but not sealed. Yasin and Erkan were in the kitchen, drinking tea, lost in deep thought.

Yasin thought about his room. What state was it in now? Had they found the computer he had imported from Russia? Were they examining his books? If they managed to crack the encrypted files on his computer, it would spell trouble for him. What had Can and Melisa done to unleash the djinn? Which djinn was it, and why was it so angry? Would it go after Bahar and Pelin? His questions remained unanswered...

They were drinking tea one after another. Yasin was trying to gather his courage and prepare his mind. As the sound of the tea glass hitting the saucer rang out, he said, "Erkan, brother."

Erkan lifted his tired and swollen eyes from the glass to look at Yasin.

"Erkan, brother, I don't know exactly what happened upstairs, but I think the djinn killed Melisa and Can. We have to destroy this djinn, or it might go after Pelin and Bahar too."

Yasin's words had the effect of a cold shower. "What do you mean 'go after them'? What are you saying?"

"Erkan, brother, calm down so we can talk."

Erkan propped his elbows on the table, rubbing his forehead with both hands. He needed to stay calm and understand what was going on.

After pausing for a few seconds, Yasin continued, "Brother, I think they tampered with my books and notes. Somehow, during this, a prayer's code was broken, and the djinn was released." He was about to say it killed both of them, but he couldn't bring himself to say it. He swallowed hard. "When the djinn appeared, they didn't know the protective prayers, so the outcome wasn't good," he added. Yasin checked Erkan's reaction. Was there any sign of anger or an imminent attack? Seeing Erkan listening calmly, he continued, "This djinn needs to be destroyed, but without my books and computer, I don't know how."

"Won't it just go away on its own?" Erkan asked.

"It probably won't go away on its own," Yasin said after a moment of thought. "In fact, it's more accurate to say it definitely won't."

"How do you know the djinn will go after Bahar and Pelin? Is it certain?"

Yasin had an answer to this question, but he didn't know how to explain it.

"It's highly likely."

Actually, he was sure of it, but...

"Why Bahar and Pelin? Why not you or me? Why the girls?"

Yasin was at a loss for an explanation until he noticed the gender distinction in Erkan's question. He decided to shape his lie around this.

"Djinn rarely target men. They prefer young women."

Erkan wasn't satisfied.

"But with so many young women around, why Bahar and Pelin specifically?"

Yasin had an answer ready.

"Because they came into my room. The djinn must have sensed their presence. If other girls had come, it would have targeted them."

Erkan felt like he was going to lose his mind. What a ridiculous conversation this was! The brutal murder of two of their closest friends and the danger to his girlfriend seemed to be met with nonsensical explanations.

"So what are we going to do?" he asked angrily.

"Erkan, brother, first I'll write a talisman for the girls. When they wear it, the djinn won't be able to harm them, even if it comes. But this is only a temporary solution. It just buys us time. We need to destroy the djinn in the meantime."

"How do we destroy it?"

"If I know which prayer the djinn serves, that will be enough. Once I know that, the rest is easy."

"Then do it!"

"I need the books and my computer in my room, but it looks like we won't be able to get them."

"What do we do then?"

"There are codes written on a lambskin by Imam Ja'far al-Sadiq, the grandson of Prophet Muhammad. If we don't know which prayer the djinn serves, the only way to destroy it is through those codes. We need to get our hands on either the books or that lambskin! It's probably kept among Imam Sait's personal belongings at the Tariqa center."

"Imam Sait," "Tariqa"... Yasin was using new terms. He noticed Erkan's puzzled look and provided a brief explanation about the Tariqa and the Imam. Since he had already started, he also mentioned the Black Shrouds, warning that if they got involved, they would kill them both without question.

Chapter

61

Trip to Bursa

In the morning, they left the house with a backpack. Yasin had said it was dangerous to stay at a fixed address. Danger could come from anywhere, from the Black Shrouds, from the Sect...

They stopped by the bank in Taksim. Yasin had hacked into the Sect's accounts and transferred a large amount into his own. After securing the money in the backpack, they went to a car dealership.

The owner didn't take the two young men seriously at nine in the morning. Erkan and Yasin had no time to lose.

"We're looking for a Mercedes Vito or something similar, no more than a year or two old. We'll pay cash," Erkan said. The owner, preparing to tell them that they wouldn't be making any business cards, saw that the young men were not just customers but 'valuable customers.' A broad smile spread across his face.

"Welcome, my princes! Command me! The gallery is at your service." Rubbing his hands together, he led the two 'princes' inside.

There was no haggling. The owner stated the price, and Yasin took the money out of the bag and counted it. The dealer asked how they would handle the transfer. "We'll do it later," Yasin said. "For now, let's just handle it between ourselves."

They made a document showing they had bought the car and paid for it. Bahar and Pelin had said they would be leaving the hospital and moving into the dorm. They got the address.

The white Mercedes Vito glided smoothly on the roads. Erkan, an excellent driver, felt a bittersweet sense of happiness behind the wheel despite the recent events.

"Whose money was that in the bank?" he asked, one eye on the road and the other on Yasin.

"Mine," Yasin said. He understood perfectly well what Erkan meant, but he didn't want to go into detail.

"And where did you get it?" Erkan asked. His first question had been for the same reason.

"It's a long story. Let's just say hacking."

"Alright then," Erkan said, focusing on the road.

—⁓—

They got back into the car after leaving the phone store. Yasin had bought a few SIM cards and two new phones. Erkan didn't understand what was happening. As they got back into the car, his confused expression was evident.

"Is all this really necessary?"

"Abi, just drive the car and listen to me."

Erkan started driving, and Yasin began to talk.

"Look, brother, I'm telling you one more time. I'm a member of a tariqa, and this tariqa is extremely ruthless. If they find out about our situation, they'll kill both of us. And that's not our only problem. There's also the Black Shrouds. If they find out from the books and computer that I'm involved in occult practices and connected to the tariqa, they'll shoot us on sight. You might say, 'Let's just run away,' but remember, the djinn is still active. If we don't destroy it, it will kill the girls. Do you understand, brother? Stop bombarding me with questions. My head is already a mess."

Erkan hadn't been scolded like this in a long time. He could barely recognize Yasin, who was once a shy kid who couldn't even look people in the eye.

They arrived at the dormitory.

Erkan called the girls from his old number since the new SIM cards hadn't been activated yet. The girls quickly came down to the dorm's cafe. Bahar embraced her boyfriend with longing. Pelin also hugged Erkan. They were cold towards Yasin, only saying "Hello".

Erkan explained that Melisa and Can had been killed by the djinn.

"You are also in danger because you entered that room before," he said. He talked about the possibility of the djinn haunting them as well. In the middle of the conversation, he subtly scolded his girlfriend, "I told you not to get involved in these things!" Bahar was ashamed.

Yasin listened for a while longer. As Bahar and Erkan talked, he noticed Pelin's furtive glances. He decided he needed to join the conversation and took out the amulets from his bag. He placed one in front of Bahar and the other in front of Pelin. The girls looked at him in astonishment.

"The djinn that killed Can and Melisa might haunt you too. Until we destroy it, I want you to wear these amulets," Yasin said. Unlike before, he wasn't looking at his feet or hands. He looked directly into Bahar and Pelin's eyes.

Both of them refused. Wearing the amulets meant accepting that the djinn could also kill them. They didn't want to believe it. Erkan intervened: "This time it's serious. I understand it's hard to accept. I couldn't accept it either, but you're in danger. Come on, my love, wear this. Come on, Pelin, you too."

Yasin also taught them a short prayer. He told them to close their eyes and recite it if they were in danger. He made them repeat it several times. Once he was sure they had memorized it, he said, "Repeat it every two hours so you don't forget."

Chapter

62

Anatomy of the Murder

The homicide detectives examining the evidence found no leads. There were numerous old books written in strange languages. They couldn't read these books, nor could they immediately find an expert to interpret them.

The autopsy reports were intriguing. According to the report, there were no marks from any cutting tools, and the intense oxygen burns under the skin were caused by high air pressure. Whatever flayed the children's skin was "air".

The detectives thought this bizarre murder might be related to the strange killings that started with Faruk Altan and Osman Karahan. When they examined the property's deed records, they found that it had changed hands two months ago and was purchased by someone with ties to Konya. This person was flagged for radical Islamic activities. A note was added to the murder file suggesting it might be a "tariqa conflict."

The Black Shrouds meticulously relayed the police's findings to Ali Fuat. The details of the murder and the mysterious books caught his attention.

Ali Fuat ordered the books mentioned in the report to be brought to the headquarters. He also set out to visit the house where the murder occurred.

The inside of the house piqued his curiosity. He had various angles of the Star of David photographed. He also took photos of the posters on the wall. Turning to Kenan Ferit, he asked, "Kenan, there was a kid living here. What was his name?"

"Yasin, Commander."

"Yes, Yasin! Where is he? Is he in custody?"

"He was taken into custody but was released when it was found he had no connection to the murder."

"What do you mean? How could they let someone like that go? Look at this room! Is he a Satanist, a sorcerer, or a tariqa member? It's not clear!"

"There's nothing the police could do, Commander. You know, the European Union compliance criteria."

Ali Fuat looked out the window at Istanbul, squinting as if he could see Europe on the horizon.

"Fuck their criteria!" he shouted angrily.

He lit a cigarette. "These bastards protect their own. They tell us to release the scum. But if something happens in their own country, they immediately issue a shoot-to-kill order."

"You're right, commander," said Kenan Ferit, understanding that Ali Fuat was referring to the bombings in England. The commander continued talking to himself: "Damn bastards! We've had minorities living under our protection in these lands for 700 years. Non-Muslims. Have we ever issued a shoot-to-kill order?"

The conversation had shifted to the European Union. Zekeriya was uninterested, preferring to examine the Star of David and the books. Aydin listened attentively to Ali Fuat while also thinking about the movie posters.

"Kenan, bring that kid in. Let's find out what these symbols and books are about. I don't care about detention periods! When national security is at stake, laws and regulations are just details."

"Yes, commander," said Kenan Ferit.

—m—

Erkan and Yasin started driving their car toward Bursa. Yasin wanted to examine the house. There could be very special books or codes in the forbidden room. Maybe even the lambskin… He was surprised at how long he had avoided entering that room. How scared he had been of the Imam. That fear was the iron cage of his colorless life.

As Erkan drove, he was wrestling with various thoughts. He had seen Yasin as a young man with mental issues and social deficiencies, obsessed with djinn and other supernatural matters. He had considered the show Yasin performed at home to be some sort of illusion or bioenergy trick. Pressing the gas on the long, narrow roads, he muttered to himself, "How wrong I was about him." In fact, he realized he had never really known Yasin. 'Connection to a sect…' 'A secret organization he calls the Black Shrouds…' What were all these? And where did Yasin fit into these connections?

"Yasin, why did we buy a Mercedes Vito? Wouldn't a taxi have been better?"

"I thought we'd be more comfortable sleeping in this, brother."

"Why would we sleep in it? We have plenty of money; we could stay at a hotel."

"No, brother, we can't stay at a hotel. There are records and all, it would be dangerous."

"What if there are records? Are we fugitives?"

"Officially, we're not wanted, but unofficially, we might be."

"Are these Black Shrouds you mentioned looking for us?"

"I don't know if they are right now, but they could be."

Whenever the road was clear, Erkan glanced at Yasin for a split second, then back at the road.

"Yasin, who exactly are these Black Shrouds?"

"All we know is that whoever they are, they don't like us very much…"

"What do they do?"

"They protect the revolutions. They are a very ruthless organization. Many Islamist intellectuals have perished at the hands of the Black Shrouds."

"Who are they composed of?"

Yasin got slightly annoyed by this question.

"How should I know, Erkan? They don't have an organizational chart on a website that we can check," he said sarcastically.

Erkan realized Yasin didn't want to talk much about it and probably didn't know much either. He decided to change the subject but keep asking questions.

"Is your sect membership new, or does it come from your family?"

"My father is also in the same sect. I've been in it as long as I can remember. I started in the community's schools. I was very successful, so the sect took an interest in me!" His last sentence sounded very unhappy. It was as if, given the chance to turn back time, he would never have let the sect take an interest in him.

"Is the sect and the community different from each other?"

"Yes, they are different. The community is an organization nationwide, even worldwide. The sect is a smaller organization. It was founded by two mujahideen named Hadji Halit and Imam Sait."

"Are all the sect members interested in djinn like you?"

Yasin smiled.

"Yes, they are, but not like I am."

Erkan sensed the pride in his words.

"How did you get involved in dealing with djinn?"

"I was directed into it. The community wanted to put me in law school or political science."

"Why law or political science? You're great at physics and math." He remembered the incident at home. "You could have gotten into engineering or medical school."

"You're right, on an individual level, engineering or medicine would be better, more profitable careers. But the community guides its students not based on individual benefits, but on the community's benefits."

Erkan frowned. "I don't see how that relates to the community's benefits."

"Of course, it relates. You can't take over the state with doctors, engineers, physicists, and chemists. But if you have judges, prosecutors, district governors, governors, commissioners, and directors, you can take over the state."

"Does the sect want to take over the state?"

"The sect wants to take over the state too, but not with the method I described. That's the community's method."

"What's the sect's method?"

"The sect... well..." Yasin paused and thought for a moment. "In short, let's say they want to take over the state by summoning djinn and such."

Erkan sensed that the matter was much deeper. The dirty web of relationships he had fallen into made him sick.

He overtook the truck in front of him and focused on the road for a while. When the road was clear, he glanced at Yasin for a moment.

"Was dealing with djinn your choice instead of studying political science or law?"

Yasin sighed deeply at this question. It was as if salt had been rubbed into his wound.

"What choice? The sect didn't even let me take the university entrance exam. In these kinds of structures, there is no choice. There is obedience to authority. Someone makes decisions for you. And you..."

Erkan noticed that Yasin was troubled. To open up the subject a bit more, he said, "What's the matter? You don't seem very happy with the decision about you."

"What's there to be happy about...?" He was about to swear, but stopped himself. It was a habit from the past. He couldn't curse the sect or Imam Sait, but this time he forced himself: "Damn it," he said.

"Isn't there any positive side? Look, it's a sect, but they taught you to control djinn, taught you hacking. As soon as you came to Istanbul, they bought you an apartment."

"Yes, brother, I understand you. People always look at intelligence agency members, gang leaders, or mafia members the same way."

"What kind of look?" Erkan cut him off.

"Let me give you an example. Is driving a Ferrari good or bad?"

"Of course, it's good."

"Yes, I think so too. But let me ask you another way."

"Is it good or bad to be forced to drive a Ferrari for 18 hours a day for 25-30 years?"

Erkan thought for a moment.

"It's bad," he said. He was curious about where this conversation was heading.

"So, brother, a Ferrari is good, but only if you can drive it when you want, to go from home to work, to take your girlfriend or family for a ride."

"I understand."

"Since you understand, let me ask you one more thing. When you think of driving a Ferrari, why did the positive side come to your mind first and not the other side?"

Erkan thought for a while. Indeed, the concept of 'driving a Ferrari' had evoked good things in his mind. When no answer came, Yasin started talking again:

"Because that's the general perception of the public, just like you had a moment ago. People think intelligence agents, mafia members, sheikhs are happy and prosperous. But they don't know that most of those people are condemned to that Ferrari."

"So, what about your situation? Are you condemned to the Ferrari?"

"Yes, I was. But now I'm slowly taking control of the wheel."

"So, are you going to leave the djinn business? Is that why you're preparing for the university entrance exam? To start a new life?"

"No, it's not about the university exam. I'm not saying I'm going to get out of the Ferrari and run away. I'm saying I'm taking control of the wheel. So the Ferrari that made me unhappy until now will make me happy."

Erkan took Yasin's metaphor and made it literal.

"So you're saying: I dealt with djinn for the sect until now. From now on, I'll deal with them for myself."

"Yes, brother. That's exactly what I'm saying," he smiled.

"Honestly, talking with a smart person is different. After talking with the sponge brains of the sect, we became speech-impaired. We missed talking to a normal person."

"No, Yasin. You're no speech-impaired! You talk like a professor."

"Only recently, brother. Think about the first days I came here!"

"Didn't you have any friends in Bursa?"

"No, what kind of friends!"

"Didn't you have any friends from the sect?"

"May the devil see their faces," he thought. "I did, but they always talked about the same things, and they were all men!"

The "all men" part caught Erkan's attention.

"You never had a girlfriend?" he asked.

"No, not even one. Neither a friend nor a girlfriend."

"Of course, that bothered you."

"You have no idea how much."

"Why didn't you find a friend?"

"The sect didn't allow it, fearing I might share information about djinn or disrupt their work. They kept me under pressure until I came to Istanbul."

"You were afraid of the sect in the past. Now, you're not. I guess it's Istanbul that made this change."

"Actually, I might not have been afraid in the past either. Because I am knowledgeable about djinn. I could have used them to protect myself. My past cowardice was psychological. It was ingrained in me since childhood. We couldn't rid ourselves of this fear because we never saw a different environment. Coming to Istanbul and meeting you guys opened my eyes."

"Don't you accept the sect's ideology anymore?"

"I do, but what's important to me now is not the group ideology, but individual attitudes and behaviors. I'm saying I never even had a girlfriend, brother. If I'm not going to have a girlfriend, it doesn't matter if it's communism, fascism, or an Islamic state."

Yasin kept focusing on the theme of having a girlfriend.

Erkan didn't miss this detail.

They arrived at the ferry. After buying their tickets, they lined up behind a bus to board the ferry.

Chapter

63

Investigating Yasin's House

Ali Fuat and his team pondered the strangeness of the room as they returned to headquarters. The books, scrolls, prayers written on parchment, and computers were all brought back to the base. Ali Fuat spread everything out on a large table. He, along with Aydin and Kenan Ferit, began examining the items. They picked up the books one by one, trying to understand what they were or what they said, but they couldn't even recognize the alphabet, let alone decipher the content, so they set them back down on the table. Their efforts were as futile as a eunuch trying to enter a harem. No matter how hard they tried, they got nothing from it.

"Does this kid not read anything in our language?" Ali Fuat muttered, lifting his head to look at Kenan Ferit. Kenan had turned pale, his face drained of color, and he was slowly flipping through the pages of one of the books, a strange unease evident on his face.

"Kenan, what's going on? You look like you've seen a ghost."

Struggling to regain his composure, Kenan replied, "I'm not sure, Commander. I think my blood pressure dropped."

"Sit down and rest."

Kenan pulled a chair over and pushed the books in front of him toward the middle of the table.

Meanwhile, Aydin was examining the posters, trying to find a connection between the movies. His constant focus on the posters caught Ali Fuat's attention.

"What's up, Aydin? You seem lost in those films." Aydin lifted his head to respond.

"There's a similarity between the films, Commander. All three of them revolve around a common point where the plot reaches a climax -based on the concept of a significant division that occurs at the moment of death. In ancient Egyptian civilization," he paused for a moment, "and in Hinduism and Buddhism, it's believed that when a person dies, a major division occurs."

Ali Fuat interrupted him.

"Do you mean the separation of the soul from the body?"

"No, Commander. The soul does leave the body, but then the soul itself divides. This is the crucial point. They believe that one part of the soul remains in the world. This part is called the soul's consciousness. It's the part that maintains the physical connection with reality—places the body has been, connections with friends, family, colleagues. The soul's consciousness maintains these connections in the form of a ghost. Then there's the essence of the soul, which inevitably moves on to the unknown."

Ali Fuat interrupted again.

"So, when a person dies, they split into three parts: the body, the soul's consciousness, and the soul's essence. Is that right?"

Feeling uneasy, Aydin wondered if his explanations sounded ridiculous. He answered cautiously, "Well, that's what they say, Commander."

Ali Fuat smiled.

"Alright, go on."

"After this division occurs, in some people, the part we call the soul's consciousness continues its connection with the real world. This theme is explored in these films. In 'The Sixth Sense', for example, Bruce Willis's character exists in the state of the soul's consciousness. The boy in the film has the ability to perceive entities in this state. The movie 'Ghost' is similar—Patrick Swayze's character doesn't die completely and returns to the mortal world in the form of the soul's consciousness. 'What Dreams May Come' also follows this theme. Robin Williams's character dies and exists in the form of the soul's consciousness."

This time, Kenan Ferit interrupted.

"I've seen the first two, but I haven't watched 'What Dreams May Come,'" he said. Then Ali Fuat asked a question:

"Are these subjects a personal interest of yours?"

"When I was a student in Ankara, we went to the movies every weekend, Commander. My knowledge of cinema comes from that time."

"I'm more curious about your knowledge base on concepts like the 'soul's consciousness.' Where does that come from?"

"Again, from my student days, Commander. My girlfriend was very interested in these topics. She constantly read books about ancient beliefs and would explain them to me."

"And of course, you listened and memorized everything without question, didn't you?" Ali Fuat smiled. Now he knew that Yasin Omen was interested in movies about life after death, to the extent that he even put up posters of them on his walls. The situation was getting more intriguing.

Ali Fuat ordered that Yasin's belongings be examined by experts. The Black Shrouds had no idea what the books in their possession were about, so they didn't even know what kind of experts to consult. To avoid revealing any thematic connections among the evidence -if there were any- they divided everything into five parts, each of which was taken by a different member of the Black Shrouds to university departments of linguistics, history, theology, and archaeology for further examination.

Chapter

64

Erkan and Djinn

Erkan and Yasin were carefully watching the people entering and leaving the apartment. They had arrived in Bursa around two in the afternoon and had headed straight to the Yavuz Selim neighborhood. Yasin, considering the reason he had been forced to leave Bursa, decided to be cautious about entering the house. The killers from the cult, the guards, and the police -all could pose a threat. The thought that tightened his chest the most was the possibility of encountering the Imam. Though he was skilled in spells and could physically protect himself, and although he had shed the fear that even the thought of the Imam once induced, he still wasn't sure if he was ready for a face-toface confrontation.

Erkan neither recognized the people coming and going nor could identify the dangerous ones they were worried about. Despite all this, he didn't take his eyes off the door. The street, filled with cars parked side by side, camouflaged the Mercedes Vito like a chameleon among green leaves. They waited for a long time. At one point, Erkan got out to buy some water. Finally, as darkness fell, they decided to move.

"If you want, you can stay here." Yasin suggested cautiously.

"Why?" Erkan asked.

"Well, I don't know, abi. You're not used to this; something might happen," Yasin replied, hesitantly.

"Get moving, kid! Something might happen? What could happen?" Erkan snapped, irritated.

They entered the building and quickly ascended the stairs. They reached the door of apartment number nine. Yasin unlocked the door. As the steel door slowly opened, the light from the stairwell spilled into the house. They stepped into a small two-square-meter area. Yasin closed the door and turned on the light inside. He inserted the key into the slot next to the inner door and turned it. As the key turned, the lights on the security panel lit up. He punched in some numbers. After pressing the enter button on the panel, he said, "Brother, don't make a sound." He lifted the door handle and brought his mouth close to the parabolic microphone. He counted the beeps and, after the ninth beep, said, "As-salamu alaykum." The 'click' sound of the steel door in his ears indicated that the door had opened.

As they took careful steps, Yasin muttered prayers one after the other in a low voice, holding Ercan's hand tightly as he followed two steps behind. Being dragged along like a child by Yasin seemed pointless to Erkan.

"Hey, kid, let go of my hand. Can't I walk by myself?" he said.

Without giving Yasin a chance to reply, he pulled his hand away. The moment he did, he felt a hand on the back of his neck. The university leader, who had punched him with brass knuckles and split his head open, grabbed Erkan by the hair and slammed him against the wall. There was a terrifying emptiness in his eyes. Erkan felt like his bones were breaking. Pain, shock, and curiosity swirled in his mind. The leader quickly lunged at him and grabbed his long hair, lifting him toward the ceiling. Yasin hastily began reciting a long prayer starting with "Rabbi inni massaniyash shaytanu…" The emptiness on the leader's face slowly disappeared, replaced by pain. As the prayer continued, the leader started shaking as if stricken by malaria. The hand that had grabbed Erkan's hair released him, and Erkan collapsed at the leader's feet. The room was suffocating with heat. The djinn, disguised as the leader, began to die in agony.

As Yasin finished reciting the prayer, the intense heat in the room vanished. The djinn that had suddenly appeared and flung Ercan against the walls was gone.

"Brother, are you okay?" Yasin asked.

"Yeah," Erkan replied weakly. But his body, unable to rise from the ground, and the pained expression on his face asaid otherwise.

Chapter

65

Ventures in Inquiry

Ali Fuat was sipping his fourth cup of tea. Seven cigarette butts, some burnt down to the filter, others extinguished before reaching the "2000" mark, lay in the black glass ashtray before him. He leaned back in his chair, gazing at the files on the desk from a few inches away. He had finally finished reading the reports containing the opinions of professors on Yasin's books. He picked up the sheet where he had noted the most interesting points. The first report that had impressed him was from Prof. Dr. Seray Birkan, who had shared her thoughts on the 'bowls.' According to the guards, Professor Seray had almost swallowed her tongue when she saw the bowls.

> *"The Arameans believed that by lighting candles in these bowls, inscribed with prayers, they could destroy evil spirits. This is frequently mentioned in the clay tablets from the Arameans that have survived to this day, and later in various parchments. In fact, one dimension of lighting a fire in the bowl is the sacredness attributed to fire…"*

After reading the report again, Ali Fuat picked up the bowl, examining it closely from all sides. The second report that caught his interest was from the professor who had analyzed the book titled "Risale of Buni"

"The Buni's Risale is one of the most important Havas books. It was written in the 1200s by Ebul Abbas Ahmed Bin Yusuf el Qureshi el Buni from Algeria. Buni meticulously studied the Havas science down to the finest details. It is one of the most fundamental books in the world on topics such as magic, spells, talismans, and djinn. Throughout history, many adventurers have tried to obtain the Buni's Risale. However, the mysteries within the book remain deep and unresolved..."

Ali Fuat picked up the 1200-page Risale of Buni, flipping through the pages haphazardly.

He then took another report he had set aside.

"The book titled Davetname was written by 'Uzun Firdevsi' in the 15th century. Uzun Firdevsi was the greatest djinn scholar of his time. His interest in djinn was inherited from his father and grandfather, both of whom were well-known Huddams in their communities. Uzun Firdevsi included his father's and grandfather's works in his book. The title 'Davetname' is meaningful. The term 'Name' refers to the recitation of certain prayers in a specific order. If these prayers are recited correctly, djinn can be used as slaves. The foundation of Huddam practices is based on this logic. 'Ebced', 'Remil', and 'Cifir' are used to calculate the numerical value of written texts. These values are then used to create codes. While the Davetname explicitly explains how to subjugate many djinn, the methods to influence the most powerful and significant djinn are explained in code..."

The same professor had also made explanations about the parchments found within the book. Ali Fuat read through these explanations as well.

"Three scrolls, each detailing how to command three significant djinn. The first one is 'Ishtarel.' This djinn's

*function is to make people fall in love with each other. If we
can command it correctly, we can make anyone fall in love
with us…"*

He started reading the notes on the second scroll:

*"This parchment also contains the summoning codes of a
powerful djinn. It is believed that the djinn named Azazel
specializes in killing enemies. Whoever can subjugate this
djinn will see their enemies devastated, as Azazel is said to
spill their blood in the blink of an eye…"*

He moved on to the last parchment, which concerned a djinn called
Zamradun:

*"This parchment pertains to Zamradun, who is considered
the most important and powerful djinn in the djinn realm.
If this djinn can be subjugated, the person controlling it
would inevitably become a ruler of a state. In ancient times,
Zamradun was also known as the 'Sovereign Djinn.'
According to the book, the code to summon Zamradun is the
most difficult to decipher…"*

The professor had concluded all his explanations with a statement:

*"These books and parchments should be considered as
remnants of folklore from the past. Much of it stems from
the curiosity of the people of that time. There is no verified
djinn book, nor has any such book proven to be accurate.
Respectfully, Professor."*

Ali Fuat set the report aside and reached for another cigarette. His
mouth felt like mud, but he lit it anyway. "What is this kid's goal?" he
wondered aloud. According to the professors, the texts were in various
languages—some in Arabic, others in Hebrew, Chaldean, and Aramaic.
Where had Yasin learned so many foreign languages? While Arabic and

Hebrew were still in use today, Chaldean and Aramaic were ancient languages.

"Yasin, Yasin, Yasin, Yasin, Yasin," he muttered to himself. "As if we didn't have enough problems, and now you..."

What was Yasin trying to achieve by mastering these djinn? Was he trying to take over the state? Or was he planning to kill someone? The most intriguing part was the love djinn, Ishtarel. Was Yasin interested in affairs of the heart while trying to conquer the state? Among the evidence taken from his house were photos of three girls, with Arabic inscriptions around them. Was he trying to make these girls fall in love with him? One of them was already dead. As his thoughts began to coalesce, it became increasingly clear that this boy was no ordinary person. It was imperative to find out what his activities were aimed at and what kind of organization might be behind him.

He shuffled through the reports on the desk and picked up the one titled "The YHVH Man."

"YHVH is a four-letter word in Hebrew. These four letters are believed to represent the true name of God. Its pronunciation is considered the greatest secret in the world. It is assumed that whoever can unlock this mystery will become the master of the world. For years, adventurous Kabbalists have wasted their lives on mystical research, trying to discover the correct pronunciation. In fact, entire schools of Kabbalah have been founded on different interpretations of YHVH's pronunciation. It is believed that the secret of human creation is hidden within this name. When YHVH is written in Hebrew and the letters are placed one below the other, they form a human figure. Yod represents the head, Hed the shoulders and arms, Vau the waist and sexual organs, and finally, Hed represents the hips and legs. The mystery of the 'YHVH Man' was one of the most popular topics of that era. Despite many Kabbalists wearing out their elbows with study, none could reach a conclusion..."

He set the report down with thoughtful eyes. Whatever Yasin's activities were, they were not limited to Islam alone. There were studies related to Judaism as well. He picked up another report and leaned back in his chair.

The report was about Yasin's book, the Zohar. "The Zohar, which can be translated as 'The Book of Splendor', delves into the mysteries of creation. It is written in Aramaic and primarily focuses on mysticism. The Zohar is one of the most important books for Kabbalists, some even consider it a rival to the Torah. The Zohar is divided into seven parts, each of which has been the subject of extensive study, leading to the formation of different Kabbalistic schools. Through research using gematria and other methods, attempts have been made to determine when the Messiah will come..."

He gently placed the paper on top of the piles of documents. The sheet slid across the desk and came to rest in a crumpled heap. Taking a drag from his cigarette, he stubbed it out in the ashtray. He reflected on what he had read. There were elements of Islam, Judaism, magic, and the world of djinn. There was also this intriguing study system called Kabbalah. So many strange things had been gnawing at his mind in recent months, and the dilemmas in his personal life only added to the confusion. He doubted he could reach any conclusion without interrogating Yasin.

Chapter

66

About Djinns

Erkan walked to the car with a thousand aches and pains, finally managing to get inside. He lay down on the back seat as much as he could, taking a deep breath, feeling a bit of relief. "Let's sleep here tonight. I don't have the energy to drive," he said. Yasin replied, "Alright." He was in a bad mood, having found nothing useful in the house.

"What was that thing that attacked me?" Erkan asked. The answer was short and direct: "A djinn!"

"How did it take the shape of the guy I beat up?" Ercan continued.

"It can take any form it wants," Yasin replied.

"But how did it know I beat up the school leader?" Ercan pressed.

"Djinns exist in a different dimension and have very powerful abilities. That's why they can know all the details of your past life," Yasin explained.

"Speak more plainly," Erkan demanded, shifting slightly to ease the pain on the side he was lying on.

"Alright, the topic is complex, but I'll try to explain a bit," Yasin said, gathering his thoughts. A few minutes passed in silence.

"Yes, brother," Yasin finally said, taking another pause. "Humans perceive the world through their five senses. Our brain's ability to perceive the world is limited to these five senses."

"For example?" Erkan asked.

"For example..." Yasin pondered, his eyes distant. "Think about radar waves or the waves that create television images. We can't perceive them, but their existence has been scientifically proven. Just because we can't perceive these waves with our five senses, we've ignored them for years. But once science proved the existence of radio waves, we said, 'Yes, they exist.' But they were there before science confirmed them. Do you know what the difference is between being able to see and not being able to see?"

"Being blind?" Erkan guessed.

"No, not in that sense. The difference between being able to see and not being able to see is three ten-thousandths of a centimeter."

"I don't understand," Erkan admitted.

"The human eye starts to see at a wavelength of 0.0004 cm, where ultraviolet rays begin, and stops seeing at 0.0007 cm, where red rays begin. Beyond this small range, we can't see or perceive anything. When we get an X-ray, X-rays pass through our bodies. Can we perceive the passage of Xrays?"

Yasin answered his own question. "Of course not. But can we deny their existence just because we can't perceive them?"

"What does this have to do with the leader who threw me against the wall?" Erkan asked.

"Brother, that wasn't the leader; it was a djinn that took his form."

"Then what's the connection between all this and djinn?" Erkan asked.

"Did you understand what I've explained so far?" Yasin asked.

"Yes," Erkan replied.

"Now, let's move on to the djinn," Yasin said, pausing to consider how to explain it in a way Ercan could understand.

"The Quran states that djinn are created from smokeless fire and can penetrate every pore. 'Min mearicin min nar' means smokeless fire, and 'Min nar is semum' refers to something that penetrates the finest pores. The fire mentioned in the Quran is light or radiation. In other words, djinn exist in a wavelength beyond our five senses. The rays that make up djinn are beyond our perception range. Humans tend to see certain things as 'impossible' or label them as 'nonsense.' As science has advanced, it has often thrown these notions back in our faces, but in areas where science hasn't yet developed, human prejudices persist. One of these areas is djinn. Since no djinn-sensing device has been invented yet, humans don't accept the existence of djinn. But we know they exist and are composed of certain rays or waves. Because djinn are in a different form, their memories, lifespans, speeds -everything about them is different from us. They can know everything about you, they can appear in different forms- in short, don't try to apply your logic when thinking about djinn. Your logic is shaped by your five senses and the society you're in."

As Erkan listened to Yasin, he realized that lying on his back was easing his body's pain. His scalp still ached, though.

"I understand," Erkan said. He had more questions, but thought it was time to take a break. He was hungry.

"Yasin, how about we grab something to eat and then continue talking?"

"Sure, brother, whatever you want."

Chapter

67

The Sanctum of Command

Ali Fuat entered the large, computer-equipped room, lost in intense thoughts. When the guards saw their commander arrive, they quickly straightened up. His lack of a clear objective at that moment caused him to hesitate after taking a few steps into the room. What was he going to do? Who was he going to look at? Who was he going to ask?

Kenan Ferit was focused on the computer in one corner of the room and didn't notice Ali Fuat until he was right next to him. "Kenan, what are you doing?" Ali Fuat asked as he glanced at the screen.

"I'm reading the report MIT prepared on the 12's murders, Commander."

"Anything noteworthy?"

"Unfortunately, no."

"I believe all these events..." he paused for a moment, "might be connected to that boy named Yasin." Kenan Ferit didn't respond, but he looked at his commander with attentive eyes.

"There's something about that boy, Kenan. We have to find him."

"We're investigating, Commander, we're close..."

"Do you think he's hiding?"

"Why would he hide? The police questioned him and released him."

"Maybe he's not running from the law but from something else. For instance, could there be a group trying to kill him?"

Kenan Ferit didn't share Ali Fuat's suspicions but tried not to show it.

"I suppose we won't know what's real until we interrogate him, Commander."

"Doesn't this kid have classmates, a girlfriend, or something? Tap their phones. The entire intelligence service can't track down one boy?"

Again, Kenan Ferit didn't respond, but he looked disheartened. Ali Fuat regretted scolding him and changed the subject by saying, "The reports from the professors are fascinating!"

"This kid is deeply involved with jinns, spells, and such. He's working on an interesting system they call Kabbalah. According to the professors, these matters require deep expertise and knowledge. Where did he acquire this background? Who trained him? How did he get his hands on those ancient books in his room?"

Kenan thought for a moment, "Are you saying there's a group behind him, Commander?"

"Absolutely. But some elements suggest the boy might be working independently."

"Then we can't say 'absolutely', Commander."

"There's no chance there's no group involved. Just think about the computers in his room..."

"Could it be a religious community?"

"I doubt it. We know a bit about how they operate. This is a different group."

As their conversation continued, a guard approached. After saluting, he handed over a confidentially stamped file. Ali Fuat had requested a report summarizing the latest developments.

He flipped through the pages quickly -details on the murders of Osman Karahan and Faruk Altan, then the murders in Bursa, the 12's murders... Nothing new. The last section was about Yasin. His identified cell phone had been off since the incident, his bank accounts were monitored with no transactions(!), he hadn't crossed any borders, nor had he received any traffic tickets or other records. He hadn't gone to his tutoring center, nor had he been home. He didn't have any identified friends. It was assumed he was friends with Erkan, Bahar, and Pelin, who were connected to the two deceased kids. Bahar and Pelin were staying at a private dorm, but Erkan hadn't been located. The report was long and frustrating to read. His desire to speak with Yasin grew stronger every second.

He ordered a more thorough investigation of his friends and instructed that their phones be tapped.

Chapter

68

Yasin

Yasin entered the car with bags in hand. Erkan struggled to sit up. They ate in silence.

The conversation resumed where they had left off, with Erkan's question. "Is the djinn that attacked me the same one that killed Pelin and Can?"

"No," Yasin replied, locking eyes with him.

"One of the djinn that the Imam left behind as a guardian attacked you. I didn't know it existed either. It seems that after I left, he prepared some 'pleasant' surprises for uninvited guests."

"What a pleasant surprise indeed," Erkan said with a smile, as if trying to ease his mind before asking another question.

"Yasin, why did the djinn attack the moment I let go of your hand?"

"At that moment, I was reciting a prayer that repels djinn. Because you were holding my hand, the prayer's protection extended to you as well."

"So it didn't attack because of the prayer?"

"Partly that, and partly because of the amulet I was wearing."

Erkan thought for a few seconds. He already knew what he wanted to say, but he still weighed it in his mind.

"Is there a chance we might encounter it again?"

It was a preliminary question; he had a different point he wanted to reach. "Yes, it's possible," Yasin said.

"Then I should learn how to protect myself from djinn."

Yasin hesitated for a moment, unsure of what to say. His facial expression made it clear that he was preparing to tell a lie.

"Well... Sure, brother, but," he paused briefly, "it's not easy to learn the prayers all at once. I don't have an extra amulet with me. I'll teach you over time," Yasin added, forcing a smile.

Yes, it was as he thought. Yasin wasn't telling him how to protect himself from djinn. He wasn't even willing to give him an amulet. It wasn't hard for Erkan to figure out why.

Yasin was afraid.

They sat in silence, watching the cars pass by. With each passing minute, they relaxed a little more, spreading out on the seats. Eventually, their eyelids closed, ending the day's vigil...

Chapter

69

Pelin

She started the day with a strange unease. Despite going to bed early, she hadn't slept well.

On the top bunk, the fear of falling and the stuffiness of the room made every sleep feel like she was lost in a foreign neighborhood, causing unease. She threw the blanket with the duvet cover aside and carefully climbed down, making sure not to step on any part of the girl sleeping below. At that moment, Bahar also sat up, blinking, "Good morning," she said.

Pelin replied with a "Good morning" and headed toward her wardrobe. She took a bar of soap and a towel, stepping out into the corridor. The first thing she felt was her lungs filling with fresh air. She entered the large bathroom at the end of the corridor. A student was washing her face. Pelin placed the soap on one of the sinks and wedged the towel between her legs. She washed her hands, splashed a handful of water on her face. As she washed her face, the thick string of her amulet dangled down. To avoid getting it wet, she took it off and placed it on the sink. After thoroughly washing her face, she dried herself. She moved to the section with the stalls and pushed open one of the doors, entering. She lifted the toilet seat and wiped the spot where she would sit with a tissue. The toilet was the part of dorm life she found most challenging and despised the most.

She shuddered at the cold between her legs. When she looked down, all her muscles tensed. In a sudden reflex, she tried to pull herself back.

A massive snake was slithering out of the toilet, rubbing its cold skin against her legs and between her thighs. Unsure if she was dreaming or if this was real, she quickly tried to escape the stall. The snake, as if reading her thoughts, coiled around her waist, not letting her rise from the toilet. She began to scream. The snake tightened its grip, causing her screams to become short and filled with pain. The snake raised its head, bringing it level with Pelin's face. Its slit pupils were aimed directly at Pelin's eyes. Its forked red tongue flicked in and out. Pelin was on the verge of losing her mind. She screamed as much as her breath allowed.

The girls outside the stall couldn't make sense of the screams coming from inside. They knocked on the door and asked, "Pelin, what's going on?" but heard nothing more than short cries like "Ah" and "Help..." The pressure the snake applied to her lungs prevented her from shouting any louder.

One of the girls waiting in front of the stall giggled mischievously, "What are you doing in there, girl?" The others laughed as well. The sounds still came out in short bursts from inside. Bahar, who had come to the door, though she couldn't understand what was happening, felt a wave of fear wash over her. The horror of Melisa and Can's deaths came to her mind. She didn't want to lose Pelin. She began to bash at the door, driven by instinct. Meanwhile, she was reciting the prayer Yasin had taught her. After a few hits, the flimsy plastic door broke at the lock and opened.

The snake quickly slipped back into the toilet as Bahar started reciting the prayer. The girls found Pelin in a terrible state. She was out of it, her entire body trembling.

They rushed her to the hospital. The doctor wanted to keep Pelin under observation until her condition stabilized. He said she had experienced a deep trauma and was seeing visions.

Bahar didn't believe it was just a vision. She had also seen the snake slither back into the toilet. Were Yasin's warnings true? Was the djinn trying to kill them? Bahar felt the need to talk to her boyfriend. She took out her cell phone. The ringing in her ear abruptly stopped as Erkan answered, "Yes, my love?" At that moment, Bahar broke down and began to recount the incident through her tears.

Erkan immediately decided to go to Istanbul. From the start, he felt he had made a mistake. He should never have left the girls alone.

"Yasin, I'm heading back. I think the djinn attacked Pelin."

"What? How did it happen?" They were both in shock. Yasin knew the djinn could haunt them, but he had believed the amulets and prayers he had given them would protect them.

Erkan relayed what his girlfriend had told him to Yasin. "The girls are in a bad state. I need to be with them."

"I understand, brother. You go. Take the car. I don't know how to drive anyway."

"What will you do?"

"I'll catch a bus to Konya. I'll check out the neighborhood where the Imam and the sect live and see what's left after the bombing. Hopefully, I can find a few useful books."

"Let's do whatever it takes to get rid of this curse."

After dropping Yasin at the terminal, Erkan turned the car towards Istanbul.

At the Black Shrouds' headquarters, the day began with new developments. One of the guards knocked on Ali Fuat's door with a report in hand.

"There are new developments, commander," he said, handing over the file. Ali Fuat began to review the report. He first read the transcript of the phone conversation between Bahar and Erkan. The part where the girl named Bahar said, "The djinn attacked Pelin," caught his attention. He underlined the part where Erkan said, "I'm coming to Istanbul," and made a note beside it: "Erkan should be taken."

The intelligence had also noted Pelin's condition. According to the information obtained from the doctor, the girl claimed that a djinn in the form of a snake had attacked her.

Ali Fuat gave the order to the operations unit to "Be ready."

Chapter

70

The Black Shroud Claims Erkan

Erkan didn't notice the black-tinted minivan as he parked his car in front of the hospital. He got out of the car. Ali Fuat and his team compared the man in front of them to the photo they had. Pale face, long wavy hair, and handsome… it was a perfect match. Ali Fuat recalled the report prepared about Erkan. It mentioned that he made a living by buying and selling second-hand musical instruments and worked as a cook one or two days a week. If the report was accurate, there was no way this guy could own a Mercedes. We'll find out everything soon, he thought. The order was short and clear.

"Take him!"

Erkan was heading towards the hospital when he noticed a medium-height, very handsome young man and a giant of a man approaching him. Kenan Ferit pulled out his navyblue ID card and said, "Mr. Kurak, hello." He was smiling. "We're from the National Intelligence Organization. We need to ask you a couple of questions. Could you please come with us to the car?"

His blood drained! His face took on an expression of shock mixed with fear.

Kenan Ferit, used to situations like this, tried to calm him down.

"Mr. Kurak, I understand that MIT (Milli Istihbarat Teskilati: National Intelligence Organization) can be a scary name, but remember, we're not a mafia or a gang. We are an official organ of the Republic of

Turkey. Please, stay calm and come with us!" he said, gesturing towards the car.

Erkan, though unwilling, began to walk. Kenan Ferit, satisfied with having handled the situation smoothly, got into the car after Erkan. Since the name Black Shrouds was never publicized, they would use MIT, JITEM, or police IDs during arrests.

They began to drive towards the villa where the interrogations with torture took place. "Where are you coming from?" Ali Fuat asked.

Erkan wavered between telling the truth or not. This question didn't matter much, but soon there would be many more. What would he do? Should he tell them everything? He couldn't decide.

"Bursa..." he muttered quietly. The fact that Erkan hesitated before answering caught Ali Fuat's attention.

"Look, young man, we are professionals. You can't lie to us like you would to any other person. We already have a lot of information about you," he said, showing the file with Erkan Kurak's name on it.

"From what I gather, you're a young man who, despite leading a fairly ordinary life, has found himself entangled in complex situations. Give us the right information so we can help both you and your friends."

Erkan waited until Ali Fuat finished speaking. Yes, he had considered lying but hadn't done so. Feeling somewhat relieved, he said, "I didn't lie."

"True, you may not have lied, but you hesitated. Otherwise, you would have answered immediately when I asked the question."

Erkan thought the man he was talking to—this sternfaced, broad-shouldered man with large eyes—was reading his mind.

"What were you doing in Bursa?" Ali Fuat asked, this time framing the question in plural. Erkan didn't know how to answer. He wasn't going to lie, but the truth was more absurd than the most outrageous lie. He felt the need to give a brief explanation.

"I'll tell you the truth, but I'm sure you'll think I'm talking nonsense," he said.

Ali Fuat noticed the tension in the young man. "Relax, just tell us everything without leaving anything out. Let us be the judge of it."

"Alright," Erkan said. He took a deep breath and looked into Ali Fuat's eyes. "So, let me tell you why we went to Bursa."

"We went to Bursa to find prayers that would destroy the djinn!"

Of the four people in the car, only Aydin was surprised. But he quickly composed himself. Ali Fuat didn't show any change in his expression.

Erkan recounted what had happened to him in Bursa. He mentioned that Yasin had headed to Konya.

Ali Fuat, growing more curious, asked about Yasin:

"Why is this Yasin so involved in these djinn matters?"

"He learned it from the sect when he was a child. When they saw how intelligent Yasin was, they gave him special training. There were many children in the sect who dealt with djinn, but according to Yasin, he was the most talented."

"And what was the sect's goal?"

"I don't know exactly, but according to what he said, they wanted to take over the state and establish a caliphate."

Suddenly, everyone in the car became more attentive.

"A caliphate? How do they plan to do that?"

"I have no idea. According to Yasin, they plan to control the djinn and use their help to establish it."

"Are they insane? Is that how they think they can establish a state?"

"How should I know, sir! Ask him yourself."

Ali Fuat realized for a moment that he had lost control and quickly composed himself again.

"Let's return to headquarters," he ordered. He had decided there was no need to go to the interrogation house.

The boy was already singing like a canary.

He was beginning to think that the events of the past few months might be connected to this incident. There were factions within the community that they hadn't yet unraveled. This could be one of them. He didn't find Erkan's stories about the djinn strange at all. He had personally experienced something similar when Halit was killed. They needed to find Yasin immediately.

"Sir, may I call Bahar?"

"I returned from Bursa today just to see Bahar. I didn't give her a specific time, but she might still be worried. She's going through tough times as it is."

Ali Fuat looked at the boy's embarrassed expression. He thought that he really did care for the girl.

"It's unlikely, but go ahead and call her! Just don't mention us. Tell her there's an important issue and that you won't be able to come today."

Erkan reacted in surprise.

"Why can't I go?"

"You're coming with us to Konya."

Erkan grew angry. Was this the reward for telling the truth?

"My girlfriend needs me," he said in a firm tone.

"Alright, young man. We didn't say you'd never see her again. You'll meet tomorrow."

"I need to go today."

Ali Fuat dropped his previously calm demeanor.

"Shut up! Do you think this is a game? You're talking about overthrowing the Republic and establishing a caliphate state. You're not going anywhere until this matter is cleared up."

Erkan couldn't respond, though he was seething inside.

Chapter

71

Yasin and Black Shrouds

They left Erkan in the vehicle and entered the headquarters. Ali Fuat ordered the helicopter to be prepared. He called Selin and briefly explained that he wouldn't be able to come that evening.

While waiting for the helicopter to be ready, Kenan Ferit wanted to share the thoughts that were bothering him:

"Commander, do you believe in these djinn stories?"

"Well, what can I say, Kenan? Let's get that boy to talk. I'm sure a lot will become clear."

Aydin, who had just entered, said, "The helicopter is ready."

"Get the boy on board; we're coming."

"Yes, sir."

Erkan was seated in a corner of the helicopter. Kenan Ferit boarded with a small bag in hand, followed by Ali Fuat, Zekeriya, and Aydin. Once all the passengers were in place, the rotor began to spin faster. The helicopter took off with slight tremors.

Ali Fuat once again bombarded Erkan with questions. Erkan spoke about the incident at home, how Yasin's face suddenly turned to stone when he punched him. This part particularly caught Ali Fuat's interest. He made Erkan recount every detail down to the finest points.

Erkan was curious about the direction things were headed. He decided to ask outright:

"What are you going to do with Yasin? Are you going to kill him?"

Everyone's attention focused on Erkan. It wasn't Zekeriya's habit to speak, and Kenan and Aydin also remained silent, thinking it wasn't their place to answer. Ali Fuat looked at Erkan with a slight smile.

"Where did you get that idea?"

"Aren't you going to kill him?"

The commander laughed.

"Well, where did you get that idea?"

Erkan didn't know what to say. He decided to mention what Yasin had told him. He couldn't think clearly.

"Yasin talked about you."

The smile on Ali Fuat's face instantly gave way to seriousness.

"What did he say?"

"He said you're a secret organization, that you don't like them at all, and that your sole purpose is to protect the reforms and the Republic."

Ali Fuat listened carefully to every word that came out of Erkan's mouth.

"Where did he get that information?"

"I don't know."

"What else did he say?"

Erkan hesitated but decided to tell. "He said you were ruthless killers."

Ali Fuat didn't respond. Yes, they had killed many people. But no one had ever stood in front of him and said, "You're a murderer," and he had never questioned that side of himself. He felt the need to defend himself.

"Whatever we did, we did it for the survival of the state. We never killed anyone without reason. Today, if the people live in a modern Republic, we have a significant role in that."

Erkan looked on, unsure of what to say. He wanted to know what would happen to him. Would he be arrested, killed, or would he ever see Bahar again?

"What's going to happen to me?" he asked. It was a straightforward and thorough question. Ali Fuat was convinced that the boy had stumbled into these matters by coincidence.

"Look, young man, first of all, know this: we're not an organization set up to kill you. We exist to ensure that you live your life in a modern, secular, and republican system. If you can grow your hair out, wear nice jeans and shirts, hold a girl's hand and walk down the street, and not be forced to don a beard, turban, or robe, it's partly thanks to us."

Erkan began to grasp the situation. The stress he was under prevented him from thinking clearly. As far as he could tell, the mysterious organization in front of him was concerned with those who wanted to overthrow the Republic. He had no issues with the regime. He wanted to make that clear.

"I'm not against the Republic."

Ali Fuat understood the boy's fears and wanted to move on from the topic.

"We know. Relax, cooperate with us, and once we solve this matter, you'll be free, provided you forget everything you've experienced!"

"Of course, sir. I don't even understand what's happening right now. I won't talk to anyone. All I want is to return to my normal life and my girlfriend."

The commander nodded meaningfully.

Erkan's desire to return, and the fact that his primary reason was his girlfriend Bahar, caught Kenan Ferit's attention. The two handsome men exchanged looks.

The helicopter sped along. Ali Fuat thought about that strange night in Sakarya. Hadji Halit had muttered something under his breath. Everything had happened after that. Could the secret lie in those few whispered words? Erkan had experienced something similar. He had said that just as he was about to punch Yasin, Yasin's lips moved as if he were reciting a prayer. After that, Yasin had turned into a man of steel. The punch hadn't fazed him.

What troubled Ali Fuat was whether Yasin or other members of the mysterious sect possessed supernatural powers. He wouldn't have believed it if he hadn't seen it with his own eyes, but... Djinn, spirits, or bioenergy... If the people he was dealing with had such powers, he would need to be cautious. Though he had no idea how to go about it.

The helicopter landed in the courtyard of the farmhouse. A guard greeted the commander and his team.

The commander wanted to reach Yasin without delay. The first method that came to mind was to call him on his cell phone. Erkan would call and ask Yasin where he was. They rehearsed what he would say a couple of times.

"Hello…"

"Yes?"

"Yasin, hello, how are you?"

"Getting by, brother, no developments yet. What about you? How are the girls?"

Erkan was momentarily stunned. He hadn't seen the girls at all. They hadn't anticipated that Yasin would ask about them.

"They're good, they send their regards."

The fact that they sent their regards surprised Yasin. The last time they had met, they had been very cold. He had only briefly made eye contact with Pelin, and that was it.

"Brother, is Pelin with you? Can I talk to her?"

"What do you mean Pelin, Yasin? I'm in Konya. Where are you? Tell me your location so we can meet up."

Yasin was surprised once more. In just a few seconds, he weighed the situation in his mind. He measured, assessed, and made a quick decision.

"Where are you, brother? I'll come to you."

"You tell me where you are, and I'll come."

"Brother, isn't this your first time in Konya? How will you find my place?"

Erkan was at a loss. He looked at Ali Fuat, who was listening to the conversation through the earpiece, with a silent plea for help. The commander quickly wrote something on a piece of paper and showed it to Erkan.

"I'm in the city center, in front of the statue," Erkan said. The conversation was brief. "I'll be there in half an hour," Yasin said, and hung up the phone.

Ali Fuat, Kenan Ferit, and Zekeriya quickly got to their feet. They gathered all their equipment—stun sprays, weapons, and so on. Aydin got up with them. The word "yaniniza" (to your side/to you) in the conversation had caught his attention. He wondered if Yasin had meant "yaniniza" or if he had said it intentionally.

When they arrived at the statue and spread out around the area, it was 14:50. By the time Ali Fuat asked, "When is this guy coming?" it was 16:20. His cell phone was also off. No matter how long they waited, he didn't show up. They had no choice but to return to headquarters.

"Kenan, do you think he figured it out?"

"I don't think so, commander."

"Why do you think he didn't come?"

"Something must have gone wrong."

Ali Fuat wasn't satisfied. He didn't want an explanation that involved chance.

"Erkan, do you have any idea?"

"No, I don't," Erkan said. What could he have possibly guessed? Everything was out in the open.

Aydin considered joining the conversation that was looping in its own circle. What had Yasin meant by "yaniniza"?

"Commander," he called out, but his words were cut short.

The commander of the Black Shrouds, Pasha Vefik, walked in. Except for Erkan, every guard in the large room immediately stood up at attention. Although Erkan didn't recognize the man who entered, he sensed his importance from the way everyone else stood up, so he got to his feet as well.

Pasha Vefik scanned the room and said, "Hello, everyone." In unison, they all responded loudly, "Hello, sir."

Ali Fuat couldn't believe his eyes. He kept looking at Pasha Vefik's face, unable to comprehend why he was in Konya. Pasha Vefik sat down in one of the chairs and began to gaze sternly at everyone in the room. He looked at Erkan for a long time.

"Who is this boy?"

"Commander, this boy will lead us to Yasin Omen," said Ali Fuat.

"And who is Yasin Omen?" Pasha's response was sharp.

"He's a student whose two friends were killed in a strange manner at his home, sir. We believe he's connected to a sect."

"Hmmm…" Pasha mumbled some words under his breath and thought for a while. Finally, he fixed his gaze on Ali Fuat.

"What are you going to do with this boy? Are you going to kill him?"

Ali Fuat was taken aback. What kind of question was that? In all the years he had known Pasha Vefik, he had never spoken like that. Something was wrong. Pasha Vefik didn't use the word 'kill'; he would say 'have coffee'. And secondly, wouldn't Vefik Sancaktar, who had commanded the Black Shrouds for years, know what to do? Ali Fuat couldn't make sense of what was happening. "As you command, sir," was all he could muster.

Pasha Vefik continued to ask questions that baffled Ali Fuat.

"Before I gave an order, what were you planning to do, kill him?"

Ali Fuat was at a loss for words. "We were going to interrogate him, sir."

"Just interrogate?"

"Yes."

"And after the interrogation, were you going to release him?"

Ali Fuat began to wonder where this incomprehensible conversation was leading.

"Yes, sir, we were going to release him."

Pasha leaned back in the chair, deep in thought, rhythmically tapping his fingers on his knee.

"So, you were going to release him after interrogating him," he muttered.

Everyone in the room was stunned, but no one dared to ask, "Sir, are you feeling alright?"

It was clear from Pasha's expression that he was processing something. He seemed troubled. For what felt like a long time, he sat in silence. The silence was finally broken by Pasha Vefik.

"Have you found Yasin?"

"No, sir. We found his phone number and called him, then..."

Ali Fuat's words were cut off by Pasha.

"I know, I know. You don't need to explain."

Ali Fuat fell silent in shock. How did he know? Who had informed him?

"I can find Yasin for you."

Ali Fuat was utterly confused. "How, sir?" was all he could ask.

"It doesn't matter how. I can bring Yasin right in front of you, but I hope you won't act differently than what you've told me."

Ali Fuat couldn't find a response. He chose to remain silent.

Pasha Vefik's lips began to move slightly, whispering something. Suddenly, the temperature in the room rose. Erkan jumped up from his seat, his face filled with terror.

"The djinn is coming, the djinn is coming," he shouted as he rushed towards the door, but Zekeriya, the only one in the room who managed to keep his composure, blocked him.

The heat had intensified, and everyone was sweating profusely. The room was filled with panic.

At that moment, Ali Fuat noticed something. Aydin had his gun pointed at Pasha. Pasha Vefik, completely indifferent, continued staring ahead, silently moving his lips. Ali Fuat quickly lunged at him. "Aydin, what are you doing? You're going to shoot the commander."

"He's not the commander," Aydin said, trying to free his arm from Ali Fuat's vise-like grip and empty the magazine into Pasha.

Suddenly, the intense heat that had turned the room into a furnace vanished as quickly as it had begun. The room's normal atmosphere now felt like a Siberian chill against their bodies. They were freezing.

In the chair where Pasha Vefik had been sitting, there was now a short, blond young man in his twenties.

Ali Fuat, who had been restraining Aydin, immediately reached for his own weapon. When he pointed his gun at the blond young man, he saw that Kenan Ferit also had his hand on the trigger.

"Who are you?" he shouted. He couldn't stop his body from trembling. The hand gripping the gun's handle felt like it was touching ice. The blond young man leaned back in the chair and calmly said, "Yasin Omen."

Ali Fuat scrutinized Yasin from head to toe. Without lowering his weapon, he turned his head towards Erkan, looking him in the eyes as if seeking confirmation. Erkan nodded and said, "Yes."

After a while, the atmosphere in the room returned to normal. The guns were put away, and their sweat-soaked clothes were changed. The calming effect of the tea they drank together was becoming more and more evident.

Ali Fuat felt his heartbeat return to its normal rhythm.

The others in the room also appeared calm and composed. It was time to talk.

"Zekeriya?"

"Yes, commander."

"Take Erkan outside."

Chapter

72

Ali Fuat and Yasin

When Arab Zekeriya left the room with Erkan, only Ali Fuat, Kenan Ferit, Aydin, and Yasin Omen remained.

Ali Fuat, in a calm tone, said, "Alright, Yasin, where should we start?"

"It's up to you, sir, but I'd prefer to discuss everything from the beginning."

"We're listening."

Yasin had thought carefully about how he should speak before coming here. He had chosen every word meticulously, crafted every sentence with precision. This conversation was crucial, as it would impact the rest of his life. He took a deep breath, whispered a prayer to himself, and began.

He explained how his first contact with the sect had been through his father, how he was a successful student who was recruited for code-breaking activities, and how his university entrance was obstructed. He also spoke of the sect's goal to establish a caliphate state using djinn, among other things.

As Ali Fuat listened patiently, he interjected with a question.

"Yasin, isn't this irrational? Have you ever seen a state founded with the help of djinn or spirits?"

"Sir, logic is limited by what you know. Trying to be rational in an area where you have no knowledge is the greatest irrationality. If you were to tell one of your friends about the moment I entered the room as your commander, Pasha Vefik, they would likely accuse you of spouting nonsense. There have been states established and wars won by activating the djinn Zamradun in history. To give a recent example: During the Cyprus War, although the technology of the Turkish planes wasn't at a high level, it was astonishing to see that they hit all their targets precisely. After the war, some pilots openly stated that old men with white beards appeared in the cockpit and told them when to drop the bombs, but the state covered it up. Similarly, in the Battle of Gallipoli, a large cloud descended upon the British soldiers, and the entire British unit was wiped out, as is clearly recorded in the Royal Library of England."

Ali Fuat couldn't take it anymore.

"Stop talking nonsense. The Cyprus War and the Battle of Gallipoli are miracles created by the heroic Turkish nation in history. The stories you're telling are fabricated by certain Islamist and liberal circles to deliberately weaken the Turkish nation's reflexes."

Although Yasin had enough information to support his arguments, he realized that getting into a debate would be unproductive, even harmful. He knew he wouldn't get anywhere by arguing. He needed to soften the atmosphere.

"Sir, the sect believes in these ideas and is deeply involved in activities related to djinn. They think there will inevitably be a reckoning one day," Yasin said, taking a few sips of water from his glass before continuing.

"The sect's aim of controlling djinn was to establish a caliphate state. However, as they gained control over the djinn, they began to use them for different purposes. The turning point was the murder of Hadji Halit Nurullah, one of the founders of the sect. From that moment on, the sect declared war on the community."

"What's the sect's issue with the community?"

"Sir, you know about the community's foundation, development, activities, and goals, right?"

"Of course. But go ahead and explain as if we don't."

"Sure, sir. I only mentioned it to avoid repeating the same things."

As the others in the room listened attentively, Yasin began to explain the conflict between the sect and the community.

"When the community was first established, they operated with an amateur spirit. They were deeply committed to the ideal of the caliphate and ready to die for it. Under the leadership of the Demirkaplan family, many attempts were made in the name of the caliphate, but none were successful. The illegal guards and the legal Independence Courts eliminated all identified members. All attempts in the early years of the Republic ended in failure. This situation led to changes in the community's strategy. Their activities became more covert, and their methods changed. Initially, they planned to assassinate the founders of the Republic or organize a large-scale popular uprising, but these methods were abandoned. For many years, the community remained inactive. But when the DP (Democrat Party) was established, there were stirrings within the community as well. Community members began to organize in all provincial and district organizations. With the victory in the 1950 elections, the community's efforts reached new heights. They believed that the caliphate was near, but the May 27th coup disrupted everything. After that, the military administration replaced all identified cadres. All of the community's efforts were wiped out at once. They began to dissolve day by day. The community was on the verge of fading into the dusty pages of history when, within a few years, surprising developments occurred. The leftist winds that began to blow worldwide also took hold in Turkey. This situation presented a new opportunity. The state apparatus was no longer dealing with religious organizations but with revolutionaries. In fact, because they were anti-communist, the religious factions began to gain sympathy."

"And then came America's Green Belt Project."

"Yes, sir. To prevent the Soviet Empire from accessing oil reserves and warm seas, America initiated the Green Belt Project. Results were achieved quickly in Afghanistan and Iran. In Turkey, the Islamic factions gained more power than they could have ever dreamed of."

"Did the CIA have direct contact with the community?"

"I couldn't find that information, sir. There was certainly some interaction, but I don't know in what form."

"How do you guess there was interaction?"

"I'm thinking about the change in their organizational structure. The emphasis on education, the placement of trained students into government positions, and the establishment of a commercial structure to finance this cycle. I don't need to go into details; you know it well. With the Green Belt Project, the community became more professional than ever before."

"Do you think this organizational structure has a CIA patent?"

"Yes."

Ali Fuat was aware of the CIA's activities in Turkey and its connections with the community. However, the fact that they were allies within NATO and that America was the world's most powerful country prevented a harsh response.

Yasin noticed Ali Fuat's silence when the word 'America' was mentioned. He assumed this attitude reflected the general policy of the state. They would torment veiled girls trying to enter university and poor revolutionaries who wanted nothing but independence for their country with torture and exile, but when it came to America, even when they knew the country was working to destroy their nation, they would sit quietly. Yasin glanced at Ali Fuat with a cynical smile.

Yasin remained silent for a while, waiting for Ali Fuat to ask a question, make a comment, or say something, but when nothing came, he decided to speak himself.

"The community was living its golden age with the Green Belt Project. The private tutoring centers, schools, finance companies, and holding companies were making money. You are well aware of the developments up until the February 28th process."

"Yes, everything went the way the community wanted until February 28th."

"If the military had delayed its intervention a little longer, we would have experienced an Islamic revolution similar to the one in Iran."

Ali Fuat was familiar with the period leading up to February 28th. Yasin had recounted everything correctly, without hiding anything. The point Ali Fuat really wanted to focus on was the process after February 28th. Because after February 28th, the community had stopped displaying its usual behavior. Initially, it was thought that they had gone silent out of fear of the military, but as the silence dragged on, it became more puzzling. After February 28th, the community didn't engage in any active operations against the Republic. They couldn't understand this situation. However, Pasha Vefik seemed to be at ease, as if he knew everything. Ali Fuat was searching for a reason. Why had the community become passive? What was their new strategy? Which intelligence groups were they working with? More broadly, what had been happening since February 28th?

"Alright, Yasin. You've summarized the period up to February 28th very well. Go on."

Yasin took a sip of water from his glass.

"February 28th was a matter of life and death for the community. The military did the necessary cleanup. A significant portion, though not all, of the community's organization within the security forces was dismantled. Key officials in the state apparatus were sidelined. More importantly, the military coup taught us that when people feel the pressure, they can suddenly abandon their beliefs."

"Are you talking about those who betrayed?"

"They're included, of course. But what I'm really referring to are those who did nothing. Those who acted as if they had no connection to the community."

Ali Fuat didn't quite understand.

"What do you mean?"

"Sir, as you know, the community trained many people and brought them to very important positions. They made them wealthy. The community had various goals in training and promoting these people. The primary goal among them was to serve the ideal of the caliphate. When February 28th happened, all the members of the community, especially those in high positions, put their hats in front of them and thought. They calculated what they might face. They could lose their positions. They could be subjected to torture. They could be killed or live a miserable life in exile, far from their country and nation. But if they didn't get involved, no one would touch them. February 28th was a turning point. Until then, the members of the community had always seen the benefits of being part of the community, but now they realized there could be drawbacks as well."

"Was it the fear of death, torture, or losing their positions that led to the community's dissolution?"

Yasin's response was brief and to the point.

"Yes."

"That doesn't make much sense. They had endured various hardships before; they were killed, tortured, but the community always survived."

"No, sir, it's not the same. The members never had so much to lose before."

"What kind of things?"

"Holding companies, educational institutions, finance companies, millions of dollars, a luxurious lifestyle."

"So, they began to move away from radicalism to protect what they had?"

"Yes, sir, that was the first factor."

"What's the second factor?"

"The second factor is a sociological situation. After the 1980 coup, Turkey was subjected to a very strong depoliticization process. People were distanced from politics, science, and production. Consumption, plundering, and an economy based on exploitation became prominent. Of course, this also left a cultural legacy. The youth began to look for ways to get rich quickly. So, it would be wrong to equate the structure of the community with the members from the 1930s or 1960s."

Ali Fuat pondered what Yasin had said. What Yasin was explaining were noteworthy things. However, the community they knew had a systematic way of thinking. What was being described didn't match the community's traditions. To explore this further, he asked a question:

"Yasin, what you're saying contradicts the community's history. We've been monitoring the community for about a hundred years since its establishment. Even in difficult situations, there has never been a dissolution process like the one you're describing."

Yasin silently prayed for patience. He had just explained this a moment ago.

"Sir, it didn't happen before because the conditions weren't ripe. The community is undergoing rapid change. The recent developments are entirely related to this internal change within the community."

Ali Fuat couldn't make the connection.

"What do you mean by recent developments?"

"The murders of Osman Karahan and Faruk Altan, the 12's murders, the bomb that exploded in Konya. Everything that has puzzled and eluded you in the last three or four months…"

The commander gave a meaningful look. Yasin was right. They hadn't been able to make sense of the recent developments, but he didn't want to admit that they were clueless.

"How do you know we couldn't figure it out?"

"Sir, it's obvious. If you had figured it out, you would have reached the responsible parties."

"How do you know we didn't reach them?"

Yasin replied calmly.

"Because I'm the one responsible, and no one reached me. I reached you."

Ali Fuat took a deep breath. This kid knew much more than he had anticipated and was very intelligent.

Yasin had devised a three-part plan. He had completed the first part, which was to explain the history of the community up to the present. Now, he would talk about the birth and development of the sect.

"Sir, the period from the February 28th process to the present is crucial. During that time, the community faced a fundamental problem: 'To be or not to be…' Either they would continue pursuing the goal of the caliphate, or they would pretend to do so while protecting their economic interests. The Council of the Exalted was aware of this dilemma. If they continued pursuing the caliphate, the community would be destroyed. Because on the international stage, there was no longer any sympathy for radical Islam. Until the fall of the Soviet Union, radical Islam was always championed because it was an enemy of communism. However, the absence of the communist threat eliminated this sympathy. The generals who carried out the February 28th coup were aware of the situation and wanted to destroy the community while they had the chance."

Yasin swallowed before continuing to speak.

"The Council of the Exalted secretly convened after the February 28th process. Most of the members who attended the meeting believed they would be discussing how to respond to February 28th with various actions. However, things didn't go as they expected. The leader of the community, Cihangir Demirkaplan, along with two key members, Osman Karahan and Faruk Altan, spoke of a very different policy. They opposed protest demonstrations and wanted to expel radical groups from the community. Some members of the Council of the Exalted, particularly Hadji Halit, strongly opposed these suggestions. They believed that a great uprising was the appropriate response to February 28th. In the end, Demirkaplan's view prevailed. Everyone who opposed the new policy, except for Halit and Imam Sait, was quickly marginalized. The expelled members were replaced by people who were both religiously conservative and liberal. Although Hadji Halit and Imam Sait were not ousted, they were effectively neutralized."

Ali Fuat took a deep breath. "Damn, we're completely in the dark," he thought to himself. The blond kid in front of him, with his small stature, was recounting the process flawlessly.

He pulled out a cigarette and offered it to Yasin. "Light it up," he said.

Yasin politely declined, "I don't smoke, sir."

After lighting his own cigarette, Ali Fuat said, "Let's continue."

Yasin nodded and began to speak again.

"Cihangir Demirkaplan, Faruk Altan, and Osman Karahan, who led the Council of the Exalted, chose life at the crossroads of their decision. The concept of 'caliphate' no longer existed in their minds. The caliphate was just a word. The three leaders began by excluding radical elements and cutting off support for some extremist religious groups. Those who were deeply committed to Sharia and the caliphate, those who were willing to die for their ideals, were expelled one by one. All the community's companies were filled with religiously conservative liberals, turncoats, and cowards. Now, the important thing for the community was to protect its multi-billion-dollar economic empire. It was about maintaining their interests. The religious structure in educational institutions was reduced. In other words, the community was secular enough not to offend its members but religious enough not to provoke the state. In return for these policies, the state granted the community the right to exist."

"Why would the state grant the community the right to exist?"

"I don't know, sir. You'd have to ask yourself! You are the state."

Yes, he was, but he knew nothing. He thought the person who should be answering this question was Pasha Vefik. He felt very inadequate. It seemed that all he had done until now was kill.

Yasin continued.

"The strongest reaction to the community's new policy came from Hadji Halit and Imam Sait. Under Hadji Halit's command, the sect intensified its activities."

"What activities?"

"Those related to the djinn! The sect accelerated its existing activities to bring the djinn under control and establish a caliphate state. They began to gather the extreme elements who were starting to resent the community's new policy. As soon as this force started to threaten and alarm the community, Hadji Halit was killed. We suspect this was done by the Black Shrouds."

Yasin looked into Ali Fuat's eyes, waiting for a response.

"Yes, your suspicion is correct. I have a question for you on this matter. Could Hadji Halit also control the djinn?"

"Partially, yes."

"What do you mean by partially?"

"I mean, only to the extent that I taught him, yes."

Ali Fuat pointed to Arab Zekeriya. "A few seconds before Hadji Halit died, he threw Zekeriya around like a rag doll. Does this have anything to do with the djinn?"

"Yes, it does. I can do the same thing. If you want, I can show you right now!"

"And what's the secret of this power? Halit suddenly became very strong. He broke his handcuffs but couldn't stop the bullets."

"He probably didn't have time to complete the prayer fully. Otherwise, bullets, swords, fire, bombs—nothing would have affected him."

Ali Fuat didn't respond immediately; he was deep in thought.

"Let's talk about the murders of Osman Karahan and Faruk Altan."

"Of course, sir."

"Did you commit those murders?"

"No, sir, let me explain."

"..."

"After Hadji Halit was killed, the sect went on high alert. The followers were as grieved as if their own fathers had died. Everyone was filled with extraordinary rage and hatred. Imam Sait held an important meeting with the leadership of the sect."

Ali Fuat interjected with a question, "Were you at the meeting?"

Yasin smiled slightly. "No, sir, I'm only 22 years old."

"I understand," said Ali Fuat. Aydin found the dialogue puzzling. What did the question "Were you at the meeting?" have to do with the answer "I'm only 22 years old"? He looked around in confusion. Kenan Ferit, understanding the situation, leaned over and whispered softly in his ear.

"He means it's impossible for someone his age to be part of the leadership."

Aydin was annoyed with himself. How had he not thought of that?

He refocused his attention on the conversation continuing with Ali Fuat's questions.

"So, you don't know what was discussed at the meeting?"

"No, sir, I do know. I wasn't at the meeting, but I heard everything."

"How?"

"Through my special methods."

"You mean the djinn, right?"

"Yes."

"So, what was discussed at the meeting?"

"They spent a long time discussing Halit Nurullah's murder. The conversation continued about the need to take revenge and cleanse the upper management of the community. Finally, they said, 'It's time to push the button.'"

"What does 'pushing the button' mean?"

"To start the activities to establish the caliphate state. The first step is to take control of the community, then all of the country."

"Were Osman Karahan and Faruk Altan killed as part of this plan to take over the community?"

"Yes, sir."

"Why didn't you kill Demirkaplan?"

"We wanted to, but the young men couldn't get into Demirkaplan's mansion."

"Because it was heavily guarded?"

"No, it has nothing to do with the security. Osman and Faruk were also heavily guarded. You must have examined the details of the murders—the camera footage, the witness statements..." Yasin paused for a few seconds and then added with a slight smile, "Or rather, the lack of statements."

"Yes, we've seen them," said Ali Fuat.

Aydin silently cursed himself. Once again, he hadn't understood anything. Kenan Ferit, who caught Aydin's confused expression, struggled not to laugh. "I'll explain it to you later," he said.

"If it wasn't a matter of security, then what was it?"

"I don't know. Something prevented our agent from entering the mansion."

"Can't you make a guess?"

"That mansion is about 200 years old. The Demirkaplan family has always lived there. Something inside could have caused this effect."

"Like what?"

"It could be a handwritten Quran written by a blessed figure, a talisman, or a prayer. The Quran might have been recited that night. Demirkaplan could have been wearing a djinn-repelling armor."

"What's that?"

"A type of shirt that repels djinn, made of special fabric with hundreds of prayers written in ant script. Sultans used to wear them too. There are still examples on display in Topkapi Palace."

"Did the sect send the djinn?"

"Three followers who had jinns within them were sent. The djinn involved was an djinn Zamradun?"

"Were the 12's murders also carried out by djinn?"

"Yes."

Ali Fuat didn't comment. He leaned back in his chair and thought deeply. This was one of the most complicated moments in the history of the Black Shrouds. Silence stretched on; no one spoke.

He realized there were a few more points that hadn't been addressed.

"Yasin!"

"Yes, sir."

Ali Fuat's eyes were staring into space. He was trying to recall a name.

"Davut something... dere... but..."

"Davut Buyukdere."

"Yes, that's it. He was burned alive and left near Osman Karahan's villa. Do you know anything about this murder?"

"Davut Buyukdere was responsible for the sect's student organization in Bursa. Somehow, the community identified him."

"Did the community kill him?"

"Yes, of course. Who else would it be? The community's crazed enforcers have killed many people. The bomb that exploded in Konya was also their doing."

Ali Fuat noted Yasin's use of the term 'killer' to describe the community's enforcers.

"Yasin, remember, indirectly or not, you're a killer too. According to what you've told us, many people were killed through your involvement."

"You're right, sir. Even if I didn't kill them personally, I'm also a killer."

Yasin smiled, letting his gaze drift over the people in the room. "I guess there isn't anyone among us who isn't a killer," he said.

He was right. Except for Aydin, everyone in the room was directly or indirectly responsible for killing.

Finally, the negotiation phase was beginning. Ali Fuat asked a question, smiling.

"So, Yasin, we've discussed everything thoroughly. Now tell us, why did you share all of this with us? What's your purpose or offer?"

Yasin responded to Ali Fuat's smile with a chuckle of his own.

"Do you think I have an offer?" The mutual smiles continued.

"Allow us to assume that much, kid. We didn't start this work yesterday."

"You're right, sir, I do have an offer."

"Well, then, go ahead, we're listening."

"I'm offering to help neutralize the sect, in exchange for everything related to me being forgotten."

Ali Fuat responded without hesitation.

"Let's say we agree to forget everything about you. What then? What do you plan to do?"

"I want to build a life of my own."

"From what I see, you have various powers. You can change your appearance to get here, you can hack into a bank to withdraw money. Aren't these enough to create a life of your own?"

"Under normal circumstances, yes, they would be enough, sir."

"What's not normal?"

"What's not normal is the sect and the Black Shrouds being very interested in me. I can't build the life I want while living on edge."

"You want to get the sect out of your life, but you know your ties are too deep for that to be possible. The only way is for the sect to be destroyed, its cadres scattered, arrested, or even killed. Is that correct?"

"Yes, sir."

"And you see the Black Shrouds as the power capable of doing this."

"Yes."

"You know that the Black Shrouds have no tolerance for radical organizations like the Djinn Sect, so you plan to help them crush the sect with the logistical support you provide, thereby freeing yourself from that burden."

"That's correct."

"In return for the information you provide, the Black Shrouds will erase any negative thoughts they have about you, and you'll also escape their scrutiny."

"Yes, sir."

"Bravo, I'm impressed by your intelligence. This is what they call killing two birds with one stone."

Yasin remained silent.

"But I have two questions that are bothering me. First, why did you come directly to me? You know very well that the commander of the Black Shrouds is Pasha Vefik. The final decision rests with him. Maybe I'll accept your offer, but he won't."

Yasin didn't wait for the second question and began answering the first.

"I couldn't make this offer to Pasha Vefik because there's no chance he would accept it."

"How did you come to that conclusion?"

"I suspect he has connections with the community. Even if he were to accept my help in destroying the sect, I don't believe he would follow through on the second part of the agreement."

"And how do you know I would follow through on the second part? Maybe I'll just order your arrest."

"Yes, maybe you will, but there's also a chance you might accept."

"How do you know that?"

"I don't know, I'm just guessing."

"And what if I order your arrest and prefer to extract the information about the sect through interrogation?"

"You know that's not a realistic option."

"Why not?"

"If you order my arrest, I'll leave just as I came. I have the power to do that."

Ali Fuat smiled.

"Fair enough. I suppose I got an answer to my first question. Now for the second."

Yasin said nothing, listening quietly.

"If you have such powers, why don't you take care of this yourself? Why not use the djinn to eliminate both the sect and us?"

"I have the power to escape both you and the sect, but I don't want to live a life on the run."

"That's not the answer to my question. Do you have the power to destroy us and the sect?"

Yasin hesitated to reveal this information. He didn't want to damage the fragile relationship with a lie.

"No. I don't have the power to destroy you and the sect. Right now, I only know some simple and intermediate-level prayers. The long and difficult prayers and the books that contain them are in two places. One is with the sect, and the other is with you. Even if I had those sources, it wouldn't make sense to start the life I want to build with a problematic process."

"So the process where the Black Shrouds do all the work and then forgive you is more logical, is that it?"

"Yes, sir, it is."

Ali Fuat let out a cheerful laugh.

"Hey Kenan, maybe we should recruit him into the organization? He's got a terrifying intelligence."

Kenan calmly replied, "As you command, sir."

Yasin felt a brief surge of anxiety.

"You said you'd forget everything about me."

Ali Fuat grew serious.

"I accept your offer."

Chapter

73

Erkan's Tempest of the Soul

Arab Zekeriya and Erkan went down to the tea room. They were drinking tea and watching television.

Erkan seemed to be staring blankly. His eyes were fixed on the television, but he wasn't truly seeing it. He kept watching every ad, news segment, and program that appeared on the screen with the same level of attention. Even when the channels were changed, he remained unresponsive. His eyes were on the screen, but his mind was elsewhere. He wondered what was being discussed inside, why Yasin had come, if they would release him, and if he would ever see his girlfriend again. A voice from deep within seemed to be saying, "Pelin." He couldn't make sense of it. Yes, Pelin was in a terrible situation as well.

"Pelin, Pelin, Pelin," the voice kept insisting, "Pelin."

Erkan was snapped out of his daydream by the deep voice of the news anchor. "...Pelin Korhan, a student staying at a dormitory, committed suicide by jumping from the seventh floor of the hospital where she was being treated for psychological trauma. The chief physician expressed deep sorrow over the incident..."

Every word hit his brain like a sledgehammer.

The anchor seemed like a demon in human form, announcing the reign of death. It was as if he was saying, "We've taken Pelin; Bahar is next." A mysterious fog began to envelop him as he turned to look around. Everything was disappearing into a black smoke. He turned his eyes back to the television. He saw Bahar running toward him, sobbing, but the more she ran, the further away she seemed to get. Panicked, he stood up and managed to say, "You won't die," as he tried to reach Bahar, but... He felt a sting in his arm like a mosquito bite and saw all the images begin to blur...

"What happened to him, Zekeriya?"

"Commander, we were watching the news. He suddenly started feeling unwell, began shouting, and moving uncontrollably. We gave him a sedative."

"What news was he watching?"

"It was about a girl's suicide. I didn't catch the details."

"Find out!"

"Yes, sir."

Ali Fuat left the infirmary. Erkan's situation was no longer important. After the operations were over, he would keep his word and release Erkan.

Chapter

74

The Unfolding Gambit

While the Black Shrouds conducted a comprehensive investigation based on the information provided, they did not cooperate with the police at all, following Yasin's warning. The Imam was very well-organized within the Konya police force. The students he had trained had now become commissioners and chiefs.

A long list was compiled. The names of the sect's leadership and fanatic followers were categorized. A priority group led by Imam Sait Nurani was established. The names of those killed in the big explosion were crossed off. The Imam was not among the dead. However, there were bodies that could not be fully identified—burnt or dismembered. The Imam could be among them. The goal was to cross off his name as soon as possible.

After the explosion, the sect had scattered across various locations in the city. The houses where the followers were staying were identified. The operation units were prepared. A villa outside of Konya, belonging to the Black Shrouds, was designated as the operations command center. After the final preparations were completed, Ali Fuat gave the signal.

The city was asleep, as the day traded shifts with the night, and the sun, faithful to its ancient promise, began to rise with its billion-year weariness. The light beams became small groups of friends, breaking away wildly from the sun and scattering toward the earth. The sun's children, with yellow flowers in their hands, new hopes, illuminating the skies of Konya, descending joyfully to pierce the darkness, meeting every leaf, every insect. They entered houses swiftly through slightly open curtains, without discriminating between race, gender, rich, or poor. They flickered without distinction. Perhaps those eyes belonged to a general, a president, or maybe a leather worker.

The operation began at dawn. The Black Shrouds entered the designated addresses with their death lists in hand. Doors were broken simultaneously, and thresholds were crossed at the same time.

Ali Fuat lit his second cigarette. He took a deep breath, filling his lungs, and then blew the bluish smoke onto the paper in his hand, as if to say, "Well, here we go." The smoke dispersed as it hit the paper, revealing a list of names. The names, duties, and nicknames were neatly written one under the other. At the top was Imam Sait Nurani – Sheikh. Some of the names were crossed out. The commanders of the operation units were reporting the names of those killed in real-time. With each report, Ali Fuat moved his pen to the top of the list, but then he would cross off a name or two from the middle or bottom.

With a small movement of his index finger, he knocked the ashes of his cigarette onto the villa's parquet floor. The beep of his multifunctional watch caught his attention, and he looked at it. The stopwatch had stopped at 4:37. The time calculated for getting out of the vehicles and back in was four minutes and thirty-seven seconds. It was the most critical part of the operation. All fourteen squads should have been in their black vans, ready to drive back to the command center.

In the large room, the guards at the satellite-connected computers were receiving the latest updates on the operation.

Ali Fuat asked, "What's the situation, guys?"

A guard with a large nose pointed at his computer screen, "Commander, nine squads boarded on time." On the screen were fourteen boxes, each containing the names of the squad commander and six soldiers. Nine of them were lit. The squad commanders pressed a button on their satelliteconnected watches as soon as they boarded their vehicles, sending the "Boarded" signal to the command center. Ali Fuat noted the names in the boxes. None of them were red, meaning he hadn't lost any of his men. If a Black Shroud operative died during the operation, their heartbeat-sensitive watch would notify the command center.

After a few seconds, four more boxes lit up. Only one squad had not boarded its vehicle.

"Why hasn't the sixth squad boarded? Is there a problem?"

"They haven't sent any danger signals, Commander." Ali Fuat took a drag from his cigarette.

"Establish a voice connection."

"Yes, Commander."

He put on the headset with a microphone and waited for the connection to be established. Voice connections were not the preferred method for the Black Shrouds. Although the radio system they used was highly secure, the frequencies could be intercepted. They only used it in urgent situations. Thirty seconds had passed since the sixth squad had not boarded, but no danger signal had been sent. There was no immediate emergency. He was ordering the voice connection out of a gut feeling that something was wrong.

Ali Fuat sensed that something was amiss. The connection, which should have been established in eight seconds, had not been made.

"Why isn't the connection established?" The tension in his voice made everyone in the room uneasy. The guard at the computer swallowed nervously, "We can't reach the frequency, Commander."

"Why not?"

"Technically, it's impossible not to reach it. We should always be able to connect, Commander."

"Then why isn't it connecting?"

Something was definitely wrong. Ali Fuat looked over the names in the sixth squad. Squad Commander Tunay Gencer, Ilker Ensari, Semih Kiremitci, Halim Hasan Altinoluk, Caner Iscioglu, and Sertan Doganay. All of them were very skilled and experienced. He was afraid that something might have happened to his colleagues.

"You can't even establish a simple connection!"

The tension in the room was palpable. There no logical explanation for the failure to connect. They kept trying repeatedly.

Ali Fuat brought his cigarette to his lips, took a deep drag, and angrily threw the butt to the ground.

"Which address did the sixth squad go to?"

A guard, seemingly anticipating the question, responded immediately, "A farmhouse, Commander."

"What's the status of the other squads?"

The guard pointed at the map on the screen.

"You can see it here, Commander."

The map of Konya's main roads was displayed on the screen. There was an "X" mark outside the city with the word "COMMAND" written, indicating the villa where Ali Fuat and his team were located. There were also small blue lights moving millimeter by millimeter along the roads. Three of the vehicles appeared to be very close to the villa.

"Is the sixth squad's vehicle visible?"

"Yes, Commander." The soldier touched the screen with his finger, pointing to a small blue dot. According to the map, it was outside the city and not moving. It appeared that the sixth squad was still inside the house. Ali Fuat checked his watch. Two minutes had passed since they should have exited the house and boarded their vehicle. That was a long time. If there had been a firefight or any other difficulty inside, they would have sent a danger signal to the command center via their watches. If there were no problems, why hadn't they boarded their vehicle yet?

Yasin had suggested managing the operations and getting directly involved. "If you encounter a team that can use djinn, you might find yourselves in a difficult situation," he had said. Ali Fuat didn't want their operational methods and working structures to be exposed. Yasin already knew many things about them. Revealing their working principles and the technology they used could be turned against them in the future. Because he didn't fully trust him and despite his concerns about djinn, he had taken the risk and carried out the operation with his men, excluding Yasin's influence.

He was worried about the safety of his men. His nerves were frayed. In a voice low enough that the guards in the room couldn't hear, he muttered, "I think I'm losing this gamble."

The large-nosed guard at the computer suddenly shouted, "Commander!" There was a tone of displeased excitement in his voice. Ali Fuat, sensing this, looked at the screen.

His worst fears had come true.

The room froze, no one wanted to be the first to speak. Ali Fuat stared at the name Ilker Ensari. It was glowing red.

His man was dead.

Questions flooded his mind. If there was a problem, why hadn't they sent a danger signal? Pressing a button on their watches would have been enough. What were the other guards in the squad doing? Had his man been killed by djinn?

Before he could answer these questions, which had appeared in his mind in a split second, he turned to the guard monitoring the road map.

"Which squads are closest to the incident?"

"3rd, 12th, and 14th squads, Commander."

"Give them the address and inform them that the 6th squad needs assistance."

The large-nosed guard shouted again, though with less intensity this time, "Commander!"

Ali Fuat looked at the screen as if he had expected this.

Another guard from the 6th squad, Semih Kiremitci, was dead.

Desperate, he reached for his cigarette. He lit one. One of the soldiers was communicating Ali Fuat's orders to the 3rd, 12th, and 14th squads. The squads that received the orders were changing their directions.

Four men were left inside the mysterious house. He hoped the other squads would arrive before anything happened to them. He looked at the road map on the screen. Three blue dots were slowly advancing towards the target from different locations.

"How long until they arrive?"

"At least 10-12 minutes, Commander."

"Damn it," he muttered to himself, knowing that was too long.

"Tell them to hurry."

"Yes, Commander."

He took a few puffs from his cigarette. He wondered if sending backup was a mistake. If the force that killed his men was djinn, the other teams he sent would also be in danger. Perhaps he had made a mistake by keeping Yasin out of the operation.

"Commander, the 4th, 7th, and 1st squads are currently at the command center."

The screen showed three blue dots near the command center. A few seconds later, the squad commanders entered the room. The military seriousness on their faces was mixed with the joy of having successfully completed their mission. At first, they did not sense the tension in the room. Ali Fuat said, "Wait in your vehicles until further orders."

All three squad commanders responded in unison, "Yes, Commander," and left the room.

Another light turned red, and then another. Ali Fuat clenched his fist so tightly that it bled. The enemy inside the house seemed to be right in front of him.

Two of his men were still inside. The backup units had to arrive quickly, or he would lose them as well.

"How much time is left until they arrive?"

Before the soldier monitoring the map could answer, another one spoke up.

"Commander, we've lost another soldier."

One of the last two names had turned red. Only Squad Commander Tunay Gencer remained. What was going on? They couldn't establish a voice connection, couldn't send a danger signal, yet the death signals were still reaching the command center. If there was a malfunction, wouldn't it affect all the signals coming from the same device?

The soldier monitoring the vehicles said, "Commander, four squads are about to enter the command center." Ali Fuat didn't pay much attention to this information. "Tell them to stay in their vehicles and wait for further orders," he said.

The soldier carried out the order. The soldier at the radio system stared at the screen in shock. Tunay Gencer was sending a voice call signal. Despite repeated attempts to establish a connection, it had failed, but now it had connected on its own. He turned excitedly.

"Commander, the radio connection has been established. Tunay Gencer is signaling for a voice call."

"Accept it immediately."

With a click of the mouse, the room was filled with Tunay Gencer's terrified screams. Among the screams, only the word "Don't come closer" could be made out.

"Tunay, Tunay, Tunay… What's happening there? Tunay…"

"Don't come closerrrr…"

"What's going on, Tunay?"

"God help me!" The screams, filled with pain, were earpiercing. "It's entering me, it's entering me…"

Ali Fuat didn't know what to do. He was drenched in sweat. What kind of thing was this?

The loud sound of the radio amplified the screams even more. It was as if the room's windows were about to shatter.

"My veins are bursting, my veins are burstiiing." The sound suddenly cut off.

"Commander, the radio connection has been lost."

Just as Ali Fuat was about to look at the radio system's monitor, the other soldier spoke up.

"Commander!"

The soldier was pointing at the computer screen. The name of Squad Commander Tunay Gencer was glowing red.

Ali Fuat stared at the screen. Six elite Black Shrouds were dead. He turned his eyes away, searching for some sense of justice in the technology. News of death shouldn't be delivered like this… He looked back at the screen. The red light was searing his eyes. "Six of my men are dead, six of my men are dead, six of my men…"

"Turn it off!"

The soldier, his voice trembling, responded, "Yes, Commander," and turned off the part of the screen that displayed the dead soldiers.

"Have the three squads reached the site?"

"They'll arrive in about two minutes, Commander."

"Tell them not to enter the house and to wait for us outside."

"Yes, Commander."

"Zekeriya!"

"Yes, Commander."

"Bring Yasin and Erkan to the courtyard."

"Yes, Commander."

Ali Fuat quickly headed for the exit. In the large courtyard of the villa, surrounded by high walls, ten black vans were waiting for him with their six-person squads inside. Yasin and Erkan were brought to the courtyard, blindfolded and handcuffed. They didn't want the young men, who they planned to release later, to know the location of their headquarters in Konya.

Ali Fuat said, "To the vehicles." The destination was the farmhouse. Yasin and Erkan were placed in the first squad's van with Ali Fuat. After leaving the villa, their eyes and hands were unbound. Ali Fuat explained everything in detail and asked for Yasin's opinion.

"Well, sir, what can I say? It's hard to comment without seeing it firsthand," Yasin said, feeling annoyed that they had been blindfolded. As if, if he wanted to escape, the handcuffs on his wrists or the cloth over his eyes would stop him.

Ali Fuat, perhaps due to the intense stress and excitement he was experiencing, didn't pick up on the hint of reproach in Yasin's words. He continued his questions in the same manner.

"Could it be related to djinn?"

The question was quite simple. "Yes, it's entirely related to djinn," Yasin replied. There was much more to say. He had repeatedly tried to warn them, saying, "Don't conduct such a hasty operation, these people are not like the ones you know," but Ali Fuat hadn't listened to any of it. Now he was asking, "Did djinn kill my men?" Yasin thought, "No, sir, it wasn't the djinn. You killed them. You threw them into the fire with your eyes wide open."

All these thoughts flashed through his mind, but he didn't express them. Because saying them wouldn't benefit him in any way. But it could harm him.

Erkan, on the other hand, was the most indifferent to what was happening. He was in a trance, thinking about his girlfriend.

The vehicles were speeding toward the farmhouse. The 3rd, 12th, and 14th squads had surrounded the farmhouse. They were in a defensive position, waiting for the other teams to arrive.

The sun was shining on the suspicious convoy of black vans. Ali Fuat kept asking the same questions over and over, wearing Yasin down.

"Did djinn kill my men?"

Yasin sighed inwardly and answered once more. "I don't know, sir. Based on what you've described, it seems so, but it's hard to say without seeing it firsthand."

"The guards in the squad are the best-trained operational teams in the world. They use the latest technology weapons. I can't comprehend it."

"I don't know much about operations, teams, or the quality of their weapons, sir. But I can say this: if djinn have been set in motion, all of that loses its importance."

"What do you mean?"

"I mean, without the proper knowledge, it's very difficult to stop them."

His anger was increasing by the second.

"Is Imam Sait inside? And those three young men you mentioned?"

"I don't know, sir, but it seems likely."

The three squads that had spread out and surrounded the house were waiting anxiously for the other team to arrive.

There was no sign of life in the house. This made the squad commanders uneasy.

It felt as though something unusual was happening. They looked at each other. Yes, one of them removed his ski mask as the temperature rapidly increased. They couldn't make sense of it. They were shaken by the noise that pierced their eardrums. The door and windows of the farmhouse had shattered outward. It was as if a tornado had passed through the house. The soldiers caught in the path of the wind were thrown into the air, breaking their arms and legs as they fell. Each one was scattered, crying out in pain. The intense heat that had drenched their bodies in sweat had disappeared. While Ali Fuat was imagining the terrifying scene that awaited him inside the farmhouse, he hadn't considered the tragedy unfolding outside. The two-story, rustic farmhouse was in ruins. Its doors and windows had exploded, and the roof tiles had been scattered. Whatever had emerged from inside hadn't fit through the doors or windows, tearing apart the edges of the walls as well. Ali Fuat wasn't getting a satisfactory answer from his men. "The heat suddenly increased, we started sweating, and then this crazy wind tore everything apart." This explanation wasn't enough, it wasn't satisfactory.

Ali Fuat ordered the wounded to be taken to the hospital. They drew their weapons and began walking toward the house. Yasin followed them, reciting prayers.

The interior of the house, which had been reduced to rubble, was also a heartbreaking sight for the Black Shrouds. It was the picture of a disaster… Ali Fuat looked at his fallen men with tears in his eyes. Their necks and eyes were burst open, and blood was pouring from their mouths. Those sharp eyes, which once glared mercilessly when carrying out death orders, were now moist with the sight of their comrades' state. None of them could speak for a long time.

Yasin was aware that an explanation was expected. After all, he was the expert on this matter!

"It seems that Imam Sait and his three followers were in this house."

Ali Fuat glanced at Yasin for a moment. Hearing the Imam's name reawakened the deadly expression in his eyes.

"They used the djinn Zamradun. The great wind that tore the house apart, as described by your men, was also caused by them. It seems that the Imam has greatly improved his abilities. It won't be easy to stop him."

Chapter

75

Issues of the Moment

The country, already rattled by recent murder reports, was shocked by a mass suicide in Konya. According to the news agencies, 46 of the 48 men, believed to be members of a religious sect, committed suicide by ingesting cyanide, seemingly coerced into doing so. The other two men had been shot to death.

Was it really a suicide, or...? Commentators, who always seemed to have opinions on everything, couldn't make up their minds. Experts remained vague, and television panels were filled with idle chatter.

"Clearly, this was not a simple suicide. You don't need to be a scholar to understand that. In fact, the two who resisted were shot dead..."

"It's said that the entire sect committed suicide, believing they would go to heaven afterward. First, we must clarify this point -no one who commits suicide goes to heaven. As Allah (s.w.t) says in His verse..."

"It would be more prudent to wait for the criminology report before making any assumptions. But, if we are to engage in mental gymnastics..."

"Let me answer your question with another: Is there sufficient religious education in Turkey? Clearly, there is not. If the state does not teach its citizens about our beautiful religion, someone else will. Among those stepping in, some will be pious souls, but others will harbor deviant ideas."

"Once again, we see that Ataturk was a great leader. The secularism he established shields our society from these backward sects, preventing them from growing and gaining influence. I want those who dream of a theocratic state to take a good look at this scene. Here is the reality of those who embrace systems far removed from secularism, science, and democracy. These sects do not even spare their own followers..."

And so, the discussions dragged on, with everyone concluding, "Didn't I say so?"

The news of the suicides -or murders- was met with very different reactions in two places.

Mr. Demirkaplan hadn't been this pleased by any news in a long time. The fanatical followers of the troublesome Imam Sait were finally off the stage.

"With Allah's permission, our congregation will prevail forever."

"Inshallah!"

Even though Alp couldn't fully grasp what was happening, it was clear to him that these developments were favorable for the congregation.

"Father, who are these men that killed themselves?

Mr. Demirkaplan glanced at his son.

"Were killed," he corrected, starting his sentence with a note of precision. His son's disposition often left him feeling hopeless. Could this boy really manage to run this great empire, he wondered.

"My son, who else's death would bring us this much joy other than Sait's followers?"

Mrs. Demirkaplan, joined the conversation.

"May his name be cursed, and may he die as well..."

"That will happen too, my dear. His time is coming."

Pointing to the head of intelligence for the congregation, Mr. Demirkaplan added, "The Black Shrouds is nothing like our fools. They'll find Sait soon enough and take care of him."

The intelligence chief lowered his head in displeasure. Mr. Demirkaplan was right. They had indeed failed to make any significant progress against the sect.

"Mr. Demirkaplan, we should secure our position and seize this opportunity while Imam Sait is weakened."

"He's already a walking corpse, my dear. Don't worry."

Chapter

76

Ali Fuat & Pasha Vefik

The red phone on the edge of the desk was ringing. It was the voice of a five-star general from the summit. His hand trembled as he reached for it.

"Yes, sir."

"Pasha Vefik."

"At your command, sir."

"What is the meaning of all this?"

Beyond what he had seen on television, Pasha Vefik only knew that six of his men had been killed. It was a development completely outside of his control. He was shocked. This was the third phone call demanding answers, and this time, it was from the very top.

"Sir, the Black Shrouds has nothing to do with this incident."

"The Black Shrouds was established precisely to deal with such matters. What do you mean, nothing to do with it?"

"Sir, we didn't kill those 48 people. I didn't give such an order."

"It doesn't matter who did. You're an illegal organization, you should be conducting your activities more covertly."

"Sir, this was not our operation."

"Then who is running wild in your territory?" The voice on the other end grew increasingly enraged. Pasha Vefik continued his explanation quietly. The more he was reprimanded, the more he fumed, biting his lip in frustration.

Sweat beaded on his forehead, and his energy was utterly drained. Slowly, he leaned back in his chair. "Damn it, Ali Fuat, what are you up to behind my back?" he muttered.

Pasha Vefik checked the time; it would take Ali Fuat and his team at least another two hours to arrive. He turned on the TV and focused on the news. The debate about whether it was suicide or murder raged on.

"Dear viewers, the events in Konya have also garnered significant attention in the global media."

The news anchor disappeared, and the screen changed to show the CNN Turk logo alongside CNN's own logo. A bespectacled woman was reporting something in fluent English, with images from the incident appearing on the side of the screen. The channel, as if trying to be more credible, didn't translate her words for a few seconds, before finally lowering her voice and starting the Turkish translation.

"... 48 individuals, suspected to be part of a fundamentalist group, believed they would enter heaven..."

The CNN logo faded, replaced by the Al Jazeera logo alongside its serious-looking host in a suit. For a few seconds, there was only Arabic, then the Turkish translation began.

As the Arab newscaster's whispery voice faded, she was suddenly replaced by a Greek beauty, marble-skinned and slightly revealing in her attire. A few words of Greek were heard before the Turkish translation followed:

"... Neighbor in shock after 48 suicides. An internal struggle among radical religious groups..."

The world's media was abuzz with the events in Konya. The stock market opened on a downward trend, continuing its recent decline. Economists found the market's reaction normal and spoke of maintaining stability.

With nothing left to enjoy, the final blow for Pasha Vefik was the decision announced by the global giant Nocxal Medical.

"... Our company has decided to remove Turkey from our investment priorities and will instead consider the invitation from the Hungarian government..."

The massive blonde CEO of Nocxal, who appeared to be Scandinavian, delivered the statement that shattered Pasha's nerves.

Economic commentators linked Nocxal's decision to the deteriorating stability in the country. Hungary's offer of "free land, infrastructure, and a ten-year tax exemption" was considered a clever program. Turkey had lost a project that would have directly employed 2,000 people and at least 10,000 through its suppliers, all due to the recent image of instability.

Pasha Vefik muted the TV and stood up. He began pacing the room, trying to pass the time.

Ali Fuat was well aware that the events in Konya had not pleased Pasha. First, the operation had been carried out without his knowledge. But in the end, he was the second in-command of the Black Shrouds. In a rapidly developing situation, he had to have the authority to make decisions. The second thing he thought had angered Pasha was the loss of six Black Shrouds. Yes, the casualties were significant, but the enemy they were facing was extraordinary. He was sure that once he explained the situation, Pasha would understand. Besides, it wasn't all bad. A very dangerous, radical sect had been dismantled. This was a serious gain for the secular republic. Pasha couldn't overlook that.

"Pasha Vefik is a difficult man. He'll definitely have something to say," Ali Fuat muttered to himself. That was the extent of the reaction he expected: a few words.

But the scene he encountered was different from what he had imagined. Pasha was seething with rage.

"A decision to kill 48 people was made without even informing us. For God's sake, at least pick up the phone and ask for advice. Ask how an operation should be conducted! Then they say a storm came, our men were martyred, and they blew up! You idiots don't even understand what's happening. A storm blew them up?!"

Ali Fuat stood at attention, silently listening.

"Do you just kill this many people in one go? Are we at war? You might as well have set up a gas chamber."

Pasha paused to catch his breath, only to continue berating him.

"Have you forgotten your training, or are you having a stroke? Are you even thinking straight?"

Ali Fuat remained silent.

"Answer me, are you thinking straight?"

"Yes, sir."

Pasha grew even angrier.

"How do you just kill 48 people like that?"

Ali Fuat couldn't hold back any longer. He had to respond.

"Sir, they were all fanatic followers of a highly dangerous sect."

"So what! Even if they all needed to die, you could have killed them gradually, one by one, over time, without attracting any attention."

"Sir, we had to finish it all at once. This sect has supernatural powers."

"What supernatural powers? Don't talk nonsense."

"Sir, the strangeness of the recent events..."

"Shut up! Don't you have a brain? You've ruined the economy and the stock market! Look, the Nocxal company has decided to cancel its investment. Why? Because of your stupidity. I've been working tirelessly to maintain stability in this country, building alliances, and then you go and do this!"

The line had been crossed. Ali Fuat momentarily daydreamed about drawing his gun and shooting.

"I'm removing you from your position as commander of operations and intelligence. If you pull a stunt like this again without informing me, I'll rip those stripes right off your shoulders."

If he didn't respond, he'd die of shame:

"Sir, this country was built by a generation that tore off their epaulets. We are their children. If necessary, we will serve the nation even without our ranks."

"Serve the nation? Ten thousand people lost job opportunities because of your so-called patriotism! Is that what you call serving the country?"

"Sir, I..."

"Get out!"

"Yes, sir."

Ali Fuat stormed out of the headquarters, nerves frayed. He began driving aimlessly. He missed Ceyda and Ece terribly, but if he went home in this state, he'd only spoil their mood as well. "I need to clear my head," he muttered to himself. He turned the steering wheel toward Beyoglu[40]. Carefully, he pulled out his cell phone and called Ferit.

"Hello, Ferit."

"At your service, sir."

"If you're free, meet me in Beyoglu. Let's grab a drink."

---

[40] Beyoglu is a vibrant district in Istanbul, Turkey, located on the European side of the city. It's known for its historical significance, cultural diversity, and lively atmosphere. The area is centered around Istiklal Avenue, a bustling pedestrian street lined with shops, cafes, restaurants, and cultural venues. Beyoglu is home to many important landmarks, including the Galata Tower, Pera Museum, and various historical churches and consulates. The district is popular among locals and tourists alike for its nightlife, art scene, and blend of modern and traditional Turkish culture.

Chapter

77

Ali Fuat & Kenan Ferit

As the night deepened, the neon lights of bars, nightclubs, and strip joints became more pronounced. Ali Fuat and Kenan Ferit wandered around, glancing left and right. The pleasant weather, marking the start of summer, had brought out more of the night crowd. They checked out a few places but didn't enter. Kenan Ferit suggested grabbing some kokorec[41]. They ate at a casual spot. After walking around a bit more, Kenan Ferit finally spoke up:

"Commander, should we go inside somewhere?"

They started paying closer attention to the glowing neon signs. Ali Fuat spotted a nice-looking place with a wooden entrance decoration. The name caught his eye: *Havlin Pub*

"Shall we check out that place, Kenan?"

"Where, Commander?"

He gestured with his hand. "There."

"Commander, they probably play foreign music there." Ali Fuat crossed the street toward the venue, with Kenan Ferit right behind him.

"What's the program like? Do you play foreign music?"

The burly bouncer, acting like he hadn't heard the question, replied, "We don't let in men without women," while shifting his gaze to a girl passing by on the street.

---

[41] A traditional Turkish street food made by grilling lamb or veal intestines wrapped around sweetbreads. It's usually chopped into small pieces, seasoned with spices, and served either in a sandwich or on a plate.

Ali Fuat and Kenan Ferit exchanged a glance. The shorthaired, muscle-bound bouncer was now staring at the girl's backside.

"Buddy, we're not asking who you let in. We're asking if there's foreign music."

The bouncer didn't take his eyes off the swaying hips of the girl, now a bit farther down the street.

"Yeeees, foreeeiiign musss…" he mumbled incoherently.

Ali Fuat's eyes widened. It was as if the gears of a deadly machine had started turning.

Once the girl's figure had faded into the distance, no longer pleasing to watch, the bouncer lazily turned his head. The moment he locked eyes with Ali Fuat's bulging stare, he shuddered. Trying to ease the tension, he added:

"Look, man, we can't let you in without a lady."

"Well then, maybe we'll make you our lady!"

"Watch your mou—"

The bouncer didn't get to finish. Ali Fuat slapped the back of his head, hard, right where his earpiece was. His connection with the world was instantly severed, leaving a look of shock and pain on his face. He reached for his ear, staggered, and collapsed to the ground.

Ignoring the fearful glances of onlookers, Kenan Ferit tapped the bouncer's head with the tip of his shoe. "I hope you've got good health insurance!" he joked, smiling. The bouncer, half-conscious and writhing on the ground, would likely suffer from chronic ear problems for the rest of his life, as the blow had either ruptured his eardrum or caused irreparable damage.

Inside, people started rushing out. Seeing the growing number of men, Kenan Ferit reached for his pistol.

The first to emerge was a tall waiter, shouting, "What the hell's going on here?" A bearded man followed, yelling, "Who the hell are you guys?"

The bar staff crowded around the door. Though they approached like hawks, the cold sight of the gun froze them in place. Ali Fuat was livid.

"Who owns this place?"

A middle-aged man stepped forward. "I do."

"Then don't hire idiots like him."

The man couldn't respond.

They looked around a few more spots and finally found a lively tavern filled with women, wine, and raki. The first glass was sipped while observing the surroundings, the second while chatting, and the third while toasting, before they got down to business.

"Commander, you left right after speaking with Pasha. Did something upset you?"

"Kenan, the man practically accused us of treason." He took a sip of his raki. "Pasha's reaction was strange and completely out of proportion."

Ali Fuat lit a cigarette and left it in the ashtray. Sensing an opportunity, Kenan Ferit quickly asked a question:

"What do you mean by 'strange', Commander?"

"For example, apparently, we're destabilizing the country! The stock market is dropping! And 10,000 people have supposedly lost their jobs because of us! Some company decided not to build a factory, supposedly because of us!"

Kenan accidentally let slip:

"Nocxal."

"Yes, that's it. Did he mention it to you too?"

He followed economic news closely but didn't want to show it.

"No, Commander, I was just looking for a music channel in the car, and the news came on by chance. I heard it there."

"Whatever! The man is talking nonsense. Stability is supposedly being disrupted, and the stock market is dropping. We're the Black Shrouds. What do we have to do with the economy or the stock market?"

"You're right, Commander. Pasha must have lost his mind. What are we supposed to do, let the fundamentalists take over the republic just to keep the economy stable?"

"Exactly!" They clinked their glasses and ate a couple of appetizers.

The conversation continued with growing intensity:

"He's evaluating the fact that we killed 48 fanatic followers not in terms of dismantling a highly dangerous sect, but in terms of disrupting economic stability. Is he a Pasha or an economics professor?"

Ali Fuat reached for a cigarette. He scanned the room, but there was nothing unusual.

"There's one more important point, something that just came to mind." Kenan Ferit leaned in attentively.

"While Pasha was yelling at me, he let slip something interesting."

Kenan Ferit asked curiously:

"What did he say, Commander?"

"He said, 'You've ruined the economy, while I'm working with certain people to maintain stability.'"

"Hmmm..."

"What does that mean, Ferit?"

"..."

"When he says 'working with certain people,' what is he referring to?"

"..."

Kenan Ferit fell into deep thought. Taking advantage of the brief silence, Ali Fuat sipped his raki and took a drag of his cigarette.

"Pasha has been changing over the last three or four years. The man who once slaughtered people without a second thought is now scolding us for killing. If we threw a stone for every person he's killed, we'd fill the sea! He probably doesn't even know the count himself. Suddenly, the butcher Vefik is gone, and now we've got Vefik the economist. He's talking about the stock market... What's going on, Commander?"

Ali Fuat spread his hands wide as if to say, "If only I knew."

"Something is definitely going on, but..."

"Commander, I think he's trying to change the structure of the Black Shrouds. He wants to slow down our dynamic, always-ready-for-operation organization that shows no mercy to Sharia. Except for the last couple of months, we haven't had any proper operations in the last three or four years. We were in total silence until that coffee meeting with Halit Nurullah."

"Yeah, there's that matter too. With hardly any information on the man, he suddenly ordered us to have coffee with him. According to Yasin, this man is the leader of the Djinn Sect and the political rival of Cihangir Demirkaplan. He's the rising star of the congregation."

"So, did we end up being Demirkaplan's hitmen?"

"That's what it looks like."

"Looks like Pasha and the Demirkaplan family are in cahoots, Commander."

"Seems so."

"What could their aim be?"

"I don't know, money maybe."

"Commander, how about we take a look at Murat's records, his balance sheets?"

"Why?"

"To see who he's doing business with. Does the congregation have any companies? Who are they selling to?"

"Well, there might be a connection between Pasha and Demirkaplan."

"He could be referring to that when he said, 'I'm collaborating with certain people to maintain stability.'"

"Of course, Commander, you're right, but wouldn't it be better if we confirmed it with evidence?"

"What are we going to do with the evidence, Ferit? Take Pasha to court?"

The tavern was in full swing now. A voluptuous belly dancer was captivating the room. They watched for a few minutes. As their eyes followed the dancer's curves, both men continued to mull over the conversation they had just had. Kenan Ferit, while listening to Ali Fuat, was trying to formulate his own theories.

"Ferit, the more I think about it, your theory makes perfect sense. The removal of Commanders Zeki and Tuncay, the lack of operations—it's all part of a plan to neutralize the Black Shrouds. But why is he doing this? Pasha used to be one of the fiercest protectors of the Black Shrouds. What's changed that he's now trying to dismantle them himself?"

"I don't know what's changed, but having ties with the Demirkaplan family is a betrayal of the cause. It's outright treason."

Ali Fuat nodded.

"Yes, it's treason."

He didn't retrieve his car from the parking lot. Whenever he drank, he preferred to take a taxi. He did the same this time. It was late, and as he gently turned the key in the lock, the familiar scent of his daughter and wife hit him. He had missed his home.

The hallway light flicked on. "They must have heard the door," he thought, as Selin appeared. Half asleep, she gave him a sweet smile, blinking her eyes, wearing a silky nightgown that beautifully showcased her curves—a seductive sight.

"I've missed you so much."

"Welcome home, love."

They kissed.

"You've been drinking."

"Mmm-hmm."

They kissed again and again.

"Is Ece asleep?"

"Yes."

They kissed more and more...

—m—

Kenan Ferit didn't want to go home alone. He pulled out his phone, opened his contacts, and typed "P" to find the names starting with that letter. The first one on the list was "P. Ali."

"Hello!"

"Hey, brother."

"How's it going, Ali?"

"Good, brother. Just busy with work as usual."

"Got anything for me?"

"Oh, absolutely, I've got two university girls for you— both beautiful and cultured. Top-notch, I tell you."

"Let's make it international this time!"

"Of course, brother, however you like. Lithuanian, Ukrainian, Russian—just say the word."

"Send me a fresh Russian girl, and do you have anyone from the Far East?"

"I don't, but give me half an hour and I'll have girls from every country in the UN at your feet."

Kenan Ferit laughed.

"What, you don't deal with non-member countries?"

P. Ali was pleased that his joke was appreciated.

"No, brother. I've got principles. Let me send you one Russian and one Chinese girl."

"Alright, get them ready. I'll be there in 15-20 minutes."

"The Russian's ready, I'll call my contacts for the Chinese girl."

Kenan Ferit began driving slowly, thinking about Pasha's recent changes. Was it just about bribes from the Demirkaplan family? Could it really be that simple? He didn't think so. Pasha's rhetoric about stability and the economy swirled in his mind. For the last three years, the Black Shrouds had been undergoing a quiet transformation. Those who resisted this change were removed, one by one. First Colonel Tuncay, then Colonel Zeki, and soon, Ali Fuat. This trajectory didn't bode well. Pasha was playing with fire. To what extent did his plan to reshape the Black Shrouds go? Was he trying to create an organization that prioritized stability and economic interests? That couldn't be allowed. If this was Pasha's vision for change, it had to be stopped. The Black Shrouds must remain as they are—striking, breaking, and killing.

The dim sign for the "Kardelen Hotel" flickered in the darkness, as if it wanted to hide the immoral activities taking place inside. He pulled over and called P. Ali.

"I'm outside."

"Alright, bro, I'm coming down."

He pulled 800 dollars from his wallet. P. Ali sauntered out with two girls. He immediately recognized the Porsche. There was no hurry, no fear, as if P. Ali was just a store clerk placing two loaves of bread and a kilo of rice into a basket.

Kenan Ferit handed over the money, turned to glance at the girls in the back seat. As usual, P. Ali had made excellent choices. The Russian girl was stunning enough to bring the dead back to life, and the Chinese girl was an exotic contrast. The girls, in turn, were impressed by Kenan Ferit. The Russian thought about how fascinating Turkey was— here, even a handsome young man had to pay for sex. In Russia, girls would be all over him. Typically, they slept with older, overweight men, due to their high prices. Men like Ferit were rare.

As the car moved through the light traffic of the night, Kenan Ferit glanced at the girls in the rearview mirror. In fluent English, he asked, "What are your names?"

The Russian quickly responded, "Natalia."

The Chinese girl followed suit: "Jian."

"Nice to meet you. My name is Stavro."

He felt a secret pleasure from the inside. "Say my name."

"Hello, Stavro."

"Stavro, darling."

"You're very handsome."

Kenan Ferit smiled. "Don't forget my name. And when you talk to me, make sure you use it, okay?"

Clients often had peculiar requests. Both girls replied, "Okay." Turkish men were quite something. You never knew what they'd do next. They'd sleep with you, then sit down and ask, 'How did you end up like this? Can we help you?' Most of the reports to the prostitution hotline came from men who'd slept with girls forced into the trade. A "love it and hate it" kind of culture.

After a short drive, they arrived at Kenan Ferit's house. The dublex house had a stunning view of the Bosphorus and was tastefully furnished.

"Girls, take a shower. I have something to take care of."

The girls laughed and replied, "Okay." Kenan showed them to the bathroom, then went to his office and shut the door.

"Hello, are you in bed?"

"No."

"I spoke with Ali Fuat today. Pasha scolded him, saying we need to prioritize economic interests and that our actions are destabilizing things. What is this guy trying to do?"

"I don't know, you're the one in the thick of it."

"The Demirkaplan family was buying construction materials from Pasha's son's company, right?"

"Yes, they are. In fact, they made another purchase worth a million dollars in honor of the 48 people killed."

"What?!"

"Exactly what you heard."

"I don't understand. If Pasha's making a million dollars off the deaths of 48 people, why is he scolding us? What's he unhappy about? What's he trying to do?"

"I don't know, maybe he's sincere in his talk about the economy and stability."

"Can you get me the records of the purchases? The invoices?"

"The invoices?"

"Anything—ledger, balance sheet, invoice. I want proof of the bribe."

"Consider it done."

"I'm starting the operation, slowly."

"Okay."

He hung up and left the office. The girls were relaxing in the jacuzzi. He grabbed a bottle of champagne and three glasses and joined them.

Chapter

78

The Architect's Game

The day had started off busy. The operations unit was assigned to Kenan Ferit, while intelligence was connected to another guard. Ali Fuat had been sidelined. Once the second in-command, he had suddenly fallen into obscurity.

The door to the room was knocked, and the new operations unit commander, Kenan Ferit, entered.

"Oh, come in, commander," said the person across from him.

Kenan Ferit had expected this level of sensitivity and was somewhat pleased by it.

"Commander, it's just Pasha's nonsense! You've always been the real commander."

Black Shroud once again reaffirmed his loyalty. "The organization is still loyal to you, just like me, Commander. No one cares about what Pasha says."

"I understand, thank you."

"Pasha can no longer give orders to the Black Shrouds. The Black Shrouds do not take orders from traitors."

Black Shroud placed the file on the table.

"What is this, Black Shroud?"

"These are the accounting records from Murat Sancaktar's company, the proof of Pasha's betrayal! When examined, some interesting things come to light. The biggest customers of Pasha's son are the construction companies tied to the congregation. And the goods were sold well above market price. The latest transaction was a one-million-dollar purchase. What was that a commission for, I wonder?"

Ali Fuat looked over the accounting records. Everything Black Shroud had said was accurate. He examined the items sold one by one. Since he didn't know the market value of construction materials, he couldn't make a comparison, but if Black Shroud said it was expensive, it was expensive.

"Yes, Black Shroud, it seems there has been close to a ten-million-dollar transfer over the last three years."

"That's about when Pasha started changing."

"..."

"Isn't it surprising, Commander? It's pure bribery."

"Look at what the great Pasha Vefik has done! I suppose this is what they mean when they say humans are inherently flawed."

"Commander, Pasha can no longer lead the Black Shrouds. We need to take action, Commander."

"You're right."

"We must retire Pasha. You should take over the organization."

"How? If he realizes we are plotting against him, he'll have us executed by the end of the day. We're not dealing with an ordinary person; he's a special operations expert, Pasha Vefik with years of experience."

"The knife has reached the bone, Commander. We can't stand by while the Black Shrouds are left to rot."

"..."

"Commander, we must start the process of retiring Pasha, but this retirement must happen in the grave."

"Are we going to kill him?"

Ali Fuat reacted as if the act of killing was completely stranger to him. Black Shroud continued speaking calmly.

"If we don't kill him, he will kill the organization first..." "Yes, let's kill him," "The commander of the Black Shrouds can't allow this nonsense," "Let's kill him, he's deserved death many times over," "Can we actually do it?" "How will we pull this off?" "He must die, no question," "Should we consult Commander Tuncay?" Dozens of thoughts swirled through his mind, and he swallowed hard, glancing indecisively at Black Shroud.

"Commander, I know this is a difficult decision. But we are the children of a nation renowned for performing miracles under impossible circumstances. Our ancestors have done what we need to do countless times before. This is an order, Commander. It's an order from our glorious history. 'You will not consider the odds or obstacles in front of you when taking on your duty.' The Black Shrouds are the foundational bastion of the Republic. We cannot allow this bastion to be undermined from within."

Ali Fuat listened carefully.

"Yes, this mission is a secret order from the proud history of the Turkish nation. Even if it leads to death, we will not shy away from undertaking our duty to defend the Republic."

"Under your command, we can restore the Black Shrouds to their former glory, Commander."

The conversation was kept brief, and they agreed to meet in the evening. Kenan Ferit arrived in his Porsche, which he claimed he bought with lottery winnings, while Ali Fuat came in his Laguna. The headlights of the cars reflected on the sea. The air had turned quite cool. Ali Fuat lit a cigarette without stepping out of the car. As soon as he opened the door, the sound of the waves filled his ears. The place was remote and safe from being overheard.

Both had been thinking a lot up until the meeting. Ali Fuat was focused on securing Tuncay Sipahi's support, even hoping to bring him back to the organization. Meanwhile, Kenan Ferit was suggesting dealing with things by hiring a toptier assassin.

"Commander, after the Pasha's death, the Black Shrouds will rally around you. I don't think we'll need Colonel Tuncay. Besides, I doubt he'd approve of us in this matter. Colonel Tuncay has a different approach. You know this. His perspective on the Pasha was not the same as ours."

"Colonel Tuncay didn't like Pasha either. In fact, he left the organization because of him. We all went through that together, as you know."

"You're right, Commander. He didn't like the Pasha, but his dislike stemmed from differences in their approach to duty and the Pasha's attitude. It wasn't because he ever saw Pasha do anything that could be considered treasonous."

Ali Fuat took a drag from his cigarette, letting the smoke blend with the sea breeze as Kenan Ferit continued speaking.

"The Pasha started changing three or four years ago. But even before that, he had been laying the groundwork. By creating the impression of personal problems, he managed to push Colonel Tuncay aside, or he sidelined Colonel Zeki with the excuse that he didn't like the intelligence he gathered. And when you should have been awarded a medal for killing 48 enemies of the republic, he came up with nonsensical excuses like 'you're disrupting stability' to get rid of you. All of this was deliberate."

Ali Fuat listened intently, nodding in agreement. Kenan continued: "Colonel Tuncay will never believe the Pasha is a traitor. He's stubborn and will assume that we've become paranoid

because of the pressure we're under."

"What if we show him the documents we have?"

"During his time, the Pasha's son wasn't involved in business yet. He'll be suspicious of the document and will want to investigate it. The chances of such an investigation being detected are very high. The Pasha could sense that there's a plot against him."

Ali Fuat cut him off:

"And if he senses something like that..."

"He'll wipe us out immediately!" Kenan finished.

They pondered for a while. Ali Fuat broke the silence.

"So, you're saying we shouldn't involve Colonel Tuncay at all?"

"That's what I'm saying, Commander. But, of course, the decision is yours."

Chapter

79

Erkan Raving

Ali Fuat woke up early. After having breakfast with his wife and daughter, he left the house. By the time he got into the car, he still hadn't decided where to go. He hadn't fully opened up to Dr. Taner yet, though he wanted to. However, he wasn't sure if his mind was ready for that conversation. Two people needed to have coffee with him—Imam Sait and Pasha Vefik. But neither of them enjoyed coffee, which would make things difficult.

He decided against going to the psychologist, thinking he hadn't made an appointment. Instead, he drove towards the villa in Samandira. The chaos in Konya had ended with six men dead and a friend wounded, forcing him to respond positively to Yasin's persistent demands about the books. For the past two days, Yasin and Erkan had been kept under surveillance.

The guards at the villa, led by Aydin Sipahi, recognized the car as belonging to Ali Fuat. Still, their training kept them alert. When Ali Fuat pulled up and rolled down the window, the tension dissipated.

"Is there a problem, boys?"

"No, commander."

"Stay sharp. Report immediately if anything unusual happens."

"Yes, commander."

Ali Fuat had reminded them at least fifty times. He feared Imam Sait and his three bodyguards might attack the villa. He glanced at Aydin, the officer in charge of the guards.

"How are things, Aydin?"

"I'm fine, sir."

"Bored here?"

Aydin paused, "No, commander," though after a brief moment of reflection, he added, "Well, a bit, sir."

"That's intelligence work, son. You'll get used to it."

"Yes, commander."

When he entered the villa, he was met with Erkan's hopeful gaze. Erkan longed to hear the words "You're free." He couldn't take it anymore. Yasin was buried in books, flipping through pages, jotting things down. He didn't even look up, assuming it was a guard coming in to ask if they needed anything. Unconcerned, he kept working. Erkan's gaze remained fixed, as if pleading: "Say we're free, let us go…"

"Hello, friends," Ali Fuat greeted them. Erkan braced for the blow but didn't waver. He still had hope. "Say we're free. Say the next word…"

"Please, say we're free!" he begged silently. But the second blow came from Yasin.

"Hello, sir. How are you?"

Why did he have to interrupt? He was about to say we're free.

"Thank you, Yasin. How are you?"

Yasin smiled. "I'm fine. We're just working."

"Working? What work? Just say we're free!" Erkan screamed inwardly. Ali Fuat noticed Erkan's strange posture—sitting with his hands on his knees, slightly hunched, staring at him intently.

"Erkan, how are you, my boy?"

In a low voice, Erkan muttered, "Let me go."

"What?"

Erkan repeated louder, "Let me go."

Now Ali Fuat heard him clearly. He studied Erkan's face carefully. Something was off.

"We'll let you go, of course. Just wait until this is over…" But Erkan didn't let him finish.

"Let me go!" he shouted, leaping from his chair and charging toward Ali Fuat. Ali Fuat shook off his momentary shock and, with a swift judo move, grabbed Erkan by the shoulder and slammed him against the wall. Blood was trickling from Erkan's head as he screamed in pain, thrashing uncontrollably on the floor. The guards, alerted by the noise, burst into the room with weapons drawn.

"Take him out, patch him up, and give him a sedative," Ali Fuat ordered.

"Yes, sir," they responded.

Erkan was dragged out of the room and taken to the villa's makeshift infirmary. His frantic cries still echoed in Ali Fuat's ears: "Let me go!" "Bahar, my love, you won't die."

Ali Fuat stood silently, listening to the fading screams, then turned to Yasin.

"What's wrong with him?" he asked.

Yasin shrugged, pursing his lips. "I don't know."

"Is it because he hasn't seen his girlfriend?"

"He hasn't spoken since we came back from Konya. He just sits in the corner all day."

"Well, he'll have to hold out for a few more days." Ali Fuat settled into a chair, crossing his legs. He hadn't come to the villa for Erkan; his real focus was Yasin.

"How's the work coming along? What stage are you at?" From behind a desk piled high with books, Yasin smiled confidently.

"I'm ready," he replied in a calm, assured voice.

"Good!"

Yasin had reviewed his texts thoroughly. He had memorized the incantations he had deciphered, ready for the showdown with the Imam. The only problem was that the Imam and his three bodyguards were still elusive. Once their location was confirmed, the Black Shroud death squads would finish the job, aided by Yasin's prayers.

Before leaving, Ali Fuat checked on Erkan. He was lying unconscious, sedated.

"Aydin"

"Yes, commander?"

"Make sure this boy meets his girlfriend, safely."

"Yes, sir."

"And be extremely cautious. Nothing can go wrong." Ali Fuat had calculated that Erkan couldn't be released for at least a few more days, but he thought seeing Bahar might help preserve his sanity. In truth, he felt a bit sorry for him.

Chapter

80

Ali Fuat&Tuncay Sipahi

Ali Fuat closed the gap between himself and the car ahead until there wasn't enough room to slide a matchbox between them. On the ferry, the etiquette was to park as close as possible to the car in front, but he might have overdone it this time. "Oh well," he muttered to himself. There was nothing he could do now anyway; the car behind him had parked equally close.

He hadn't told anyone about his trip. Neither his family nor his men knew he was heading to Bursa. Not even Colonel Tuncay had been informed of his visit.

Kenan Ferit had opposed the meeting, but Ali Fuat was determined to speak with his former commander, Colonel Tuncay. Although he didn't entirely disagree with Kenan's reservations, he planned to be cautious. He would never mention the plans to assassinate the Pasha. He intended only to discuss the strange behavior of the Pasha and listen to the colonel's perspective.

By the time Ali Fuat arrived in Bursa, it was 1:30 p.m. When he reached Karacabey, the clock showed 2:45 p.m. Colonel Tuncay had moved to the Bogazkoy holiday village in Karacabey after leaving the organization. Following the directions he had been given, Ali Fuat arrived in Bogazkoy around 3:35 p.m. It was a beautiful place, with the sea on one side and the forest on the other. Since the tourist season hadn't started, it looked like an abandoned town—quiet and still.

He pulled out the address he had written down earlier by Aydin: "Izci Neighborhood, Kuyu Street, No:26, Bogazkoy/Karacabey-Bursa." Ali Fuat asked one of the few people he saw on the street for directions to the neighborhood and followed their guidance. There were no large estates, massive apartment buildings, or luxury villas. The area was surrounded by village houses—this must have been the original settlement, where the true locals of Bogazkoy lived.

He found Kuyu Street and then house number 26. It was a quaint house with a large garden. Ali Fuat opened the iron gate by pulling on the string and walked inside. The pathway was paved with marble, with a faucet on one side and a shower on the other. The garden was well-tended, with various fruits and vegetables growing. Walking along the half-meter-wide marble path, he reached the entrance of the house. Wooden beams about 2.5 meters high were placed over the marble, creating a trellis covered in grapevines. Using his height to his advantage, Ali Fuat plucked a couple of grapes and popped them into his mouth.

Just as he was about to approach the door, he saw the curtain move aside, and a shotgun was aimed directly at him. Whoever was behind the curtain kept their face hidden. The barrel of the gun glistened in the sunlight filtering through the grape clusters. For a moment, Ali Fuat considered reaching for his own weapon, but it wasn't a smart idea. At this distance, he had no chance against a shotgun. He hesitated, shifting slightly to the side, but the barrel instantly followed his movement. Whoever was behind the curtain was alert and wasn't about to fall for any cheap tricks. A single pull of the trigger, and Ali Fuat's chest would be torn apart.

Had he come to the wrong house? Was the homeowner angry because he had eaten their grapes? Did they mistake him for a thief? A wave of fear shot through him. What if Imam Sait and his bodyguards had stormed the house, killed Colonel Tuncay and his wife, and set up an ambush for him? Sweat dripped from his brow. He regretted not bringing his men with him.

The gun's barrel moved rhythmically, up and down. For a moment, Ali Fuat was puzzled. The gun rose and fell two more times in quick succession. They were signaling him to raise his hands. He obeyed, raising his hands until his fingers brushed against the grape clusters.

Laughter came from inside. A woman's voice behind the curtain said, "That's enough, Tuncay. The poor boy is about to have a heart attack." The curtain opened. Colonel Tuncay stood there, his expression stern, while his wife smiled warmly.

Ali Fuat was taken aback. This was not the kind of welcome he had expected.

Since we last met, the Colonel's sense of humor had changed considerably. The Colonel smirked, "Don't eat someone else's grapes without permission again, Fuat," he said. The couple chuckled. Mrs. Sipahi added, "Put your hands down, child. Look at him, he's in shock." His hands were still raised in surprise.

Colonel Tuncay and his wife prepared a fine raki table in honor of Ali Fuat. They enjoyed an array of mezes and grilled fish that was seared to perfection. Glasses clinked, and the conversation drifted from one topic to another.

The sky had started to turn red, and the sun was gradually setting. After enjoying coffee brewed over the embers, Commander Tuncay suggested going for a drive in his Jeep. His wife encouraged it, "Go up to Malkara Hill[42] before it gets dark to take in the view," she said. Ali Fuat remained silent; this was what he wanted anyway. He was eager to be alone with his commander to discuss matters concerning Pasha Arif.

Without his wife noticing, Tuncay Sipahi took two cigars. Doctor had forbidden him from smoking, but he allowed himself small indulgences. They hopped into the open Jeep and sped up to Malkara Hill. Reaching the top, Tuncay veered off the road toward the edge, coming close to the cliff. He turned off the engine, silencing the roar.

The crimson glow of the setting sun hit their faces, with endless blue waters stretching beneath them. The Colonel removed the cigars from their tubes, cut the ends, and handed one to Ali Fuat. "Moisten

---

[42] A hill located in the Thrace region of Turkey, within the district of Malkara in Tekirdag province. Known for its surrounding natural beauty and agricultural fields, the area is famous for its vineyards and sunflower farms, playing a significant role in the agricultural economy of Thrace.

it a bit before lighting it. I've been saving these for a while; they might have dried out."

Ali Fuat used his lighter to ignite the cigars. They sat in silence for a minute or two, watching the view as they puffed on their cigars. Tuncay Sipahi was the first to break the silence. "So, tell me, Fuat, what brings you here?"

Ali Fuat started from the beginning, recounting the murders of Faruk Altan and Osman Karahan, the oddities surrounding the killings, and Pasha's constant refrain of "Let's not disrupt stability." He shared everything on his mind, excluding details of the bribes Pasha had taken and his thoughts of killing him. Tuncay Sipahi listened intently, taking frequent puffs from his cigar.

When he finally finished, the Colonel said nothing at first, taking time to think.

"Pasha is a peculiar man," he remarked at one point, before falling silent again. Ali Fuat remained quiet as well, lost in thought.

After a long pause, Tuncay spoke with an uncertain tone.

"Honestly, I don't quite understand it, Fuat. Pasha Vefik has always been an eccentric. He was a constant obstacle to us back in the day. I left the organization because I couldn't stand his whims. But stability and economics? Those were never topics he talked about. Must be his latest obsession."

"How do you interpret Pasha's talks about the economy, Commander?"

"What's there to interpret, Fuat? It's nonsense, plain and simple. Every institution has its own functions. Hospitals treat patients, schools educate students, police catch criminals... The Black Shrouds were established to protect the republic and its reforms. Every institution has a distinct role. The country has plenty of agencies that deal with the economy and stability— Treasury, Central Bank, Ministry of Economy. With so many expert organizations, it's sheer lunacy for Pasha, with no relevant background, to make the Black Shrouds pursue an economy-driven policy."

"Yes, Commander, but still, he's enforcing his will."

"Pasha Vefik is a stubborn man, Fuat. No matter what you tell him, he won't deviate from his path."

"Commander, could Pasha have a personal interest in these matters?"

"No, son, what interest could he have? It's just stubbornness. He's not the type to pursue personal gain. We worked together for years."

"I understand, Commander."

The conversation stretched on. Kenan Ferit's predictions had proven correct. Yes, Colonel Tuncay didn't like Pasha, but he didn't view him with outright hostility either. He would never approve of any plan involving Pasha's death.

Finally, Ali Fuat asked, "Commander, would you consider returning to the organization?"

The response was firm and definitive. "No."

Ali Fuat spent the evening at the Colonel's home. Despite insistence to go fishing in the morning, he set out for Istanbul.

The day had also started briskly in Istanbul. The intelligence officers of the congregation had unexpectedly located Imam Sait and three of his followers. The deadliest hitmen were prepared, plans were drawn, and the news was rushed to Demirkaplan. However, the expected approval did not come. This time, Mr. Demirkaplan did not want to leave anything to chance. He didn't trust his men.

After consulting with his wife, he decided to call the Pasha.

"Hello."

"Yes?"

"Good day, Pasha. This is Cihangir Demirkaplan"

"Hello, Mr. Demirkaplan."

"How are you, Pasha? I hope you're well."

"Saying I'm fine is just habit... Lately, I've had neither morale nor joy."

"Pasha, I think the news I have will lift your spirits."

"What news?"

"Pasha, we have located Imam Sait and his men."

Far from lifting his spirits, the news only seemed to make him more tense. He said nothing, remaining silent.

Cihangir continued with his explanations. "Pasha, this man is a thorn in our side. Even though his followers in Konya were killed, he remains a serious threat to us. If we don't act quickly and eliminate him, he'll reorganize soon enough, recruiting new youths to poison. He'll be a plague for both the congregation and your organization. Let's crush him while he's lost all his strength, Pasha."

Pasha Vefik's face grew even more serious.

"Mr. Cihangir, I don't want any more killings. The country has suffered too much. Perhaps you've heard—a major international company has decided not to invest in Turkey. The stock market collapsed. The entire world believes Turkey is a land of chaos. This image is harming us greatly. I don't want any more turmoil or murders. We'll arrest the man by legal means and be done with it."

"On what charge will we arrest him, Pasha?"

"We'll fabricate something. Don't worry about that."

"Pasha, what's done is done. Killing one more person won't change anything. We can't contain this man with mere imprisonment."

"The matter is closed, Mr. Cihangir."

Pasha Vefik wrote Imam Sait's and his followers' location on a piece of paper. He planned to capture and interrogate him first, then hand him over to the authorities with the label of a sect leader responsible for the suicides in Konya. If Imam Sait were tried on these charges, he would likely receive a life sentence. This way, both the Imam threat would be neutralized, and the public would be reassured as the perpetrators were found.

He immediately summoned Kenan Ferit.

Kenan knocked on the door, entered, and, after giving a nod in salute, said, "At your command, Commander."

The Pasha handed him an address, saying, "Assemble a team. Go discreetly, without causing a commotion, and bring in the four people from this location."

"Who are these four people, Commander?"

"Imam Sait Nurani and his three followers."

Although Kenan tried to hide it, he was visibly surprised. How had the Pasha learned Imam Sait and his men's location? He needed to get this information to Ali Fuat immediately.

After listening to the Pasha's instructions to "Be cautious, let no one see or hear," he left the room.

His first move was to head to his office and call Ali Fuat.

"Commander, where are you?"

"I'm driving at the moment."

"Commander, there's a major development."

"I'll be there in two or three hours."

"Can't you come sooner?"

"I can't; I have a personal matter to attend to."

Kenan muttered a curse under his breath.

"Commander, Pasha Vefik just gave me Imam Sait's address."

"No way... Where did he get it from?"

"He didn't explain. He just said to go capture them."

"Don't do anything until I arrive. Take Zekeriya with you, go to the villa, and wait there."

"At your command, Commander."

Chapter

81

Mournful Demise

As Kenan Ferit and Zekeriya headed toward the villa in Samandira, a group of men under the command of Aydin Sipahi was leaving the villa with Erkan in tow. Acting on Ali Fuat's orders, Aydin was arranging for Erkan to meet his girlfriend. To avoid any complications, he had brought three men with him. Erkan was handcuffed and blindfolded before being loaded into the minivan.

Despite it being a simple task, Aydin was excited. This was the first operation under his command. Even after repeated instructions, he reminded his team once more, "Alright, everyone, be careful. Let's handle this flawlessly."

The three seasoned agents, who had been part of intense operations before, chuckled to themselves. "Don't worry, nothing's going to go wrong," they reassured him, amused by Aydin's inexperience, his fumbling hands, and his nervous energy.

Aydin then turned his strict instructions toward Erkan.

"You'll see your girlfriend like a gentleman, and then we'll head back, okay? No funny business. We wouldn't want to hurt you."

Erkan, thoroughly irritated, sighed and replied, "Alright, there won't be any issues." He was happy; he would soon see Bahar. His heart raced, like a bride lifting her veil.

They arrived at the hospital where Bahar was being held under observation. As the minivan pulled into the parking lot, Aydin issued

343

a final round of instructions. They unlocked Erkan's handcuffs and removed his blindfold.

They exited the vehicle and entered the hospital. At the reception, they asked the short-haired girl with glasses for Bahar Tekin's room. Finally, they arrived at Room 116. After Pelin's attempt to jump out of a window, the hospital had moved Bahar to a first-floor room as a preventive measure. Her sister stood in front of the door with a one-liter water bottle, chatting with the companion of a patient in the neighboring room.

Berrak didn't notice them until Erkan called out, "Hey, Berrak."

"Oh, hello, Erkan." She was momentarily surprised. They had been considering the possibility that what happened to her sister Pelin and Bahar might be connected to Erkan. After Pelin's suicide attempt, the police had been searching for him. How had he managed to get here? And who were these men with him?

Erkan sensed the displeasure in Berrak's expression. "I've come to see Bahar."

Berrak didn't respond. She considered calling hospital security but found herself unable to act. At that moment, the door opened. Bahar had heard the voices. Despite her pale face and downcast spirit, she looked dreamlike. She was dressed in pajamas, her feet bare, standing on the floor without slippers. The moment she heard Erkan's voice, she leaped out of bed and threw herself into his arms, sobbing. Erkan, moved by the reunion, felt tears streaming down his face. Embracing each other, they entered the room.

Aydin was about to enter the room with his men when Berrak blocked their path.

Aydin stammered, "We're Erkan's friends."

"Fine, then wait here," she replied.

They had no choice but to wait, not wanting to cause any trouble. Berrak couldn't enter either; the sight of her sister tearfully embracing Erkan had stirred her emotions. It was a positive sign. Perhaps seeing her boyfriend would have a shock effect, helping her return to normal.

Bahar continued to cry. "Where were you, my love? Why didn't you call? The djinn killed Pelin. They're going to kill me too."

"Don't be afraid, darling. Nothing will happen to you."

"Please don't leave me, stay by my side."

"I won't leave, my love."

Erkan got up and looked out the window. There were no bars, and it wasn't too high. He might never get an opportunity like this again.

"Come over here, my love."

He placed Bahar on the window ledge, facing outward with her back to him. He moved close behind her, holding her by her underarms. He spread his legs for stability and braced himself against the wall. Slowly, he began lowering her, whispering quietly, "Be careful; I'm letting go."

Bahar landed on the hospital lawn. Along with her, a talisman, tied to something unknown, fell to the ground.

"I'm fine! Come on, you jump too," Bahar called, looking up at the window. But what she saw froze her in place. Erkan's face had rotted; his flesh was peeling off. His clothes were torn to shreds. Tiny worms crawled out from his skin, falling from the window. One of his ears hung down, bloodied. Bahar felt her breath hitch, her whole body shaking.

As Erkan was about to jump from the window, he noticed Bahar standing beneath, unmoving, her face twisted in horror.

"Move, love, so I can jump."

"..."

"You're going to dieeee!"

The monster at the window spoke in a grotesque voice. Bahar started running.

"What's happening, my love?" Erkan asked, panicking. He quickly leaped from the window and chased after Bahar.

When Bahar looked back, she saw the creature had jumped from the window and was now chasing her.

"Help!" she screamed.

The cries startled Aydin and his men, who exchanged looks. Berrak, alarmed, said, "That's my sister's voice." They burst into the room, rushing to the window, then quickly jumped out and started running after them.

A man who had brought his wife to the hospital was driving at a normal pace when, suddenly, his gas pedal was pressed to the floor. The steering wheel moved on its own.

Bahar ran with all her might, trying to escape the creature closing in on her. She left the grassy area, hurtling onto the curb and then onto the road. Erkan's scream of "Nooo" blended with the sound of screeching brakes. The road was marked with tire tracks and blood. Aydin was frozen, unsure of what to do. The seasoned members of the Black Shrouds quickly rushed to Erkan's side. As people nearby began to gather around the accident scene, they used a spray to knock Erkan unconscious. Taking advantage of the chaos, they carried him to the minivan.

"Where's Aydin?" one of them asked. They looked around at each other. Aydin wasn't with them. While one waited with Erkan in the minivan, the other two ran back to the accident site. They found Aydin looking around in confusion. Approaching him, they said, "Let's get out of here immediately." Aydin nodded absently, still dazed.

When Ali Fuat entered the villa in Samandira, he saw Kenan Ferit's Porsche parked outside, confirming they had arrived. He parked his own car next to it and went inside.

Kenan had already prepared the operation team, and the villa's interior resembled an armory. As Ali entered the room, Kenan and his men stood at attention.

"Hello, everyone!"

"Thank you, sir," they replied in unison.

He motioned for them to sit down, then called Kenan aside into a separate room.

"What's going on, Kenan?"

"There's been a small problem, Commander."

"What kind?"

"Aydin took Erkan to see his girlfriend, as you know."

"And?"

"They tried to escape. Then, the girl got hit by a car."

"So?"

"The girl is dead, Commander."

"Our men—are they okay?"

"Yes."

"Good, then it's not a big deal. You should've given Aydin a scolding. He's already messed up his first task."

"Well, I didn't say anything, Commander."

"Never mind, forget about it. What's the situation with Imam Sait?"

"The Pasha gave us the address and ordered us to capture him, Commander."

"To capture him or to kill him?"

"To capture him, Commander."

Ali Fuat thought for a moment. He had already made his plan on the way.

"Kenan, tonight we'll take care of both the Imam and the Pasha. By tomorrow morning, the Black Shrouds will be completely under our control."

"How? Do you have a plan?"

"Yes. First, we'll handle the Imam. The rest is easy."

"Commander, what will we do with Yasin and Erkan?"

"We'll release them after the job is done."

"Commander, Erkan is fine, but I'm worried about this Yasin. He's too clever."

"He's clever enough not to cause us trouble. Let him live his life in peace."

The team boarded the minivan, while Kenan, Ali Fuat, Zekeriya, and Yasin got into the Jeep. The address provided by the Pasha was a farmhouse in Akfirat.

They arrived at the location, took positions, and started watching the house. This surveillance could take hours, but they needed to be sure the Imam was inside. Yasin distributed talismans he had prepared earlier. In his hand, he held a parchment inscribed with various prayers. Once inside, he would burn it to scatter the djinn.

After a long wait, they saw a young man entering the house with bags in hand. Yasin recognized him immediately; he was one of the Imam's three loyal followers. This meant the Imam was indeed inside.

Yasin explained the plan.

"We're going to make a sudden entry." Holding up the parchment, he added, "I'll burn this parchment immediately. When it burns, all the djinn in the house will flee. At that moment, you need to kill the Imam and his men. If they manage to escape outside, they could reunite with the djinn. As I light the parchment, things might get chaotic inside. Don't be afraid; the talismans around your necks will protect you."

Ali Fuat added, "Attach the silencers."

Silencers were fixed onto the automatic rifles. They circled to the back of the farmhouse and jumped into the yard. A guard dog began to bark, but a bullet zipped through the air, shattering the dog's skull.

They approached the windows. None of the lights were on. They aimed a thermal camera at the rooms but detected no signs of life. If the walls were too thick, the camera might not pick up anything inside. They carefully positioned themselves by a window. One of the men used a suction cup to affix to the glass and cut it with a diamond, creating an entry point. They slipped inside quietly. Ali Fuat activated the listening device attached to his left ear, capable of capturing even faint sounds. His ear was filled with the hum of insects and the faint murmur of voices from the room, though not clearly. He turned off the device, finding it ineffective.

They exited the room cautiously, moving silently through the hallway until they reached a door with light seeping from under it. Ali Fuat activated his device again.

"...and this is how we can view the martyrdom of our lord Hamza..." He switched off the device. There was a discussion going on inside. He signaled with his hand, and the men took positions on either side of the door.

With a swift kick, they burst in, and gunfire erupted, filling the room with blood. Around twenty to twenty-five men inside were quickly cut down in the crossfire. Only the Imam and three young men remained standing, untouched by the bullets. Their eyes held a terrifying emptiness. Frustrated by the bullets' ineffectiveness, Ali Fuat turned to Yasin, shouting, "Damn it, light that parchment!"

Yasin was frozen, paralyzed by the gruesome scene of blood-soaked bodies sprawled on the floor. Kenan grabbed the lighter and set the parchment ablaze.

The Imam's voice erupted in fury. "Yasin, what are you doing with these infidels?"

Yasin couldn't answer as the Imam glared at him with a terrifying intensity.

As the parchment burned, the three young men began to tremble. With growls, they lunged at the Black Shrouds, throwing those they caught against the walls. If this went on any longer, not a single guard would be left unbroken. But as the parchment continued to burn, their strength weakened.

The Imam took advantage of the chaos and began to flee. Ali Fuat was immediately in pursuit. The parchment burned slowly, and the men's strength waned with it. The Imam rushed down the stairs to the basement.

"Don't run, you treacherous dog!" Ali shouted, his words hitting the Imam like a nail. The Imam stopped, turned, and attacked Ali. Though Ali resisted, he was no match. The Imam was as strong as a bull, throwing him harshly to the ground.

"Betrayal, cowardice—these run in your filthy bloodline," the Imam sneered.

The parchment continued to burn.

The Imam's body began to tremble. His voice took on a demonic tone.

"Commander... You're preoccupied with unnecessary things, Commander. You should be focusing on your family, facing your fears!" The Imam's voice shifted to sound exactly like Selin's.

"Oh, keep going, darling, keep going," he mimicked.

Ali's face turned pale.

"I want you behind me, my man. Come on, come on."

Now, the Imam was imitating Serkan Cenet's voice.

"Haha, can Fuat even manage it from here?"

"Oh, don't bother, darling. It's not like it's anything worth doing anyway!"

Ali was on the verge of losing his mind.

"Enough, you son of a—!"

Then came the mocking voices of dozens of children: "Fuat, little Fuat, tiny little Fuat!"

The parchment continued to burn.

In a frenzy, Ali squeezed the trigger with all his strength. The last few bullets in his magazine whizzed into the Imam's body, knocking him to the ground, though they didn't fully take effect.

The parchment continued to burn.

As the djinn prepared to leave his body, the children's taunting chants mixed with Selin's moans. Serkan Cenet's voice joined in, along with a psychologist's, each belittling Ali, speaking of his wife's infidelity. They justified Selin's actions. "Of course she'd cheat. No one could put up with that for a lifetime…" the psychologist sneered.

Ali pressed the gun to his chin and pulled the trigger. The bullets were gone. He drew his sidearm and held it to his temple, but Zekeriya kicked his hand away just in time.

The parchment continued to burn.

Zekeriya aimed his shotgun at the Imam and pulled the trigger. The blast shattered the Imam's neck. The sound echoed, deafening in the empty room, as a thick cloud of gunpowder filled the air.

Ali dropped to his knees, sobbing. Kenan and his men had killed the three followers.

The parchment had burned to ash.

They quickly got into their vehicles. The first part of the plan was complete.

Ali remained silent, speaking to no one.

Kenan Ferit gathered his courage and asked, "Commander, is something wrong? You don't look well."

Ali gave no response. He pulled out his phone, dialed a number, and held it to his ear.

"Yes?" came the answer.

"Doctor, I need to see you immediately. Tell me where you are, and I'll come to you."

Dr. Taner recognized Ali's voice and sensed a serious problem.

"Mr. Ali, I'm at home right now. It's quite late. Perhaps it would be better if we met at the clinic tomorrow."

"We need to meet now, doctor! I'll come to your home if necessary."

The voice was angry and commanding. Had it been an ordinary patient, he would have refused, perhaps even reprimanded. But Ali Fuat was a dangerous man. If he said he would come, he would. Dr. Taner felt he had no choice.

"Alright, Mr. Ali. Let's meet at the clinic in half an hour."

"Fine," Ali replied, abruptly ending the call.

Turning to Kenan, he instructed, "Take the men and go back to the villa. Release Yasin and Erkan as planned." Then, looking at Yasin in the back seat, he added, "Yasin, thank you for everything. Go and build the life you want. But forget all of this—forget us, the djinn, everything. The books will stay with us."

"I'll honor our agreement to the end, Commander. Thank you for everything. I hope you'll forget me, too, and that we never meet again."

Kenan felt uneasy. He disagreed with letting Yasin go and felt he needed to do something about it.

"Commander, are you sure you don't want us to come with you? What if there's danger?"

"No need. I'm only taking Zekeriya."

Kenan flinched. If Ali was taking Zekeriya, it likely meant blood would be shed. What was going on? Why had the plan changed? Weren't they supposed to kill the Pasha together?

"Damn it," he cursed inwardly.

The vehicles pulled over. Ali took the driver's seat with Zekeriya beside him, while Kenan and Yasin transferred to the minivan, which turned back toward the villa. Ali and Zekeriya headed toward Dr. Taner's office.

Dr. Taner anxiously waited in his office, unsure of why Ali wanted to see him. It was 11:17 p.m., and Ali was late. After a ten-minute wait, there was a knock at the door. Dr. Taner rose from his leather couch in the lounge and opened the door to find Ali, his face tense, accompanied by the hulking figure he had seen once before. Ali got straight to the point.

"Doctor, tell me everything."

Dr. Taner could see that Ali's mental state wasn't conducive to calm conversation. Trying to buy time, he asked, "Would you like something to drink?"

"No."

It was an angry no.

"We don't have much time. I need to know everything about my wife and daughter right now."

Dr. Taner was taken aback, realizing that further delay might set Ali off. He decided to make one last attempt, then reveal everything if it failed.

"Mr. Ali, you don't look well. Maybe we should talk when you're calmer?"

Ali didn't even let him finish.

"I want to talk now," he demanded, his voice sharp and commanding.

Dr. Taner felt he had no other choice. Anxiously, he began to speak, sensing that what he was about to reveal would not be met with calm acceptance.

Ali's intense eyes were fixed on him, waiting.

Dr. Taner finally began. "Ece's primary fear was related to her mother's death. Over time, we discovered that her fear wasn't of a natural death but of being murdered."

Ali Fuat knew this part already. "Yes, I know all this," he said.

"Ece believed that someone was going to kill her mother. Until the very last moment, I couldn't figure out who that person might be. I thought it could be an ex-lover who was pestering your wife, or perhaps a neighbor you had argued with. Maybe Ece had witnessed a minor argument and internalized the idea that her mother would be killed. Until now, I couldn't identify the person Ece feared. But now, we know the name."

Ali's excitement grew. "Who?"

"It's you, Mr. Ali!"

Ali was utterly shocked. "Me?"

"Yes, you."

Ali remained silent for a few minutes, unable to process it. "How is that possible?"

Dr. Taner, as if anticipating the question, began to explain.

"My first impression, based on my conversations with your wife, was that there was a romantic connection between your wife, Selin, and your neighbor, Serkan Cenet."

Ali's breath hitched. He wanted to shout, "No," but he couldn't. Words failed him.

Dr. Taner continued, "Do you remember the drawings your daughter made?"

Ali nodded.

"Those drawings contained hidden messages. Ece was trying to say, 'I saw something through the crack in the door. But I can't tell anyone!' Please recall the drawing of the eyes inside a rectangle and the girl with her mouth crossed out."

Ali remembered both drawings very clearly.

"One night, thinking Ece was asleep, Serkan Cenet came to your house. He and Selin were left alone. At that moment, your daughter got up, and as she was about to enter the room, she saw something. Something she shouldn't have seen…"

Ali interrupted, "Like what?"

"I don't know. Maybe they were embracing. Maybe they were doing something more. But it was definitely something she shouldn't have witnessed. She kept this to herself, fearing that if you found out, you would kill her mother. Perhaps you did something that gave her this impression. Maybe you drew your gun in front of her or hit a third person. It could be anything…"

Ali's face was ghostly pale.

"Why didn't you tell me this before, doctor?"

"I was going to tell you in our last session. But after you shot that thug in the knee in my clinic and ordered that mafia boss to be captured and tortured, I became afraid. I felt that you would react impulsively upon hearing this. I would have told you over time, in a more suitable manner if you hadn't forced my hand."

"You waited too long, doctor!"

Ali stood up and turned to Zekeriya. "I'll be waiting in the car."

Dr. Taner looked at him, panic in his eyes. He watched as the massive figure of Zekeriya approached him, silent and intimidating.

"Mr. Ali, please!" Dr. Taner cried, disbelief evident on his face. "What's going on, Mr. Ali? I was only trying to help you. Are you going to kill me because I delayed the news?"

Ali turned back to look at Dr. Taner, contemplating for a few seconds.

"Psychologist, my mind is in chaos, and unfortunately, the thing I'm best at is killing. I'm sorry!"

Ali locked eyes with Zekeriya, then turned and left. Zekeriya approached Dr. Taner.

"Get a grip, what's happening?" Dr. Taner pleaded, his voice laced with desperation.

Zekeriya, calm and unfazed, walked toward Dr. Taner, who was sitting in his chair. Ignoring his struggles and cries, he clasped Dr. Taner's neck firmly and twisted it with a sharp motion.

Dr. Taner collapsed lifelessly.

When Zekeriya got into the car, he summed up the entire situation in one word.

"Done!"

They headed toward Ali Fuat's house.

Chapter

83

The black minivan drove into the villa's garden, enclosed by high walls. Kenan gathered all the men and ordered them to return to headquarters, leaving him alone with Yasin and Erkan. He didn't want any witnesses to what was likely about to happen.

Yasin waited impatiently in the villa's garden. All his plans had been executed perfectly. His first priority now was to free Bahar from the possession. "Hopefully, she hasn't taken off the talisman from around her neck," he thought. Although he wouldn't be allowed to keep the books and computer, it didn't matter much; he had already memorized the most crucial codes. He felt an overwhelming urge to shout, "What a beautiful night, God!" He had freed himself from both the sect and the Black Shrouds. It was as though he'd cast off the weight of the grave and he felt like he had gained a new personality, a new character. He could have lovers now. Maybe even Bahar would fall in love with him. She was technically Erkan's girlfriend, but Erkan was losing his mind. "There are plenty of girls in the world," he mused to himself, smiling. The university entrance exam was also approaching. "I'll get into Bogazici University, the department with the prettiest girls," he thought. And the sect's money was his now; He could live off it for the rest of his life.

"Pack your stuff and get out of here," said Kenan Ferit.

Yasin rushed toward the villa, quickly entering a room and stuffing his clothes and notebooks into his bag. Ali Fuat had forbidden him from taking the books.

Kenan then went to the room where Erkan was locked up. He unlocked the door.

"Erkan, you're free now, my man."

"What good is freedom after my girlfriend is dead, you... you son of a..." He wanted to spit back, but instead, he glared angrily. Kenan sensed that his news hadn't been well-received. It suited him just fine; it was another advantage for him.

"My man, why are you mad at us? The fault lies with..."

Meanwhile, Yasin was hurriedly tossing his things into a bag. He felt someone enter the room and quickly turned to see that it was Erkan. He turned back to his packing, focusing intently.

"Are we leaving, Yasin?" Erkan asked.

Yasin was lost in the pile of books on the desk, checking each one for any hidden papers. Sometimes he'd tuck away important codes between the pages related to them.

"Yes, my friend, we're leaving," he replied.

He noted how Erkan was suddenly calling him "friend." Yasin was growing up. Slowly, Erkan moved closer behind him.

"So, did the Imam and his men die, that they're letting us go?"

Yasin glanced back. "Yes, they're dead."

"Don't you feel any sadness? You grew up under that man's wing since childhood."

Yasin examined a few scraps of paper he'd found. He tossed the important ones into his bag and focused on the remaining books.

"Sadness? That man ruined my childhood, my youth. He stole my best years of my life. I spent my life studying physics and math, praying and chanting among men. I never got to hold a girl's hand. I wrote pages of codes but never a love letter to a girlfriend. Thank God I'm free now. Freedom... oh, God, how beautiful it is. Just thinking about it makes me crazy! I'm done working for the sect. I'll use all my skills for myself now..."

For a moment, Yasin turned around. Erkan was looking at him with a cold expression. Yasin smiled. "You know, Erkan, you're my only friend from the normal world. I'm cutting off everyone else from the sect. Let's build a new life together. We'll go through girls like no tomorrow! We won't even have to work," Yasin winked. "You know my skills with banks. Let's travel the world, go to university, maybe even earn a degree, then study for another. Let's start a music band, buy a production company, become producers and do anything that brings us women."

Yasin laughed. Erkan remained silent, his face a mask of icy composure and replied calmly, "Maybe."

Yasin turned back to the table, flipping through the remaining books.

"Wow! This whole ordeal has brought about incredible personal growth in me. I've shed all my restrictions. I've found myself!"

Erkan could no longer hold back his anger.

"So, my closest friends had to die for you to 'find yourself'."

"What?"

Erkan swung a blade he'd hidden at Yasin's right hand resting on the table. Yasin eyes wide with pain and shock, looked back at Erkan in disbelief, screaming in agony. Erkan grabbed him by the hair and dragging him to the floor, pinning him down and bringing the blade to his ear. The ear didn't come off with a single strike. Yasin was writhing in pain, screaming. Erkan gripped the skin, tearing at it with all his might, ripping it toward the mouth—but it still wouldn't come off completely. Yasin opened and closed his mouth in agony, as though trying to say something, his entire body shaking.

"What's the matter? Are you trying to pray? Can't get the words out, huh?" Erkan picked up the torn flesh and stuffed it into Yasin's mouth, wanting to silence him. He had things to say.

"Surprised, aren't you? Surprised… You scumbag! My friends, my girlfriend, all died because of your twisted fantasies. And you don't even care," he sneered. "You've 'found yourself,' have you?"

Yelling, he spat, "Bastard! You knew Bahar was my girlfriend, so why did you cast a spell on her, huh? You wrote her name in the love spell notes you were decoding! Kenan told me just a bit ago. He even showed me the paper. You're a sick maniac!"

Erkan looked down at the blade in his hand. Both the blade and his hand were covered in blood. His anger rose.

"You've turned me into a psychotic killer with a blade in his hand."

Just then, Yasin managed to open his eyes and meet Erkan's gaze. Erkan interpreted the look as if Yasin was asking, "What does that have to do with anything?"

"It has everything to do with it, friend, yes, everything. When Kenan told me what had happened, I knew I had to kill you. I thought I'd do it quickly to stop you from praying over me. Maybe I'd kill you in your sleep or shoot you in the head. But when Kenan handed me the gun, I couldn't take it. I knew it wouldn't bring me peace if you died too quickly. I asked for a blade instead to make sure that filthy mouth of yours couldn't utter a prayer. That's why I asked for a blade. Do you get it now? Do you understand what you turned me into?"

Erkan raised the blade high and, without hesitation, brought it down on Yasin's neck. Blood sprayed onto his face...

Chapter

84

Zekeriya and Ali Fuat entered the complex, parked the car, and headed towards the apartment building. They began to climb the stairs, stopping outside Serkan Cenet's apartment.

Quietly, Ali Fuat instructed, "Handle this, then meet us upstairs. Wait by the door." Zekeriya nodded in acknowledgment.

Ali Fuat continued up the stairs while Zekeriya drew his silenced pistol and waited for the hallway lights to go out. Once everything was cloaked in darkness, the peephole in Serkan Cenet's door stood out, illuminated from inside. Holding his gun about a hand's width from the peephole, he carefully aimed. Keeping his position steady, he rang the bell. He pressed it again and again, holding it longer each time, intending to unsettle the person inside and make them think about security.

The sound of the bell repeatedly ringing at midnight would make anyone inside rush to the door, then feel uneasy, instinctively peeking through the peephole. A single, soft ring might be interpreted as "just a neighbor," but the continuous ringing triggered urgency.

Using his other hand to brace his gun-holding arm, Zekeriya wanted to ensure the bullet hit its mark. The light from inside momentarily dimmed, and as the peephole darkened, he pulled the trigger. The bullet pierced through the peephole, hitting Serkan Cenet directly in his left eye and embedding itself in his brain.

Zekeriya didn't feel the need to check. Even if there had been a guest inside, it would have been the homeowner who answered the door. And with a bullet to the eye, there was no chance of survival. It was all done.

Ali Fuat left the door slightly ajar as he entered, moving silently. He headed straight to the bedroom. As he opened the door, Selin awoke.

"Is that you, darling? I didn't even hear you come in."

"Yes," he replied.

He turned on the lamp. Selin blinked, her eyes adjusting. She looked beautiful, as innocent as a sleeping child. The sight of her softened his resolve. His heart pounded wildly. Seeing her face chipped away at his determination.

"Don't just stand there, come here. I missed you."

Ali Fuat obeyed. They lay together on the wide bed, entwined like a cat curled up with a ball of yarn, kissing passionately. Selin was already trying to slip off her nightgown, and as they continued, she removed her pajamas and bra, lying on her back as she embraced him between her legs. Their kisses continued, but then, abruptly, Ali Fuat stopped.

With his eyes now adjusted to the darkness, he leaned on his elbows, hovering about 15-20 centimeters above her, gazing down.

"I want you behind me, love…" he whispered.

But then came the echo in his mind, the words of the psychologist: "Mr. Ali, your wife has been involved with Serkan Cenet."

The voice rang in his ears.

"What's wrong, sweetheart? Can't you hold back?" she teased playfully.

Ali Fuat shifted his weight to one elbow, using his free hand to brush her eyebrows, an act of innocent delight.

"Can't hold back?" he thought. Maybe that was the whole summary of it. He should never have married. He knew it would come to this, he'd decided long ago never to marry… but then, he fell in love. He thought she was different.

None of it mattered anymore.

He stopped adjusting her brows and instead, like a vice, placed both hands firmly over her nose and mouth. Selin's eyes widened in shock. She struggled, letting out muffled sounds, scratching desperately at his back. Tears filled Ali Fuat's own eyes. He could already feel the regret of each second, knowing he would never love anyone like this again and would live the rest of his life in misery.

The two or three minutes felt like a century. Selin finally stopped moving, her eyes staring blankly.

Ali Fuat, sobbing, stood up. He dressed, went to Ece's room, and gently lifted his sleeping daughter into his arms. At the door, he saw Zekeriya waiting.

"Take her to Feridun's house. Let her stay there tonight. I'll come by in the morning and explain. And then, go home yourself."

"Yes, sir."

Ece stirred slightly. Ali Fuat pulled a small vial from his pocket, uncapped it, and held it near her nose for a few seconds before pulling it away.

"She won't wake up now."

"Commander, should we cover her with something?"

"Oh, right. Good thinking."

They fetched a blanket from inside, wrapping Ece in it. Zekeriya gently took the girl into his arms and began descending the stairs. Feridun's house wasn't far.

When Ali Fuat entered the villa, he was startled to find Yasin's lifeless body.

"What happened?"

"Commander, I sent the men off and told the two of them they were free to go. Then I stepped away for a moment, went to the bathroom. In the blink of an eye, Erkan killed Yasin and then escaped."

The black van pulled into the villa's garden, enclosed by high walls. Kenan gathered all the men and ordered them to head to the headquarters, leaving only Yasin and Erkan with him. He wanted no witnesses to the events about to unfold.

"..."

"What shall we do? Should we have him caught?"

"Forget it, what will we gain by catching him? We already have enough trouble without adding him to the list."

"Commander, what should we do about the Pasha Vefik situation?"

"Here's what you'll do: call him up, tell him, 'Commander, we've caught Imam Sait, but we have a serious problem, and you need to come here immediately.' He'll ask what the problem is, and you'll say, 'The man has planted bombs at seventeen locations across the city. If we don't release him, his men will detonate all of them, and thousands will die.' That'll make him panic and rush over here. Got it?"

Kenan Ferit looked at him with suspicion.

"Will he really buy it, Commander?"

"What's not to believe? You are Kenan Ferit, one of the commanders of the Black Shroud. If he won't trust you, who will he trust?"

Ali Fuat's instructions were followed to the letter.

The Pasha set out at once. Half an hour later, he was at the door. Both men felt a surge of excitement.

The security chief read the message on his phone and deleted it immediately. He attached a silencer to his gun and went up to Cihangir and Feyza's bedroom. As he entered, they awoke to the sound, but before they could rise, he fired his weapon. The bullets whispered through the air again and again. He quietly closed the door, returned to his room, and went back to sleep.

From now on, the new leader of the congregation was Alp Demirkaplan.

The Pasha entered the room, visibly distressed. Seventeen bombs would spell catastrophe.

Expecting a large group of Black Shroud members, he was instead greeted only by Kenan Ferit and Ali Fuat. He was surprised.

"Where is that man? I need to speak to him immediately!"

"What man?" Ali Fuat replied.

The Pasha found the response odd. And what was Ali Fuat doing here? He had sidelined him; he wasn't supposed to be part of this operation.

"The Imam," he said, irritation coloring his voice.

"We had coffee with the Imam," Ali Fuat answered, an ironic smile playing on his lips.

"Didn't I tell you to bring him in alive? And why are you here at all?"

"It doesn't matter what you ordered! Because we don't take orders from traitors."

"Watch your mouth, you filthy animal."

Ali Fuat flung a blue dossier in the Pasha's face.

"These are the documents of the bribes you've taken."

The Pasha's face flushed with rage.

"I'll have you shot, you rebellious dog."

Ali Fuat, weary from the overwhelming stress, decided not to drag it out any longer. He drew his gun, ending the conversation for good.

The legendary Commander Vefik Sancaktar fell lifeless to the floor.

Ali Fuat tossed his gun onto the table, then collapsed into a chair. He opened the bottle of cognac he had brought and took a few sips. The taste was bitter. Finally, it was over.

He had eliminated the Republic's enemy, Imam Sait, and his followers. He had killed his treacherous wife and had given the bribed Pasha his final "gift"…

"Four bullets, free of charge."

The next day, he would take command of the Black Shroud and adopt a more aggressive approach.

The room echoed with the sound of a message notification. Kenan took out his phone and looked at the screen for a long moment.

"Who's the message from?"

Kenan looked up, paused for a few seconds, and answered, "From Dimitri."

He took a few more sips of cognac, smiling.

"You have foreign friends too?"

"A necessary friendship, Commander."

He took another sip.

"What do you mean?"

"Work friendship, Commander."

The smile faded from Ali Fuat's face.

"What kind of work does he do?"

"He's the head of the Northern Polar Council's Turkey branch."

"What's that?" he asked, half-rising from his seat, only to freeze as Kenan pointed his gun at him.

Ali Fuat couldn't comprehend what was happening.

"Kenan, what's going on? Have you gone mad?"

"Commander, call me Stavro. I never quite embraced the name Kenan."

"What Stavro? What are you talking about?"

"It's a long story, but I believe you deserve to hear it."

Stavro pulled up a chair and placed it about three or four meters in front of the chair where Ali Fuat sat. He turned the back of the chair to face forward and sat carefully, his eyes never leaving Ali Fuat. He braced his arm on the chair, watching him with unblinking intensity. The conversation began.

"In your opinion, Commander, who really rules the world?"

As he listened, Ali Fuat's eyes darted around the room. His gun was on the table, out of reach. He had another one on his belt, but there was no way to draw it. Kenan—no, Stavro— was renowned for his marksmanship. Unless someone suddenly burst through the door, an earthquake hit, or one of Yasin's djinn decided to stir up trouble, he had little chance. He was hoping for a miracle.

"You're taking too long to answer, Commander. If this is boring you, we can end the conversation," Stavro said, aiming his gun. Ali Fuat replied hastily:

"The master of the world is America. And America is controlled by the Jews. All the big corporations belong to them."

Stavro relaxed his gun arm, resting it on the chair again.

"Like everyone else, you're mistaken, Commander. The rulers of the world are the Anglo-Saxons. England, the United States, Canada, Australia. These four nations, led by England, shape the world's destiny. They all descend from the same race—the Anglo-Saxons. After World War I, these nations formed the Northern Polar Council, led by England. This council is the true command center of the world. British Intelligence and the CIA operate under this council's orders, positioning thousands of agents in every country, every corner, ready to be deployed when necessary. Writers, statesmen, soldiers, spies—you see, even in the most covert organization in your country, the Black Shroud, we have infiltrated. You know, my father was in the Black Shroud, and so was my grandfather. His father was a great Kuva-yi Milliye leader in Giresun. But, in truth, they were all agents for British Intelligence and, later, the Northern Polar Council. We are not really Turkish. We're Pontic Greeks. My name is Stavro."

Stavro flashed a handsome smile. "Life is fascinating, isn't it, Commander?"

Ali Fuat gave no reply.

"As for the issue of Israel; no state can dominate the world with a population of six million and a handful of land. Not long ago—only fifty years back—Hitler burned five million Jews. Is this what dominion looks like? Would a nation that truly ruled the world allow five million of its people to be burned?"

"Come now, we're talking about today, not 1945."

"Commander, dominion cannot be established in such a short time. Only Genghis Khan achieved that, but the conditions were vastly different. Such a thing would never happen now. For the past three hundred years, since the fall of the Ottoman Empire, England and America have ruled the world. Sometimes England took the lead, and other times it was America. But it didn't matter much, because in the end, they are both Anglo-Saxon. The appearance of Israel as the controller of the world is an illusion carefully crafted by the Northern Polar Council. It was done deliberately to distract the world's peoples and direct their anger toward the Jews. A calculated strategy, if you will."

"So your Council has a hand in everything, then."

"Yes, Commander, almost everywhere."

"And what is your objective?"

"Our objective is to prevent rivals from emerging against England and America, to stop the rise of new powerful nations and alliances."

"Then it seems you haven't been very successful. The European Union and the Shanghai Cooperation Organization are coming on strong."

"Indeed, we're actively working to hinder the development of both."

Ali Fuat fell silent for a moment. After a sip or two of cognac, he reached into his shirt pocket. Kenan Ferit immediately aimed his gun at him. Ali Fuat froze.

"I was only going to take out a cigarette."

"Do it slowly and announce every movement, Commander."

Kenan lowered his gun and rested his arm on the chair. Ali Fuat lit his cigarette.

"And what about Turkey? Do you intend to divide us?"

"We've already divided you."

"What do you mean?"

"You were a colossal empire, and we broke you into pieces. Initially, we had plans for a Kurdish, an Armenian, and a Pontic Greek state, but Mustafa Kemal shattered all of those."

"So you don't have any goals to divide the country now?"

"No, we don't. Instead, we have a policy of keeping Turkey weak in a controlled manner. Pushing you into utter chaos and fragmentation wouldn't serve our interests."

"Why not?"

"Because when local powers lose their hold, a country turns into a swamp. We made that mistake in Afghanistan. From that swamp came a swarm of mosquitoes, and those mosquitoes bit us. You remember what happened on September 11."

"So, you're saying the governments of Third World countries function like local municipal workers, spraying the swamp from time to time?"

Kenan Ferit smiled, finding the metaphor amusing.

"Precisely," he replied.

As Ali Fuat took another drag from his cigarette and sipped his cognac, a question lingered in his mind.

"If you're an agent, and you don't care about Turkey's well-being, why did you help kill the Pasha? You could've looted the country together with that traitor."

Kenan Ferit smiled.

"That's the point you've never understood, Commander. Not just you—none of your people understood it. You've always seen the Pasha and others like him as traitors. But the Pasha wasn't a traitor. In fact,

I might even say that, in his recent years, he became a patriot because of his views."

"Patriotism through bribery?"

"Don't get hung up on the bribery. Every person has flaws. Don't confuse their personality with their political outlook. History is filled with leaders who served their nations greatly despite having personal shortcomings. Take Winston Churchill, for example. Some say he was homosexual. Once, during a speech in the House of Lords, a member of the opposition taunted him, saying, 'You're gay; you shouldn't be in government.' Churchill replied, 'Yes, I may be gay, but I govern the state with my mind, not with my backside.' Maybe he was homosexual, but what difference does it make? He rendered the greatest services to the British State and its people. You have similarly flawed leaders in your history, too. Perfection is unattainable in politics. What matters is that a leader can advance their country forward. Minor flaws are inevitable. An impeccable leader only exists in legends because every nation needs such a myth. They look back, pick one, strip them of all faults, and elevate them to an idealized, almost divine state. But that leader never really existed—they are a creation of the imagination."

"And what does any of this have to do with the Pasha's patriotism?"

"Let me be clearer, then. The Pasha took bribes, yes. But his ideas were critical for Turkey. He realized that the path forward lay in stability and economic strength, not in violence. That was the truth. Cities like New York, London, Paris, and Zurich attract the wealth of the world precisely because of their stability. Parts of London are practically filled with Arabowned villas. Arabs invest their fortunes there instead of in their own countries. Why? So they have a place to live if something goes wrong at home. All the dictators of the world channel their nations'resources into our lands. Why? Because if there's a regime change, they need a Plan B. Tell me, Commander, why don't the wealthy of the world invest in your country, in Turkey or Russia, for example? Because we have stability. The rich know that if they buy property in England or America, no one will confiscate it. There won't be any problems. Now look at your own situation: you make a fuss just because a few thousand British and German retirees have bought apartments in Alanya. You should be celebrating that foreign currency is entering the country through tourism. As a nation, your economic knowledge is nil. If you weren't a country prone to coups every decade, many of the world's wealthy would buy homes or land here, simply for the unparalleled beauty of your landscape. You never understood the magic of stability, Commander. Do you remember the thrill in the organization when news arrived of the murders of Osman Karahan and Faruk Altan? Everyone was buzzing with excitement. You and your Black Shroud have started feeding on blood, Commander. Patriotism is no longer your goal; you're like a vampire, unable to find peace without bloodshed, without murder, and chaos. The Pasha recognized this and began by replacing the top officials in the organization. First, he removed Tuncay and Colonel Zeki. Then, you. His goal wasn't to dismiss you and then feast on bribes undisturbed. Rather, he sought to replace militaristic leaders like you with quieter, softer..."

Stavro paused, thinking. "Perhaps it's bold to say, but he wanted to find individuals who were, ideologically, more liberal and free-thinking. He was aware of how each act of violence was damaging the country's economy."

"In his youth, he too harbored fascist views, but he came to realize that such a path would lead nowhere. His association with Cihangir Demirkaplan began with these new realizations. As for the bribery—it was something that appeared unexpectedly, partly due to the pressure from his son. The Pasha's weak link was his son. In other words, this alliance wasn't built on bribery but on defending national interests through a different means. And let me tell you, it's not a misguided approach. The true misguidance lies in your tactics of breaking and smashing. Arif Pasha's emphasis on economic stability was crucial. If he could have implemented his vision, it could have brought tremendous benefits to Turkey. But we couldn't allow that. A stable, strong Turkey, with its strategic location, natural beauty, and Muslim identity, would attract all the wealth and real estate investments of the Middle Eastern rich. That's why we had to remove Pasha Vefik. Though, if we hadn't taken care of it, you would have anyway—that's another matter."

Kenan Ferit swallowed and continued:

"There's a difference in our understanding of patriotism, Commander. Patriotism isn't necessarily about sacrificing your life and living in poverty. Serving the people doesn't mean putting on grand ceremonies and making them sing anthems of heroism. True service to the people is ensuring they can commute from their homes to their jobs in private cars, that they can support their families with a single job, that no child is left without an education due to lack of money. Patriotism isn't about choosing T.2000 cigarettes over Marlboro; it's about producing a cigarette as high-quality as Marlboro. You've always equated patriotism and heroism with dying, Commander. These lands have produced many heroes. All of them died."

"I have a question."

"Please, go ahead, Commander."

"If the Pasha's mindset was beneficial to the country and mine was harmful, I understand why you killed him. But why are you killing me? If I'm harmful to this country, wouldn't it benefit you for me to remain at the head of the Black Shroud?"

Kenan Ferit laughed briefly.

"Controlling you, Commander? Impossible. You're like a wounded lion. If you take over the Black Shroud, you'll tear apart anything in your way. And besides, the Pasha's death needs an explanation. Otherwise, people might suspect the existence of an infiltrated organization within the Black Shroud."

"And how will you explain that by killing me?"

"Quite simply. Ali Fuat couldn't accept his dismissal and killed the Pasha. He shot at me too, but the bullet only grazed me. In the chaos, I killed him."

Ali Fuat was hoping for a miracle. If only the gun would jam. If something happened and he managed to escape, he would tear Kenan to pieces... but he tried to prolong the conversation.

"Who is Dimitri?"

"I told you, he's the head of the Northern Polar Council's Turkey branch. He's also the security chief for the Demirkaplan family. His father and grandfather worked with that family too. Just a short while ago, he killed Cihangir and Feyza Demirkaplan, Pasha's allies. Now that we've taken control of the congregation and placed Alp Demirkaplan as its new leader, everything will be back on track, at least from our perspective. As for Turkey, who knows."

"And you'll be the head of the Black Shroud, then!"

"No, Commander, not at all... These lands have never granted us a sultanate. At most, we've been viziers. But we've always chosen the sultan. Remember the child-sultans in your history who weren't even circumcised yet. We'll crown another one of them in the Black Shroud."

Ali Fuat muttered in astonishment, "Aydin."

Kenan Ferit smiled.

"Right on the mark, Commander. Aydin Sipahi."

Although he rested his arm on the chair, Kenan Ferit felt tired. This fatigue was dulling his reflexes. He needed to be cautious; after all, he was facing the deadly Ali Fuat.

"Commander, that's enough talk. I have no personal grudge against you. I've always liked and respected you. But duty is sacred. I must carry out the order I've been given."

He aimed his gun and took careful aim.

"Any last requests?"

Ali Fuat couldn't say a word. He wanted to say "my daughter," but before he could, a single bullet lodged in his forehead.

www.ingramcontent.com/pod-product-compliance
Lightning Source LLC
Chambersburg PA
CBHW030241030726
47493CB00023B/311